THE WOLFSE

Richard D. Handy is the au
Danny Nash adventure serie.. ... . v..u..., *The Reich Device*, was published in 2015, with good reviews. The storytelling is set at a time when German scientists led the world with discoveries on atomic physics, rockets, and other inventions of intrigue. Espionage inevitably followed. In addition to being an author and editor, Richard is also a scientist with an international reputation. He travels extensively and meets interesting people, sometimes in the darker corners of the world. He lives in England in the beautiful county of Devon.

Find out more about Richard D. Handy by visiting http://www.richardhandy.com and for The Reich Device http://www.reichdevice.richardhandy.com/

The Wolfsberg Deception

Richard D. Handy

A Danny Nash Adventure

First paperback edition: 2020 in the United Kingdom.

Paperback ISBN 978-1-9161499-2-2

A catalogue record for this book is available from the British Library.

Cover design by Berni Stevens.
Resilient Books UK is an imprint of RichardHandy.com

Web: http://www.richardhandy.com/

For the people who work in the shadows.

CHAPTER 1

Ukrainian Border

Something wasn't right. Major Danny Nash froze, then dropped behind the nearest fir tree and clicked the safety off his Thompson sub-machine gun. He squinted down the snowy bank, listening and smelling the air. Blood pulsed strongly in his veins, and trusting his gut, he took up the binoculars. Two troopers plodded back and forth in the slush. Sentry duty. Or at least that's what it looked like.

He shifted the binoculars over the terrain. There were no footprints and the snow-laden branches were undisturbed. It all looked pristine, but looks can be deceptive. The bank of trees descended steeply on to the single track road below. The narrow track curved out of the forest into tundra-like grassland. A thin blanket of snow cloaked most of the ground with only the occasional tussock grass protruding through the melt. It was an ideal spot for an ambush. But what choice did he have?

Nash zoomed in on the pot-marked road. It was swimming with iced water. Had any vehicles been through that morning? It was hard to tell. A shiver ran down his spine. He was lean and toned, but his muscles ached beyond his thirty-plus years. The cold seemed relentless, sapping his energy. He pulled up the collar on his grey coat and weighed up the odds. The assault on the train in the Carpathian Mountains had been costly. If it hadn't been for the new-fangled plastic explosive

1

from Section D and the professionalism of his men, he'd be dead – they'd all be dead. He owed them. His rucksack full of half-burnt identity cards, some technical drawings and a few fragments of metal alloy were the only evidence of the Nazi device, or any other super weapon. He had to make it across the border – it was the only mountain pass for miles – and if he didn't everything would be lost: the war, Emily, and his future along with it.

Nash waited as the ragged band of commandos took up position along the rise. He glanced across at the stocky frame of his second in command. The man gave a brief nod and a quick smirk through his frost-damaged features, then patted his Thompson.

Nash smiled to himself. Despite being in a rough state, out of rations and low on ammunition, the men still offered a keen spirit. Nash tugged his woollen commando scarf-cap over his short, dark hair and cold ears, then pushed the binoculars against his chapped skin. He adjusted the focus. The two sentries had stopped. They stood sharing a cigarette. Their worn rifles were slung casually over the shoulders of their grizzled overcoats. Muddy slush covered their boots and trousers. Nash worked the binoculars along the road. A log cabin sat some fifty yards away, smoke curling from the chimney. Somebody was at home. More soldiers.

He tracked the binoculars across to the Lithuanian side. It was a good five hundred yards of open ground beyond the lodge. The hammer and sickle fluttered tantalising in the breeze. The Red Army – who'd have thought it? Two Russians paced in front of a rough sawn tree trunk resting on wooden trestles. It did the job, but there was nothing make do and mend about their brand new Tokarev semi-automatic rifles. Nash flashed a silent hand signal to his Number One. The commando acknowledged and crouching low, moved over to Nash's position. He huddled his weapon against his chest and with his index finger resting on the trigger guard, whispered quietly. 'Sir?'

'Take two men. Give us covering firepower on the left flank between the border post and that mountain lodge. Then drop down behind the sentry box.'

'Yes, sir. What about the Russians?'

Nash shrugged, 'Let's hope the Ruskies don't get too itchy on the trigger finger.'

The sergeant nodded.

Nash watched in silence as the commando selected two gunners from the squad, then waited as the trio moved off along the tree line. He returned his attention to the German position. With two troopers on sentry, and at four or five hours a shift, that would leave at least eight men inside the lodge – fairly even odds under normal circumstances. But things were about as far removed from normal as you could possibly get. The remaining eleven commandos were exhausted, frost-bitten and bloodied, and needed to conserve rounds.

He fisted a few silent orders to the remnants of his troop and then eased to a standing position, sliding a finger under the trigger guard of his weapon as he did so. He worked down the contour, keeping to the thinning tree line and finding respite behind a scrawny pine at the side of the road. With adrenalin pumping, Nash remained poised, like a panther preparing to strike at its prey.

The sentries stood at ease, still smoking.

Nash estimated the distance – *thirty feet.*

He pointed briskly at two commandos on his flank and then walked his fingers in the air before jerking a hand in a cutting motion over his throat. They got the message and beavered across the road into the sparse tree cover on the other side.

Then working parallel on the nearside. Nash advanced. Snow crumped softly under his boots. The smell of tobacco smoke drifted into his nostrils. Snippets of foreign tongue

3

amplified in the proximity. German feet squelched in the slush.

Twenty feet.

Gingerly slinging his Thompson, Nash reached into his thigh pocket and produced a stiletto throwing knife. He balanced the blade across his palm, instinctively feeling the weight of the weapon. Then quickly stepping into the open, he launched the stiletto in a single fluid movement. It found its target.

The German gargled surprise, clawing at the knife protruding from his windpipe. The second sentry hastily unshouldered his rifle, fumbling the bolt on his weapon. 'Scheisse! Scheisse!'

Nash made ready with a second blade – but didn't need it.

A huge hand covered the German's mouth. The sentry stiffened, then slumped silently to the floor with blood gushing from a wound to his kidneys. Nash nodded thanks to Number One and simultaneously reached for his Thompson. The commandos were already moving at a pace towards the lodge. Nash prayed they'd make the distance.

Suddenly the rattle of a distant truck filtered into the valley. Nash swung round into a knee-firing position, Thompson at the ready. The lorry emerged around a bend in the forest road, lurching momentarily as the gears crunched. Its canvas top brushing snow from the nearest fir trees overhanging the route.

Nash fired.

Glass shattered. Breaks squealed. The vehicle broadsided off the road, smashing into a tree trunk. Steam erupted from the engine block. Oil and water spewed on to the snow. Troops tumbled from the rear, taking cover behind the tailgate and adjacent spruce trees. Nash held them with short bursts of the Thompson and bellowed, 'Rear guard from the right flank! On me! Left flank – maintain the advance on the lodge!' He fired again, ricocheting bullets around the wheel arches. Rifle shots rang out as the German troops organised their defences.

Nash hollered across the road, 'Move it!'

Two commandos duly broke from the tussock grass, and keeping to a shallow depression at the side of the road, moved to the rear delivering bursts towards the enemy vehicle. Rounds splintering bark and found flesh amongst the metalwork. Nash pressed harder into his Thompson, with his bones rattling and nostrils filling with cordite.

The weapon clicked empty.

He crouched to the deck with the Thompson hot in his palms. 'Reloading!' He slammed in a fresh magazine.

The revving of a second diesel engine suddenly penetrated the din. Nash bolted upright and grimly worked the Thompson, discarding any notion of conserving ammo as a second troop carrier came into view. Shell casing decanted into the snow. The barrel smoked, scorching hot.

The second lorry shuddered to a halt at the edge of the tree line, disgorging more German infantry on to the road.

Nash roared, 'Fall back! Fall back! But hold them!' He sidled backwards, firing in an arc towards the enemy and pumping out rounds until the magazine was spent.

He dropped to one knee, balling. 'Move back! Go! Go! Go!' Then slamming home his last magazine, he let rip with another burst, before turning on his heels. Accelerating to a sprint, he passed his fellow commandos and then skated to a halt some ten yards to their rear. He instantly returned covering fire. A staccato of deafening rounds issued from his Thompson.

'Move! Move!'

The men scootered past in seconds.

Abruptly, gunfire opened up from the lodge. A German trooper hunkered down in the doorway, offering death from his MP 40 sub-machine gun.

Nash fired a burst from his Thompson and splintering bullets about the trooper's position, then crouched and roved an eye over the battlefield. It wasn't looking good. German soldiers advancing quickly from the rear. Flanking fire now pouring from the defended building. He felt the weight of his weapon and fumed at the declining choices. Get slaughtered here. Or take our chances with the Soviets. What's not to like?

He suddenly yelled orders, leaping to his feet. 'Move faster! Towards the border post! Bloody well move it!' He rattled his last magazine empty across the tussock grass as German rounds snapped at his feet; then tossing the spent machine gun, he pulled a canister from his webbing and lobbed it towards the enemy.

He bellowed, 'On the double!'

Thick orange smoke swirled low in the air. He tossed another smoke grenade and pulled the Sauer 38 automatic pistol from under his grey coat, firing double taps towards the advancing Germans. He retreated, bringing along the two commandos on his right flank, firing his pistol and conserving ammunition for the surest of kills. He glanced towards the side of the lodge. 'Number One, move it! You can make it!' Nash fired covering shots at the building.

The sergeant pushed his four-man team towards their objective. One commando dropped holding his guts. Another fell clutching his chest. A hail storm of German rounds cut across their position. Miraculously, the sergeant and two men made it to the porch. They stopped, keeping low in the corner of the veranda. Nash fired more pistol rounds into the ground floor window and screaming, 'Number One! Take them out! Take them out now!'

The Sauer clicked empty. Nash dropped back into the snow, systematically changing out the magazine in his pistol as a burst from a German MP 40 machine gun tracked through the slush. Automatic rounds smashed into his position and rendering the chest of the commando to his left. The man flew backwards, bleeding heavily and writhing a last effort from his Thompson.

Nash hunkered down with his fresh magazine and firing steady double taps from his pistol. Suddenly, heavy machine gun fire issued from the hillside, cutting a swathe through the advancing Nazi troops. Ripping flesh and fragmenting bones mixed with screams. Men fell dead and injured amongst the tussock grass. Nash rallied at the muzzle flashes from the hillside – but knew it couldn't last – the gunners would soon be out of ammunition. He squinted towards the lodge. Number One crouched at the sidewall.

Boom!

The windows exploded, showering the veranda with dust and debris. Nash seized the opportunity and leaping to his feet, gestured frantically with his pistol arm. 'The Ukrainian border! On the double! Fall back!' He turned towards the hillside, sweeping his arms over his head amid the dispersing drifts of orange smoke, shouting himself hoarse, 'Fall back! The border!'

The door to the lodge abruptly flew open, almost smashing off its hinges. German soldiers spilled on to the veranda, spraying automatic fire in all directions. Nash held, standing in the snow, placing carefully aimed double taps through the orange smoke. The nearest trooper collapsed dead on to the boardwalk. He took aim on another, and began walking towards the target, squeezing the trigger as he did so.

His weapon clicked empty.

He shoved the spent side arm into his waistband and quickly drew a stiletto throwing knife and charged towards the veranda as a Thompson sub-machine gun blurted loud from the corner of the building. Blood and vital organs sprayed on to the timber panelling as the last of the German defenders from the lodge expired.

Nash scuttled to a stop on the edge of the porch, cordite and orange smoke filling his nostrils. Panting, he held the knife at the ready and gaped at the twitching corpses.

Number One emerged at a trot from the side of the building. 'Sir!' He jerked a thumb over his shoulder towards the tussocks, 'We can't hold them!'

'Get going, Number One!' Nash hastily stowed his knife and then stooped, relieving a dead infantryman of his Mauser rifle. 'I am right behind you! On the double, Sergeant!' Nash gritted his teeth and pushed the weapon into his shoulder. He worked the bolt action, firing at selected targets, then turned and sprinted after the commando. The sound of small-arms fire picked up from the German line.

The commandos shifted to a run, slipping in the ice and slush as they did so. Nash estimated the distance as he caught up with his band: some three hundred yards to the border. He flashed a look to the rear.

Fuck it!

Slithered to a halt, and standing firm, he took aim at the nearest target and fired a shot from his rifle, then retreated four yards and fired again. He focussed on the drill: fire, retreat, fire. Germans advanced at a pace. Nash took a breath and gave his men a final glance, then dropped to a knee-firing position. With renewed determination he worked the rifle bolt.

The German line moved at speed towards his position. Nash kept firing. Two more German infantryman fell in the snow.

Abruptly, the smoking-hot roar of a Thompson machine gun deafened his ear. Shell casings bounced off his rucksack and shoulder, scattering to the ground. Commandos fell in on either side of Nash, firing their weapons in bursts.

Nash shouted, 'I thought I told you to double it to the border, Number One?!'

The sergeant rammed his last magazine into his weapon. 'Yes, sir! Of course you did, sir!' He let rip, whittling a few more casualties from the advancing enemy.

Suddenly, the ground shuddered to a deafening boom, then another. Ice, snow and loose earth rained down.

'Mortars! Cover!' Nash pressed himself into the snow, shielding his head as best he could. Soil and fragments of ice bounced off his back and shoulders. His bones vibrated with each explosion. Shell after shell pounded the terrain. His jaw jolted violently with the seismic proximity of the detonations, smashing his molars together and chapping bloody strands of flesh from the insides of his cheeks.

Miraculously, the shelling stopped.

Nash lay in the snow, his brain fogged by the heavy artillery. He remained prostrate on the frozen ground waiting for the delirium to pass or the next barrage to begin; but none came. Instead, the rhythmic squeak of a heavy, tracked vehicle filtered into his ears.

He looked up at the approaching Russian T-34. The tank paused, firing a shell into the distance – the German trucks erupted in a ball of orange flame. The T-34 rolled forwards, stopping in front of the lodge. Its heavy calibre machine gun delivered slaughter to the German infantry.

Outgunned, the Germans ran for the relative safety of the tree line.

Nash staggered to his feet, using the Mauser rifle for support. He leant on the weapon, breathing heavily, grubby and perplexed. He glanced around at the surviving commandos – only five of the original band of forty, including himself. The men rested on their weapons, panting and bloodied, sharing uneasy glances towards the Soviet tank.

A Russian armoured car trundled into view from behind the Lithuanian post. Nash watched cautiously as the vehicle approached. The light armour of the BA-20 with its machine gun turret on the roof looked almost comical – a civilian motor car with some steel plate bolted to the sides and a weapon slapped on the top. The BA-20 halted a few feet away. The passenger door opened and a smartly dressed man in a Red Army uniform stepped into the snow. Nash recognised the insignia – a polkovnik – equivalent to a British colonel.

Nash lifted his rifle as he eye-balled the Soviet. The man stood, about average height for a Russian, forty-five, perhaps fifty years of age. The Polkovnik took off his shiny peaked cap and shoved it under his arm, then gave a broad smile. His slicked-back dark hair and penetrating eyes gave an air of authority. Nash sensed some intellect or comradery about his persona.

The officer took off his leather gloves and extended a hand. He spoke in good English, with a slight Moldavian accent. 'Major Nash, we've been looking for you. I hope I am not too late.' The Polkovnik raised an eyebrow. 'What is it that you English say – in a bit of a pickle – no?' The Russian chuckled to himself, 'I am sorry, let me introduce myself, Sergio Korolev at your service.'

CHAPTER 2

Steinhoff

octor Steinhoff carefully positioned the last section of the carbon-coated alloy plating on to the elegant curvature of his device. Despite the chill of the cavern, sweat dripped from his brow making his black round spectacles slide down the bridge of his nose. He absently pushed his glasses back into position with his index finger and swallowed hard, then tentatively secured the last of the precisely engineered titanium screws with an Allen key. Satisfied, he dropped the key into the pocket of his oil-stained laboratory coat. A rush of adrenalin gave a crimson hue to his cheeks as he stepped back to overview the construction. He nodded appreciatively and then smiled to himself. Water filled his bloodshot eyes as his heart skipped a beat. It was beautiful; an elegant master piece of advanced engineering.

The steel gantry above suddenly rattled with the rhythmic clunk of boots. Steinhoff glanced upwards, ignoring the gritty moisture soaking into his shirt collar from his short, dark hair. Two troopers, each in pristine uniform and sporting sub-machine guns patrolled the walkway. He sneered in their direction as they did their usual circuit past the small shed that served as a temporary office area for his many papers. The soldiers paused at the railings a few yards along from his office, casting keen eyes over the workshop below. Steinhoff held their gaze for a couple of seconds and then watched them clank along the gantry to continue their patrol into the expanse of the underground complex.

Damn the soldiers – always interrupting things. He shook his head in disgust and thrust his hands into his laboratory coat pockets. The oversized garment hid his somewhat soft and undernourished, but otherwise average torso. He paced slowly around the shiny exterior of the alloy tube. At some ten feet long and two feet in diameter, it was bigger than the last prototype. He rubbed the bristles on his chin with deep satisfaction as he muttered to himself.

'Out of adversity is born opportunity.' He paused to take in his miraculous achievement. Who had he stolen that poetic phrase from? Einstein? It didn't really matter. The glory was now his for the taking. The Führer would not be disappointed. A new technology for the new Reich. A world-changing technology that would give the Führer command of not just Europe and Africa, but the whole planet. The Führer would rule as the Caesars did over the known world. Then, and only then, would he take his place at the Führer's side as the first Plenipotentiary of Global Scientific Research, and the most honoured of Nobel Prize winners.

Steinhoff paused at the end of his device and bent over, staring into the blackness of the hollow tube. He tried to fix his eye on the centre. The utter darkness gave no reference point. His eyes recorded no shadow or light; save the flickering white noise of his own retinas. The special carbon-coating seemed to absorb reality itself – but then his discovery of carbon sixty; hollow spheres made of neatly arranged pure carbon atoms was nothing short of genius. These minute footballs made of exactly sixty carbon atoms had remarkable quantum properties. The hidden power of these nano-scale structures was his to control. Enormous force could be generated with the right application of voltage. *His* device *was* the Holy Grail of Physics – perpetual motion, an unlimited supply of free energy. Today, his device would propel a new generation of intercontinental rockets, and more, much more. New York, London, Washington – all would be annihilated, wiped from the face of the earth.

He dragged his gaze away from the device and removed his glasses, then rubbed his eyeballs. He repositioned his spectacles, blinking several times as the starting plate on the side of the device came into focus – once primed, the device would run forever.

He picked up the end of the industrial power cable that snaked across the concrete floor and inspected the square grid of brass pins that made the elaborate plug. The connector seemed almost alien in the glow of the overhead lighting. Satisfied that everything was in order, he carefully married the pins to the specially machined socket that sat flush within the curvature of the device. He turned towards the control box sitting on an adjacent workbench. The control panel, with its Bakelite dials and switches, looked cannibalised. The regulation grey paint of the German Army had added nothing to its dour façade.

Steinhoff swallowed and then tentatively rested his index finger over the primary switch.

He pressed the power supply on.

Needles flickered to life on the display. He caressed the dials in turn, adjusting each Bakelite knob to the required setting. A green luminescence emitted from the panel, marking the first stirrings of his atomic beast. His palate dried as he moved his palm towards the primary ignition. He reached out for the large red button and, half-turning towards his beloved device, punched the button on.

A crisp electrical drone gave life to the machine. The hairs on the back of his neck stood up as the electromagnetic field of the device kicked in. The blackness of hollow tube was suddenly replaced by an emerald glow on its carbon surface. He slowly turned up the voltage, shifting the radiance to a yellowy-orange hue.

A shiver of adrenalin shot through his chest, flushing more perspiration upon his brow.

It's working! My God, it is actually working!

He edged the dial up a few more volts.

The orange colour intensified, becoming somewhat focussed. Like a gelatinous worm running down the centre of the tube.

That's it! That's it. The voltage aligns the molecules. With each colour the quantum properties of the device are revealed.

He took a long, slow, breath. Then puffing his chest in triumph, he turned the voltage up a final step. The orange worm gave a sudden flash and transformed into a sharp crimson plasma along the length of the tube. Steinhoff stood in silence. His jaw partially dropped open in awe of the laser-like spectacle. He calmly reached into his pocket, pulling out a small glass vial of the finest carbon dust. He held the container up against the backdrop of laser light and rolled the powder around in the glass.

Pure carbon sixty. A wonder of the natural world – harnessed for the Reich.

He stepped towards the anterior end of the device, then slowly removed the ground glass stopper from the vial, habitually shoving the stopper between his fingers to keep it clean. He searched in his laboratory coat pocket with his free hand, producing a small glass pipette sporting a rubber teat. He squeezed the bulb to create a vacuum and sucked up a few milligrams of the precious carbon sixty powder.

He stood poised, pipette in hand, in front of the machine.

Let there be light!

Steinhoff puffed a small cloud of the carbon powder into the device.

The bolt of red plasma transformed with a lightning-like flash into a pure brilliant white. The device jolted on its moorings. The cradle groaned under the monumental force, barely holding the thrust generated by the plasma beam.

Steinhoff clenched his fist in the air. His face reddened. Tears fell from the corners of his eyes. 'Yes! Yes! Yes!'

Surely, the Nobel Laureate would now be his, and his alone. All would follow his new world order, or fall to oblivion and despair.

Nash sat casually against the pile of mooring ropes, looking the part in a threadbare woollen jumper, working trousers, and a tattered pair of leather boots. His surviving commandos were similarly dressed and dispersed around the boathouse. Nash kept a firm eye on the slippery Polkovnik – it just didn't make any sense – why did the Russians come to their aid? The German-Soviet pact was well-known. They'd already shared the spoils of war; annexing parts of Poland, Romania and Lithuania into their respective German and Soviet territories. It was official: the Nazis and the Russians were allies. So why help the British?

If the Russians knew about the German secret weapons programme, then perhaps they wanted a slice of the action? But there had been no sign of Soviet collaboration at the Peenemünde rocket facility in Germany. Had the Germans soured their special relationship with Stalin by not being willing to share weapons technology with the Russians? Possibly, but it just couldn't be that simple: the Soviets *already* had some major hardware of their own. Whatever, the Russians were double dealing under the table: being Germany's friend when it suited and now helping the British – or so it seemed. If that was the case, then the Soviet Colonel couldn't be trusted, or had British Intelligence been working with Korolev all along?

Nash watched as the Polkovnik shoved his Soviet officer's hat under his arm and slicked back his dark hair with the palm of his hand. The Russian took another quick drag on his cigarette, flicking the ash into the air, then exhaling a stagnant smog of rough tobacco. His black overcoat flapped in the breeze as he paced up and down. Nash shook his head: the Soviet was impossible to read. There was one other possibility – the British had something that the Russians needed. Under the circumstances, there was no prospect of Whitehall handing over intelligence to the Russians, or anyone else allied to Germany – unless of course the Soviets were about to change sides. Nash dismissed the thought. Perhaps it was something of a more personal nature – something that Korolev *himself* required. But what?

Salty water mixed with a sheen of spent diesel oil as the Black Sea lapped at the moorings in the confines of the boathouse. Nash broke from his train of thought as the Soviet approached.

Korolev sucked another caustic breath of cheap Russian tobacco and looked down at Nash. 'I don't like it. The fishing boat should have been here by now.'

Nash folded his arms and smiled briefly at the Polkovnik, 'Colonel, the breeze is up. We should stay with the plan and wait.'

Korolev clicked his jaw and winced, 'Alright, English. We wait another ten minutes, but not a moment longer.'

Nash nodded slowly, 'Yes, we wait.' He eyed the Russian up and down. 'I am curious. Why are you helping us?'

Korolev formed a slim smile, then frowned. 'It's not like the old days, Comrade Nash.' He waved his cigarette in sudden disgust. 'This collaboration between Comrade Stalin and Hitler. I don't like it. What possible allegiance does Mother Russia owe Germany? Besides, we have enough of our own domestic problems. This isn't a time to be dragged into a war with the rest of Europe.'

Nash countered, 'So, you are helping us. And other officers in the Soviet Army?'

Korolev chuckled bravado. 'Comrade Nash, Russia has been at war with itself for years. We don't need anyone else's fight. I just hope Comrade Stalin remembers the old allegiances. After all, it was Britain that maintained trade with us after the glorious October Revolution, not the Kaiser and his Germanic lapdogs.'

Nash leant forwards, 'So *you are* sympathetic to the British?'

Korolev waved a finger and spoke with a nonchalant tone. 'I have my orders, as do you. It's just a simple boat ride from Odessa to Istanbul, and from there your contacts will see you back to London.'

Nash shrugged, 'I am still alive, so let's say I trust you. What do you want from me, from Britain, in return?'

Korolev dropped slowly on to one knee. With his cigarette dangling from his lips, he spoke in a harsh whisper. 'You ask too many questions, English. You should be more careful.'

Nash kept a blank expression. 'I am just a soldier.'

'Of course you are, Comrade.' Korolev stood up and took a last gasp of his cigarette, then stubbed it out with his boot. 'The British do not want Germany to proliferate new weapons of any sort. So for now, that's all you need to know – but the times *are changing*, Comrade Nash.'

Nash risked outstaying his welcome, 'What weapons?'

Korolev pulled out another smoke from his overcoat and shoved it under his top lip. 'Don't worry yourself, English. You think we Soviets have no fucking intellect? We know about the National Socialists, German aspirations.' Korolev prodded a finger towards Nash, 'And we know about you!'

Nash sat in silence.

Korolev bent over to light his cigarette. He puffed a glowing ember as the sound of an outboard motor drifted closer. 'At last! Your ride home, Comrade Nash.'

A small wooden dingy putted into the shed. A weather-beaten man sat at the tiller of the small two stroke petrol engine. The noise of the motor echoed around the boathouse. Plumes of blue smoke discharged from the exhaust, clouding the stern of the boat.

Korolev gabbled in Russian as he took the short mooring line from helmsman and pulled the small craft alongside. He held the boat firm and turned to Nash. 'Go, quickly now! A small trawler will meet you in the bay and take you to Turkey.'

Nash signalled for the men to depart. They loaded efficiently into the boat. Nash shoved on his rucksack and tightened the straps. He stared at the Polkovnik for a few seconds, then shouted in his ear over the noise of the outboard. 'Perhaps we will meet again in different circumstances.'

Korolev stood, poker-faced. 'I doubt it. Goodbye, Major Nash.'

Nash jumped into the boat, as the coxswain flipped the outboard into reverse. The Black Sea and a rendezvous in Istanbul beckoned.

CHAPTER 3

Eavesdropping

E mily Sinclair sat elegantly with her back straight on the utilitarian office chair and focussed on her work, pleased to at last be doing something that really could make a difference to the war effort. The hours were long and the offices of the Radio Security Service were somewhat drab compared to her previous desk job in Whitehall, but that didn't matter. Besides, she'd made things a bit more homely with a few odds and ends of personal stationery and a blue quilted cushion to give a little comfort on the wooden chair. She scribbled on her notepad. Her slender fingers pressed hard onto the pencil as she cross-checked every fragment of information from the last radio transmission with the various intelligence codes, wireless operation procedures and dictionaries piled on her desk. Satisfied that the call had been properly recorded in her notes, she picked up the headphones, then paused as a hot flush washed through her chest.

The room suddenly felt very stuffy. Or maybe she was just tired? She placed the headset back on her desk. Then leaning backwards over her chair, she pushed her fingers through the knots forming in her long, slightly wavy, brown hair. She stood up and turned towards the sash window behind her desk. The south-facing window overlooked the River Thames, offering a modicum of brightness in the otherwise dull room. She paused at the glass, taking in her pale complexion against the whiteness of her blouse. The narrow black skirt didn't help much either, hugging her thighs a little more than her liking. She huffed at her average bust, and slim but too athletic figure, before opening the window a crack. She inhaled a deep lungful of air and then exhaled. Thankful for the fresh air, she brushed down the front of her blouse with the flats of her palms and quickly adjusted the waist on her black skirt. Then turning, she gazed absently about the room. The other three girls were working hard at their desks. They weren't a bad bunch. Beavering away late into the evening on most days, translating, or listening to their allotted frequency. Despite the cramped conditions amongst the oak bookcases and the cardboard boxes full of half-processed intelligence, morale was good.

Emily picked up the headphones and adjusted the large dial on her wireless to the next Soviet frequency. She closed her eyes momentarily to concentrate on the familiar, but at the same time alien, Russian dialect crackling into her headset. The weight of the solid-state headphones pressed the flesh of her ear lobes, causing a sticky sweat. Despite the encroaching discomfort, she listened; eavesdropping on the conversation and writing down the exchange as best she could.

A sudden flurry of speech crackled into her ears. She scrawled down the words in Russian, and deliberately skipped every other ruled line on the notepad to provide enough space for the subsequent translation. Instinctively, she rolled the tip of the pencil around to keep the keenest edge of the soft lead to the paper, scrawling frantically to note every nuance of the conversation. Abruptly, the tip of the pencil gave way. She tossed it aside and, still listening, stretched over her papers grabbing another HB from the pot. She whispered in Russian to herself as she picked up the thread, mouthing the dialogue in real time and pressing the pencil to paper. The headset crackled a deep Soviet voice. She estimated the age.

More than thirty? But experienced. Older perhaps?

It was hard to tell. She listened intently to the Soviet.

'We are not selling potatoes in a famine, comrade. These are matters of some importance, I am sure you understand.'

Well spoken. Educated – Moscow – possibly Leningrad. Has authority ... but there's something else?

The Russian voice continued, 'The fires of German industry need raw materials. So, let us be pragmatic. The Soviet Union has oil, coal, timber, precious metals – all manner of natural resources ...'

White noise filled the earpiece momentarily.

Some kind of trade deal, but with whom? And that voice ... strange, but somehow familiar ... An intangible, uneasy feeling diffused from her abdomen. A knot formed in her stomach; perplexed, she tried to concentrate.

A new player piped up on the airwaves. 'Well, it seems we both have our orders. In the spirit of cooperation, it might be possible to come to some arrangement.'

Emily scrawled down the Russian language as fast as she could. *Speaking Russian, but as a foreigner – not a Soviet – German? Or Austrian? Male, age – not sure, but sounds confident, intelligent.*

The Muscovite gave a reply, 'Comrade, you can be sure of discretion on my part, but my superiors will want something in return.'

Definitely a trade deal; and between the Germans and Soviet – but for what? Her mouth suddenly parched, the headphones pressed uncomfortably on her ears.

The Germanic voice phased in and out. 'I am authorised to offer ...' Emily tentatively adjusted the dial, squelching in and out of the frequency. '... if that would ... satisfactory.'

The tone changed as the Soviet broke into her earpiece. 'Comrade ... Krauch, we will consider ... superiors ... no need of ... gold ...'

The radio crackled in silence for what seemed like an eternity. *Comrade Krauch.* She underlined the name and

21

furrowed her brow as she concentrated on fine tuning the wireless.

The German voice erupted through the headphones. '… Berlin will … invitation to talks …'

A blast of static broke the transmission. She frantically gripped the dial, willing the frequency back to life.

Abruptly, the Soviet voice returned. 'Very well, in Tabriz.'

'Yes, the Reich is open for business. In Tabriz …' The German voice faded as the frequency went dead. Dumbfounded, Emily listened to white noise and random whistles for almost a minute. She circled her pencil around the words, *Berlin* and *Tabriz*.

The Germans and Russians are going to Tabriz. Where the hell is Tabriz?

She ditched the radio headset and leapt to her feet, almost running across the room. She grabbed a leather-bound atlas from the bookshelf and stood frantically flipping through the pages. She mumbled to herself. 'Tabriz, Tabriz, where are you? I should know this! Come on …' She found a Mercator projection of the Middle East and traced her finger across the map. 'There!' She stabbed her index finger into the page and then stared into space.

It made sense. Northern Iran, not far from the Caspian Sea and The West, but also close to the Soviet border. What better place for the Germans and Soviets to meet?

But *when?*

The German character seemed to be a man called Krauch, but who the hell was the Russian? A shiver ran down her spine, her stomach churned. *It makes no sense but I've heard that voice. Who are you?*

She wandered back to her chair in deep thought, still carrying the atlas. She dropped the book on her desk and sat down, absently tapping a pencil against her lips. She eased back in her chair, staring at the headset slung on the table and exhaled. 'Bloody hell. Who are you?' She learnt forwards, reaching for the dial on the small radio receiver, and steeled herself for the next transmission. The wireless crackled. The occasional high pitched whistle squealed from the speaker between bands of white noise.

Suddenly, a brunette poked her head around the office door. Ruby red lips smiled in Emily's direction. 'Emily! Something for you on three thousand kilohertz.' The girl gave a mischievous smile and then disappeared from view.

Emily raised an eyebrow and then tuned to the new frequency. The whine of the airwaves turned to static and then snippets of Arabic as she made fine adjustments to the dial. Abruptly, a crisp signal snapped into place. The speaker issued forth a melodic chant, and despite the odd crackle, the exotic sound was very distinctive: the call to evening prayer for the Muslim world.

An English voice come over the radio. 'Station Indigo Three Seven calling Lima One Zero, over.'

Emily stiffened with a wave of adrenalin. Her heart missed a beat.

Danny!

She grabbed the receiver, her voice quavering with uncertainty. 'One Zero receiving, over.'

'Lima One Zero, this is Indigo Three Seven. Situation report, over.'

'Go ahead, Indigo Three Seven ...'

'Operation accomplished. Target destroyed, over.'

'Indigo Three Seven, it's good to hear your voice. Report your ETA to Lima Base, over.'

'Good to hear yours also. Three, maybe four days, over.'

Emily kept a calm exterior. 'Indigo Three Seven, casualty report, over.'

Nash hesitated, 'Lima Base ... negative on the latter request ... await RTU, over.'

Emily changed tack. 'How many for evacuation to Lima One Zero, over?'

'Zero five, over.'

Emily closed her eyes.

Only five men?! My God!

Emily leant urgently on the transmit button. 'Indigo Three Seven, confirm. Was that zero five? Over.'

'Affirmative, zero five, over.'

Emily spoke in a controlled voice. 'Understood. Await further instructions, over.'

'Lima One Zero. This is Indigo Three Seven, awaiting RTU. Indigo, Three Seven; out.'

The speaker fell silent. Emily slumped back into her chair.

Only five men left? Out of how many? ... Thirty at least: the poor fellows, the poor, poor fellows.

She rubbed her brow, holding back the tears.

Oh Danny! I prayed for you. Please, I hope you are not hurt.

She pinched the bridge of her nose and forced herself to think rationally.

Don't be stupid. If he was injured badly, he would not be coming home in three or four days. Don't be selfish! Think of those men who will not return.

A silent tear rolled down her cheek.

One day Danny ... you can't go on beating the odds. Please, please don't leave me all alone. You must *come home ... this time and the next.*

CHAPTER 4

Major Weiner

The gigantic, six-foot-five frame of Major Karl Weiner filled the doorway. The unkempt nature of his *SS* uniform, blond stubble and his bloodshot eyes gave testament to a busy night. His square-set muscular jaw kept a firm expression as his blue eyes pierced in Steinhoff's direction. He regarded the scientist with contempt and spoke in a gruff matter-of-fact voice. 'Good morning, Doctor Steinhoff, what news of the construction?' Weiner stepped into the small office, towering over his charge.

Steinhoff looked up slowly, remaining expressionless and silent.

Weiner took the bait, 'Well? Progress report, Doctor Steinhoff. Is your machine ready or not? Or have you forgotten the little matter of the Führer's personal interest in your work?'

Steinhoff sneered a reply, 'Good morning, Major,' and returned to the business of reading the notes on his desk.

Weiner stepped up to the desk and leant on the table. The flimsy construction creaked under his massive bulk. Thick veins stood out on his neck. 'Berlin was expecting the results over two weeks ago. What news should I give the High Command?'

Steinhoff shrugged, 'Tell them the truth.'

Weiner swept the papers off the desk and bellowed. 'Are you insane?! The Führer was expecting a working device and a production line by now!'

Steinhoff backpedalled against the wall, cowering in his chair. He swallowed and fiddled with his glasses. 'Tell Berlin that we are almost there.'

'I'll need a little more than that for the two-million Reichsmarks that your little project has had this month.'

Sweat erupted on Steinhoff's brow despite the chill of the cavern. 'Alright! ... Tell them that one machine is ready. Tell them that we will catch up time and have things in production by the end of next month.'

Weiner stood upright, glaring. 'Doctor Steinhoff, if we don't go into mass production now, it will be the Russian front for me – and likely the hangman's noose for you – or us both. You *have* to stick to the timetable! There can be no more delays!'

Steinhoff suddenly jumped to his feet, exasperated. 'Yes, of course, Major Weiner. I realise the gravity of our situation, but I am working as fast as I can!'

Weiner menaced, 'Then work faster! Damn you!'

Steinhoff boiled, but held back his anger with a firm, almost tearful reply. 'I can't. We are out of materials.'

Weiner furrowed his brow, 'What? I don't understand? Why didn't you tell me this before?'

Steinhoff pushed his glasses on to the bridge of his nose and cleared his throat. 'I did, but you weren't listening as usual.' He bent down, retrieving a wad of paper from the scattered documents. 'Shall, I read it to you?' Steinhoff waved the bundle, and creasing his forehead, recounted his notes as if taking the school register. 'Titanium dioxide, sixty ... no one hundred and sixty kilograms, ninety-nine percent pure carbon sixty – not with any charcoal contamination – and aluminium sheeting; lots of it. Spun copper wire for the starter; the finest that money can buy. And general chemicals … solvents … liquid oxygen.'

He tossed the notes on the table and huffed, shaking his head. 'Where the hell am I going to get these materials with a war on?!'

Weiner stood like a Neanderthal, processing the information, then mustered a retort. 'Herr Doctor, Berlin has considerable resources at hand, do you forget that the Reich now controls most of Europe?'

'Yes *Europe*, but that's no damned use to me!'

Weiner snorted, 'So?' He picked up papers, scanning the details of the shopping list. 'It doesn't seem problematic. We have heavy industry all along the Rhine, including chemical plants. We just order what is needed – and do it quickly.'

Steinhoff rubbed his chin wearily. 'I will need a steady supply of aluminium to make the alloy sheeting, but most of our steelworks have gone over to iron and ship building for the navy – I can't get the special alloy locally. Then there's the titanium, without it, we're finished!' He paced behind the desk like a caged animal, kicking out randomly at the detritus on the floor.

Weiner growled. 'Alright! Don't make a meal out of it. We still have our contacts in South Africa with a plentiful supply of titanium dioxide.'

'Yes, but can you get it here? The British control large parts of the continent.'

Weiner shook his head. 'Not where it matters. We control North Africa and the Mediterranean ports. Materials can be moved by rail to Algeria, or by road to Tripoli. The metal ore can then be flown from there, or more likely shipped with an escort.'

'Yes, for the British to sink!'

'It matters not – whatever the British can do, the U-boat fleet will revisit on them tenfold. You will have all the metals you need.'

'But not on time. I need them now. And what about the special carbon?' Steinhoff gave a sweep of his arm.

'We do it the same way?' Weiner puzzled.

'But that's just it, we can't! The South African government has allied with the British, who now occupy most of Zululand! The only suitable geology for digging up the carbon!' Steinhoff slumped, 'The carbon sixty supply is out of reach: without it we *cannot* mass-produce the machine.' He shook his head. 'We have to face reality. It's over ...'

Weiner stood in silence, searching for a solution. It had been one headache after another. Need this, need that, more men, more supplies. The little upstart had him running around in circles. Baby sitting a bunch of overgrown spoilt brats wasn't such a good route to promotion after all – not that it mattered now – making the rank of Commandant seemed even further over the horizon. Still, a decent rank, salary, and some fucking respect wouldn't go amiss. Fate had landed him in *Wolfsberg*. Every grunt in the German Army knew that even hearing about such a secret facility was a one way ticket. He'd have to face the music sooner or later; it was either help Herr Doctor Steinhoff or face the firing squad. The front line in North Africa suddenly felt very appealing, but the thought of regular soldiering was nothing but a pipe dream. Besides, after the debacle at the rocket facility at Peenemünde and the sabotage of the supply lines through the Carpathians, he had a score to settle. The death of his own Commandant at the hands of the British had put him in charge of security and logistics. The pressure was on, but how the hell was he going to secure the special chemicals needed?

Weiner suddenly stiffened. Of course! Why hadn't he thought of it before? 'Doctor Steinhoff, the carbon. You made it once from burning charcoal, no?'

Steinhoff stopped pacing. 'Yes, in the small furnace at Peenemünde, but it was only some experimental batches. The process was too inefficient, with only a tiny fraction of the right kind of carbon being produced.'

Weiner rallied, 'So that's the answer isn't it? You know how to make it. Germany has some of the largest blast furnaces in Europe; get someone to make it locally, no matter how must wastage from the process.'

Steinhoff picked up the train of through. 'Yes, I suppose so … in theory.' His eyebrows lifted. 'Actually, there is one possibility. I. G. Farben have a big chemical plant at Merseburg. It's not far from Leipzig. The last I heard, they were making ammonia and other general chemicals; but they would certainly have the right facilities.' Steinhoff gaped, then mumbled to himself. 'Yes … we just make a few changes here and there, adjust for scale up in the chemical reactions …' Abruptly, he dug amongst the papers littering the office, frantically moving from bundle to bundle.

Weiner stood moronic, observing. If the spectacled lunatic had something, he'd go along with it for now.

Steinhoff produced a large folded sheet of paper from the detritus and opened it out on to the desk.

Weiner leant over the complicated-looking diagram. 'What is it?'

Steinhoff looked hopeful, 'Schematics of the carbon synthesis. If we can adapt the furnaces and pipework at Merseburg, then we are in with a reasonable chance. If we can't, then South Africa is our only other option for a usable natural source of carbon sixty.'

Weiner nodded at the grim reality, 'Then it has to be I. G. Farben. Come what may, I'll find everything on your shopping list. Berlin might even help – you know, with the Captains of Industry. Either way, it has to work or we are both condemned. Remember, Herr Doctor, the price of failure is a rope around both our necks.'

Weiner turned and headed for the gantry without waiting for a reply. If I. G. Farben couldn't make the precious carbon sixty, then the whole project might be in jeopardy – but that wasn't the only problem. The destruction of the train in the Carpathian Mountains hadn't just wiped out the last of their supplies and technical drawings. German scientists were thin on the ground – finding more physicists and expert engineers to work on the production line was crucial – but where the hell was he going to get them from?

He had no idea.

CHAPTER 5

British Intelligence

Nash stepped into the small lobby on the fifth floor of SIS headquarters, clunking his steel toe capped boots across the parquet flooring towards the receptionist. He stopped short of her desk, realising he stank – there hadn't been time to change out of his crumpled trousers: navy-issue number eights. The grubby cable stitch of the fisherman's pullover and his soiled grey coat completed the look. He threw a stubbly smile at the curvaceous young lady, 'Is the old man in?'

She smiled politely, 'He's expecting you, go straight in, Major Nash.'

He nodded a quick thanks and slipped through the large mahogany doors, simultaneously wiping the smirk from his face. He walked a few paces into the empty room, halting at a respectable distance from the conference table, then cleared his throat. He stood, eyeing Sir Hugh Sinclair stooped over a manila folder on the desk. As usual, Sinclair wore a three-piece pin stripped suit, cut perfectly by the Saville Row tailors to fit his tall, lean frame. The silk tie, pressed white shirt with gold cufflinks, and his slicked-back neatly trimmed hair sold the image – and it was no illusion – Sinclair was a man of genuine breeding and distinction. He carried himself with ease.

Nash kept a blank expression and almost regretted his grubby attire amongst the pristine atmosphere of beeswax, the wooden panelling, and the posh carpets in the conference room. 'Sir, you have orders?'

Sinclair waved him forwards, 'The intelligence analysts have finished with the items you recovered from the Carpathian Mountains.'

Nash dropped beside his superior, frowning, 'Sir?'

Sinclair shook his head gently, half-peering at the top secret document. 'I am afraid it's not good news. The identity cards you recovered were mostly of lowly technicians and other engineers. At least, that's the opinion of our own boffins – no one we would recognise as a scientist of international standing was on the train.'

Nash tensed a little, feeling the hawk-like mind of Sinclair penetrating his thoughts. 'Sir, what about the military personnel?'

Sinclair pursed his lips. 'You see that's really odd. A few middle ranking Germans, albeit seasoned troops as you reported, but no Commandant, *SS* Brigadeführer or even an *SS* Sturmbannführer. The fact is, they barely had anyone of a decent rank on the train.'

Nash exhaled palpable tension and disappointment. 'The train was obliterated. It's likely that some of the bodies simply disintegrated in the explosions.'

'Yes, quite so, but still, I remain suspicious.' Sinclair brightened, 'Though it looks like we finally have some decent technical drawings of the German device and its components.' Sinclair patted a fist against his lips, revealing his gold Rolex. 'Whether that helps us or not is unclear. It's a rather top-notch piece of technology. Our chaps have nothing like it. We have to face facts, Major Nash, the blasted Germans are way ahead of us; even ahead of the Americans.'

Nash gritted his teeth, seething. Was that it? Some thirty-odd of his best men dead, just so the eggheads could tell him what he already knew: the Germans had perfected some kind of super weapon and were intent on moving it to an underground location, likely for the purposes of mass production. The absence of high ranking Nazis and senior scientists on the train, along with the dearth of any intact devices did only mean one thing – he'd been too late – the Germans were already installed in their damned fortress. And if that was the case, it was over. There was nothing to be done to stop them. The facility was under hundreds of feet of solid rock in the most difficult of terrain. A ground assault on the fortress, or even a bombing raid on the mountain, would be futile.

'Sir, what are your orders?'

Sinclair paused before replying. 'There's been a bit of a development.'

Nash puzzled, 'Sir?'

'We must assume the worst. The Germans are hiding underground and moving towards production of their device. It seems the Russians have even gleaned the Führer's name for the place: he calls it his *Wolfsberg*. But the Germans have a weakness.'

Nash rallied, 'They've trapped themselves like rats in a hole – we starve them out, sir?'

Sinclair nodded appreciatively, 'No, not exactly, something with a little more finesse. We know the Germans and Soviets are bedfellows. The Russian desk at SIS has been rather busy of late; and it seems that my Emily has stumbled on to something.'

Nash flushed with adrenalin, 'Emily?'

'Yes, clever girl. We're not entirely sure, but the Russians maybe planning a little get together with the Germans in Iran – a place called Tabriz.'

Nash gave a blank look. 'So?'

'Ordinarily, we might not have given the report much credence, but a German by the name of Krauch was mentioned.'

'I am sorry, sir, I don't follow you.'

'This Krauch – if we've got the right man – is known to us. He's an industrialist and a man of influence in the higher circles of the Third Reich. He runs a huge chemical company, one of the biggest in the world. The I. G. Farben conglomerate; and has done so for some years. He set the business up before the war and, as you can imagine, he's now a very wealthy man.'

Nash rubbed his chin thoughtfully, 'So you're wondering why one of the most powerful German industrialists might need the help of the Soviets?'

Sir Hugh shrugged, 'It could be nothing, but the timing is rather suspect. So, we need to know a little more about this Krauch and the resources at his disposal.' He flipped through the loose pages in the manila folder, producing a photographic print. 'Fortunately, the RAF have been collecting reconnaissance on a variety of industrial sites of interest in Germany; shipyards, steelworks and so on.' He handed the black and white to Nash then continued, 'Including chemical plants, several owned by I. G. Farben.'

Nash examined the image. A large smoke stack or tower sat amongst an expanse of long single storey buildings. A myriad of pipework and gantries seem to connect the factory floor to a collection of huge storage tanks – but storage tanks for what? Petroleum spirit? Gas? Ammonia? Some other industrial chemical? He flipped over the aerial snapshot: 3rd November 1940. Taken a few months ago.

'There's more,' Sinclair handed over another photograph.

Nash absorbed the contents. The same factory – but something was different – more pipework and a new building going up. He scanned the edge of the building, squinting at the detail in the image. Sandbags? Machine gun posts? Troops guarding an industrial plant? He turned over the image: 1st February 1941. Nash glanced a puzzled look at his superior. 'Sir?'

'It's a chemical factory belonging to Herr Krauch. At a place called Merseburg, a few miles west of Leipzig.' Sinclair pulled another sheet of paper with a small portrait photograph pinned to the corner from the file.

Nash examined the document. A lean-looking man, perhaps in his early forties, wearing a double-breasted suit, silk tie, handkerchief folded neatly in the left pocket and a gold pin announcing his membership of the Nazi party on his lapel. Nash read the caption. 'Director Carl von Krauch, I. G. Farben, industrial chemist and business man.' Nash looked up, 'Sir, what is it that you require?'

'We need to give this Krauch more attention. He made his fortune before the war from synthesising novel chemicals for pest control, developing industrial catalysts and various petroleum-based products. That expertise can be reapplied and this possible meeting with the Soviets is worrying.' Sinclair paused.

Nash swallowed, waiting for the good news, but remained silent.

'I am sending you on a reconnaissance mission. There are some details to arrange – but pack your kit for a solo drop behind enemy lines – you're leaving at the end of the week.'

'Yes, sir.'

Nash withered inside. It wasn't the enemy that left an uneasy feeling. Had Sinclair's judgement been impaired this time? It was possible, especially where Emily was concerned. Or maybe Sinclair wasn't telling the whole story. Either way, it made no difference, the job was on – and there was only three days to get ready.

Sergio Korolev stiffened in his chair, throwing the hand-held radio microphone on to the desk. The radio hissed back with static. He folded his arms tightly, snorting through his nostrils as he bit into his own lip. The bitter metallic taste of warm blood teased his palate. Abruptly, his chair was swung around. He stared defiantly at the senior official from the People's Commissariat for Internal Affairs, the NKVD. The investigator stood in his crisp uniform, towering.

Korolev felt the spade-like palm of the NKVD on his shoulder. The man spoke in a quiet, but harsh tone. 'The old alliances are dead, Comrade Korolev. New ones are afoot. You understand the game of course …' He patted Korolev on the shoulder.

Korolev shook his head. 'Game? This is not a game.'

The NKVD menaced, his rancid tobacco breath filled the Colonel's nostrils. 'Oh, I think it is, comrade. A deadly one, nonetheless. Your friends in London were listening in? No?'

Korolev shrugged, 'Probably …'

'Good, then you have done your duty for today.'

Korolev spoke in a monotone. 'And tomorrow?'

'For you?' The NKVD smiled, 'The game is to stay alive, is it not? You will make your bed with our new German friends.'

'And if I don't?'

The NKVD pushed his face closer to Korolev and hissed. 'Siberia is very cold my friend. How long do you think you would last in the Gulag? One month? Maybe less?' The official broke into a smile, patted Korolev gently on the shoulder once more, and then sauntered towards the door.

CHAPTER 6

Merseburg

The brakes of the staff car squealed as Weiner brought the vehicle to a halt at the main gate. He pushed the gear level into neutral and took a drag from his cigarette, then glanced across at his charge. Steinhoff sat in the passenger seat, grasping a leather satchel and looking more like an impromptu mourner in his ill-fitting dark suit than a scientist visiting one of the largest chemical plants in Europe. Weiner took another rasp, exhaling smoke in Steinhoff's direction. 'What the hell is wrong with you?'

Steinhoff sulked, 'I am not sure this is a good idea. My work is highly sensitive.'

Weiner gave a disdainful look. 'Do you want your raw materials or not?'

Steinhoff countered, 'Well, of course.' He pushed his glasses on to the bridge of his nose.

'Hallelujah,' Weiner shook his head slowly and turned his gaze towards the approaching sentry. He wound down the window and then fished inside his breast pocket, producing a folded sheet of paper. Weiner spat a fragment of tobacco from his lip as the guard arrived at the driver's door. 'Major Weiner for Director Krauch. We have authorisation from Berlin.' He thrust the document out of the window.

The foot soldier read the letter quickly, taking in the signature and official stamp of the Reich Chancellor. He click his heels to attention and stuttered a reply, 'Yes, yes, Major

… Weiner, but I am sorry, sir. I also need to see your identity cards, sir.'

Weiner flicked an impatient hand in Steinhoff's direction and quickly gathered their worn passes. He handed them to the sentry, 'Come on, we don't have all day.' Weiner drummed on the steering wheel as the guard checked their documents.

The trooper held out the cards, 'Thank you, Major. Please go straight ahead for about three hundred metres and then left at the first intersection. Herr Krauch is expecting you.' The guard waved a hand and within seconds the iron gates parted. Weiner crunched the vehicle into first and accelerated through the entrance. The chassis rattled along the narrow cobbles of the access road. A spaghetti of industrial pipework engulfed the thoroughfare. Steam vented overhead, mixing with soot and the spent vapour of chemical solvents. The volatile cocktail quickly infiltrated the cab.

Steinhoff took a slow, deep, sniff and mustered a superior look. 'Esters, the sweet smell of organic chemistry.'

Weiner jeered a reply, 'Crud if you ask me. Cordite on the battlefield – now that's a test of a real man. Have you ever *smelt cordite, Herr Doctor*?'

'Unfortunately, yes, when your predecessor failed to prevent sabotage at Peenemünde. It isn't an experience I would like to repeat, but that depends somewhat on you. *Doesn't it, Major*?'

Weiner shot a deathly glare as he pulled up at the entrance to a long brick building. 'This looks like it.' He applied the handbrake. A man of average build, with neat brown hair parted at the side, and wearing a blue pin-stripped suit stood in front of the building. A heavy steel door suspended on a sliding rail marked the entrance. Narrow gauge tramlines disappeared under the structure and into the factory. Weiner stepped from the car, taking in a lungful of the damp, polluted, air. He walked briskly over the cobbles towards the director, not bothering to wait for Steinhoff, and clicked his heels politely. 'Herr Director Krauch? Major Weiner reporting, sir.'

The man smiled and extended a soft, manicured hand. 'Ah! Major Weiner, yes, I am Carl Krauch, chairman of the board, at your service. Welcome to Merseburg, part of the I. G. Farben Corporation.'

Weiner shook hands firmly and scrutinised the chairman's features. His brown eyes and facial expression gave little away; he was clearly a man of intellect, but there was also something less tangible – a steeliness of character, or was it deviousness? Weiner wasn't sure. Either way, he was a man of some influence and politically adept. He hadn't got to the position of Plenipotentiary for Special Issues in Chemical Production for the Reich Chancellery by being nice to people. That made him a dangerous man and one with absolute authority bestowed by the Führer himself.

Weiner clicked his heels and smiled, 'Thank you, sir, we are keen to proceed.' Steinhoff appeared at his side, still carrying the leather satchel tucked under his arm. Weiner forced politeness. 'Herr Director, may I introduce Doctor Steinhoff.'

'Doctor Steinhoff, welcome. I am sorry, I am not too familiar with your work,' Krauch lied. 'Liquid fuels I believe?'

Steinhoff offered a limp hand. 'Yes, I have worked on fuels in the past, Herr Director.'

Weiner flashed a glance at his charge, then quickly cleared his throat. 'Thank you for agreeing to meet us at such short notice, sir. I appreciate you have a busy schedule.' He formed another polite smile.

Krauch pursed his lips. 'Indeed, Major, the war keeps us all busy. Shall we?' Krauch gestured towards the heavy steel door and then pulled it open a few feet with surprising ease.

Weiner and Steinhoff followed as Krauch switched to business mode. 'Well, gentlemen, this way. I am sure you'd like to see the factory floor …' He waved an arm indicating the expanse of the installation. 'As you can see, the Reich Ministry and of course I. G. Farben, have invested heavily in new furnaces and machinery for the war effort. This section is dedicated to the refinement of metal ores. We're processing aluminium at the moment – mostly for the Luftwaffe, but we can make other things. Titanium dioxide isn't it?'

Weiner stepped in, almost shouldering Steinhoff aside. 'Sir, that's correct. We need five hundred kilograms a month. I am hoping you can refine or source that for us.'

Director Krauch smiled, 'Major, I expect we can help you, depending on the type and quality of the finished powder you need.' Sensing the tension between his two guests, the director turned to Steinhoff. 'Herr Doctor, your specification?'

Steinhoff spoke as he ferreted amongst the documents in his satchel, 'It has to be the anatase crystal form of titanium dioxide, and extremely pure – ninety-nine percent purity.' He offered a crumpled sheet to the director.

Weiner stood in silence, observing as the director studied the sheet.

Krauch looked up with a blank expression. 'Gentlemen, this is challenging you understand. With the raw materials I have now, I can produce about two or three kilos a day – at best seventy kilos a month.'

Steinhoff blanched, 'But Herr Director that is nowhere near enough. We need more, much more.'

Weiner scowled at the scientist and offered a matter-of-fact clarification, puffing his chest in military fashion as he did so. 'Forgive me, Director. Berlin is imposing a firm timetable and Doctor Steinhoff here is keen to deliver, sir.'

Krauch allowed a polite reply. 'Quite so, Major, but even I must work with limited resources.'

Weiner reeled at the suddenly dour prospects. Everything depended on help from I. G. Farben; without it the hangman's noose would surely tighten around his throat. Weiner threw caution to the wind. 'Yes, sir. I hear from the Reich Ministry that you are building a new factory at Monowitz. Labour is hard to find, perhaps I can cut you a few units?'

Krauch maintained the polite façade. 'The Reich Ministry is placing demands on us all. I understand there were problems at Peenemünde and now you have your new facility, but it isn't a question of labour – our main problem is raw materials.'

'Yes, sir.' Weiner pressed for a reply, 'But you can make the titanium dioxide, Herr Director?'

'Yes, we can.' Krauch stood measuring the demeanour of his guests. 'Major, let me wrestle with that little problem for now. You also need a particular type of carbon I understand?'

Weiner feared more bad news, 'Yes, sir. A carbon material, sir.' He stood warily.

Krauch broadened into smile. 'Please, this way gentlemen. Let me show you our other production lines.' Krauch turned towards the heart of the factory.

Weiner held back, keeping a respectable distance and steered Steinhoff by the elbow. He hissed into the scientist's ear. 'Let me do the damned talking. Don't make this more complicated than it needs to be!'

Steinhoff glared back. 'I must have enough material to make at least seven or eight devices a month.'

Weiner shook his head in disgust. 'Leave the negotiations to me. You'll work with what I can get!'

'One or two machines a month isn't enough! There has to be more raw materials …'

Weiner gritted his teeth. 'You think I don't know that? It's my head on the block as well you know! Just follow my lead. I am in charge of logistics!'

Machinery clunked and hissed on each side of the main gangway as they followed the director some fifty yards into the factory, eventually coming to a stop adjacent to a bank of brand new furnaces. Weiner eyed the director with caution, whilst keeping Steinhoff at his side.

Krauch continued the tour, 'Gentlemen, this section of the factory is dedicated to carbon products and various extractions of chemicals from coal. Of course, we will give priority to your particular needs ...' He stood with his hands on his hips, gazing with satisfaction into the depths of the factory. 'Impressive, is it not?'

A bank of furnaces lined the left wall. Men in brown coats worked at benches a few yards in front of each fire, weighing and sieving black ingredients. 'Here, we process good quality German coal to obtain various carbon-based products. We make a range of graphite materials for example.' Krauch smiled back and forth his visitors, 'I am sure we can adapt our process to your needs.'

Weiner replied, 'Thank you, sir. It is a spherical carbon. Doctor Steinhoff, the specification if you please.' He discreetly nudged the scientist.

Steinhoff lifted his brow, then unbuckled his satchel, pulling out a wad of papers. He offered a bundle of pages to their host. Krauch read through the first page in some detail and then flicked through several others. 'A most interesting process, Doctor. I must congratulate you. I don't believe anyone has made this type of carbon before – carbon sixty – intriguing.'

Weiner intervened, 'Sir, are you able to synthesise it?'

Krauch examined the notes again, then stood thoughtfully. 'Yes ... I think so, but it's rather specialist stuff requiring a particular type of coal. The wastage will be very high. We might only get a few hundred grams of material from burning several tonnes of coal. Some might argue the coal is better spent in the shipyards of Hamburg; and I would be inclined to agree. Unless of course, we can find our own supply of high quality coal for special chemical production.' He pushed the wad of notes in Steinhoff's direction.

Steinhoff took the worn pages and busily crammed them back into his satchel.

Krauch, with his expression hardening, turned to Weiner. 'Major, perhaps we can help each other after all.'

Weiner stiffened, 'Sir?'

'Walk with me.' Krauch furrowed his brow and moved off.

Weiner followed. Both men ambled a few yards and then huddled together with their backs to Steinhoff.

Krauch spoke quietly and calmly. 'You obviously have security clearance and certain capabilities, so indulge me for a moment.' The director paused, 'We are both challenged by the need for raw materials, and as you know, Germany has several trade agreements in place with our Soviet allies.'

Weiner stood with his jaw firmly set. 'I am listening, go on, sir.'

'So perhaps German coal is not the best for our purpose here. Our supply of metal ores for producing titanium alloys is also stretched thinly across the needs of the Luftwaffe, the U-boat fleet, munitions production and heavy industry. The list goes on; and there are special projects to consider such as yours.'

Weiner absorbed the notion. On one level it made sense. Trading with the Soviet Union might provide the critical raw materials needed for the device, but what would the Russians want in return? A slice of the action? Weiner dismissed the thought. On the other hand, the prospect of delivering another meagre progress report to Berlin would certainly bring the wrath of his superiors. The Reich Chancellery was fickle and there'd been plenty of middle ranking officers who'd suddenly found themselves at the gallows. Time was now a limiting factor and the options were running out. He took a deep breath. 'Alright, Herr Director, we can agree that both of us are tested by dwindling supplies, but do you really want to trust a bunch of communists?' He shook his head slowly, pursing his lips. 'I just don't know, they're slippery bastards, sir.'

Krauch placed a friendly hand on the Major's shoulder and continued in a harsh whisper. 'The truth is, Major, we need better quality starting material and in larger quantities than we can achieve domestically. The Soviets are our only prospect – don't believe the rhetoric coming out of the Reich Ministry – the German war effort is on its knees. We *need* access to the vast mineral wealth of the Soviets, and we need it *now*!'

Weiner explored the concerned features of the director. It seemed a little too convenient, but where else was he going to get the special carbon sixty and the high purity anatase form of the titanium mineral needed for the device? If there was any chance of getting the production going, then he'd have to take it, even if it meant clandestine dealing with the Russians. He exhaled and looked the director in the eye. 'What would you have me do, sir?'

Krauch paused lifting his hand free from Weiner's shoulder, 'Good, Major, we will have to trust each other in this shared endeavour – but no one else.'

Weiner nodded cautiously, 'Agreed.'

Krauch spoke in a matter-of-fact tone, 'What I am about to tell you is classified …' He scoped the Major up and down.

Weiner stood poker-faced.

Krauch continued, 'The Soviets are ready to trade with us, but only under certain conditions.'

Weiner gritted his teeth. 'Conditions? What conditions, sir?'

'There is a meeting planned on neutral ground – in Tabriz.'

Weiner struggled to maintain his composure. 'Tabriz?'

Krauch confirmed, 'Yes, officially, it's just another trade delegation to the Middle East, but unofficially … I will be speaking to my counterpart in the Soviet Union about our special needs in chemical production. A Soviet Colonel will attend. A man of particular interest to the Reich, a Colonel Korolev.'

'Korolev?'

'Yes, he's a military man like yourself, but he's also an engineer of some repute. He's intimately involved with the Soviet rocket programme. It seems both sides have something to trade. The Soviets want superior German propulsion technology in exchange for raw materials. So, it is suggested that yourself and Doctor Steinhoff attend the delegation.'

Weiner blanched, 'Sir, you want me and the good doctor to go to Iran?' He swallowed and glanced back towards Steinhoff then at Director Krauch, 'That's a bit of a security risk isn't it, sir? I mean, we are already behind with production.'

Krauch nodded appreciatively and stood upright. His features remained grim. 'Quite so, Major, not that it matters – the Führer has decreed it. We are all going to Iran. Your job will be to use Doctor Steinhoff and to appeal to this Russian, Korolev. Feed them scraps of credible technical information from Doctor Steinhoff's work, then we make the exchange.'

Weiner stiffened, struggling to process the new information. Go to Iran? Actually *hand over* information on the device to the Soviets, contrary to all directives from the Reich Chancellery to maintain *absolute secrecy*. It made no sense. Besides, Steinhoff would never agree to it. Had Krauch known about the problems at Wolfsberg all along? If so, who else knew about the facility? Weiner felt the diminutive stature of his rank. In the end, he was just another lump of meat in the food chain. He took a deep breath and ventured a reply. 'Sir, respectfully, for reasons of national security, I would need to see written orders.'

'Indeed,' Krauch produced a sealed envelope from his inside breast pocket.

Weiner stared at the eagle on Swastika stamped in red ink over the closed document. 'Sir, this is a dangerous course of action.'

Krauch nodded. 'Of course it is. That's why you're coming along. The Russian delegation must never make it back to Moscow.'

CHAPTER 7

Attic Room

Emily laid on the bed with sweat trickling down her back and a sticky dampness clinging to her skin. She propped herself up on her elbows and kicked the disarray of sheets back, allowing the relatively cooler air of the attic room to access her torso. Her bare nipples hardened. She pushed aside her fringe with her palm and stared up at the single skylight in the sloping roof. Dried splodges of green and white on the glass marked the ever-constant presence of the pigeons of Bermondsey. She looked around the room taking in the peeling wallpaper that was browning at its edges, the discoloured paintwork, and the moth-eaten rug on the floorboards. Some grubby utensils and a portable petrol stove sat on a small table in the far corner of the room.

She stretched, pushing her arms against the iron of the bedstead and relaxed back into the pillow. 'Danny, how long have you rented this room?'

She studied Nash as he stirred the solitary mess tin on the stove. He stood wearing a green army-issue pullover, but was otherwise naked from the waist down. The odour of fresh coffee began to drift across the room.

He stopped stirring momentarily and half-turned towards her. 'I dunno, seven years I guess … maybe eight. Why?'

She formed a mischievous smile. 'Oh, nothing really. I was just wondering; why don't you get your own place?'

Nash shrugged, 'This is my own place.'

Emily tutted, 'No, not like this. I mean, *your own* home. You could buy a flat in London or something.'

Nash stared absently at the shape of her breasts while stirring the mess tin. 'Coffee?'

Emily sat up, suddenly pulling the sheet over her modesty. 'Danny Nash, *do not* change the subject. Come on, why not have your own place?'

Nash poured a tin mug full of the steaming brew. 'There's no point. I am either at the barracks most of the time, or away on a job; besides I don't have any furniture or anything to put in a place of my own.'

'It's a bit chicken and egg isn't it? If you had a place of your own, you could buy some things to go in it.'

'I could, but why bother? I eat, sleep, drink and shit mostly at the barracks. I don't need a place of my own. Besides, this suits me fine to get away from the army. I can pretend to be a civilian for a few hours here.'

She sat up as he passed her the cup. She took a sip of the hot liquid. The taste of coffee and sugar washed away the saltiness in her throat. 'Danny, I guess that's my point really – you pretend to have a life.' She shuffled over a few inches, trying not to spill her brew, as Nash settled on the edge of the bed. She felt his index finger caressing her fringe.

He spoke quietly. 'Emily, I do have a life. I am in the army and when I am not at work, I can be with you …'

'Be with me …' she titled her head, eyeing him up and down. 'What more could a girl want?'

Nash squinted a mischievous look. 'What exactly does a girl want?'

She laughed nervously. 'Oh, I don't know. Most girls want a husband, a home …'

Nash brushed her cheek. 'What about this girl?'

She flushed, 'A husband – yes, *a husband* eventually, and a home; some place where *we* could belong.'

Nash furrowed his brow and spoke softy. 'And what then? Children? An ordinary life?'

Emily raised an eyebrow and gave a wry smile. 'Is this a marriage proposal, Major Nash?'

Nash looked sheepish. 'Well, no, but we could … I mean, I love you, you love me. We could get married, eventually.'

Her smile faded. 'Eventually? After the war?'

'Yes, they say it won't last much longer. Perhaps in two or three years' time …'

Her face soured. 'You'll be dead and I'll be …' Moisture filled her eyes. 'I'll be lonely.'

Nash eased forwards. 'No Emily, I will not be dead. I will survive this war, and when it's done we can be together.'

'How can you know that when so many are already dead?'

'I am here, aren't I?'

Emily shook her head, still holding the coffee cup. 'No, you've just beaten the odds once or twice. What will happen with your next roll of the dice?'

Nash took a deep breath, he exhaled, shoulders sagging. 'No, it isn't a game of chance – it's a matter of careful preparation, fitness, training and a state of mind.'

She pursed her lips, her eyes filled with water. 'You go off and I sit and wait, feeling useless. Unable to influence the outcome.'

'No, you mustn't think like that. You *are already* helping with your new job on the Soviet desk. There's no question that good intelligence makes all the difference. Men come home alive because of the work you do.' Nash looked her in the eye for a few moments, then shifted his gaze to the far corner of the room.

Emily leant out of the bed, placing the coffee mug on the wooden floor. She eased up on her left elbow, 'Danny?' She frowned, but spoke softly, 'You're leaving again, aren't you?'

49

He shook his head slowly. 'Yes, your intercepts on the Russians have given us some fresh leads. I am away again – the day after tomorrow.'

She leant forwards, rubbing his shoulder gently, 'I see … You know it's strange. I could hear the call to prayers over the radio. It sounded so … romantic and melodic. Istanbul … What would Germany want with such a beautiful and exotic place? Why the Middle East?' She hugged into his muscular back.

He stared at the floor, 'That's what your father would like to find out,' and then looked up. 'The German you identified in the radio transmission as a Herr Krauch; you heard him speak. What did you make of the man?'

Emily continued caressing his shoulder, 'Not a young man, not old either, but confident – the kind of surety that comes with experience. Also authoritative, but comfortable with it, not aggressive.' She furrowed her brow and then suddenly sat upright. 'Danny, you know who this Krauch is, don't you? You're going after him?'

Nash turned to face her. 'You know I can't say, but if it's the same Krauch – and that's a big if – he's a well-known industrialist. It's no secret. He runs Germany's biggest chemical company, I. G. Farben; or at least he did before the war.'

She flushed with a sudden clarity. 'The German are organising talks, or some sort of negotiation in a place called Tabriz.'

Nash nodded, 'Yes, I know. It was in the transcript.'

Emily concentrated, 'So, somebody called Krauch, a German industrialist, is negotiating with the Russians for something. Christ!' She jolted stiff on the bed. 'The Soviets want chemicals from Germany? But that doesn't make any sense. Besides what would the Germans want in return – tanks? Planes?'

Nash interceded, 'Emily, you know I can't discuss operations.'

She massaged the lines in her brow, almost whispering to herself. 'No! It's the other way around, the German industrialist needs something from the Russians – supplies, raw materials – Germany is running out of supplies …' She gaped at Nash, 'Danny, the Russian … the one in the transcript.'

He gave a puzzled look. 'What about the Russian?'

"I know this sounds daft, but I *know* that voice. I've heard it before. I am sure.'

Nash sharpened, 'In other conversations over the wireless?'

Emily shook her head vigorously. 'No, it's not like that, not from the radio. It's a voice I have *actually heard in person*, perhaps a long time ago; from my childhood.'

Nash countered, 'Nah, you've spent hours transcribing messages. The mind plays tricks when we're tired; besides your father has moved in diplomatic circles. You're just misremembering Russian voices you may have heard, or a story. Your mother is Russian after all.'

'Yes, I know, but *this voice* – its educated tone, polite yet with a measure of gruffness, and the pronunciation – it's overwhelmingly familiar.'

Nash leaned in closer, stroking her hair. 'Emily … leave it, you're over-analysing a scrap of dialogue … Besides I can think of better things right now.' He pressed closer.

She pushed him away with the flat of her palms. 'Danny, I am serious! *I know this man.'* She pursed her lips. 'If he's middle-aged now, he would have been in his twenties, maybe thirty when I was a child. I have vague memories, someone acquainted with my mother …'

Nash squeezed her hand. 'Emily, where's this going? Promise me that you won't do anything rash.'

She sat with a blank expression as her mind processed the information. What would her father do with the intelligence? Where would he send Danny, and what for? She suddenly squinted unable to conceal her irritation, 'You're going to bloody Germany. Aren't you?' She studied the details of his face.

Nash tried to keep a closed expression.

'You are! Danny! You're going to this chemical factory in the heart of Germany?! What for? To blow it up or get yourself killed?!'

Nash held up his hands, 'Easy … easy, Emily. I am under orders, like everyone else!'

She pierced a reply. '*Yes, you are*. Daddy says jump, and you ask *how high*?! If it wasn't this war, he'd go and find another one for you to fight!'

Nash stood up, pleading, 'No, Emily, that's not how it is. I am a soldier and there is a chain of command.'

She threw back the covers, growling as she abruptly pulled on her clothes. 'No wonder Mother left him and went back to Russia – he's doing the same to us! *You're* doing the *same* to us. You're always away on some job. Bloody hell, Danny!' She hastily buttoned her blouse and straightened her skirt.

Nash rubbed his brow, exasperated. 'Where are you going? Come on, it doesn't have to be like this?'

She slipped on her heels and grabbed her coat. 'Don't you see, Danny? This is all an illusion. There is no you and I – it's just *you, Daddy*, and your *blasted war*!'

'Emily! No! That's not fair, I …'

She sniffed back tears as she headed for the door. She pulled the door open and abruptly paused. 'Danny, there has to be more. *I want more* – not just this.'

She gave a piercingly brutal stare, took a sharp breath and then stepped over the threshold, slamming the door behind her.

CHAPTER 8

The Poelzig Building

Nash crouched amongst the shrubs, taking advantage of the cover behind the low retaining wall. A vast expanse of paving slabs comprising the front terrace of the I. G. Farben building lay ahead. A cool breeze blew in from the south west, gently rustling the treetops of the formal parklands. No vehicles had entered or left the site since dusk and, apart from the main lobby and ground floor corridors, the lights were out. Hopefully, Fritz had knocked off for the day. Nash glanced up at the sky taking in the glow of the moonlight. It was the perfect evening for walking the dog or taking the girlfriend for a stroll – not exactly the greatest for a break in.

He rubbed his fingers along the itchy collar of his German uniform and tried to ignore the churning in his guts, then pulled the Mauser from its holster. He flipped off the safety and checked the magazine. The balance and grip of the foreign pistol felt a little bit chunky, but was otherwise well crafted. Satisfied, he re-holstered the weapon, leaving the leather cover open. He stared reluctantly at the German rifle leaning against the rhododendron trunk. The bolt action weapon fired well enough, but rifles were cumbersome when it came to close quarter battle. Still, a trooper walking about the building at night without his rifle would look odd. Nash pulled on his haversack and tightened the shoulder straps, grimacing to himself as he silently placed the rifle on his left shoulder.

He peered cautiously over the low wall, squinting towards the main entrance and the adjacent machine gun nest. A cheroot glowed amongst the ordered pile of sandbags. The metallic barrel of an MG34 heavy machine gun offered oily destruction to anything that moved on the open ground – there would be no going in the front door tonight.

Nash sunk behind the wall and checked his watch.

One a.m. It was now or never.

He eased forwards and immediately registered movement. Two soldiers came into view at the far west end of the building. He crouched back into the shrubbery, remaining motionless. He stilled his breathing. They walked steadily along the terrace with their rifles slung at ease. He timed their traverse in his head.

One, two, three, four, five, six, seven, eight …

The odd muttering of German drifted on the wind. The soldiers reached the cross-section in front of the lobby and continued along the front of the building, passing a few yards from Nash's position as they made their circuit of the perimeter. He counted them out as they disappeared around the far corner.

Bloody hell! Five minute interval at best.

Stooping with the Mauser at the ready, he worked quietly along the shrubbery away from the machine gun nest; keeping behind the wall and maintaining a parallel track to the building. After some fifty yards, the shrubs petered out. He dropped on to one knee, with sweat dripping from his brow despite the cool night air. A lawn neatly bisected the corner of the building. His heart pumped harder at the prospect of the open terrain, but there was no other choice. He'd have to brass neck it. Holstering his pistol, he checked the rifle on his shoulder, took a deep breath and then stepped on to the grass.

He moved purposefully over the damp, springy substrate; willing himself to stand upright and to hold a steady pace. He gripped the shoulder strap of the long weapon, trying not to walk too stiffly as he took a wide arc around the corner of the building. He scanned ahead, seeking the relative solace of the eastern wall, hoping to make the distance before the next patrol appeared on the veranda.

The side of the building loomed. He maintained his stride. Only the swish of his clothing and the squeak of his boots on the wet grass revealed his presence. He peered into the darkness, but nothing lurched into view. He allowed himself to be swallowed up by the dank shadows of the façade, and took refuge with his back to the wall. Breathing sharply, wiping sweat from his brow, he listened.

Nothing.

He took a deep breath and exhaled, then slowly dropped the rifle off his shoulder and into his right palm. He pushed the stock comfortably into his armpit, then delicately chambered a round and sidled along the wall to the next corner.

He held the weapon at the ready across his chest and gritting his teeth. Then, walking tactically and taking an arc a few yards wide of the concrete, he rounded the final corner, bringing the pavement at the rear of the building into view. He lifted the weapon, probing his arc of fire for targets; taking in the footpath and the neatly trimmed back lawn.

Silence.

The straight lines of the German architecture offered no cover. Taking rapid, shallow breaths, he kept the weapon up, shifting himself sideways off the grass towards the rear wall of the building. Light suddenly emitted from an office window some twenty yards ahead. He increased his pace, almost trotting on to the flagstones.

He pressed himself against the rear wall.

Damn it!

He re-shouldered the rifle and closed his eyes for a second, then took a calming breath. He set off along the pavement, forcing himself to a patrol-like plod, hoping to look the part. His palate dried, his heart raced. He closed one eye to preserve his night vision as he approached the brightly lit office. Shadow turned to stark contrast, revealing the details of his uniform. He felt naked and exposed, but kept walking straight ahead with his heart in his mouth, resisting the urge to glance through the pane. He passed the occupied office and receded once again into the comfort of twilight. A small porch of steel and glass marked the modest rear entrance up ahead. A single lamp lit the doorway. Nash marched the last twenty yards with his heart pounding. He drew up adjacent to the door, forcing himself to remain upright. He glanced to the left and the right, then delicately applied pressure to the art deco handle. He winced, gritting his teeth as the metal alloy of the doorframe scrapped gently across the concrete.

He stepped inside finding a utilitarian stairwell. He crouched, easing the door shut and then checked his rifle strap over his chest to neatly stow the weapon. He took out the Mauser pistol, it was a much better piece for the confined space, and tilted his head, mouth open, and listening.

Nothing, so far so good.

He moved up the stairs, letting the Mauser lead the way, rolling his feet to minimise any disturbance. Despite his best efforts, the soles of his boots scuffed against the floor. The stairwell opened up, only amplifying the noise. He cursed at his prospects and went for broke – increasing the pace. After several flights the concrete gave way to marble stonework. His boots screeched on the polished floor as he made the last step. He instantly dropped back behind the clean lines of the art deco bannister, pistol at the ready. A big number six beckoned overhead, announcing the top floor of the building. He listened while trying to quieten his breathing.

No movement, no sound.

He peered into the long corridor. Internal night lighting gave orientation to the scene. Apart from a few pot plants and the odd statue, nobody was home. Nash crept into the open, moving forward strategically, arcing his weapon and searching for targets. He sidled along the hallway, passing closed office doors, making some thirty yards before arriving at an intersection. He paused with his shoulder against the wall. Sweat trickled down his spine. His palms felt sticky as he gripped the German weapon. He craned his neck, following the long curve of the corridor into the west wing.

Damn it!

He stretched out with the weapon, scanning the way ahead, but it was no good. The sleek curve of the Nazi architecture served the enemy well.

Shit!

He stepped out into the middle of the hall to get a better view, pistol up in a double-handed grip. He shuffled forwards in a firing stance, probing with the weapon, watching and listening for the enemy. Working systematically, he traced the Mauser along the right-hand wall, checking the adjacent doorways in the exterior of the curve.

Nothing.

Something snatched at his peripheral vision. His pulse raced. He swept the weapon to the left, tensing on the trigger.

Statue!

He exhaled gently, easing off the firing mechanism.

Jesus!

He shook his head at the marble relief and refocussed, edging forwards, working the pistol from left to right.

The curve widened. A shaft of light shone under a door, some ten feet ahead. Nash swallowed, frantically darting his weapon back and forth. His mind raced, and feeling suddenly vulnerable in the open, he made for the nearest statue. He took up position behind a *Venus de Milo*. And shoving the pistol under the crook of her porcelain arm, he traced the weapon around the doorway.

Despite the shaft of light, the door remained closed.

Nash exhaled. *Get a grip!*

He glanced at the nameplate on the wooden façade. A Doctor Henrik Hauser – not a name he recognised. He snorted back tension, and then shifted from cover to continue on down the corridor.

Come on! Come on! Where the hell are you?

Time was running out. Sooner or later security would patrol this sector of the building, but he couldn't leave without documents – some evidence of what Krauch was up to. Maybe the schematics he'd seen of the building were out-of-date and he was searching the wrong floor. In the end, the intelligence was a couple of old photographs and a sketch of the Poelzig building made by some hobbyist architect. God only knows how Sinclair had conjured up that source of information. Risking his neck on the say so of some architectural equivalent of a train spotter didn't seem like a good idea, but what choice did he have? Then there was the little matter of the rendezvous – it was only three hours before first light and the Lysander wouldn't wait.

He made another fifty feet, wondering if he'd missed the director's office. The last section of the hallway came into view. The decor provided a fresh slice of neoclassicism, with an honour guard of ferns, mini-palm trees and a few more fake Michelangelo's. The double doors of the boardroom at the end of the corridor showed their status with twin statues of Hercules and Prometheus.

Nash worked the pistol over the entrance, then leant gingerly with one ear against the door.

Nothing.

He gripped the door handle, rotating it gently, with the Mauser at the ready.

The door clicked opened. Nash froze.

No alarm.

He inched open the door, and eased himself through the gap, then arced the weapon about the room.

Still nothing.

He kept the weapon up and closed the door carefully with his free hand. He stood in silence, breathing gently and waiting for his eyes to adjust to the gloom. His speckled night vision revealed a modest reception area with a desk guarding the entrance to the director's office. Several four-draw wooden filing cabinets lined the wall to the right. A small sofa and coffee table comprised a waiting area for visitors on the left. An oversized painting hung above the sofa. Nash moved silently across the deep carpet towards the inner sanctum. He tried the door handle.

Voices suddenly emitted from the exterior. The clump of boots got louder.

Soldiers!

Nash whirled around, dropping to a knee firing position as he did so. He took aim at the double doors and waited for the assault.

The door handle rattled and turned slowly.

Nash depressed the trigger, taking up the slack on the firing mechanism. His mouth shrivelled. He instinctively closing one eye to preserve his night vision and judged the best angle for a head shot. The first two men through the door would die, maybe he'd get a third – after that it didn't matter. His mind cleared. Only the pistol and the target area remained.

The door opened barely a crack. Voices got louder, then the door clunked shut. Nash waited, moving his weapon back and forth across the double doors. Boots scuffed and slowly faded as the patrol worked its way back along the corridor, checking door handles as they went.

Nash exhaled, relaxing his grip on the pistol momentarily. Sweat dripped from his nose. He rubbed his palm over his face, wiping it on the sleeve of his German tunic and stood, turning his attention to the inner door.

He slowly turned the handle, pushing the door ajar. Moonlight bathed the room. His eyes adjusted quickly after the relative blackness of the reception. He took in the odour of furniture polish and expensive tobacco as he pointed the weapon around the place. A large oval table occupied most of the space. A two feet high bronze made a centre piece: a German eagle with a few miniature red flags bearing Swastikas protruding about its talons. The usual paraphernalia of office life: a telephone, notepad, a few pens, and a diary sat neatly on the far end of the teak structure, next to a substantial carver-style chair. The sixth floor window filled most of the wall behind the desk, giving a bird's eye view of the parkland below. A bunch of filing cabinets, piled with loose papers sat behind the door. A portrait of Hitler adorned the adjacent wall, competing with a life-sized bust of Zeus himself.

Nash moved towards the filing cabinets, staying well clear of the window and the open drapes. He placed the Mauser carefully on top of the nearest filing cabinet, then fished into his pocket, producing a small flash light. He covered the bulb with his index and forefingers, then switched it on. He opened the first drawer, finding suspension files crammed with loose leaf papers. He picked up a random document protruding from the masses of paper and stuck his face close to the contents. The diffracted luminesce of the torch offered just enough light. He read the first page and then tossed it aside – it was just a memo. He exhaled, then placed the torch between his teeth and hunted through the files with both hands, finding more dross – monthly financial reports and general administration. He closed the drawer, and held the torch close to labels on the outside of the filing cabinet, checking each metallic stack as he did so.

Agrochemicals, Dyes and Detergents, Product Management, Client Portfolios, Suppliers ... Special Chemical Production. Bingo!

Nash carefully opened the drawer, scanning the contents with his torch. The files seemed to be in alphabetical order. He pulled a manila file from the latter third of the drawer. Red ink stamped the Nazi eagle on the front cover, another rectangular stamp read *Reichssicherheitshauptamt* –the main security office for the Reich – and the words, *Zyklon B*.

He opened the file. A skull and crossed bones stared back. *Sehr Giftig!* Nash translated under his breath – *very toxic*. He flicked through the first few pages, finding chemical equations and other mumbo jumbo, then stopped abruptly at a diagram. It appeared to be some kind of canister with the words *hydrogen cyanide* written in the small print.

So, Krauch *was* up to no good, making poisonous chemicals for the Reich. But were the canisters intended for military use? Nash shuddered at the thought. He placed the torch on the open drawer and removed his haversack, taking out his camera. He weighed the chunky item in his hand, then placed the torch in his mouth before snapping away; hoping the boys back in London would be able to develop useful images from the film. He photographed a handful of the pages, then shifted his attention to the files at the front of the drawer. He hung the camera around his neck and walked his fingers over the index labels.

His eyes frantically flitted from label to label. Abruptly, he paused, his heart skipped a beat.

Carbon sixty.

He dug the brown folder from the draw and pulled on the red silk closure, then balancing the document on the open drawer, he read the contents. It seemed to be instructions for the purification of carbon from charcoal and other materials. He eyed a schematic. It showed furnaces and pipe work, the legend read: *Carbon 60 chemisch produktion, Merseburg.*

That was it! The German were producing special chemicals at Merseburg. He busily snapped away with camera, capturing as many pages as possible. Satisfied, he closed the file and carefully re-tied the ribbon. He checked his watch.

Two fifteen a.m.

His gut told him it was time to leave, but then, the opportunity for this amount of intelligence might not come along again. He swallowed his doubts and continued searching through the drawer.

His brow suddenly furrowed.

Monowitz: Buna Werke Arbeitsausbildungslager. He translated. *Monowitz: Buna Works Labour Camp? What the hell?*

He opened the file.

Some kind of factory – a big one.

He turned the first few pages, collecting evidence with the camera.

Synthetic rubber, oil, petrochemicals … just the sort of things an army would need.

The edge of a black and white print caught his attention. He eased the photograph from the document wallet.

Nash blanched.

A group of skeletal-looking workers, dressed in striped rags, carried a heavy length of pipework. At least one worker lay facedown in the mud, apparently dead.

Sweet Jesus! What are the bastards up to? Forced labour? Poisonous chemicals? Clandestine production of special chemicals for the Reich?

He shoved the photograph into the haversack and returned the file to the draw.

Bastards!

He tackled the remaining files with renewed effort. If this was right, the Germans were using forced labour for their special chemical production – another good reason for the RAF to flatten the likes of Merseburg – but on the other hand who were the workers? Prisoners of war? Nash rifled through the remaining documents, seething, when a familiar phrase caught his eye.

Titanium dioxide?

Rockets – the Germans were getting their special titanium ores from South Africa before the war, but not any more, thanks to the Commonwealth contingent. Nash weighed the heavy, worn file in his hand. It looked like Krauch had maintained his interest in procuring titania. Nash opened the folder and scanned the contents page with the torch. He read, mumbling to himself. He raised an eyebrow.

Anatase? … *The same form of titania used at Peenemünde.*

Light suddenly flooded under the office door. Nash roused from his thoughts. A youthful male voice tentatively spoke. 'Herr Director? Herr Director, is that you?'

Nash hastily returned the file and tentatively closed the drawer. He carefully extinguished the torch, shoving it in the waist pocket of his tunic, then stretched for the Mauser resting on the adjacent filing cabinet.

The voice called through the door. 'Herr Director?'

Nash took up the weapon. He applied pressure with his thumb, painstakingly cocking the pistol.

'Herr Director, sir?'

Then he had a better idea.

Nash slowly released the mechanism on his pistol, and clicking on the safety, he returned the gun to its holster. He sidled up behind the door and reached under his waistband, finding the pouch of throwing knifes secreted in the small of his back. He grasped the hilt of the nearest blade and slowly withdrew the razor sharp stiletto, registering the familiar balance of the weapon.

The voice got louder. 'Herr Director?'

The office door opened ajar. A solid tranche of light illuminated the desk and the adjacent surrounds. Nash held in the shadows behind the door.

The young trooper stepped into the room. Zeus stared back.

Nash pressed himself against the wall, raising his blade, pulse racing and muscles tensed ready to pounce.

'Herr Director?'

The spotty recruit stood beanpole-like in his oversized uniform, carrying his rifle awkwardly on his shoulder.

Nash gritted his teeth, breathing steadily through his nostrils, but remaining motionless behind the door.

Go on kid, get lost! *Walk away while you still can*! He moved the stiletto a fraction closer to the target.

The recruit looked about the room, taking in the tidy desk and closed filing cabinets.

An older gruff voice echoed from the corridor. 'Amaud? Amaud is that you?'

The young recruit hesitated a reply. 'Yes, yes, I am ... I am in the director's office.'

'Come out at once, we are not allowed in there. Didn't anyone tell you that?'

'No, sorry ... sorry, Dieter, no they didn't. I thought I heard something, that's all ...' The boy soldier looked around the room again.

Nash gripped the blade.

The older voice enquired from the hallway. 'Amaud, are you alright?'

The lad turned towards the reception. 'It was nothing.'

The older man chuckled. 'Your first week on patrol, and you're hearing things already. Come on ...'

The recruit look about the room, with his hand on the door.

Nash smelt cheap cologne, but held.

The door gently closed. Nash watched as the shaft of light from the reception area vanished with the click of a light switch. The clunk of the double doors marked the departure of the two soldiers.

Nash stood motionless in the darkness, listening to the footfalls of the patrol recede along the corridor. He took a deep breath and exhaled, and visibly slumping his shoulders, he eased the throwing knife back into its pouch. He'd outstayed his welcome long enough. He grabbed the haversack from the floor, stashing the camera for safe keeping, and slung the pack, tightening the straps as he did so and taking care not to tangle it with the rifle still on his back. Then drawing the Mauser, he open the door carefully, sweeping his weapon over the reception room.

Relieved to find the room empty, he sidled across the carpet and opening one of the double doors a crack. He peered into the hallway.

Nothing.

He stepped into the hall, weapon up, and gingerly closed the door with his free hand. He worked back along the sixth floor, passing the *Venus de Milo*, and eventually finding the eastern stairwell. He peered over the edge with the Mauser, listening.

Nothing stirred in the void.

He moved tactically down the stairs, checking his descent on each landing. Sweating and fatigued, he reached the ground floor. He worked methodologically in the twilight, slipping silently from the narrow concrete staircase and out of the back door. He crouched momentarily in the porch, sweeping his weapon from left to right, before breaking into a trot. He headed across the rear lawn into the mist, hoping to make the rendezvous before first light.

CHAPTER 9

Iranian Border

Weiner squirmed in his seat, resigned to the heat and the hard wooden slats that dug into his thighs. Sweat trickled down his neck, mixing with the dust and grime that seemed to stick to everything in the desert. He wiped the unpleasantness from the back of his neck with a spent handkerchief, and winced as another bead of sweat contoured over his brow to sting a warm saltiness into his eye.

The train suddenly jolted, the brakes squealed. Weiner lurched forwards, only just managing to stay on the bench by grabbing the edge of the slats and pressing his heels into the floor for purchase. The train stopped. Momentum threw Weiner back against the hard frame of the seat. Luggage swung back and forth in the cargo netting above each bench.

'What now?' He rubbed the lump emerging on the back of his head and then mopped liquid from his temple. 'Damned hot. Too damned hot. I am beginning to hate this country already.' He glanced across at Steinhoff sitting slumped on the opposite bench. Perspiration soaked the armpits of Steinhoff's grey shirt. A tidemark of salt stains gave testament to the arid conditions.

Weiner wiped dust from his lips with the back of his hand. 'Why the hell have we stopped?'

Steinhoff gave a wiry shrug. 'I've no idea. Perhaps I should consult my crystal ball.'

Weiner menaced, 'Less of the fucking sarcasm. You won't be unexpendable forever you know.' He stood up, peering through the utilitarian wooden shutters. An eddy of hot air touched his cheeks. He squinted against the sudden brightness of the baking sun and surveyed the horizon. 'I can't see a thing. Just rocks, sand and more fucking desert. How far are we from Tabriz?'

Steinhoff deliberately busied himself, rubbing moisture off the rim of his glasses using his shirt tail. He reset the sticky spectacles on to the bridge of his nose, habitually pushing them into place with his forefinger. He composed an intellectual look. 'Major, it is some four hundred kilometres from the Black Sea to Tabriz, and through the rough terrain of Armenia. I would say we have about another hundred kilometres to go. Two, perhaps three hours …'

Weiner huffed, then continued looking through the blinds. 'Two hours too damned long. It would have been much quicker by plane.'

Steinhoff gave a sarcastic smirk. 'Major, think about it. Iran is barely holding on to its status of neutrality with the Russians moving in from the north. What's more the British are jockeying for position in the south, playing the old card of empire.'

'The British and their pathetic empire. It would still have been quicker by plane.'

Steinhoff raised an eyebrow, 'And risk being shot down by the British?'

Weiner turned, towering over the scientist. 'The British have a nasty little surprise coming their way. They have greatly misjudged things.'

Steinhoff shrugged, 'Perhaps.'

'And so do the bloody Soviets … Stalin is no match for the Führer. The arrogant bastard speaks as if he's on equal terms with Germany.'

'So why are we going to the Russians with our begging bowl?'

'Begging? No, this is a trade. An exchange of raw materials for German ingenuity.'

Steinhoff, battling with another trickle of sweat, pushed his glasses back on to his nose, 'I do not believe the Soviets are so foolhardy. We are wasting time, Major.'

Weiner shook his head and squatted back on to the wooden bench opposite. 'The Soviet Union may be vast with ample reserves of coal and oil, but the communists are sheep.'

'Sheep? Maybe, but the flock is being guarded by a wolf. We should not underestimate Herr Stalin, or the Soviet Technocrats.'

Weiner leaned forward and spoke in a flat tone. 'What of them? What do you *really* know about your counterpart in the Soviet Union?' He stood up, jeering. 'See, you're talking out of your arse as usual.'

Steinhoff ignored the quip. 'A little … we have suspected that the Russians have had their own rocket programme for sometime – that you already know – but there will be other technology-led projects. The Soviet engineers are some of the finest. Of that I am sure.'

Weiner spoke with a distain look. 'Yes, but what *do you know* about the Soviet scientists – nothing – so we tread carefully. Don't fuck it up.'

Steinhoff raised an eyebrow, all hoity-toity, 'Actually, before the war …' Steinhoff gave a sweep of hand, 'Before *all of this*, we used to talk about science.'

Weiner pantomimed a smirk. 'We used to talk about science.' He repeated, then scowled abruptly. 'What do you mean, talk?'

Steinhoff remained aloof. 'I am sure you wouldn't understand. We were a scientific community once, an international one. We would meet periodically at the Physics Society, or other academic conferences. Over the years, I have

68

met American, Swedish, English and Russian scientists of course.'

Weiner, suddenly poked an accusing finger in Steinhoff's direction. 'So you've travelled a bit – before the war – that doesn't mean anything. All we know about your Russian counterpart is what everyone else knows – he's an engineer and holds military rank. At least the Soviets have the balls to make their engineers soldiers.' Weiner shook his head and turned towards the window slats in disgust.

'Actually,' Steinhoff pressed his glasses back on to his nose and cleared his throat. 'I do know him of sorts, Sergio Korolev.'

Weiner spun round, towering over his minion. 'What! Why didn't you tell me this before?!'

Steinhoff shrugged. 'I've only just remembered. I was a lowly PhD at the time. I saw him speak at a meeting in Stuttgart about fifteen years ago.'

'We have half the Reich Chancellery breathing down our necks and you decide to tell me this now?' Weiner scowled and skulked to his bench. His mood seemed to soften, or perhaps it was the heat. 'Tell me. What was he like, this Korolev?'

'Educated of course, well spoken. Factually correct. He certainly knew about propulsion systems and ballistics; but there was something else about him … something disciplined, almost military, even then.'

Weiner gave a sideways look. 'That doesn't surprise me. Every young Soviet has a spell in the army. Stalin is paranoid. I hear that children are taught to strip down weapons in the classroom from the age of twelve – we could take a leaf out of his book on that score. Still, we don't know much about Korolev's military career – except that he is a middle ranking officer and a scientist.'

'Yes, I've read some of his early work – brilliant, just brilliant.' Steinhoff pushed his glasses back on to his nose and shifted forwards in his seat with a sudden enthusiasm. 'Fuel calculations, aerodynamics, engineering with new materials – he was there early – one of the first. I would go so far as to say that Korolev's papers have influenced my own work.'

Weiner grimaced as he wiped sweat from the back of his neck. 'So, you've read his work. If you've had a measure of the man, what do you think the Russians are building now?'

Steinhoff paused, 'He seems well-placed to bring a military angle to the use of technology – but I don't really know – just rumours.'

Weiner's bulk creaked on the slats as he leant forwards. He spoke in a conspiratorial tone. 'Rumours? What rumours? You know what's at stake here. A minor detail here or there could be crucial – you know what Berlin has said. We succeed or feel a rope around our necks.'

Steinhoff flurried in harsh whispers. 'Alright, alright – consider the facts. The Soviets are good at mass producing hardware: tanks, planes, armoured vehicles. They can take a prototype and mass produce it quickly. *Ipso facto*, if they have a special project at an advanced stage, we can expect them to be manufacturing at the earliest opportunity; certainly within months.'

Weiner gritted his teeth, hissing, 'Then we had better get a move on. The Führer will not tolerate the Russians being ahead of us in such matters. You *will* get to know this Korolev. Find out what drives him. Find out what he is working on, and I pray the Soviets do not have a working rocket, or other weapons. This would not please the Führer.' Weiner sank his tall frame back on to the bench. He folded his arms, fuming.

'And how do you suggest I do that? Korolev is no fool and we need to be careful so as not to put our own technology at risk.'

'Christ, do I have to do everything? Make use of your common interest in propulsion systems. Get him to talk … I don't care how.'

'That's easier said than done.'

Weiner suddenly pounced forwards. 'Look, *you really don't get it*, do you? Can that brain of yours calculate how many soldiers are in the Russian Army?'

Steinhoff hesitated a reply, 'I don't know, some five hundred thousand men?'

Weiner contrived a laugh. 'Exactly! You have no idea. They have over two hundred rifle divisions alone, armoured divisions, and much more. We are talking *millions* of men, not thousands. For me – that's what's behind Berlin's trade agreements with the Soviets. They out number us, by some five to one – so the Führer keeps the Soviets sweet until they're not needed anymore.'

Steinhoff spoke as if addressing a room full of wayward undergraduates. 'Politics … oversimplifications … linear thinking. You cannot possibly know the Führer's mind. You understand nothing, Major. No matter what the Russian's have to offer us, I will not trade a single scrap or morsel of my work – and that is that.' He sat back, forcing a dignified pose.

'Stick with the plan. You'll give them something credible to sweeten the deal.'

'And when our Russian friends find out you're a double crossing, lying bastard?

Weiner leapt forwards, pressing a forearm across Steinhoff's throat, giving just enough leverage to crunch the windpipe, but allowing a rasp of respiration. He rammed the barrel of his pistol against Steinhoff's forehead, twisting the weapon, creating a bruise. He hissed tobacco breath. 'Like I said – stick with the plan. It's all arranged. Lose your nerve and I'll blow your fucking brains out. Do we understand each other, Herr Doctor?'

71

Steinhoff crackled, wide-eyed, hunting for air, but finding none. Weiner put his full weight on the scientist's windpipe and repeated. 'I said, do we fucking understand?'

Steinhoff squeezed a staccato nod and gargled noises of submission. Weiner released his grip and stood upright, holstering his pistol and brushing down his uniform as if about to hit the parade ground for an inspection of the troops. He spoke in a matter-of-fact tone. 'I do enjoy our little chats. You will make good with our new Russian friends and hand over what you're told to hand over. We make the deal and then we're long gone before the Russians realise their delegation isn't going to make it back to the Kremlin.'

Steinhoff slumped on his seat, rubbing his throat and gave a hoarse reply. 'You'll start a war – the Red Army!'

Weiner stood grim. 'If you're as good as you say you are – should it come to that – we'll have a weapon to keep the Red Army in check – won't we?'

CHAPTER 10

England

S ir Hugh Sinclair sat resting on his elbows at the oak desk and pushing his fingers together in a crab-like fashion. He huffed, then absently brushed a fleck of dust from the lapel of his three-piece suit and furrowed his brow.

Was this a good idea or not?

He lifted the cuff of his silk shirt and checked his Rolex.

One a.m. – that would make it at least three in the morning in Russia.

He stared at the circular face of the telephone and waited.

The Germans were getting friendly with the Soviets. It was common knowledge with the various trade negotiations and public declarations of co-operation on economic matters; but what was Herr Hitler *really* up to? The economic declarations were a smoke screen – that much was obvious – but for what? What did the Germans want from the Russians that they couldn't obtain themselves with the vastness of the Reich now occupying large swathes of Europe and North Africa? Oil and steel for the German war effort? Minerals? Gold? Money? Or simply the prestige of equalling Stalin and the mighty Soviet Union? It was hard to tell. The intelligence analysts had varying opinions on the relationship between Stalin and Hitler – and it wasn't clear if the two most powerful men in the world have ever met. Would they do so at this Tabriz meeting, whatever that was about? And more importantly, *when*?

The shrill of the telephone startled Sinclair from his thoughts.

He picked up the receiver and spoke in monotones. 'Yes.' The telephone crackled. The room filled with silence.

A gruff, middle-aged voice finally spoke. A guttural Russian accent sounded in Sinclair's ear. 'A ship sails from Manchester. What is her name?'

'The steamship Treverbyn,' replied Sinclair.

'She travels to where?'

'St Petersburg – not Leningrad – but she does not make it.' Sinclair countered, 'Where does she lay now?'

The Russian gave a grunt. 'At the bottom of the ocean.'

Sinclair leant into the receiver. '*Where*?'

'West of the Isle of Skye. Forty fathoms down.'

'She went down by the stern or the head?'

The Russian gave a small chuckle. 'Neither my friend, a torpedo amidships. How did you enjoy the cold water?'

Sinclair brightened his tone. 'Damned freezing. You took your time pulling me out.'

The Russian gave a small laugh. 'Yes: but *I did* pull you out. How are you my friend?'

'As well as can be expected, comrade. What news from The East?'

'As I anticipated. The old alliances are not favoured, even within the inner circle. My masters make new friends …'

'*Friends*?'

'Ask not why the mongoose seeks the cobra. Simply ask yourself who will prevail?'

'The mongoose of course.'

The Russian gave a quiet chuckle, 'It always does.'

Sinclair continued, 'Half of Europe has fallen, and the serpent grows another head – a dangerous one.'

'Then the mongoose will bite it off, but perhaps not straight away, comrade.'

'What nourishes the serpent? Why nourish it?'

'It feeds on itself, but it will eventually run out of food. They ask for the usual materials of war: iron, coal, petroleum and grain.'

Sinclair risked probing further. 'But this serpent is seeking a new diet to create a special poison in its fangs.'

'It seems so, but the potion is not ready, and they ask for metal ores of high purity and particular types of coal dust.'

Sinclair creased his brow. '*Coal dust*?'

'Yes, but we know not why.'

'We prefer that you didn't feed the serpent.'

The Russian grunted. 'It is not in my gift … besides, what better way to catch a snake, than when it is hungry?'

'Where does the snake catcher go?'

'Iran – you know where.'

'*When*?'

'When the maidens get their feet wet and the diamond points to the east.'

'How do I get a seat at the table?'

The Russian gave a burst of false laughter, 'If only that were possible my friend, but alas it is not.'

'Then you might like to contact me afterwards – penfriends always write to each other, don't they?'

'No, the pen runs dry. I have given too much already.'

'We would be very grateful … perhaps you could pay us a visit?'

The Soviet suddenly hissed, 'Have you lost your mind? The cold water must have numbed your senses.'

Silence.

The Russian spoke hesitantly, 'Forgive me … but there might be just one way.'

Sinclair tightened his grip on the receiver, 'How?'

'Ordinarily … I would not ask this of you.' His voice dropped away, the phone line crackled.

'Tell me how?' Sinclair urged.

'She is half Russian and fluent in several tongues. Send the fair maiden of your own.'

Sinclair flushed with a rush of adrenalin. 'No! Not that!'

'It is the only way. Think on it, comrade. It was Eve who tamed the serpent, not Adam.'

Sinclair paused, his throat dried. 'How can I trust you?'

'I pulled you from the water didn't I?'

'Why her and not another?' Sinclair clutched at straws. 'I can send another.'

'No you *must* send *her*. I have my reasons.' The Russian was matter-of-fact.

Sinclair probed, 'What reasons?'

'The same reason you risked The North West Passage in the bleakest of midwinters – for love – but my masters are both astute and meticulous. I remain ahead by the slenderest of margins. You should know, Anya is alive and well.'

Sinclair sat in stunned silence. His wife? His ex-wife? No! She was a civilian, a school teacher – not part of the game – living a normal life in Moscow. All connections to him, his diplomatic circles, the service, were over; and had been for many years since the divorce.

Sinclair faltered, 'Why does the Kremlin seek her? She is of no credible value. She has no information to give, not now.'

Reality intervened – she would always be the ex-wife of a spymaster – no matter how much she'd craved an ordinary existence, or made it seem so. The Kremlin would have a man watching for old times' sake. It was just a question of which man. Maybe one of the new breed of technocrats was applying leverage even now. Sinclair cleared his throat and tried to speak calmly. 'There's no reason for her to be involved. You know she is not a current asset.'

The Soviet spoke in a placatory tone. 'I know … but you of all people must understand my dilemma.'

'Can you guarantee her safety?'

The Russian grunted, 'Anya? In Moscow? To be truthful, that depends on how my masters choose their friends in the coming days. Only if you send the girl – then perhaps there is a chance. She should come to the city where The East meets The West. Good luck, comrade …'

The click of the receiver abruptly ended the call. Static rung in Sinclair's ear. He slowly replaced the handset on its stand and eased back in his chair, dumbfounded. It was an unwritten rule – wives, girlfriends, and especially children, were never to be involved – a code of honour amongst the faithful. Unless of course in the fullness of time they chose to become players themselves. The divorce had been a bitter, acrimonious affair. Things limped on for several years. The hours at work got longer, arriving home late, then missing dinner, then not coming home at all – snatching a few hours' sleep on the sofa at the office. There was only one person to blame for her loneliness. Anya was an intelligent and gregarious woman. She wasn't made for marking time, waiting dutifully for her husband to return home. She craved and deserved something better than playing second fiddle to a civil servant – in the end that's what he'd become in her eyes. Then one day, she finally left: simply packed her things and took a taxi to the station. The 'Dear John' on the mantelpiece summed it up in as fewer syllables – she was going home to Moscow – look after Emily, she'd send for her once Emily had finished schooling. In the end she never did. Emily had chosen to stay in England anyway. The father-daughter bond somehow endured, tempestuous and full of blame at first, then mellowing to a new equilibrium. The questions about Anya become less frequent. After several moves between apartments in Moscow, he'd lost the thread of contact with Anya. He'd heard that she'd settled and found love again – he couldn't deny her that. But it had put a strain on Emily. The poor girl had gone in on herself – for Emily at least, the subject of 'Mother' somehow drifted, became taboo.

He and Emily rarely spoke of Anya now – apart from Emily's recent interest … He wondered what had triggered his daughter now, of all times; then dismissed the thought. There were more pressing matters.

He and Sergio Korolev went back a long way; since the British convoys to St Petersburg in the latter stages of the Great War. Their paths had crossed many times during his days in the Diplomatic Service, and during his tenure with the intelligence services. Sergio had been a trusted source, but the changing of the guard at the Kremlin was ever-constant, as it was in London. Adaptability and tenacity had kept them both in work – but what leverage did the new regime at the Kremlin have over Korolev? Or Anya?

The political and economic showboating made it clear that Hitler and Stalin were now bedfellows; but what of Sergio Korolev and his Russian colleagues? Could he *really* be trusted in this new climate? It sounded like Korolev's influence was waning, with only a few of the old guard remaining. Caution was required – making contact with Korolev would need to be more covert – especially if the old soak was being told to tow the new party line, or to make it appear so. *What did Sergio really want?* Should he trust the life of his daughter and possibly her mother to an old alliance? Putting Emily in harms way to get an ear at the most important meeting likely to ever take place between the Soviets and the Germans? Was there any choice?

Sinclair suddenly leant forward to the intercom on his desk and pressed the solid Bakelite button. 'Mary, bring me the Admiralty Chart for the Isle of Skype and the latest tide tables please.'

A polite, 'Yes, sir,' dampened through the speaker. Moments later his personal assistant arrived with the documents.

Sinclair looked up, forcing a bland expression. 'Thank you, Margaret, most helpful.'

She smiled and headed for the door without speaking. Sinclair waited until the latch clicked shut. He rolled the chart out on to the table, muttering to himself. 'When the maidens' feet get wet …' His finger traced the intricate contours of the west coast of the Hebridian island. 'Maidens' feet … there!' He tapped his index finger on the chart. 'McLeod's Maidens!' His mind's eye saw the giant stacks of rock rising from the sea. He dragged his finger over to the nearest table of tidal diamonds on the chart. He mumbled concentration, 'When the diamonds point to the east … a flood tide … *high water on the next flood.*'

He flipped open the small booklet of tide times and scoured down the month, looking for the next full moon. His finger abruptly stopped. 'Ten days … the Germans are meeting the Russians in Tabriz, ten days from now?!'

He slumped back into his chair.

Ten days! How can she be ready in ten days? I cannot send her!

Sinclair plummeted. If he didn't send her, then any possibility of a deal with the Russians would be off; and so would England's chance of stopping the device and the war along with it.

Major Nash stood with the flats of his palms resting on the conference table. He studied the documents scattered over the oak surface. The sleeves of his army-issue woollen jumper scruffily concertinaed about his elbows, revealing minor cuts and bruising on his forearms. The shoulder pads of his jersey remained anonymous with no insignia of rank. He casually rubbed his brow and picked up another one of the photograph of the Monowitz factory under construction. He glanced sideways at Sinclair. Something wasn't right. The old Rupert would normally take things in his stride, remaining informed, calm, logical – and most of all – in complete control. But there was an aurora about his personality this morning, a side he hadn't seen before – or maybe it was just the relentless pressure. The war wasn't going well, in fact badly, and the Cabinet Office was looking to SIS for some quick results. 'Sir?' Nash waited as Sinclair remained stooped over the intelligence, tapping his fingers spider-like on the edge of the conference table and clenching his pipe between his teeth, lost in thought. A minor smog had formed around his head, blending in with the dark blue of his pin-stripped suit. The sweet aroma of the pipe tobacco tickled Nash's throat. 'Sir, should I continue?'

Sinclair checked his Rolex – eight-thirty a.m. 'You'd better, Major. We've three hours to make sense of this I. G. Farben business before I meet the P.M.'

Nash nodded appreciatively, 'Yes, sir.' He lifted another photograph from the pile of intelligence then continued, 'Well as you know, the window of opportunity was limited – there were plenty of files in the director's office that I didn't get a look at. Nonetheless, I've recovered evidence that I. G. Farben, and likely Krauch himself, is engaged in profiteering from slave labour. Also evidence of the manufacturing of highly toxic chemicals, including gases, probably for military use.' Nash paused, unable to prevent his eye roving over the black and white, even though he'd studied it several times since the Frankfurt job. Sullen human forms in soiled, pyjamas-like rags stared back. He handed the print to Sinclair, 'Slave labour,' then fished for another document, finding a diagram, 'And toxic chemicals.'

Sinclair examined the photographic image, shaking his head. 'Slave labour for certain,' then looked at the sketch. 'Toxic gas … the arrogant bastards.' He turned the page towards Nash, 'What's your interpretation of this?'

'*Zyklon* B. You can just make out some of the small print on the label, it contains hydrogen cyanide. I am no chemist,' Nash clicked his jaw and winced, 'But I know what cyanide is for. Christ knows what else is in it, but what bothers me more is the container – it's a canister, certainly portable, perhaps for anti-personnel use.'

Sinclair gripped his pipe between clenched teeth, then took it out abruptly. 'I'll brief the staff officers. I am sure they'd be thrilled to know that Hitler is likely planning to use cyanide gas on British troops.' He prodded his pipe in Nash's direction. 'Have we a location on this *Monowitz* yet?'

Nash shrugged, 'Not much. Maps show it as a small village in the middle of nowhere – Poland. We don't have any other information at present, but look at these photographs ...' Nash passed over a handful of snaps and continued, 'The morass of pipework, cooling towers, silos and factory units – this isn't one factory under construction. It's a *small town*, and built for purposes of chemical production including cyanide.'

Sinclair squinted as he flicked through the images. 'Our technical experts can take a look, but my bet is the towers and pipework relate to some kind of fractionation or distillation. Petroleum, oil, maybe industrial alcohols.'

Nash raised an eyebrow, 'For the German rocket programme?'

'It's possible. The Germans also have a long list of armoured divisions all requiring fuel. No matter – there is just cause – we'll add it to the list of targets for the RAF. That leaves the matter of their Merseburg plant.'

Nash retrieved several documents from the mound. 'Merseburg ...' He shuffled them into some kind of order and then passed the first wad of papers to Sinclair. 'This seems to be on the money, sir. It contains drawings of lines of furnaces, instructions for burning charcoal and purifying different types of carbon – there's only one possible conclusion – the Germans are making some special types of carbon at this location.'

Sinclair studied the pages momentarily, 'Alright, but is it the same carbon you recovered from Peenemünde?'

Nash shrugged, 'I don't know, sir. The boffins will have to figure that one out. It seems likely – what's more the same factory also has plans for refining titanium dioxide.' Nash held out another file.

Sinclair sharpened, '*Titanium dioxide*?!'

'Yes, sir. And the documents mention *anatase*. They're after the same stuff they were getting from South Africa.'

Sinclair cut in, 'Only Cape Town is closed for business thanks to our efforts.' His voice dropped to a tentative whisper, 'So … the Germans must be buying it from the Russians instead? Perhaps not the only thing they want from the Russians. Why not ask for special charcoal or coal products at the same time? Then they would have everything they need to make a new device, or even several of their machines.'

Nash rubbed his chin, 'It's a probability, sir. The increased security at the plant would fit with something of a secret or sensitive nature, but I didn't find any documents that directly linked Merseburg to the Russians.'

Sinclair stared into space, holding his pipe. 'Of course not, we know from the radio transcripts that the Soviets are negotiating with Krauch – but they haven't done the deal yet.' He gaped at Nash, 'Christ! That's why they're meeting. To trade in the materials for this top secret weaponry!'

Nash furrowed his brow, 'There's a firmed up date for a meeting of the Nazis and Soviets? But, sir, even if the Kremlin is that cosy with Berlin – it still doesn't make any sense. I mean, the Russians have all the oil and mineral wealth they need. Why bother trading?'

Sinclair nodded grimly, 'The Soviets want something the German's have – perhaps they know about the device – they certainly know about the rockets at Peenemünde. Or they could be using the trade deal to fish for other intelligence.'

'So the question is, sir, are the Russians really supplying the raw materials in exchange for Nazi secrets, or are they playing Herr Hitler for a fool? And if so, what do they hope to gain?'

'That's why we need ears and eyes on the ground in Tabriz.'

Nash nodded, 'I read the transcripts. Tabriz was certainly mentioned.'

'Indeed, we have an operation going on out of the Istanbul office. The Germans and the Soviets are having a little shindig in Iran, but we are not exactly sure of the details. There'll be some generic trade agreements I expect, but behind the façade something much more technical and secretive is afoot.' Sinclair took a deep breath and exhaled, visibly slumping.

'Sir?'

'I've decided to send Emily to our Istanbul office.'

Nash swallowed and forced a calm expression. 'Sir, is that wise? I mean, you know how the Arabs are with women …'

'Exactly, they think nothing of them. She can hide in plain sight. A personal assistant to the minor diplomatic posting there, a bit of typing and subtle observation.' Sinclair forced a convincing tempo. 'She speaks Russian and her German is fairly good. She knows something of the culture of the Middle East. Ideal for the task.'

Nash spoke sheepishly, 'Yes, sir, but she's not ready for the field. It might only be a matter of time before the German Army advances into Turkey. That would put the Istanbul office, Emily, and the diplomatic staff there on the front line.'

'It's a risk we will have to take. Finding out what is going on in Tabriz is the key to the puzzle. She'll met with an old Soviet colleague, a man I hope I can trust.'

'Sir, I like how the Russians treat their women even less. Are you sure about this Russian? The potential for kidnapping in a place like Istanbul …'

'Yes, I know, but I am relying on old loyalties and discretion. If the Soviets are playing a game of double bluff with the Germans, then perhaps we can help them.'

Nash raised an eyebrow, 'And if not?'

Sinclair shrugged, 'Simple – we lose the war – and/or Britain gets wiped off the face of the Earth in the process.'

Nash stiffened, 'What would you have me do, sir?'

'Basic training for Emily – you have three days – then she's on her way to Istanbul.'

'And me, sir?'

Sinclair tightened his lips around his pipe, generating a fresh glow in the bowl. 'We hold our nerve on this one, Nash – it's just observation and intelligence gathering.'

'Yes, sir, but who's going to watch her back?'

Sinclair stopped sucking on his pipe and prodded it in Nash's direction. 'You are old chap. As soon as she's left London, you'll be on the next transport to the Middle East. Don't make me regret it.'

CHAPTER 11

The Persian

Weiner coughed the dust and dry heat from his throat as he sat down on the worn slab of stone that constituted the park bench outside the mosque. Sand and gravel scuffed under his boots. The parched red-brown earth had already began to work its way into the fabric of his khaki shorts and short-sleeved shirt. The semi-civilian clothing felt alien, but circumstances required it. He could hardly go strutting about the streets of Iran in his German uniform. Blistering heat radiated from the stone plinth. He wriggled on the monolith to minimise the scorching discomfort on his thighs, then sliding crab-like to one end of the slab, found the meagre shade of a small olive tree potted at the end of the bench. He aimlessly examined the weathered terracotta and the compacted sandy loam mixed with cigarette ends that provided a toxic mulch around the plant. He shook his head, then squinted down at his feet to relieve the constant glare of the sun.

Scheisse! God forsaken filth of a place, baked too long in the fucking sun.

He fished in his breast pocket, retrieving a crumpled pack of cigarettes, and tapped out a smoke. He shoved it between his dry lips and patted down his shorts in search of a light. His fingers caught the solid metallic feel of his Adami lighter. He flipped open the chrome lid and sparked up a petroleum flame, habitually cupping his hands as he drew the cigarette to a glowing red ember. He clicked the lighter closed, running his thumb over the embossed Siemens Halske Werke logo on the side.

Proper German engineering, none of this foreign crap.

A sudden immense shadow stirred Weiner from his thoughts. He looked up. A giant of a man stood looming. The man was dressed in a pair of black baggy Sirwal trousers crimped neatly at the ankles, above a worn pair of brown sandals. He wore a pristine shirt, apparently made of the finest Egyptian cotton. A black turban sat loosely wrapped around his head in the Arabic style, covered most of his face and one side of his muscular neck.

Weiner stood up, tentatively offering the Persian his hand, cigarette still dangling from his lip. 'Weiner, Major Weiner …' The calloused roughness of the Persian's spade-like hands grated against his palm. Weiner kept a steady formal expression, hiding his surprise at the immense power of the Muslim's grip. He continued with unaccustomed politeness, 'Thank you for taking the time to meet me.' He gestured towards the seat, 'Please …' Weiner took a glimpse into the Arab's sunken eyes, but was unable to assimilate a measure of his new exotic friend.

The Persian glided effortlessly on to the stone bench, and sat comfortably with one leg crossed over his knee, allowing the free end of his turban to flap in the heat. 'Mohammed Al-Ruzi, Emeritus Regimental Commander, Persian Cossack Brigade.'

Weiner took a deep drag on his cigarette, deliberately exhaling slowly. Acrid smoke filled the void between the two men. He stared ahead into the empty square and spoke in monotones, 'I worry for Herr Hitler … for Germany.'

The Persian gave a dismissive shrug, and spoke in an educated, surprisingly smooth voice. 'These are difficult times …'

'Indeed …' Weiner continued looking ahead across the square, roving his eye absently over the elegant blue roof tiles of the mosque. 'My superiors seek council with the Russians, or so it seems.'

'I don't see how a humble Muslim may help with your affairs.'

Weiner turned towards Al-Ruzi, studying his expression. The Iranian gave nothing away. Weiner continued. 'It bothers me … I have concerns for our interests in the Middle East.'

Al-Ruzi was unreadable. 'What is it that bothers you my friend? The Soviets, or the fact that your superiors seek their allegiance?'

Weiner shook his head slowly and took another drag on his cigarette. 'No, not an allegiance, a bargain of sorts; but the Soviets have their own interests … their own agenda.'

Al-Ruzi gently formed a polite smile, 'The Soviets indeed have many interests, as do the British, and of course, Germany.'

Weiner countered, 'Germany seeks only friendship.' He flicked ash from his smoke, 'Others from The West seek to rule all of Persia.'

The Iranian slowly lost his smile. 'That maybe true, but Allah will punish the infidels who threaten these sacred lands.'

Weiner spoke in a matter-of-fact tone. 'The English and the Russians? Why would a commander of the Persian Cossack Brigade wish that?'

Al-Ruzi allowed a smirk to return. 'Germany of all nations should know the meaning of empire. The Qajar Dynasty would have lasted a thousand years had it not been for the Russian revolution. The Soviets have rights to their lands in Russia, but *not Persia, not Azerbaijan*.'

Weiner had done his homework on the Persian. It made some sense. The legitimate royal family of Iran, the Qajar's, were wiped out in a coup supported by Soviet forces in the

1920s. The remnants of the Qajar Dynasty dispersed, and their sacred leader, Ahmad Shah, went into exile.

Weiner furrowed his brow. 'Why should I trust a Cossack?'

'Do not be deceived by the rhetoric of the English. They are mere lapdogs of their Soviet masters. They seek to divide Persia, the Russians from the north, and the British from the south. They will not prevail, the Shah's of old will return.'

Weiner recalled the information in the file. Ahmad Shah, had died in exile, in some French slum. 'Yes, but why should I trust a *Cossack*?'

Al-Ruzi grunted disgust. 'You forget, I am a Muslim first, evicted from my homelands of Circassia in the north by the Imperial Russian invaders. The Imperialists believed that they had conquered our spirit, forcing young Muslims into conscription to serve their so-called Russian masters. No, Major Weiner. The Persian Cossack Regiment may have its origins as Russian-trained Calvary, but *we are and remain* Muslims. Ahmad Shah pushed the Soviet hoards from our lands for a brief time after the Great War. I remain loyal to the cause.'

'Why? Do you not see the might of the Soviet Army? We will crush the English, the world will be divided between Herr Hitler and Stalin, and in time, Germany will prevail.'

'If Allah wishes it so, but I will die fighting the infidels. I will not stop, not matter how many they send. Persia will be a proud Muslim state once again.'

Weiner stubbed out the remains of his cigarette. 'So you hate the Russians for stealing your homelands, and the British for helping them?'

Al-Ruzi gave a deep chuckle and shook his head. 'No, Major Weiner, it is not the Muslim way to hate. We are considerate and respectful of our neighbours. This is a holy war and I am but a servant of Allah the Almighty.'

Weiner ignored the growing discomfort of religion and focussed on practicalities. 'Well, it seems we maybe able to help each other after all.'

Al-Ruzi nodded.

Weiner continued, 'Germany also has its principles, and we fight what you might consider to be a holy war in Europe. We have fought many battles, especially against the English and their allies.'

'So you are winning your holy war?'

Weiner studied the black orbs of the Muslim. The static facial expression was giving nothing away. He decided to take a chance. 'Yes, for now, but fighting a war in Europe requires materials: steel, oil, petrol, rations for a large army.'

Al-Ruzi nodded appreciatively, 'If your holy war is righteous, God will provide.'

'The Russians have huge oil reserves, coal steel, and grain – more than they need. Stalin wishes to trade part of this surplus for German technology.'

'And yet he also seeks to divide Persia with the British. I do not trust this Stalin.'

'Germany shares you mistrust.'

'Perhaps, but why should I help you?'

'We will make our exchange, agreement – call it what you will with the Russians; but they must not be able to leave Persia, alive. Of course, for diplomatic reasons Germany cannot be seen to have a hand in this; but then the mountains to the north are a dangerous place. Raiding parties loyal to the Shah have skirmishes with the Russians all the time. It would be a terrible tragedy for the Soviet delegation …'

'There would be reprisals. The Soviet T-34 is the ruin of my people, destroying homes, women, children …'

'You have great courage, but courage and a sword is no match for a Russian tank, or the British machine guns. Germany can even the odds. I will supply you with modern automatic weapons, explosives, anti-tank grenades.'

Al-Ruzi shifted his gaze towards the mosque. 'Our temples have stood for a thousand years, through many invasions. Each time we have pushed the Christians back, but this Stalin brings a new breed.'

Weiner spoke firmly, 'Stalin has no religion; he cares not for the Muslim world. Greed and fear drives the communists.'

Al-Ruzi stared sharply at Weiner, '*Fear*?'

'Yes, Stalin is a brutal master. He murders all who do not obey, including his own people … or makes them into slaves in the salt mines of Siberia.'

'This Stalin will one day learn humility.' Al-Ruzi paused, both men sat baking in the sun. The Iranian finally spoke, 'Alright. I will help you with this task in exchange for weapons to equip my men. My men are loyal, but we are few compared to the Russian hordes.'

Weiner smiled his appreciation, 'You are to kill the Soviet delegation. No witnesses must survive. The documents they carry must be returned to me intact.'

Al-Ruzi nodded slowly. 'It will be done, but tell me, Major, why do you trust me with your secrets?'

Weiner shrugged, speaking with a dismissive tone. 'Herr Hitler has the ear of Joseph Stalin, the second most powerful man in the world. If Stalin was to hear of Circassian treachery, he would wipe your race from the face of the earth.'

Al-Ruzi suddenly edged towards Weiner. The smell of Arabian spices and halitosis assaulted the Major's nostrils. The Muslim hissed. '*Power?* A man *without God* has no power. This Stalin is truly lost. I will keep to our bargain, Major Weiner.' Al-Ruzi suddenly produced a jewelled dagger from under his garments. He held the small curved weapon against Weiner's throat.

Weiner stiffened under the razor sharp blade, but maintained a calm expression.

'Major, a Muslim's word is his bond. I will kill the Russian infidels and return your documents.' Al-Ruzi pressed the tip of the dagger, drawing a small nick on the soft skin of Weiner's neck.

Weiner gritted his teeth, but held his ground, eyes fixed on the Persian.

'You also have my word, that if you should break our bargain, you will feel my blade again. This I swear.'

As suddenly as it appeared, the blade was sheathed smoothly into the scabbard under the Persian's clothing. Al-Ruzi broke into a grin as he stood up. Weiner remained dumfounded fixed to spot on the bench. 'Allah be with you my friend.'

With that the Muslim gave a courteous bow, turned on his heels, and paced across the square towards the mosque with his turban flapping in the breeze.

Weiner dabbed at the cut on his neck as the call to afternoon prayers echoed from the minuet. His muscles tensed involuntarily, his heart pounded, his head thumped with rage as he clenched his jaw.

He resolved never to underestimate the Persian again.

CHAPTER 12

Training

Nash tucked his white vest into the top of his camouflaged combat trousers and quickly adjusted the waist belt. He absently greased back his hair with a sweaty palm and took a defensive stance, with his legs slightly apart and body turned to minimise the target for his opponent. He pushed the soles of his gym shoes into the rough fibres of the hemp matting and balled his fists, raising one arm in readiness to block. The whole thing was a bad idea, but the old man had decided; she was going to Istanbul, and possible, Iran. Actually, it was madness. He'd always worked alone on covert reconnaissance – for obvious reasons. It would be worse for a woman; not just the brutality of capture, but the inevitable violation that would follow. He buried the train of thought into the 'do not open' part of his brain. It was unbearable. And then there were the practicalities – how was he supposed to maintain professional detachment on the job? Emotion was a dangerous thing. It always led to mistakes. Get the job done and get out alive had been his mantra, but having Emily in the field would change all that. He pushed the turmoil to the back of his mind, accepting the consolation prize. He had three days to train her. Three days to make a difference.

'Alright, Emily, try again. Remember, keep your balance and kick through your opponent for maximum effect. Aim for my ribs and keep going. Imagine the power of the kick going deep into my body, and make it so.'

She exhaled, sweat dripped down her face and chin, adding to the moisture already soaking the cleavage of her green army-issue T-shirt. She shuffled her feet and shrugged her shoulders like a boxer. Her firm, but strong white legs protruded through over-sized black shorts. A small red ribbon held her hair in a make-shift pony tail. She nodded, 'Right. I think I've got it.' She smiled briefly and then adopted a hard expression.

Nash anticipated the attack. 'Don't hold back, speed, power and aggression. Really try to hurt me this time.'

She yelled, simultaneously kicking out, sweeping her right leg around in a smooth arc towards the side of Nash's rib cage.

Nash blocked easily with his left arm, absorbing the shudder of the blow into his shoulder. She simply wasn't strong enough for a fist fight. One punch from a battle-hardened soldier would break her jaw. All he could do was to teach her a few distracting moves and protective stances. He jostled on the mat taking a fresh defensive position. 'Good! Try again, more power. Imagine the blow kicking my heart in the air like a football. Kick harder!'

Emily stiffened her upper torso and screamed tension into the next blow.

Nash felt his ribs reverberate with the impact.

'Excellent, that's it!' He lied, 'Again!'

Emily kicked out.

Nash blocked. 'Again!'

She shuffled a dummy move, and then abruptly thrust out with the other leg.

Nash turned and parried the blow with his lower arm, fist still clenched. He smiled. Perhaps she could pick up enough – but in three days? 'Good girl! Now really kick me. Try a double kick. Go!'

'Yeah!' Emily roared, rapidly kicking in a controlled sequence with each leg, and finishing with a punch to the sternum.

Nash gave ground and caught her fist in his upturned palm. 'Well done! Well done! Now I think you've got it.'

Emily took up position for another attack, panting heavily.

Nash glanced her up and down. 'Let's break for five minutes.' He tossed a small green hand towel to her from the edge of the mat, and picked up another for himself. He vigorously rubbed the sweat from his own face and neck.

Emily did the same, but in a more gentile fashion.

Had she got it? Perhaps. It was textbook basic training that might work against a groping, half-cut civilian; but her moves were too stiff and predictable to worry any decent soldier. Then there was her father. What would he do if Emily failed to return? Nash felt a rush of remorse. The old man was a tough bird, but Emily was the only family he had. It would destroy him. It would destroy them both. He'd be busted down to corporal or kicked out of SIS altogether – not that it would matter without Emily. He'd started in this world with nothing. Being dragged up in the slums of the East End and taking beating after beating from a vile drunk of a father. No wonder mother had left the bastard. He'd been alone and with nothing before – so what else was new?

Nash shoved his towel around his neck and took a deep breath, placing his hands on his hips. 'Right then, over to the weapons bench.' He glanced in the direction of a small trellis table that sat against the opposite wall of the gym. Emily followed, still dabbing moisture from her hairline and breathing deeply.

Nash gazed over the selection of small arms and stabbing weapons. Her sweet scent and not unpleasant sweat filtered into his nostrils. He tried to ignore it.

'Weapons training.' He stated the obvious.

'Yes, weapons …' Emily spoke vacantly while running her eyes over the bench and then off across the gym.

Nash swept his hand over the assembled tools of the trade. 'Police truncheon: used by the Gestapo and others. Boot knife: standard issue for the German Army. Designed to be worn on the leg or boot – hence the name. A selection of German pistols; the kind officers usually wear. These are all weapons that might be used in close quarter battle. Your aim of course is not to engage, but to escape unharmed. So, we will go through a few defensive moves that might temporarily disable, or even disarm, your opponent.' He gave her a sideways glance, 'Emily, are you okay? You listening?'

She suddenly fussed, 'Oh sorry, I was miles away. It's something Daddy had said. He thinks the Soviets are using their position to gain intelligence on German infrastructure and their technology.'

Nash gripped the towel around he neck. His brow furrowed. 'Yeah, that's why you're going to Istanbul; to find out.' His tone fell bitter. 'It's what you wanted isn't it? *Something more* – well you've got it alright.' He exhaled, fresh beads of sweat dripped from his brow. He stood impotent.

She pleaded, 'Danny, don't be like that.'

'Well, how the hell do you want me to feel?!'

Emily stood sour-faced. 'I don't know.' A silent pause seemed to double the size of the gymnasium. She continued, a little calmer. 'We can't defeat Germany without help from either the Soviets or the Americans?' She studied the anguish on his face. 'Danny – answer me – we need the help of the Russians, don't we?'

Nash conceded, 'Your father thinks so.' He nodded his head, 'Yes, yes, I think he's right. We do – but he doesn't have to send you – he could send somebody else.'

Her face suddenly reddened, 'Now who's bloody talking! That's what I've said all along, but you always go away –

don't you, Danny?' She closed her eyes and stifled tears, then hardened. 'Well, now the shoe is on the other foot and you don't like it!'

Nash swallowed, 'That might be so, but he *could* send someone else. It doesn't have to be you.'

Her voice quietened, almost pleading. 'That's the problem, Danny – he can't. Yes, I speak Russian and know the food, customs and culture of the region, amongst other things. I lived in Tehran for a spell when Daddy was on a diplomatic posting. There aren't any other women in SIS with that level of background. You know how it is.' She paused, looking a little sheepish, 'Also, the Russians like their men to be men, and their women ... well to be women. It's less confrontational. I can win their trust.'

Nash closed his eyes, breathing in the smell of her sweat and perfume, then pulled the towel from his neck, rubbing it on his hands. He spoke softly this time. 'Emily, there is more. There's something you're not telling me?'

'Yes ... I am sorry. Daddy wants me to win the trust of an old Soviet contact. I am to go with the Russian. If I can. The Soviet delegation needs an interpreter in Tabriz ... and a woman, a secretarial assistant taking notes would be a natural part of the delegation. I'd go unnoticed.'

'The Russians have their own people – why are you *really* going?'

Her face mellowed, almost haunted. 'It was something Daddy said, about the transcripts ...'

Nash puzzled, 'What about them?'

'The Russian voice. You know, the one I'd thought I'd heard before. Well I had – long ago. Daddy says, when I was a child ... Don't you see, Danny, I have to go ... It has to be me.'

Nash exhaled, giving her a blank look. He tossed the towel aside and selected a weapon. 'Let's start with the truncheon.' He reasoned she'd be more likely to run into trouble with the local police, or God forbid, one of the tribal gangs in the city. He lifted the short black truncheon. 'Hold out your hand.'

She hesitantly pushed out her right arm.

His brow widened, 'Don't worry.' He managed a thin smile, placing her hand through the small leather loop at the base of the truncheon. She seemed to quickly settle her fingers around the grip, then weighed the weapon against the open palm of her hand. Nash continued. 'Feels good? It's a solid lump; short, stocky, effective.' He took her gently by the elbow, 'Come on …'

They stood a few feet apart on the gym mat.

Nash watched as she adjusted her grip. 'Good, good, get the feel and the weight of the thing. Try a few swipes in the air.'

She waved the baton experimentally. First to the left, then to the right, and then down from overhead; with each swing faster than the last.

Nash forced a grin to lighten the mood. 'See, just like splitting coconuts at the funfair.'

Emily gave a nervous smile.

'Alright, attack me from above. Bring the truncheon down as hard as you can on my head.'

She held the weapon aloft, hesitating. 'Danny, are you sure? This could really hurt.'

He soothed confidence. 'Go ahead; give it a good swing.'

Tensing, she swung the baton downwards at a modest speed, but at least aiming towards his head.

Nash blocked sharply, pushing both his fists up, and crossing them at the wrist to meet the blow. He patted the truncheon against the flesh on the inside of his wrist. 'See here – this is an effective block, but you don't want a broken arm; keep the inner part of your wrist uppermost so the baton lands on the soft flesh and not the bone. Alright? Try again.'

Emily nodded and repositioned the weapon. This time bringing the cosh down with more power.

97

Nash blocked. The slap of wood against skin reverberated around the gym. He ignored the stinging sensation on his arm. 'Excellent! Now, you try at defence.'

They swapped positions. Nash took up the baton, standing with his legs slightly apart. He raised it over his head and then looked blankly at his student. 'Ready? Double arm blocking movement. Remember the position of your wrists.'

He swung the baton at a reasonable speed.

Crack!

The truncheon struck home on the side of her arm.

Emily crumpled to the floor holding her wrist. 'Ow! That really hurts!'

He admonished, 'Fight through the pain. Try to ignore it – and never lower your guard. Once you're on the floor, it's all over. Stand up, try again.'

Emily furrowed her brow, rubbing the bruise on her wrist.

Nash took up position. 'Ready? This time, block with more power. Sweep your arms up to meet me – the closer you get, the less energy your attacker has in each blow.'

She took a deep breath, shuffled her feet, then positioning her wrists in a fisted cross slightly above her chest. She spoke more firmly. 'Ready.'

Nash swung the baton.

Thump!

The weapon deflected away. Emily stood her ground.

'Good, you're getting the hang of it.' Nash wiped sweat from his palm and re-secured his grip on the weapon.

She nodded, breathing hard. 'I am ready. Again, more power.'

Nash heaved the weapon.

Suddenly with a fluid movement, she turned sideways, dropping simultaneously on to one knee and grabbing Nash by the wrist and shirt, throwing him over her shoulder.

Nash slapped on to the canvas, slightly winded, but wide-eyed with surprise. He perched up on his elbows, nodding with satisfaction. A smile crept across his face as Emily looked on from above, panting with her hands on her hips.

'Where did you learn to do that?'

She broadened into a grin. 'I don't know. Well, I kind of just remembered. God knows why. When Daddy was in the diplomatic service, I would hang around in the back garden of the embassy getting bored.'

Nash looked perplexed, 'So?'

'Well, there was this man servant. A strong-looking Iranian fellow who used to play fight with me and a few of the other kids. I've forgotten his name now, but anyway, he was *Pahlavani*.'

'*Pahlavani?*'

'Yes, it's a traditional wrestling and fighting technique. Originally, I think to entertain the Shah and to provide the various courts and palaces with amusement in the eighteenth and nineteenth centuries; but it dates back to the Parthian Empire of Iran, one hundred and thirty-two B.C.'

Nash raised an eyebrow. 'Does it now?' He sat up on the mat shaking his head. Could she learn enough to stay alive? Istanbul was a place of narrow streets and shadowy doorways. A white woman of child bearing age was a commodity like no other. The local Arabs also had an unpredictable temperament – the flash of a shamshir had severed the heads of many insolent females. Then there was the *SS*, brutality being their stock-in-trade. A girl such as Emily would be a play thing. How they would relish the prospect of slowly executing a female spy. Especially one that had been caught plotting against a room full of senior German officers; but more so because the cunning and guile of a woman should never be allowed to tarnish the impeccable credentials of the black shirts. Nash wondered how many men he could kill, how many bullets he could stop, before they got to her. He only hoped it would be enough.

99

CHAPTER 13

Istanbul

Emily Sinclair prepared for the street and took one last look at her reflection in the cheap glass panels mounted behind the registration desk. She huffed with uncertainty at the image that stared back, but took comfort from the fact that the lobby of the somewhat shabby Excelsior Hotel was deserted. She'd have to get the job done, but without drawing attention. She stood in a pair of British Army lightweight khaki trousers, the kind with a map pocket on the side of each leg. A leather belt secured the over-sized material around her waist, extenuating her hourglass figure against the folds of her short sleeve shirt. A tan coloured scarf covered her hair. A few brown locks escaped from the triangular fold at the back of head garment, but otherwise it looked respectful enough. She adjusted the canvas strap on the small Red Cross satchel that sat across her torso. The solid metallic lump of Webley revolver inside the bag rubbed the canvas fabric against her hip. She checked her blouse to ensure the buttons were done up above the cleavage and then headed for the exit.

She stepped into sweltering heat and dusty air. The smell of spices and diesel mixed with the faint odour of human waste. Suspect flakes a sun-dried detritus filled the gutters. The locals crammed onto the uneven footpaths, their hubbub competing with the toots of impossibly laden vehicles. A driver hung out the cab window of a dilapidated flat-bed, ranting in the local Arabic dialect at the traffic jam and adding to the exotic mayhem of the narrow street. She weaved amongst the vehicles and headed down the street towards the bazaar, trying to look anonymous and avoiding eye contact with passers by. Her pulse raced, sweat trickled from her armpits and an unpleasant stickiness coated the back of her neck. She concentrated on her field training and tried to maintain an outward composure. She was just another Brit from the Women's Auxiliary Force going about her business: harmless, humanitarian, and incidental.

She focussed her senses on the street ahead. A chaos of shops, street traders, and the homeless marked the route. Tatty apartment blocks towered randomly on either side of the narrow street, creating a modicum of shade in the corridor of still air that trapped the stench of humanity.

She recalled the route in her head as she went. *Fifty yards, past the basket weaver's shop ... right fork ... rusty black sign on the building ahead ... street gets narrower, go into the arch at the end. So far, so good.*

She paused under the mud and cement arch that marked the edge of the market. A donkey chewed on some rotten vegetables. A fresh pile of manure added a familiar odour to the otherwise foreign surroundings. Emily scanned ahead into the labyrinth of semi-covered gangways that made the bazaar. The cobbles were polished smooth by hundreds of years of activity. Waste paper, torn cardboard boxes and splinters of wood from a myriad of packing crates collected in the Byzantium thoroughfare. The locals didn't seem to mind and stood smiling politely, some in sandals, others in bare feet, and all haggling for a bargain. Each market stool appeared to be a home-made construction of whatever was to hand. A few lucky diehards held prime positions with solid wooden benches heaped with goods. Torn canvas and stained tarpaulin provided some cover overhead, haphazardly tied to drain pipes, gutters and anything else that would make an anchoring point. A spaghetti of power cables criss-crossed the underside of each tarpaulin, openly stealing electricity from nearby buildings to fuel the activity below.

Emily gazed through a multi-coloured array of spice baskets, each one heaped like a psychedelic termite mound. A second stall rested at an angle, groaning with dried fruits. The aromatic spices and exotic fruits filled her nostrils with sensation, jogging childhood memories from the depths of her brain. She tried to concentrate, recalling the mantra from her hastily arranged field training at SIS: *Navigate, observe, assess, move with purpose.* It didn't help. *Archway, market running roughly east ahead. What do I see? Nothing? What am I supposed to see? Man selling dates. Local women ... old, fat, buying food. Dog yapping.*

It all seemed ordinary and maybe it was? Or perhaps she'd missed something?

Emily scanned the scene again, and then satisfied that it really was just a bunch of market stalls, headed into the bazaar. She squeezed between the crowds, holding on to the Red Cross canvas satchel and ignoring the lecherous glances of old men. She kept moving.

Jewellery stall on the left, opposite carpet stand on the right. Go another thirty paces ... take the next left. Blacksmith.

She turned the corner into another gangway. The *chink chink* of metal against anvil, smoke, and the radiant glow of volcanically hot charcoal emitted from the blacksmith's stall. A muscular, greasy-looking Turk stood stripped to the waist, impervious to the heat and dripping in sweat. He continued hammering, seemingly oblivious of the westerner.

Emily allowed her eyes to follow the line of the market stalls which quickly petered out as the canvas-covered market gave way to a narrow brick alleyway, barely wide enough for one person. She focussed on the gloomy arch of stone ahead and replayed her instructions.

Alley up ahead ... enter, go forward fifty paces. Find the oak door on the right.

Her heart involuntarily missed a beat as she started pacing towards the darkness. The alleyway loomed, engulfing, like some black pit of despair. She lost sight and sound of the market as her mind's eye conjured vile creatures: lurking, primeval, clinging to the crevices of the ancient whitewashed stonework. She advanced into the alley nonetheless and then paused after a few yards, forcing her heart rate to settle and allowing her eyes to adjust to the shadows. She edged forwards, feeling a transition from cobbles to stone slabs under her shoes. The alley curved slightly. A sudden shaft of light provided a focal point some thirty yards ahead. She spied a protrusion in the brickwork.

The door!

She moved towards it. She knocked twice, then waited two seconds and knocked three more times in rapid succession, then waited another second, before giving a final, single knock.

She stood in silence, her ears burning for the slightest sound. She glanced up and down the alleyway, but there was no intrusion. She waited a few more seconds, wondering if she'd got the instructions wrong. Suddenly the sound of a heavy metal latch and the scraping of wood on stone told her that she hadn't. The door opened a crack, casting a shaft of candle light across her face.

She spoke quietly but clearly, 'London has sent me.'

The voice of an old woman growled back. 'Of course they have. My master wishes to know *who* sent you?'

Emily instantly registered the Russian accent, 'I was sent by Papa Lima Seven.'

'What for?'

'Macleod's Maidens.'

The door slammed shut. Emily stood waiting as muffled voices exchanged back and forth on the other side of the door.

Abruptly, the door opened. The hag stood blocking the doorway with her pear-shaped frame. 'My master asks who you are. What is *your* name?'

'Echo Sierra One. I am told the tide is rising in the Sound of Sleat.'

A deep chuckle emitted from the depths of the building. A man spoke with a strong Moldavian-like accent. 'That's her alright. Let her in!' Hollow laughter boomed from the man's throat. 'Olga, let her in. We have been expecting this visitor.'

The old women frowned with suspicion, but stood aside holding the door open as she was bid. 'Enter,' she spoke flatly.

Emily stepped over the threshold into a lime-washed plaster hallway, devoid of any lighting, apart from a recess by the door that sheltered a thick candle. The flame flickered gently, shedding a yellow glow. The movement of fresh air and a brightness at the end of the narrow hall beckoned. She moved cautiously over the terracotta floor towards the light, emerging into an open room. Net curtains fluttered in the breeze at the open windows, which gave a surprising view across the city. Cane furniture comprising of two single chairs and a sofa sat on the polished floor. A coffee table standing on a small Persian rug occupied the space in between. A stocky man, possibly in his late forties and with dark hair slicked-back, stood by the window. He puffed on a rather caustic Soviet tobacco and, after exhaling a plume of the toxic waste into the room, broke into a fatherly smile.

'Well, well, well. You are even lovelier than I imagined …' He took a gentle drag on his cigarette. Smoke swirled about his head.

Stunned, Emily registered butterflies in her stomach, which morphed suddenly into a gut wrenching foreboding. Her heart raced. '*You* … It is you, I *know* your voice! We know each other don't we?'

The man inflated his chest and smiled, then nodded gently as he formed a more serious expression. 'Yes, indirectly we do, but long ago. You were just a child then. My name is Sergio Korelov.'

Emily stood dumbfounded, wracking her brains for the slightest memory of the man.

The Chinese Embassy days?

Nothing.

Nanjing?

Nothing.

Come on, come on, why do I know him? Where did I hear that voice?

Emily furrowed her brow, flicking her eyes up and down the man standing in front of her.

Tehran? Yes, Tehran ... something about Tehran.

Korolev interrupted her train of thought. 'Do not be concerned, Miss Sinclair. You are amongst friends here, Russian friends.' Korolev smiled and waved his free hand towards the wicker furniture. 'Please, please ... take a seat. It is hot and you must be thirsty. Some sweet tea? I find it quenches the thirst in this dry climate.'

Korolev nodded towards the old woman who stood hovering on the threshold. She grunted disapproval and headed for the small set of saloon-style louvre doors that made the entrance to a galley kitchen on the far side of the room. Korolev waited for the domestic to disappear through the slatted doors.

Emily sat primly on the edge of the two-seater wicker sofa, squeezing her knees up before the coffee table. She took the scarf from her head, involuntarily shaking her hair free of the confinement.

The Russian gazed at her feminine perfection, then broke with a business-like cough to clear his throat. He ambled slowly to an adjacent carver chair, stubbing out his cigarette in the glass ashtray on the table. He exhaled another plume of smoke. 'So, here you are in Istanbul … How do you find it?' He waved his arm towards the net curtains billowing in the warm air, 'It's a beautiful city is it not?'

Emily spoke politely, 'Yes it is.'

'How do you find the food? Not something you English are used to eating?'

'Mr Korolev, the food is fine and Istanbul is lovely, but I am here on business. My office has sent me from London to meet with you.'

Korolev chuckled and leant back in his chair. The frame creaked under his weight. 'Direct! That's what I like! You are right, my lovely. We are here on business. Miss Sinclair … Emily? Do you mind if I call you, Emily?'

Hesitation crackled her voice, 'Well since you already know my name … I suppose that would be alright. You preferred to be called, Mr … sorry, Major Korolev?'

'Colonel, my rank would be close to that of a British colonel.'

Emily decided to keep the formality of rank, and maintaining a polite smile. She continued, 'You know my father?'

Korolev nodded slowly, 'Sir Hugh, yes of course.'

'He sent me.'

The Russian gave a smirk, 'No, I asked for you …'

Emily hid her surprise. 'You asked for a *translator*?'

'Yes, I did, amongst other things.'

She shuffled uncomfortably, 'Well, I speak Russian and can translate into English. I have some Arabic, but not much, just enough to get by. I am also competent in German.'

'I hear your Russian is fluent and your German is excellent.'

'No, not so fluent, but after a few minutes I can tune into a conversation and take detailed notes.'

'Do you think in Russian?'

'Sometimes …'

Korolev slapped his thigh, 'Good! That means you are fluent! What about your German? Do you think you could take notes, dictation, word for word as they speak it?'

Emily shifted her gaze to her shoes, and then fiddled with the scarf on her lap. 'Well, yes, I think so; provided the speaker is reasonably clear and not too fast. Some of the Germanic dialects from the Black Forest are not so easy to understand.'

Korolev nodded appreciatively, 'Well, if you can identify different dialects, I expect your German is more than enough for the task ahead.'

'What exactly is my task, Major, I mean, Colonel Korolev?'

The louvre doors suddenly swung open. Olga trudged into the room with a fake brass tray containing two tea glasses, an ornate sugar bowl and a few slices of lemon.

Korolev observed as the domestic laid the offering on the table. He spoke quickly in Russian, 'Thank you Olga, you may return to your duties.' The woman duly scurried off to the kitchen. Korolev waited for the louvres to close, then returned to English. 'We will continue to speak in English. My servant has only a few words, it is better for us.'

Emily nodded.

Korolev dropped a sugar lump in one glass of the steaming tea. 'Earl Grey,' He inhaled the steam and smiled. 'I got a liking for it back in the twenties. We would exchange goods with the British Navy in the Baltic.'

'You were in the Russian Navy then?'

'Not exactly, it was then that I became acquainted with your father, Sir Hugh. He spent some time at sea too. We were young and keen then, but that is ancient history … let us talk about the present.' His polite smile dropped to a bland expression.

Emily maintained prim formality. 'Colonel, what is it that you would have me do? I was under the impression that I would be simply taking radio communications and translating in the Istanbul office. At least to start with.'

'You will be.' He tapped out another cigarette from the waist pocket of his suit. 'But there's been a slight change of plan.'

'Change of plans?'

'Yes,' he lit the cigarette, oblivious to the choking smog it generated. 'There will be some routine monitoring of radio traffic and translation at the desk, but I also have a face-to-face meeting with the Germans – it's been moved forwards by a day.' He paused to allow the information to sink in. 'It's probably just a security precaution. I am to meet with my counterpart from Germany to discuss a trade; well, a negotiation of sorts.'

'I know about the meeting. You need a secretary to take minutes.'

'No, I need a beautiful woman to put the Germans at ease.'

Emily spoke sheepishly, 'I am sure there are many Russian girls …'

'Not ones that speak English and German, and can be trusted.'

She looked Korolev in the eye. 'And you trust me? *Why*?'

He stared back, unflinching. 'Because I must, and because you are the daughter of Sinclair. I trust him, so I will trust you.'

She doubted his reply. Yes, he had known her father and there *was* some kind of bond between them – Daddy had indicated as much. It was strange though. Daddy wouldn't elaborate. It was as if he had been wounded in some way. Regardless, their acquaintance wasn't just a long standing professional courtesy, but a subliminal connection that clearly neither would divulge. If Daddy was being economical with the truth, then it was a certainty that the Russian could not be trusted.

She tried the direct approach. 'Colonel Korolev, you don't know me really.'

Korolev eyed her carefully, cigarette dangling from his lips. 'Caution is good. You are right not to put your faith in me … is that the right phrase in English? Yes? You are under orders from SIS. I am under orders from my superiors …' He shrugged, and took another slug of his tobacco, then leant back in the chair. 'We are both under orders.'

Emily conceded the point. She *was* under instruction from London – to translate for the Istanbul office, and meet with this Russian contact, but that didn't mean she would trust him. If only Danny was here. She swallowed 'Alright,' she sat upright, 'What would you have me do?'

The Russian kept a blank expression. 'My orders from the Kremlin are to make a trade with the Germans.'

Emily sat attentively, 'I know in general, but exactly what kind of trade?'

Korolev shrugged, 'The German government has a number of trade agreements with respect to economic cooperation between the Soviet Union and Germany. My superiors merely wish to elaborate on these agreements.'

Emily tried to mask her irritation. How the hell was she supposed to do her job if the Russian was going to be evasive all the time? She needed to know the substance of the task. Who she was dealing with, what they were like, and most of all, what to do if it all went wrong. She spoke assertively, 'Negotiate on what and with whom? If I am to take notes it would be useful to know who will be at the meeting and the topic of the discussions.' She raised an eyebrow.

Korolev relaxed into a smile. 'Of course, you are right.' He waved his cigarette in the air. 'I will be meeting the Plenipotentiary of Special Issues in Chemical Production for the Reich. A man called Krauch. A civilian, but nonetheless an influential one. He is the company director for I. G. Farben; one of the largest chemical companies in the world.'

'Yes, I know of the company, at least a little. What does this Krauch want?'

'Simple – he wants raw materials for his factories: coal, metal ores, and the like.'

'And just like that, you will give them to him?'

'No, if only it were that easy. In return, Comrade Stalin seeks technical expertise from German engineers.'

Emily forced an even tone, remembering the radio transcripts taken in London. 'Engineers? What kind of engineers?' She felt the prickly heat of vasodilation flush up her neck.

Korolev politely ignored it. 'I am not at liberty to give all the details, and I am not certain which experts will be part of the German delegation, but there will be at least one scientist: my counterpart from Germany.'

Emily frowned, 'I don't understand, Colonel, you're a soldier? Your counterpart is a *scientist*?'

Korolev greased back his hair and took a drag on his cigarette. 'Everyone in the Soviet Union is a soldier at one time or another.' He gave a deep chuckle, 'I am a Colonel, that is true, but I am also an engineer. I have expertise in aeronautics and projectiles.'

Emily's frown deepened. 'I am sorry, I don't follow …'

'*Aeroplanes* Miss Sinclair. I make what one might call, very fast *aeroplanes*, for the Soviet Union. My contribution to the Soviet war effort, so to speak. My equivalent in Germany is engaged in the business of rockets and propulsion systems. A Doctor Steinhoff, originally from the Technical University in Berlin.' He shrugged confirmation, 'This Steinhoff is an engineer, just like me.'

Emily filed away details in her mind. *Steinhoff, Berlin, engineer, works on aeroplanes and possibly rockets.*

She puzzled, 'Steinhoff is also a soldier?'

'No, Germany still prefers to keep its intellectuals and scientists in reserved professions, working behind the scenes on presumably important projects for the German war effort.'

'So, what should I know about him?'

'His work on rocket motors and propulsion systems was known a little before the war. He published a few mediocre scientific papers and was doing alright – then disappeared. He seems to have resurfaced in some top secret programme. My masters want to know what Steinhoff is working on – if he's perfected a rocket propulsion system, or something else.'

Korolev maintained the façade. The NKVD had made it clear – the Soviet Union was to remain superior, more advanced than the Germans in all matters of aeronautics and rocket technology. His inspiring design of the Soviet Delta Wing was a revolutionary concept in aircraft technology. The D-Wing absorbed the entire cockpit and main fuselage of the plane. Its slender shape and swept back curves were close to aerodynamic perfection. The Kremlin wanted it, and wanted it now as a uniquely capable, almost supersonic, long range bomber. No other aircraft could match it – the British, the Americans – nobody. But there was a problem: the flattened structure of the D-wing was large and only stable at high speeds. He didn't have an aircraft engine powerful enough to fly it. Try as he might, all attempts at making a suitable engine had failed. The NKVD had made the Kremlin's impatience very apparent. He was one step away from the Gulag and starving to death in a Siberian winter.

Emily Sinclair interrupted his thoughts. 'Colonel?'

Korolev snapped back to the present, 'Yes, I was saying …'

'Doctor Steinhoff is the German's technical specialist. Presumably, there will be military representation from the German side as well?'

He picked up the conversation, 'Yes, of course. They are sending their man. A Major Weiner. I am not entirely clear on his role, but he's *SS* – I am sure he didn't arrive at his position by soothing the politicians. He's a proper soldier, so be careful. He seems to come with the required authority on military issues at least.'

Emily flushed a little more, her heart began to race. Soldiers, *SS* officers, Nazi officials, she was already out of her depth. She feigned politeness, 'Anyone else?'

'A few political officers and our Iranian hosts.'

'So you want me to play the role of a dutiful personal assistant, taking notes, and eavesdropping on the German conversations.' She picked up her tea glass to calm her nerves, and took a gentle sip of the warm sweet liquid. 'I can take notes and memorise more private discussions. Is there more I should do? I mean, how do I get close enough to listen without looking suspicious, out of place?'

Korolev nodded slowly, 'Your first time?'

'Yes,' her voice croaked a little.

'I see …' His voice dropped to a gentile whisper. 'Use your instincts. You'll be alright. Your father had good instincts. I suspect you do too.' He smiled gently.

Emily sat poised with the tea glass in her hands, heart pounding, feeling light-headed. The smell of sugary lemon drifted into her nostrils. She took another sip. Like a tonic, the hot liquid just kept the collywobbles at bay.

Korolev spoke with a more familiar kindness. 'The Germans have an arrogance, an iron façade; call it what you will – but it is also their weakness. This is what we shall exploit.'

She took another sip of tea, calmer now. 'Yes, I can see their arrogance, but getting their confidence?'

Korolev chuckled, '*Beautiful women*. This Director Krauch has a reputation for being firm and decisive, but he is also a – how do you call it – *a ladies' man*. My English is correct, yes?'

'Ladies' man, yes,' Emily repeated.

112

'Our new German friends will not deal all their cards, and like a Georgian snake, they will keep some under the table.'

'You want me to get close to Krauch?'

'Well …' He squatted forwards, glancing from side to side as if looking for conspirators. He spoke in a whisper. 'I want you to use your feminine wiles to occupy the time of this key member of the Third Reich. Steer the polite conversation, gently probe him for what he knows. Do you think you could do that for me?'

Emily spoke quietly and evenly, 'Alright, I will try.'

Korolev suddenly piped up with bravado, 'Good girl,' he leant across, patting her on the knee. 'You have the Russian spirit in you after all! We will seek the true motivations of these Germans, and perhaps one day soon Britain and the Soviet Union will be friends again.'

Korolev broke into a grin and picked up his tea in a mock salute. 'The Sinclair's it is then, for England! For England and Mother Russia!' He gulped down his tea in one mouthful, slamming the empty glass back on the table.

Emily politely sipped her tea, dredging the depths of her mind for the slightest remembrance of her new Russian friend, but the memories remained elusive. It *was* his voice on the German-Soviet transcript taken in London – but who was Korolev *really*? She had to face the plain facts: he was a Soviet on an official meeting with the Germans, and therefore the enemy – everything he says could be lies, all lies. He was there to trade in secret weapons technology with the Germans on the instructions of the Kremlin. But then, things could never be that simple. Even if that part was true, why the hell was he helping the British? *Why*? He was a Soviet spy playing both sides, but which side was he really on? Daddy trusted him, but perhaps their old friendship – if it was a friendship – had clouded Daddy's judgement. What did the Russian have on Daddy? Have on *her*? Either way, it was too late to back out now.

Children's laughter meandered into her mind's eye. She could see herself playing and giggling. She runs across the grass, hiding behind a large terracotta pot, sniggering, counting to ten. Others squeal with laughter. She scampers to another hiding place in the compound. A small olive tree amongst the manicured flower beds. The smell of flowers, a cricket hops in the dust. She sees Mother. She is beautiful, long hair curling down on to the bright orange of her silks. A man is at her side, partly obscured from view. He chuckles and speaks into her ear. She replies in Russian, they both laugh. The man chuckles again, a deep, throaty, Soviet belly laugh.

Nash hovered amongst the sheets of iron and lengths of steel rod at the back of the Smithy, and peering through a crack in the grease-stained tarpaulin that marked the boundary of the blacksmith's stall. The rhythmic *chink chink tap* of hammer against anvil filled his ears, punctuated by the general hubbub of the market. Sweat formed a V-shaped swath of dampness on the chest of his khaki shirt, almost meeting with the moisture creeping out from his armpits. A sudden cloud of steam mixed with the heat of the furnace as the huge Turk plunged a piece of glowing metalwork into a wooden bucket. Nash glanced towards the rippling morass of muscles as the Turk moved back to the anvil. A dual *chink chink tap* announced the next round of hammering. Nash shifted his focus back to the surveillance, and strained an eyeball through the crack in the canvas towards the alleyway; watching, listening and smelling the scene. Pear-shaped women dressed head to foot in black cloth, sandals, and each carrying one or more woven straw shopping baskets that seemed to be all the rage. Tradesmen dressed in turbans and cheap Egyptian-style cotton shouted encouragement, waving goods at the punters as they passed by, but rarely making a sale.

Nash roved his eye over the heaving crowd and the alleyway up ahead. He checked his watch.

Six-thirty and still nothing.

She'd been in there for hours, but what could he do?

It was a waiting game. He stared through the hole in the canvas, gritting his teeth.

Come on, Emily, you should be out of there by now. Come on … come on. What's keeping you?

A teenage boy scurried by carrying a wire mesh box under his arm. Two scrawny bantams flapped at each other, fighting for space in the confinement. Downy feathers and a whiff of chicken manure trailed behind the young lad as he disappeared into the alley. Some thirty seconds later another trader emerged with a small crate of fruit that had seen better days. No Emily. Perhaps he'd missed her?

Suddenly, as if on cue, she appeared.

Nash watched as she hesitated at the entrance to the alley. She fiddled momentarily with the Red Cross satchel and then with her headwear. Her European figure, height, and wavy brown hair protruding from her scarf, did nothing but draw attention. Old women glanced, resigned with their lot. Lecherous old men looked on hopefully for a few seconds before returning to their customers.

Emily stepped into the crowd, weaving between the shoppers at a less than gentle pace. Anguish furrowed her brow.

Nash hung back behind the curtain. *Come on, Emily, take it easy.* He waited a few more seconds, and then moved to the edge of the tarpaulin, catching a glimpse of her headscarf as she went deeper into the bazaar. Nash flashed a nod of thanks towards the Turk and moved past the small artisanal furnace towards the thoroughfare.

Suddenly, a tall, exotically dressed man emerged from the alley.

Nash froze. He shrunk back behind a crate of oranges, looking for cover.

Flowing robes of the finest black silk covered the man's body, an equally expensive turban draped loosely about his head. Polished black leather riding boots protruded as he strode purposefully along the gangway. The sea of shoppers instinctively parted as he approached, some respectfully muted, others with fear in their eyes. Nash caught sight of the curved blade under his cloak – an Iranian shamshir. The gold-yellow fastening on the ornate handle spoke of fine craftsmanship. Instinct told Nash that the sword wasn't for ceremonial use.

He checked the Webley under his shirt and, taking comfort from the gaping hole a .38 round could make in a man's chest at close range, stepped into the crowd. He followed, maintaining a careful distance from his new Arabian friend.

Nash worked through the shoppers, straining his neck to maintain eyes-on with Emily. The turbulent wake of bodies left by the giant Arab seemed to bounce like pinballs off the incoherent stacks of produce in the thoroughfare. Nash stood on tiptoes, scanning the tops of the crowds, looking for the bobbing motion of her long hair in the brown scarf.

Had he lost her?

A flush of adrenalin increased his pace and, with the application of a little attitude, Nash clambered his way forward. Black cloak and boots strode only yards ahead. Nash, placing a hand under the front of his khaki shirt, gripped the Webley. He eased the weapon free, being careful to keep it concealed under his shirt tail, but at the ready. He frantically scanned ahead for Emily.

Abruptly, the Arab turned a corner, heading for a collection of rustic stone archways that made the north entrance to the market. Nash pushed past an enthusiastic merchant, spilling a basket of peaches on to the floor. Ignoring the ranting and gesticulations of the shopkeeper, he focussed on the archway ahead. The narrow cobbles gave way to an open, marginally less crowded street. Nash assimilated what little he could see of the road as it curved uphill away from the arch. A flash of army-issue fatigues disappeared from view, some thirty yards distant.

Emily!

He increased his pace, gripping harder on the pistol as he made for the exit. The Arab seemed to be lengthening his stride and heading in the same direction.

Nash emerged on to the street, breathing deeply, and with sweat trickling down his back. He instinctively shielded his eyes from the scorching sun. The black figure crested the rise in the road and quickly slipped over the horizon. Nash pulled out the Webley and jogged up the street, weaving amongst the pedestrians and parked vehicles. Pausing on the rise, he absorbed the new terrain. The road widened, almost enough for two vehicles. Sandstone and cement apartments, some three or more storeys high, leaned haphazardly over the pavement. Laundry hung from balconies. The aftermath of a recent outdoor market fed a debris field of waste paper, cardboard, and rotting vegetables in the gutters.

Nash breathed a mixture of decaying squashes and batted flies from his face, straining to see his quarry. Emily was walking briskly from the scene, glancing over her shoulder as she went. The Arab was only ten yards behind. Her backward glances increased. She broke into a run.

Nash leapt off the pavement and pounded down the middle of the road, and pumping with his free arm, he accelerated. Throwing caution aside, revolver in hand, he powered downhill as if sprinting for the finishing tape in an Olympic final.

He couldn't hear her cries as she ran into the main square at the bottom of the hill, but the anguish on her face as she glanced back forced another burst of speed that even Jessie Owen would be proud of. Nash pelted downhill, desperate in the knowledge that black cloak and boots would close on his prey. He pushed hard, dodging vehicles. Then hand springing off a wayward motorcycle, he burst into the square and stumbled to a halt.

Half-bent, panting, he moved his eye quickly over the quadrant. Palm trees sat regimented amongst the flagstones. A thirty foot marble statue depicting Saladin the Magnificent rested proudly in the middle of the square. The black-cloaked Arab stood in the open some twenty yards ahead – but no Emily.

An echoing chant suddenly filled Nash's ears. He glanced up at the minuet across the quadrangle. The call to prayer seemed infectious, bodies hastened on to the street. A gaggle of school children emerged from the right, creating a riverine-like obstacle across his path. He hastily tucked the revolver under his shirt, bobbing up and down, he maintained eyes-on with the Arab. The man prowled about the square, uncertain, and then seemed to edge with more purpose towards the statue of Saladin.

More believers filed into the square, weaving ant-like processions towards the mosque on the far side. Nash pushed his way through the last of the school children, searching, but there was still no Emily. The Arab disappeared behind the marble. Nash made a beeline for the statue, withdrawing the Webley as he went.

This couldn't be it. They'd only really just started. Well, no they hadn't – it had been on and off over the last eight years – more on than off in the last three. She would ask, and he would dither; always finding one excuse after another to keep his pokey little room in Bermondsey. What the hell was the matter with him? She wanted commitment, that's all. What was he so afraid of? Everything: letting her down, letting himself down, an ordinary life, being trapped with the candle of his soul extinguished. Soldiering and brutality was all he'd ever known. House, home, hearth – were not for his kind.

Orders, war, death, survival – that was it. And yet there was love. He *did* love her. There had been no other. Yet, their love was eroded by a powerful defect; the soldier's, no *his* ability, to remain cold and detached – but most of all by her aspirations for the mundane. If she still wanted that.

Nash swung around the concrete plinth at the base of the statue, skidding to a stop with his heart racing, sweat dripping from his brow. He stabbed ahead with the pistol, searching the gathering crowds for a target.

Nothing.

He moved the sight of the revolver methodically from left to right, then froze, clicking back the hammer on the pistol. He took aim as black cloak and boots disappeared amongst the palms on the far side of the square. He gave an involuntary growl, staring skyward, then gently lowered the pistol, disengaging the trigger with his thumb.

Damn it to hell!

He shoved the pistol back under his shirt and stood panting with his hands on his hips. He moved his eyes amongst the ever-increasing gathering. The call from the minuet beckoned the faithful. Had she escaped into the crowd? He took a breath and began jogging, accelerating across the square, picking up the line of sight where the cloaked giant had disappeared from view. What would he tell Sinclair? How could he tell him? His only daughter subject to a summary decapitation at the hands of a savage tribesman. Or worse, sold into prostitution and slavery; never to be seen again.

He ran towards the tree marking the Arab's exit from the square.

A feminine voice suddenly penetrated his alarm. 'Danny! Danny!'

He decreased his pace, brow furrowing.

'Danny!'

Nash whirled around.

'Danny, oh my God!'

Anguish fell from his features as he registered the woman running towards him.

He jogged a few yards, stumbling to halt as they almost collided. He looked her up and down. She stood sweaty and bedraggled, still clutching the Red Cross bag. He spoke, whilst trying to calm his breathing. 'You alright? Jesus Christ, Emily. I thought I'd lost you.'

She forged a smile, then dissolved into tears. Nash remained fixed to the spot as she flung her arms around his neck. 'Oh, Danny! I was so worried, thank God. Thank God that you are here!' She squeezed in closer, sobbing.

He responded by hugging her waist, almost lifting her off the floor. A mixture of body odour, raw fear, carbolic soap, and lavender filled his senses. He brushed her hair gently through the scarf, soothing, 'It's alright … you're safe. You're safe now.' Then abruptly changing mode, he removed her arms from around his neck and held her shoulders firmly. He looked her in the eye with a blank expression. 'The Arab – have you seen him before?'

She stood, drying her eyes.

He gripped her biceps. 'Emily, did he follow you from your hotel?'

She flustered, 'No … no, I don't think so.'

He took her firmly by the hand. 'Come on, we need to get you out of here before your friend doubles back.'

Nash held on tight, marching Emily across the square, heading for the nearest side street, and keeping his free hand on the Webley and both eyes wide open, searching for signs of the enemy.

CHAPTER 14

Tabriz

Major Weiner paused on the ornate marble staircase to straighten the braid of campaign medals on his dress uniform. He brushed a fleck of hair from his lapel and glanced down at the shine on his shoes. They were gleaming. Satisfied, he puffed his chest and took in the view below. The white marble extended across the lobby of the Iranian Ambassador's residence. The historic building breathed opulence. The original plasterwork and ornate coving, along with tapestries from the building's heyday as the Shah's summer house, had been painstakingly restored.

Weiner moved down the stairs into the huge lobby. A warm breeze funnelled through some glass doors that had been wedged open at the entrance, and rustled the leaves of the potted palms and ornamental orange trees that tastefully decorated the place. He searched amongst the pot plants and leather sofas for his charge, finally spotting Steinhoff lurking in one of the arched window bays and looking awkward in a black three-piece suit. He maintained a blank expression as he walked smartly towards the scientist, with his heels clicking rhythmically on the hardstone. The grand vista through to the veranda emerged as he approached. Large arched windows gave a view across an expansive rectangular pond come man-made lake that merged to infinity with the perfectly manicured gardens. The landscaping offered both privacy and seemingly idyllic natural beauty, despite its false construction and proximity to the city centre. The last of the afternoon sun gave an orange glow in the background, silhouetting the trees on the perimeter. Nightlights, marking the formal footpaths in the garden, emitted a pleasant glow in response to the setting sun.

Weiner watched mildly disappointed as Steinhoff turned towards the sound of his heels, being denied the chance to surprise his minion with a withering remark. He came to a halt and tried anyway. 'You look like a sack of shit.' He glanced Steinhoff up and down, 'I hope you're bloody ready for this. You're representing Germany remember.' Not bothering to wait for Steinhoff to respond, he reached into his waist pocket and produced a pack of cigarettes. He punched a smoke out of the paper carton and shoved it between his lips, deliberately making a show of it and not offering one to his companion. Weiner muttered with the unlit cigarette in his mouth. 'Fucking cocktail party. Whose idea was that? Waste of time!' He clicked his petrol lighter with frustration, over-flaming the end of his cigarette.

Steinhoff stood with his hands buried in his pockets, black tie, white shirt, and a gold chain showing from the fob watch in his waistcoat pocket. 'It certainly wasn't my idea. I didn't want to come here in the first place. It's not as if I don't have enough to do back at the lab.'

Weiner exhaled a thick blue cloud, '*Scheisse*, these Russian cigarettes could stun a carthorse.' He grimaced, taking another drag all the same.

Steinhoff offered a sarcastic tone. 'Well, that's politics and diplomacy for you. It's a "getting to know you" session – right up your street. I am sure the Russian delegation will be delighted to know that you're endorsing their favourite brand.'

'What the hell do you know about diplomacy?' Weiner screwed up his face and then shook his head slowly, 'Come on. Let's get on with it.' And without waiting for the scientist, he headed across the lobby towards a corridor leading to the private dinning room. Steinhoff hurried, eventually falling in alongside his associate. They turned the corner into an equally grand hallway, lined with exotic plants and oil paintings. A pair of ebony doors stood open fifty feet ahead. A waiter in silk Persian dress stood resplendent at the entrance, smiling a welcome towards his new guests.

Weiner eased his military-style pace as he approached the door, producing an elegant-looking invitation from his inside breast pocket. He looked bluntly at the doorman. 'Major Weiner,' he jerked a thumb sideways, 'And this is, Doctor Steinhoff. Have the Russian guests arrived yet?'

The servant gave a short, but respectful bow. 'Yes, sir, a few moments ago. Please go in. There are some light refreshments waiting for you.' The man held the door open, smiling and beckoning Weiner forwards.

The Major walked cautiously over the threshold, whispering harshly to Steinhoff. 'Remember, leave security matters to me. Let me do the talking on that score. You stick to your damned science.'

Steinhoff flicked a look of irritated agreement, but said nothing.

A stocky Russian, dressed in the uniform of a colonel, turned from polite conversation at an adjacent table covered with champagne glasses for the select, but nonetheless important guests. He held a glass of bubbly in his left hand and extended the other in greeting. 'Ah! Gentlemen!' He smiled politely. 'You must be, Major Weiner?'

Weiner nodded, 'Yes, Major Weiner.'

They shook hands.

The Russian gave a measured smile towards Steinhoff. 'And you must be the great, Doctor Steinhoff?'

Steinhoff extended a limp hand. 'Yes, I am Steinhoff.'

The Russian nodded curtly. Steinhoff almost whelped at the crushing grip from the man's calloused palm. 'Colonel

Korolev, Sergio Korolev. I am an engineer by training.' He swept his free hand without spilling a drop of the bubbly and slipped a mock bow, 'But also a soldier with the glorious Soviet Army, so I believe I have something in common with you both.'

Weiner stepped forwards, partly obscuring Steinhoff behind his tall frame. He smiled briefly and then adopted a blank expression. The Soviet seemed to be too frivolous for the occasion, but no amount of soft soap from the Russian delegation would alter his position – or the Reich's for that matter. Still, a colonel in the Soviet Army didn't get to achieve that rank by winning friends and applying influence. Despite the comedy, there was a hardness about the Russian than matched his own. Weiner tested the waters, 'Colonel Korolev, I am sure you understand the delicate nature of our business. I am responsible for security in all matters.' He looked the Soviet in the eye, unflinching, 'This includes the needs of Doctor Steinhoff and his work. His security is a matter of priority with me and my superiors.'

Korolev took it in his stride, smiling, like a man seeking his death in a Siberian winter. 'Major, caution is my second nature,' he shrugged. 'But please – let us speak freely.' Korolev raised an eyebrow. 'Germany wishes to trade with the mighty Soviet Union, and so here we are to negotiate on behalf of our superiors. Does this not make us allies of a sort?'

Weiner held the Soviet's gaze. The bastard was just trying it on. Weiner gave a terse reply. 'The formal negotiations will begin tomorrow morning. Trade agreements on matters of economic cooperation, I leave to others. My interests are only for – shall we say – other resources.'

Korolev smiled, 'Forgive me, Major, I understand your needs are of a more technical nature.' He turned to Steinhoff. 'Doctor Steinhoff, you seek a particular type of titanium ore, rich in the anatase mineral form? Also some particular types of coal or carbon.' Korolev pouted, leaning his head

124

sideways, 'No problem. The natural resources of the Soviet Union are extensive, if not inexhaustible.'

Weiner fumed in silence.

Steinhoff edged forwards, swallowing contempt and hiding his surprise. 'You are well informed. I see you have been briefed on our requirements already.'

Korolev chuckled, 'Come now, Comrade Doctor, it would not do to come to a negotiation without some notion of what one is bargaining for. I am a scientist remember, not just a soldier. I do my homework, as I am sure you have.'

Steinhoff's mind raced. *Anatase*! *Carbon*! *How does this Soviet worm know*? *Who*? Weiner – it had to be Weiner. No one else could have told the Russian. Fucking Weiner, interfering Major bloody Weiner. There'd be a reckoning when they got back to Wolfsberg. He bit his lower lip, then replied calmly as if making a peripheral enquiry. 'The Major has spoken with you already?'

Korolev shook his head. 'No, my superior has spoken to your superiors, and I have received only the outline information so far.'

Weiner broke in, suspicious – surely no one in Berlin had sanctioned any dialogue of a technical nature. The Russian was a liar – he was sure of it. 'And who is your superior, Colonel?' Weiner fixed the lines of his jaw, examining the Soviet's every movement for the slightest sign of deceit, but found none.

Korolev smiled politely and held eye contact for a few seconds longer than was necessary, 'The Kremlin of course,' then broke into a grin. 'Come now, Major Weiner. No need to be so dour on account of our superiors.' He beamed a clumsy bear grin and continued, 'Look about you.' He swept an arm towards the various dignitaries in the room, and then leant in towards Weiner, placing an arm on his shoulder and steering him away from Steinhoff. Korolev glanced over his shoulder at the German scientist, then reduced to a mumbled complaint. 'Between you and me, Major; these damned officials are a pain in the arse.' He shook his head, then continued in an even more cursed tone. 'The politicians would have us running round in circles, sending our men to this or that front – and for what? Politics is politics and we soldiers have to put up with a certain amount of their horse shit. Don't you agree?'

Weiner stood, poker-faced. 'Perhaps you have a point.'

Korolev persisted, releasing his arm from the Major's shoulder. 'I do. We are soldiers, men of action. You have political officers in the Reich Chancellery too I understand. Your Director Krauch for example?'

Weiner allowed a shift in his tone to show a level of irritation befitting the differences in their rank. 'As you aptly point out, we are both in the military and Krauch is a civilian.'

Korolev nodded, 'Yes, this is so. Plenipotentiary of Special Issues in Chemical Production for the Reich, no less. The director is an important man.'

Weiner felt the presence of Steinhoff at his side. He prayed the little worm would keep silent.

Korolev continued, 'Do not be alarmed gentlemen. Director Krauch is well-known to us. He was an industrialist before the war, remember. His company traded with the Soviet Union many times, then and now. It is fitting that he should be part of the negotiations, tomorrow. A man of authority, and holding the purse strings I understand?' Korolev gave a short chortle, 'But what he doesn't know is how we soldiers like to spend money! Isn't that right, Major?' Korolev continued with his mirth.

Weiner opened his mouth to reply, but was interrupted by the *tink tink tink* of a spoon on glassware. The concierge stood sheepishly at the entrance, holding an empty champagne flute and an item of silver cutlery. Having made the required chimes, the servant grovelled backwards in deference to the local Iranian Ambassador, a rotund-looking official dressed in white Arabian robes and a neatly folded turban.

'Gentlemen, welcome to Tabriz.' All eyes turned towards the dignitary, 'As your host, it is my great pleasure to welcome you to Iran and our beautiful city. Tonight …' He paused, smiling, 'Please enjoy our hospitality. Do let me or my staff know if we can be of any assistance this evening. Iran is of course neutral in the affairs of Europe and my role will be to humbly facilitate your important meeting. So, enjoy the pleasantries for this night, and tomorrow we will begin at nine a.m. in the conference room. May I wish you all a successful negotiation.' The Ambassador gave a curt nod, raising his glass of orange juice in the air, 'Gentlemen, enjoy!'

The assembled guests politely applauded. Weiner leant closer to Steinhoff and hissed through gritted teeth and a contrived smile. 'Look at this! They are turning this into a bloody circus! We must seek a private audience with the Russians, with this man Korolev – tomorrow, first thing.'

Steinhoff poised an intellectual look and smiled, still clapping, he shouted in the Major's ear. 'What did you expect? There will be some pomp and ceremony. Krauch can talk generalities on supplies for the war effort and trade tomorrow.' He pulled back from the Major, grinning, then leant forwards again. 'We hide in plain sight, Major, then we will discreetly quiz this Comrade Korolev on our more important affairs in private.'

Weiner snarled, 'Stick to the plan. Fucking Reich Chancellery! Who does Krauch think he is? Overriding my authority!'

Steinhoff gave a withering look. The Neanderthal didn't get it. 'Major, smoke and mirrors. The British will undoubtedly be snooping about. I trust them even less than the Russians – all they will see is another boring trade negotiation, and in the background the real work will be done.'

The applause increased to a crescendo as Plenipotentiary Krauch entered the room.

Nash adjusted the zoom on the binoculars bringing the Ottoman-style arches of the palace windows into focus. The night hummed with the gentle sound of cicadas. A small, but nonetheless tangible, decrease in air temperature provided some comfort after the baking heat of the day. The waxy sheen of the cactus and other succulents in the border glistened in the starlight, giving the deception of moisture. Sedum provided a modest blanket of greenery to contrive patches of lawn. Nash wriggled in the gritty earth. Shafts of light emitted from the south-facing windows, shimmering finger-like projections across the rectangular shape of the ornamental pond come lake.

He concentrated on the *summer house* – or at least that's what the locals called it. The building's grander days served as the weekend retreat of the great Shahs. Its new role as the Iranian Ambassador's residence wasn't a bad second place. The open drapes offered a good view of the dining room. Dignitaries were still arriving, all trussed up in their best uniforms. Gold chandeliers sparkled, silver cutlery shone on crisp white table clothes. Trays sat heaped with canopies, various fruits, and artisan products from the best bakeries in town. The visual feast jolted an involuntary flush of saliva in his mouth, his stomach panged. How long since he'd eaten? He couldn't remember. He concentrated on identifying the guests.

A rotund middle-aged man chewed the fat over a glass of bubbly with two stern companions, one in German uniform.

Fat guy, Persian dress, cigar – minor local official? From the consulate? Drinking alcohol – not a Muslim. Christian? Maybe the Prophet Mohammed had given the gluttonous

128

bastard a night off. Nash shifted the binoculars to his military companion.

Korolev!

The Russian stood in polite conversation, a glass of bubbly in hand, then suddenly brightened as two new guests crossed the threshold.

German soldier, insignia of rank – a Major. Muscular, fit, very tall, possibly mid thirties. Polished uniform. Nash lowered the binoculars momentarily, digesting the new intelligence. His brow furrowed. *So not a pushover, doesn't look comfortable in his number ones, a real soldier not a ponce.* He lifted the binoculars to examine the Major's companion. *Black suit and tie, civilian shoes, stands like a civi, thick glasses.* Recognition suddenly hit home. *Steinhoff*! *One Doctor Steinhoff, lately of Peenemünde, Germany, and obviously not now working on the V1 rocket programme. Steinhoff's companion, a Major, Major who*?

It had to be the Major Weiner character that Korolev had mentioned to Emily during her briefing in Istanbul. Nash focussed on the visage of the soldier. *Looks sharp, attentive, certainly fit, and huge. Just my luck, a bloody monster.* Resigned to the inevitable, Nash moved attention back to Korolev. The Russian extended a hand and shook that of the German Major, still smiling and joking. The Major seemed to give nothing away.

Nash strained through the binoculars, getting a measure of the German officer. *Well, well, well. Thank you, Colonel, for confirming the presence of your Major Weiner.*

Something about them didn't sit right. He lowered his binoculars, suddenly lost in thought. There was a lot riding on old man Sinclair's peculiar trustworthiness when it came to Korolev. Insidious little details were emerging about the Russian. He seemed to carry more clout with the Politbureau than was reasonable for his rank. Moreover, he'd told Sinclair his influence was waning as a member of the old guard. It

129

didn't add up. What was more, he was either a bloody good showman or perhaps he knew the Germans already? At any moment, he could simply hand her over to the Nazis. On the other hand, why bother with the charade? He could have left the British out in the cold, simply by not showing up in Istanbul – but he did show up – and offered Emily a way in.

Emily. Where was she?

He lifted the binoculars and scanned the gathering.

Nowhere.

She should have been at Korolev's side. More German officers entered the room. *SS* suddenly hovered discreetly about the exits – all wearing their side arms. His mouth dried, his heart suddenly pumped with adrenalin. Had she been rumbled? If so, it was a trap.

CHAPTER 15

Negotiation

The German adjutant grovelled a thin smile and continued at a gangly pace down the corridor, beckoning his guest to follow. 'This way, Colonel, if you please.' Korolev strode at his own damned speed with his peaked cap pressed firmly under his arm. He pushed his chest out, as if marching past the Kremlin itself, and allowed his face to contort with disgust at the intrusion. This had better be good – for the love of Lenin, the Germans had some front to pull a stunt like this. They think they own half the world – well, they can think again. Their little slice of Europe could be swallowed whole by the Soviet Union. The Nazis continued to exist only because Russia allowed it.

Had they rumbled the girl or his connections with the British? Perhaps, but they wouldn't dare, not here. A colonel of the Soviet Army could not be pushed around without consequences – especially one on official business for the Kremlin.

The adjutant slowed, nodding and smiling as he approached an anonymous door at the end of the east wing of the building. He rapped politely on the woodwork and called through the door, 'Herr Krauch, sir. I have your guest, if you please.'

The door opened. The military assistant gave another nod, oozing false politeness, and waved Korolev forward. The old Soviet remained monolithic. Only his eyes moved. An inner rage tightened his jaw. He snorted a vile look at the junior rank and stepped over the threshold. The door was closed behind him.

He took in the small meeting room. White walls, silk drapes and a fine collection of rare porcelains dotted about the perimeter. The tiled floor was partly covered by a thick Persian rug. An oval table with four chairs occupied the centre. The room was empty; all except for the expensive suit standing with his back to him and apparently staring out of the window. The man turned. Korolev changed his estimation. It was a *very expensive* double-breasted suit and a pair of tan brogues that few in the Soviet Union, or Germany for that matter, could afford. The man's neat brown hair, with its regulation schoolboy side parting, fitted the snobbery of his attire. Only the steeliness in his eyes gave Korolev cause for concern.

Korolev grunted, sour-faced. 'Director Krauch,' He pursed his lips, 'You'd better have a damned fine explanation for this intrusion.'

Krauch gave a disarming smile, 'My intrusion? No, you are mistaken, Colonel Korolev.' He took a pack of American cigarettes from his waist pocket, placing one of the immaculately rolled specimens between his lips, and sparking his gold lighter. He took a tight-lipped drag and exhaled the delicate vapour. 'These Arabs are relatively well-meaning hosts, don't you think? But not so good at vetting the delegates. A minor security alert I believe.' Krauch offered the briefest of grins as he placed his cigarette pack neatly on the table, then compulsively positioned his lighter carefully on the dead centre of the box.

Korolev growled, 'The Ambassador, not to mention the Kremlin, will hear of this. What security alert?'

Emily – he'd been forced to leave her in the lobby with the other staff. Protocol dictated the arrival of the guests into the private dining room by importance or rank. The initial soirée was a select affair. Where was she now? Had she been arrested? Korolev remained ironclad.

Krauch replied, 'It seems there are some irregularities. The guest list you understand; you know how these things work. One likes to keep a tally.' He smirked and stepped forwards. 'It seems that there has been a few substitutions, as it were, in the Soviet delegation.'

Korolev met his gaze, snarling. 'Substitutions, what the hell are you talking about?'

Krauch took a functionary, almost feminine puff on his cigarette. 'Names and faces, not all the ones we were expecting, especially amongst the administrative staff.'

Korolev stiffened. So, they had been rumbled? Or was Krauch simply testing his metal? He decided to brass neck it. The smooth Nazi would feel the rough end of his bear-like attitude. Korolev offered a terse reply, 'If you haven't noticed, there's a war on.' His voice hardened, 'That's why we're here isn't it?' He gesticulated with his free hand, 'To trade for supplies. You realise of course, there are logistics. For the Soviet Army, it's tough enough to arrange supplies. Three thousand tons of ammunition here, fuel dumps for the T34s there, tins of beef – five-million – then there's the field ration packs for our infantry.'

The Plenipotentiary stood calmly, 'And your point is, Colonel?'

Korolev shook his head, placing his cap on the table, edging closer to the Nazi and keeping both hands free. 'My point is, all the bloody paperwork. If you thought Berlin was bad, you should try the Soviet Union for bureaucracy. In Russia, it's an art form, believe me.'

Krauch stood in silence, eyeing the Colonel up and down. 'Then you have an explanation?'

Korolev rubbed his chin, and spoke in a matter-of-fact tone. 'You should remember that the Soviet Army is some five times larger than the Germany Army – more divisions, more men, more heavy weapons and machinery.' He paused, letting the veiled threat sink in, 'Staffing is a matter of turnover, but I can assure you that all of my staff, down to the last secretary are accounted for. You simply don't have the current list.'

Krauch remained impassive and unreadable, his dark brown eyes penetrating. He exhaled and nodded slowly, 'Alright, Colonel. It seems this is just a misunderstanding … an administrative irregularity if you will.'

Korolev placed his hands on his hips, chest out. 'It seems it is and now we have that out of the way. Perhaps we can discuss the real reason we are here …'

Krauch smiled and tilting his head submissively, he waggled his cigarette almost laughing. 'Well, well, this has been an eventful day.' He took another delicate puff, 'You're right of course. Let's put this little misunderstanding aside. I offer my most sincere apology to the Soviet delegation, if we've caused offence.'

The Russian gave a guttural reply, 'We Russians are used to being offended, but enough.' He dismissed it with a wave of his hand. 'You want to do business with us, so let's do business. Tell me what you want, and I'll tell you if I can get it – simple.' Korolev allowed his expression to soften, but only slightly. He knew it – the bastard *was* fishing. The Nazi turd didn't have a thing, arrogant bastard. They need us, more than we need them.

Thoughts of Anya and the menace of the NKVD suddenly crept from the back of his mind: he had to do a deal with the German whether he wanted to or not. He broadened a false grin, 'Please, Director Krauch, allow me. Coal, oil and steel is a given … but there were certain other materials of particular interest that you require?'

Krauch stubbed out his smoke and switched abruptly to business mode. 'Berlin will pay an advance of two-million Reichsmarks for oil, coal and steel for the German war effort.'

Korolev shrugged, he spoke quietly, 'Come now, Herr Director, we are not trading for money. Russia has no need of currency, not even German gold.'

Krauch walked slowly behind the table, nodding appreciatively, 'It's an odd thing. Berlin tells me that the Kremlin needs cash to pay the Soviet Army?' He allowed a thin smile.

Korolev gave a dry laugh. 'You understand little of the Soviet Union. I cannot remember the last time the rank and file were properly paid for their service. We are not here to trade for gold, but I am sure Comrade Stalin might take a little of your German gold out of politeness, but the real negotiations are for armaments and above all – *special technology* – so let us be frank about our needs.' He held his palms uppermost, and shrugged false conciliation.

Krauch spoke firmly, with a hawkish expression, 'Alright – you will discuss generalities with Doctor Steinhoff at the trade meeting tomorrow morning of course – but this is what we want to happen.' He corrected, smarming, 'Would like to happen.' A pause. 'The trade agreement should conclude by tomorrow night as planned. It will show all the usual commodities, but amongst the detail will be some specific mineral resources: titania in the anatase form and some certain types of high quality carbon.'

Korolev took in a deep breath and exhaled slowly. 'And if we supply you with the requested special materials, there will be something the Soviet Union would like in return …'

It was his only worthwhile roll of the dice. This Steinhoff *was* working on something new and it had to be a propulsion system. A *new* propulsion system – the Soviet Union had to have it – the NKVD demanded it. But what if the Germans were really hampered by the absence of materials? Maybe they had nothing to trade – no prototype – no secret. Just a worthless charade to embezzle resources. If he went back empty handed, well, it was unthinkable. The NKVD … Anya

… Emily would never know the truth. For the first time, Korolev welcomed the though of perishing alone in the Gulag – if only he could save her and set things right.

CHAPTER 16

Comrade Akimov

Emily Sinclair sat forwards offering smiles and a firm cleavage to the director, all tastefully appointed in the black cocktail dress she'd chosen to accentuate her best curves. A double string of pearls, and the elegance of her hair tied up to reveal her neckline, completed the look. The ice chinked in her Martini as she forced another laugh. She looked all starry-eyed at the Plenipotentiary and spoke in almost fluent German, doing her best to add a Soviet twang. 'Why, Herr Director, it must be absolutely fascinating! However do you find the time to relax with so much to do?! Responsibility for *all those people*, and one of the largest factories in Europe!'

Krauch coughed on his Martini, 'Excuse me, mademoiselle, not *one of the largest, but the largest factory* in Europe.' He sat back satisfied with the correction, and produced a cigarillo from his waistcoat pocket. He waved the unlit cigar between his thumb and index finger as he spoke, 'You know, you are right. The work never stops! There are meetings here, meeting there, accounts, endless directives from Berlin, shortages of raw materials, and ever-increasing demands from the ministry: more oil for their tanks, more rubber for their cars and boats, more of everything!'

Emily looked on in fake awe, 'It must be inspiring, making all those things; not just for the people, but for the soldiers on the front.'

'It is a big responsibility, I agree,' Krauch smiled, 'But inspiring?' He sat back momentarily contemplating the thought. 'Yes, I suppose it is. One does not become a Captain of Industry without inspiring somebody,' he chuckled, fishing in his left waistcoat pocket for a light.

Steinhoff suddenly leaned forwards with a book of matches. He pinched off one of the flimsy pink sticks and struck a flame, cupping it with his hands towards the director.

Krauch puffed up a red ember on his cigar and gave a nod in Steinhoff's direction, then sat back observing the pleasant female at his side. 'Well, forgive me, Comrade Akimov isn't it? That business yesterday,' he gave a dismissive wave. 'All a frightful misunderstanding.'

Emily nodded politely and smiled, 'Director Krauch, please, you may call me, Nina.'

'Nina Akimov … that is a pretty enough Russian name. From which part of Russia do you come from?'

Emily forced an outward calm. 'Moscow. I come from Moscow.' The best cover stories always contained a few half-truths. Emily tried to conjure up an image of the city in her mind's eye, but nothing seemed to come. *Think*! *Mother was from Moscow*!

'Moscow? That's a bit of a coincidence. I've been there. Three years ago as a result of our last economic agreement, just before the war. It was summer, dry and hot. Which part of the city are you from?'

Emily froze and uttered the first words that popped into her head. 'Near the railway station,' she smiled, concealing hesitation.

Director Krauch furrowed his brow and glanced towards Steinhoff, then at Emily. 'That's odd. Nina, you know, I don't recall any houses by the railway station.'

'Oh, well, when I say near the station, I mean only a few minutes walk away from one of the smaller stations in the city.'

'Indeed, but I didn't catch where you were from?'

Emily sat in silence. *Think*! *Think*! *Railway station*! *Where*? 'Yaroslavsky.' She plucked a random name of a station as if from thin air.

'Yaroslavsky?' Krauch stopped smoking and abruptly leant towards her. 'Really? Now let me think … I am sorry, I don't remember a district called Yaroslavsky.'

Emily flustered and forced a small laugh. 'It's only a small patch of housing behind the station, most people don't know it.'

Krauch glanced uneasily at Steinhoff, then at Emily. 'So, you live in the centre of Moscow. How did you come to speak German?'

'My grandmother taught me. I think she was partly German, or at least Prussian, and lived in Germany for a while in the 1880s,' she lied.

Krauch slapped his thigh and gave a belly laugh. 'I knew it! You have Prussian blood in you, and a grandmother of German descent! You are a woman from fine stock, German stock!'

Emily tittered and took a sip of her Martini, desperate to change the subject. 'You are from Berlin I understand, Doctor Steinhoff, originally from the Technical University?'

Steinhoff sat blankly in his leather arm chair, his Martini untouched. 'Yes, something like that.'

'Oh, come now, Doctor,' Emily beamed a playful look. 'You are too modest. I hear from Colonel Korolev that you are quite famous for your work.'

Steinhoff offered a neutral answer. 'My work is important to me of course. It is nice of the Colonel to say so.'

Emily sat forward a little more, aware of Krauch puffing on his cigarillo and his gaze fixed on her cleavage. She continued, 'It must be *very* important, Doctor Steinhoff, but forgive me I am just a humble secretary. I am not really sure what you do?'

Steinhoff spoke flatly. 'I make propulsion systems. I am an engineer.'

'Oh! Propulsion systems, that sounds very interesting. And you do this work in Berlin?'

Steinhoff maintain his reserved composure. 'I said I was from Berlin.'

'So, you work somewhere else now?'

'Something like that.'

Steinhoff remained clammed shut. Emily tried a different tack, returning her attention to Krauch. 'So your company refines chemicals and manufacturers parts from the materials?'

Krauch sipped his drink and gave a brief smile. 'You are very perceptive, mademoiselle, yes we make chemicals and turn them into all sorts of products. Car tyres from petroleum products, and even new laminates so the housewives of Germany can have new kitchens!' He winked at her, as if to a fellow conspirator and whispered. 'In fact, I wondered if Comrade Stalin wouldn't mind if my company supplied new kitchens to the lovely ladies of the Soviet Union. Ones such as yourself.'

Emily tittered, 'I admire your sense of humour, Director Krauch. I am sure all the Russian women would love a new kitchen!' She let her laughter subside. 'But seriously for a moment, you make some very special materials. Is that how you come to know Doctor Steinhoff?'

Krauch waggled his cigarillo, 'Now, let me tell you,' he slurped the last of his Martini then continued. 'My company makes some products for the war effort. Rare metals are needed to make alloys for aeroplanes, and other shall we say, projectiles.'

Steinhoff interrupted with a flat tone. 'Herr Director …'

Krauch dismissed his minor protest with a wave of his empty glass. 'Doctor Steinhoff and his fellows are all men of great intellect, even genius, but where would they be without my chemical company?' He lifted his glass in the air, attempting to attract a waiter. 'Nowhere, that is the truth of it! Without I. G. Farben where would we be?'

A waiter in early Persian dress suddenly appeared with a tray of fresh Martinis. Krauch dumped his empty glass and grabbed another two cocktails, then dismissed the waiter. 'Nina. I hope you don't mind if I call you, Nina?' He offered a full glass, 'Have another drink.'

She smiled and accepted the refreshment. 'Thank you, you are kind. You were saying … about supplying important materials to clever Doctor Steinhoff.'

Krauch cut in with alcohol-fuelled enthusiasm. 'That's right. We make bespoke materials to very precise specifications, certain types of titania, and …'

Steinhoff briskly intercepted, 'Herr Director, I am sure that Fräulein Akimov does not wish to be bored with the technical details of our projects.'

'Not at all! It's so exciting!' Emily beamed.

Krauch slurped his drink. 'Nonsense, we are in good company …'

Steinhoff suddenly pushed his chair back from the small table, sloshing vermouth from one of the glasses. 'Herr Director! I must insist.' Steinhoff stood firm.

Krauch curled his lip towards Steinhoff, and then smiled at Emily. 'There you see! So much to think about, so much pressure. Our Doctor Steinhoff is always thinking ahead, an exemplar of the German work ethic.' He eyed the scientist up and down.

Steinhoff looked a little sheepish, and then recovered his formality. 'I bid you good evening, Fräulein,' he smiled clicking his heels together, then looked blankly at Krauch and nodded, 'Herr Director.'

With that Steinhoff moved off across the room looking for the exit. Krauch remained, smiling at his voluptuous quarry.

Nash adjusted the Soviet-made sniper rifle, bringing the luminous green cross hairs of the latest telescopic sight from the Zeiss Company into focus on the target. He had to hand it to the Russians. They recognised good craftsmanship when they saw it, and adapting the Soviet weapon to take the German telescope was a stroke of genius. Three hundred yards out in the dark, with reflecting artificial light from the target area, and yet everything was crisp and clear.

He clicked the Zeiss another notch and then zeroed the cross hairs. Nash melted. Emily sat primly on the leather sofa in her black evening dress, absolutely stunning. She was smiling and nodding attentively, apparently absorbed in conversation. Her hair bounced elegant curls with each nod. Nash buried a pang of regret and nuzzled the stock of the weapon deeper into his shoulder, taking the slack up on the trigger with his index finger.

He moved the scope slowly across the table. Cocktail glasses shimmered in the green tint of the Zeiss. It looked like Martini's all round, olives, ice and a slice. He eased the weapon sight off the edge of the table, finding a male torso dressed in a black waistcoat, white shirt, and a silk tie sporting the Nazi party logo. Nash moved the cross hairs slowly up the man's body. The visage of Director Carl Krauch stared back. Whatever had happened the previous evening seemed to have resolved, or maybe that's how the Germans wanted it.

What was Krauch really about? An industrialist for sure, and rising to some position within the Nazi party – in charge of chemical production for the regime, but was it all ideology? Not likely – war was a profitable business. How many millions had Krauch *personally* made? By any measure the I. G. Farben conglomerate was worth at least a billion Reichsmarks. Even if Krauch claimed only a percentage bonus from the profits that would amount to a tidy sum; more than any man could spend in a life time. The Monowitz factory under construction, cyanide canisters, slave labour dressed in rags and half-starved, the dead laying where they fell – the files from Krauch's office said it all. Underneath the respectable veneer was a profiteer of the worst kind.

Nash zeroed the cross hairs on the director's throat. Squeezing the trigger slowly, he took up the last of the slack on the firing pin, holding the shot. The larynx moved up and down, swallowing, warping the black and red swastika on the silk tie.

The bastard had it coming.

Nash eased off the trigger. If he killed him now, what would that gain? Nothing, apart from an unexpected promotion for the deputy director. The German infrastructure and its chain of command needed to be dismantled – but that could only be done with the right intelligence. Hopefully Krauch would be on the shop floor when the RAF bombers paid his factories a visit.

Nash adjusted the cross hairs. A man of average build came into focus. The man sat stiff in his dinner jacket, sour-faced, intermittently pushed his thick glasses into the bridge of his nose. Nash smiled to himself and whispered in harsh monotones. 'Welcome, Doctor Steinhoff.' He held the dead centre of the cross hairs on Steinhoff's skull. The Zeiss blurred as the German abruptly stood from his chair. Nash flushed with anticipation, moving his finger under the trigger guard and then adjusting his aim, allowing the Zeiss to track smoothly with the target.

Steinhoff's jaw moved forcefully, punctuated by protruding neck muscles. The silent exchange left a contrary expression on his face. Nash moved the telescopic sight on to Director Krauch – the man seemed to be smiling. His shoulders jostled with false humour. Nash moved the Zeiss over Emily. Her upright posture and artificial smile spoke volumes.

Hold it together girl, not long to go now.

Had her cover been blown? It was hard to say. Nash flashed the cross hairs at Krauch and then at Steinhoff. He tensed his index finger on the trigger. The fluorescent green image of Steinhoff clicked his heels, nodded his head sharply and then made a silent remark towards Krauch.

What was he saying? Nash regretted not being able to lip-read. The guests seemed to freeze around the table. Not just an awkward pause in the conversation, but something more serious. He worked the snipper rifle quickly around the room. The other delegates seemed to be milling about enjoying their drinks with no sign of anyone heading for the exit. Nash tracked the Zeiss back towards Emily's table, catching Steinhoff on the move. The German strode towards the door. The cross hairs followed the target across the room and stopped at the doorframe as the doctor turned right into the corridor, disappearing from view.

Nash worked the rifle sight carefully along the building, following the line of the corridor. He caught a glimpse of a dark suit as it past one of the ground floor windows. He worked the Zeiss forward to the next section of glazing. The suited figure walk briskly, but there was no mistaking it – *Steinhoff.*

But where was he going?

Nash tracked the weapon ahead. His answer stood alone on a balcony.

Major Weiner – so why aren't you at the party?

Weiner suddenly turned.

Nash shifted the zoom a few feet to the left – Steinhoff appeared.

The two Germans faced each other in the glow of the telescopic sight. Weiner's jaw moved up and down in military fashion. Steinhoff firmly punctuated the discussion with a sharp slice of his arm and vigorous shakes of his head.

An argument – Nash snuggled into the Zeiss. But what about?

Weiner seemed to pick up the pace – his jaw moved faster. Steinhoff stood, looking bad-tempered and shaking his head.

Nash went with his gut feeling.

So, Major Weiner, you're dishing out a bollocking. Has the Herr Doctor screwed up? Not following orders?

Steinhoff's jaw moved sporadically. A small notebook appeared. The scientist scrawled something with his pencil. Nash watched as Weiner leant in, nodding. The two men seemed to exchange glances, then Steinhoff continued working on his notepad. Weiner broke in, prodding a finger at the paper, then sucked harshly on his smoke.

Technical information – they're arguing over something technical. They have to trade with the Russians – Steinhoff doesn't want to – he's holding back.

Nash zoomed in, trying to pick out the notebook, but it was hopeless. At this distance not even the latest in Zeiss telescopes could manage it. He lowered the weapon – he needed to get closer.

CHAPTER 17

Deception

Emily stood drained and nervous as Korolev fumbled with keys to his suite. She glanced up and down the corridor, feeling vulnerable in her skimpy cocktail dress. The door finally opened. She took a crumb of comfort from Korolev as he slipped his arm around her waist and ushered her into the room. She heard the door click shut and the turn of a key closing the lock. She closed her eyes, took a deep breath, and tottered across the room; subconsciously seeking refuge and desperate for air. Her neckline became mottled with red blotches as she hyperventilated. She dropped her clutch bag on the mahogany coffee table in the centre of the room. Then skirting the matching arm chairs adorned with brightly coloured silk cushions, she moved towards the windows and began pacing back and forth in front the heavy curtains. Their rich tapestry mostly concealed the balcony and the outside world beyond. The authentic Persian rug over the hard wooden floor dulled the rhythmic thud of her heels.

She stopped abruptly, then strode for the drinks cabinet in the corner of the room. She removed a glass stopper from one of the lead crystal decanters and poured a generous glug of Scotch into a heavy glass. She slammed the decanter down on the silver tray, not bothering to replace the stopper. Then swallowed back the whisky in one hit, holding the empty glass against her cleavage as the alcohol burned down her gullet. She gasped, screwing up her face, then squinted

146

accusations at Korolev. 'They knew I wasn't a Russian! They played me like a fool – and *you knew* they would!'

Korolev stood with his back to the door, smiling. He removed his shiny peaked cap, placing it under his arm and walked slowly towards her, nodding his head in appreciation. 'No, you did well, Comrade Akimov. You held your nerve. We left them a message. *You* left them a message – we can choose our friends, but it is they who need us. Anyway, the deed is done. I have spoken with Director Krauch.'

Emily sloshed more whisky into her glass, 'So, you've made a deal – effectively with the German High Command – so what does that make me?' She gulped a mouthful of Scotch, 'A traitor? An accomplice?'

Korolev shook his head gently, 'No, my dear, it doesn't.'

'But you intend to give them what they want – the raw materials they need for the very projects my father is trying to stop.'

His eyes suddenly pleaded, 'It is difficult for you to comprehend – my predicament. I make the arrangements to supply the Germans because *I must*. Your father understands.' His eyes moistened, 'I wish I could tell you more, but there is something I must do first – and when it is done – well …'

'Well what?'

His voice crackled with unaccustomed emotion. 'Your father will get the intelligence and thanks to you – he'll know for sure what the Germans are doing. The British military can take decisive action, target I. G. Farben and their facilities. I cannot be seen to have a hand in what comes next, at least not yet. Officially the Soviet Union has an alliance with Germany, remember.'

Her voice dropped to a whisper, 'The Kremlin has something on you … it's something to do with my father isn't it? You've know him for many years …'

Korolev shook his head, 'No, nothing like that. This isn't about your father.'

Her brow furrowed, she looked Korolev in the eye, 'Or it's my mother? … It's her isn't it?'

Korolev turned away, barely concealing his anguish, and then rallied a reply, 'I knew your mother in the early days.'

Emily probed, 'So, it is you I remember – in the garden at the embassy …'

He almost glazed over. 'Yes, possibly. I did know her, much earlier. Moscow was a different place back then. She studied languages and the fine arts. I was a student of engineering.'

'You met at Moscow University?'

'Yes. You could say that, but it was a brief encounter. I was moved to a military establishment after my first year, where I completed my training on aeronautics. Your mother faired less well, the Party frowned up modern art, closing her Faculty. She had to find other work, or so she was told.'

'What happened to her?'

Korolev's face flattened. 'What happens to everybody – Russia. I don't know exactly, she was moved away.'

Emily placed her glass on the cabinet and ambled closer to the Colonel, 'She *was moved away* – or she left? Please, tell me what happened to her.'

'A bit of both, she was persuaded.' He shrugged, 'You understand, in those days you towed the line. Some didn't and vanished – for good.'

'So, she moved at the request of the state. Is this how she met my father?'

Korolev swallowed, grimacing, 'Look, that's something you should ask him.' He exhaled, shoulders slumping, then he forced a brighter tone. 'It's late. We are both tired. You should go – get some sleep.'

She gave Korolev a sideways glance and ambled slowly to the table, picking up her clutch bag. She spoke crisply, 'Goodnight, Colonel,' then strutted towards the door.

Korolev called after her, 'You're just like your mother, hot blooded and as fierce as a lioness. Russian through and through.'

Emily turned at the door, placing her hands on her hips. 'Why did you *really* ask for me? Why am I here?'

Korolev stood in silence.

'Answer me, damn it!'

He spoke in an even tone. 'There is a lot you do not yet understand about the Soviet Union. Mother Russia has suffered, our people have suffered, individually and collectively.'

'My mother – you know where she is? Don't you!'

Korolev spoke in a guttural growl. 'Leave it – now is not the time.'

Emily gritted her teeth, stifling a venomous retort as she turned to the door. She flipped the key in the lock, wrenched the door open, stepping through and slamming it behind her.

Korolev whispered to himself, moisture filling his eyes, 'Yes … just like your mother … exactly like your mother.'

Nash squatted behind the last acacia, making the best of the cover in the planted border. Holding the sniper rifle across his chest, panting quietly, he focussed on the raised balcony some ten yards ahead: mouth open, head tilted and listening. Sweat tricked down his neck, dripping on to the parched earth. The two Germans stood a few feet back from the edge of the veranda, the wooden slats of the decking partly obscuring the view. Nash strained at the conversation: harsh whispers, increases in tempo – an argument. He sat patiently, catching the odd word ... *my design ... it's mine ... listen to me ... in charge ...*

Nash resisted the urge to break cover. Suddenly, a pair of boots scuffed, then clumped, across the deck. The Major Weiner appeared at the railings. He leant on the wooden

149

palisade with both arms, flicking cigarette ash into the void. Definitely pissed off about something.

As if on cue, the scientist also came into view, with his arms folded, stiff-looking, and partly turned towards the Major, but with his back to the garden. Nash couldn't make out the detail, but Steinhoff was as sour as they come. Weiner shook his head, abruptly standing. His deep voice carried easily on the night air. 'For both our sakes – you heard the man! The Russians have the materials we need.' He hissed stabbing his finger towards his companion, 'You do what you're fucking told. Krauch is already breathing down our necks – or do you want to go back empty handed?' Weiner took a long tug on his cigarette, exhaling with a disgusted look.

Alright, so it's Steinhoff upsetting the apple cart. Nash caught the aroma of the tobacco, and shrunk back into the dirt as best he could, switching his attention to Steinhoff. He strained eyes and ears at the man's back.

Steinhoff spoke, 'I don't like it I tell you. That bloody woman was asking too many questions.' His feet shifted, he leaned closer to the Major. Nash got a better view. The scientist seemed to be ranting. 'This Korolev is a snake! He can't be trusted!'

Nash huffed to himself. *Tell me about it – for once – something we agree on.* The rant continued. 'Do you think I am some kind of retard? The women is no more Russian than I am! The Soviets are playing us, damned you!'

Weiner skulked, 'It doesn't matter what you think.'

Steinhoff bristled, 'No! I will *not* hand my work over to those communist bastards – No!'

Nash watched as Steinhoff pushed his glasses back on to the bridge of his nose. *So, that's the deal – the Soviets trade titania and carbon for a slice of the action. They want Steinhoff's device – or so they want the Krauts to believe.*

Weiner flicked his cigarette butt over the balcony. Nash watched the ember arc to the dirt, then studied the German officer.

'Too late. Krauch has already signed the document – he leaves for Berlin in the morning. The Russians are to get what they want – end of.' Weiner spat into the shrubbery below.

Nash stiffened. *Already signed? The deal is done – Christ! The exchange? When?*

Steinhoff rattled a pathetic fist in the air, 'No! Major, are you mad? The bastards can have what they like, but not my work. That is *not* for negotiation.'

Weiner sniggered, 'That's right. Give yourself a fucking heart attack – it doesn't change a thing – you're signed up, so hand over your notebook.' The Major extended a spade-like paw.

Sweat congealed on Nash's brow. The awkwardness of crouching with the rifle niggled. *Steinhoff's notebook! Details of the device to give to the Russians?*

'Or I could slap you about and take it anyway,' Weiner shrugged, 'Your choice.'

Steinhoff pulled what looked like a small leather book from his trouser pocket. He held the book against his chest with both hands.

Nash risked lifting the rifle to get a better angle and absorbed the exchange.

Weiner beckoned, 'Come on – orders are orders – choose a page. This Korolev isn't stupid and he's an engineer – so Krauch wants us to give the Russian pig something credible: a few designs, technical drawings – you know the sort of thing. Some detail that will satisfy our end of the bargain, then we can all go home.'

Steinhoff opened the booklet.

Nash zoomed on to the page. *A sketch. Part of the Device! Not exactly – bigger – but like the one he'd blasted to smithereens at Peenemünde. So they do have another device*

151

– and a fortress within which to produce it. He shifted the scope on to Steinhoff's face. Blind rage stared back.

Weiner held out his hand. 'We give them a copy of a few of the relevant pages – don't worry – you'll get them all back.'

Steinhoff suddenly looked puzzled, 'Get them back? What the copies?'

'Yeah,' Weiner grunted, 'The Russian delegation will leave here with their business happily concluded – all signed, sealed and delivered – but they won't get far.'

'What? I don't understand.'

'Of course you don't – you're not supposed to. The road heading east from Tabriz is full of bandits. Who knows what could happen …' He forced a belly laugh.

Steinhoff remained fixed.

Weiner tapped the side of his nose, 'It's been arranged … and for much less than I expected.'

Steinhoff baulked, 'Hired help? You're using the locals? Tribesmen …'

Weiner spoke with menace, 'There won't be any survivors, no loose ends. The tribal faction I've selected for the job have a hatred of the Russians like you wouldn't believe. The money helps of course – but vengeance – that's what really counts. They'll kill the Russian, and the woman – after they've finished with her of course.' He tipped his head back and laughed.

Nash shivered involuntarily. He lowered the rifle sight. It was a set up – and had been from the start. The Germans would hold the Kremlin to the deal – and the Soviets would keep to it, rather than lose face. The politicians on both sides would publically condemn the ongoing unrest in the Arab world. Perhaps even using it as an excuse for military action: the Nazis and Russians would carve up Iran and the region generally between themselves. How very neat. But Emily – she was in mortal danger – and so was Korolev.

Suddenly, the crunch of gravel penetrated his thoughts. Nash glanced sideways, registering a ghostly flow of black robes in the moonlight and the steely flash of a curved shamshir being drawn from its scabbard.

CHAPTER 18

Assassin

Nash rolled sideways putting as much vegetation as possible between himself and the gigantic Arab. Off-balance, he turned the unwieldy sniper rifle towards the new threat. The Persian stepped into the void, instantaneously bringing down the razor edge of the curved weapon. Steel glinted in the night. The rich aroma of exotic perfumes suddenly mixed with scent of the acacia bush as the blade clashed with the rifle barrel, sending seismic reverberations along the stock. Nash felt the tendons popping in his shoulder, like the sting of a dozen scorpions, and dislodging his grip on the trigger. He parried desperately, only just retaining hold of his rifle as the sword clacked repeatedly against the barrel.

He lost his grip. The rifle butt dropped uselessly to the gravel, leaving the diagonal shaft of polished cedar and blackened metal his only defence. He clenched the top of the rifle with his good hand, instinctively judging the angle of the next scything cut. He scrabbled to put the barrel in front of the blade and certain evisceration. Steel drove into wood. The *rip crack* of the cedar pinched his ears as the firearm almost severed in half. Nash staggered backwards with the remnants of his weapon dangling, his heart in his mouth, and his brain whirling a thousand scenarios. He edged backwards, discarding the spent rifle and flexing his numb fingers and willing his right arm to life. His eyes fixed on the Persian.

Sweat dripping from his brow as he hunted for breath in the stifling air. The Persian glided forwards with a double-handed grip on his huge sword, offering his blade with deadly accuracy. Nash dummied a move to the left, then abruptly backwards, catching his heels on the low-lying cacti. He stumbled and then scuttled crab-like to the rear, pulping cactus as he went. Sharp spines dug into his palms and the stiff fronds of the spikey vegetation grabbed at his clothing. He made a few more yards before finally snagging. He snarled, forcing himself upright, and with his clothes ripping and bleeding from a myriad of deep scratches, he probed into his waistband, drawing a stiletto commando knife.

The Persian swung.

Nash concertinaed to the floor. A sharp breeze trimmed hair from his scalp as the blade sliced miraculously overhead. Instinctively, he sprung into the smallest of gaps, jabbing low with the stiletto. Flecks of black cloth barely caught on the knife as the Persian moved, anticipating and evading each thrust.

Feeling more confident with a weapon in his hand, and with life returning to his shoulder, Nash jostled, crouching, moving his feet like a boxer, switching the knife between hands.

The Persian seemed to ignore the routine of distractive moves and expertly held himself as he flicked out again with the monstrous blade.

Nash twisted, gritting his teeth, but too late. A precision wound opened on his bicep, wicking crimson across khaki. He forced himself to ignore the searing pain and held firmly on to the stiletto as blood trickled down his arm. He jabbed out at his assailant.

The Persian parried comfortably with the shamshir. Shouts echoed from the veranda. The place would soon be crawling with troops. He pursed his lips, angling the knife, seeking the slightest opportunity – but there was no bringing the fight to the enemy.

The Persian swung savagely with a backhand upper cut.

Nash leapt sideways, almost twisting into a backwards summersault. The sword swept an inch below his ribs. Despite landing hard on his shoulder, with almost feline reflexes and a little help from hours of parachute training, he took the blow and rolled to his feet. His breath shortened to a useless hyperventilation. More blood dripped from his wound.

This was a fight he couldn't win – he'd be no use to Emily dead – the Persian had the advantage. A fighting retreat was the best option. He stabbed with the blade and instantly stepped sideways behind a stunted date palm. The jagged fronds of the large plant scratched across his torso as the shamshir felled the vegetation. Nash moved backwards as the shamshir hacked off another chunk of the greenery. The Persian stood majestic next to the sapling, sword upright, his features hidden in the shadow of his black turban, breathing steadily with no signs of exertion.

Nash eased towards the rear, one foot, then another, feeling impotent with his little blade.

The Persian lowered his blade. He spoke in a smooth, rich and deep voice, 'You fight well, but are wise enough to know when you are defeated. What is it you seek – Englishman?'

Nash remained silent, rocking on his feet, ready to move and gripping his stiletto commando knife.

'Come now, put down your weapon. Why do you spy on my countryman?'

Nash shifted a few more steps to the rear. The sound of many boots on gravel penetrated his thoughts. He glanced towards the house. Silhouettes of men scurried in small packs and skirting the obstacle of the large pond. He was out of options and out of time. He launched the stiletto throwing knife. The blade rotated, flashing through the air; only to be deflected by the shamshir. The stiletto buried itself harmlessly into the adjacent date palm. The Arab twisted the handle on the stabbing weapon, dislodging it from the tree. He momentarily examined the knife and then placed it under his belt. He looked at Nash, 'What do you seek, Englishman?'

Nash hesitated, then cupping his left hand over the wound on his bicep, he broke from the engagement; turning rapidly, zig-zagging amongst the cactus and digging deep to find acceleration. He pushed hard for the perimeter, taking advantage of the thickening shrubs and palm trees as he left the confines of the formal garden. Sweat and sticky plasma soaked the shreds of his khaki shirt, bramble-like scrub dragged at his knees. He glanced over his shoulder, catching multiple aspects of movement in his peripheral vision. He accelerated, covering another ten yards, before paranoia forced another look. The Persian was crashed through the vegetation, sword in hand and moving towards him.

Nash turned on his heels and sprinted hard. Head down, he ploughed into the thickest band of scrub. Pushing through, tattered, he emerged into clear ground, and accelerated between the palm trees. Denying exhaustion, he made for the nearest rise and the obscurity of the night beyond.

The Persian jogged into the relative clearing, rubbing his chin. He spied Nash some fifty yards ahead and almost through the perimeter. He smiled, sheathing his sword and mumbled to himself, 'Englishman, you are not the only one with the heart of a lion. God willing, Allah will allow us to both feast on the infidels.'

He looked up at the stars, took a deep breath as if cleansing himself from battle, and turned back towards the house.

CHAPTER 19

Road from Tabriz

Korolev worked the black metal rim on the heavy steering wheel. Despite doing his best to avoid the largest potholes in the dirt road, the rear springs of the GAZ M-1 Soviet staff car squeaked monotonously on the suspension. He glanced into the rear of the vehicle for what must have been the hundredth time to eyeball the whereabouts of his briefcase. His jacket, cap, and the leather satchel containing the all important documents lay on the back seat; exactly where he had left it. Sweat trickled from his hairline and mixed with the fine layer of red dust that grimed his forehead. His armpits had long since wicked sweat stains over most of his tan-coloured shirt. He wiped his forearm over his brow, adding to the iron oxide streaks on his sleeves. He peered ahead at the lead vehicle in their small convoy and winced as another cloud of dust emitted from under the rear wheels of the flatbed ZIS-5 truck. Grit peppered the car windshield. He switched on the wipers momentarily, smearing another deposit across the glass and then looked towards the passenger seat.

He yelled over the noise of the V8 engine at Emily Sinclair. 'How are you enjoying your ride in my new car?! Isn't she beautiful?!' He beamed a quick grin and then concentrated on the road ahead, trying not to get too close to the lorry in front.

Emily sat sweltering and stuck to the brown leather seat. Despite tying her hair up and opting for a loose grey skirt, she was boiled. Even her bare feet secreted a hot greasiness into the soles of her open sandals. She dabbed a handkerchief into the nape of her neck, failing miserably to prevent perspiration from dripping down the cleavage of her short-sleeved khaki shirt. She rested an elbow on the open window frame of the passenger door, the air was like an oven and full of detritus. 'You men are all the same! Cars, planes, trucks; you like your toys!' She smiled, trying to lift the mood for the long journey ahead.

Korolev chuckled, 'What do you expect? I am an engineer! But surely this is a thing of beauty, is it not?'

Emily glanced around the cabin. 'I suppose so. It looks sturdy enough.'

'Made in Russia and built to last!' He flashed another grin, 'I insisted on the leather seats rather than the usual cloth ones. Do you like the colour? It almost matches the dust!'

Emily rested her head on her palm, letting the wind catch her cheeks for a second and then she looked up. 'I imagine only the rank of Colonel and above gets leather seats from the Red Army. Did you choose the colour of the car as well?'

Korolev shook his head, 'No, regulation black with a thin red stripe down the sides – the Party colours of course.'

The suspension suddenly thumped sending a tremor through their bones. Korolev held on to the wheel. 'Sorry, it's the terrain. We still have to climb this valley.' He tapped the temperature gauge to be sure it was reading correctly – unfortunately it was. He squinted at the end of the bonnet looking for signs of steam from the massive engine.

Emily stared across the road towards the ravine, trying to glimpse the geography ahead, but the lead truck weaved back and forth blocking any decent view. The narrow dirt road had been cut into the mountainside and followed the contours of the River Aras; a shallow body of silty water that marked the border between Iran and the Soviet-controlled areas of Azerbaijan and Armenia. She risked a look down the steep

159

scree slope to the river some two hundred feet below and thought of the vehicle skidding. Then wished she hadn't. A group of buzzards circled on the thermals some thousand feet up the cliffs that enclosed the valley. Vertical scars of erosion had heaped loose stone and sand that encroached on to the dirt road and threatening a rock slide. The flapping canopy on the truck up ahead shed more dust in her direction. Two lines of troops sat opposite each other on wooden benches in the rear of the truck. They rested on their rifles, looking fatigued by the constant jolting of the suspension. The tailgate rattled each time the driver gunned the accelerator.

'How far until we cross into Russia?' Emily asked.

Korolev spoke in a jovial tone. 'We keep heading north on this road for maybe another six hours, then we find a bridge to cross the river.'

'Where are we anyway?' Emily wiped her handkerchief around the back of her neck. 'Are we still in Iran, or Turkey?'

Korolev abruptly steered around a small crater, then replied. 'To be precise, we are in the East Azerbaijan Province of Iran – bandit country!'

'Great!' She shook her head in mock dismay.

'Do not be alarmed, as Comrade Akimov, the Russian Army is here to protect you.'

'And as Emily Sinclair?'

Korolev gave a pleasant smile. 'I will protect you from the savages of the desert.'

'Why don't your words comfort me,' she smiled. 'Where do we cross the river?'

'At a little place called Nehram. We will enter the Soviet Province of Azerbaijan and then head north towards Georgia; where I catch the train to Moscow. You on the other hand, get to go home. A plane will fly you back to Istanbul and leave you in the trusted hands of your British colleagues.'

'It's a pity I couldn't have flown home from Tabriz.'

Korolev shook his head. 'Too risky, the Germans have ears and eyes in many places. We leave Iran as one – all Russians together as far as the National Socialists are concerned.'

'And the technical documents provided by Director Krauch?'

'They go to Moscow with me. We trust no one until I am inside the walls of the Kremlin itself. Besides, the information needs to be verified.'

'What then, a phone call from Moscow to London to share Germany's most important secrets? How do I know you will keep your side of the bargain?' Emily looked at him with a sly smile.

Korolev shrugged. 'You don't, besides your father trusts me. Moreover, you are still alive, are you not?' His face stiffened. 'You know our Soviet ways well enough. My masters would see all the men in this operation silenced in the Gulags of Siberia and you at the bottom of the Volga by the end of the week.'

Emily blanched.

Korolev roared with laughter, slapping his palm on the steering wheel. 'You see! Now you understand Mother Russia!'

Emily folded her arms, pursing her lips. 'Colonel Korolev, please!' She huffed.

Suddenly, a loud bang issued from the truck in front. Steam billowed from the vehicle. The rear wheels locked as the driver slammed on the brakes. Korolev responded in kind, pressing his brake pedal to the floor. Emily screamed as she was thrown against the gear stick. The car skidded towards the ravine and gouged a trench in the gravel as the back end swung out towards the abyss. A protruding rock dragged on the axle, providing the only purchase before oblivion. The chassis crunched and finally came to rest with one of the rear wheels rotated in the free air above the void.

Shadow quickly loomed, filling the car. Emily looked up, her mouth open as the second lorry that comprised their little convoy lurched towards them, wheels squealing. She tucked herself into a ball, hollering. Metal screeched on metal as the wagon smashed into the side of the staff car, buckling the passenger door. Emily let out a piercing cry and feeling zero gravity in the pit of her stomach as the truck crushed her towards the driver's seat. Glass showered from the windscreen.

The Soviet flatbed shuddered to a stop like a sedated elephant.

Korolev gripped the wheel, his knuckles white. He took short breaths for a several seconds and, realising he was still of this Earth, forced some composure. 'Are you alright?'

Emily nursed bruised ribs, breathing with difficulty. 'Yes, I am … I think so.' Involuntary tears ran down her cheek. She brushed broken glass from her lap.

The Colonel reached for the driver's door handle. It was stuck fast. He tried again, simultaneous putting the weight of his shoulder into the panel. The door sprung open, catching the Russian off balance. He lunged for the safety of the steering column as the hundred foot drop registered. Grabbing the wheel with his left hand, he pushed himself back on to the seat with the other. He spoke between laboured breaths. 'Not this way.' He looked at Emily, 'Can you open your door?'

She nudged feebly at the bent panelling, shaking her head.

'Then it will have to be over the hood.' He craned his neck over the dashboard, assessing the prospect of climbing through the smashed windscreen. Troops were already piling out of the rear of the lead truck on to the road.

A shaft of brilliant white light suddenly flashed across his face. He instinctively shielded his eyes against the glare. Then blinking off sun spots, he just about captured the swish of the curved blade across the front of the car. He gasped as the head of a Soviet trooper, helmet-and-all, spun through the air;

162

landing on the bonnet and pulsing the dregs of arterial blood on to the metalwork. A shrill war cry emitted from a dusty figure cloaked in Arabic dress. Standing tall in the confined space between the vehicles, the man skewered his shamshir into the next trooper only to retract the blade in one fluid movement and hack down another. A soldier filled the void, standing over his dead comrades and shuffling the bolt action of his Mosin-Nagant rifle to chamber a round – but too late. The razor sharp curve of the sword cut a swathe from his shoulder to his sternum, tipping the soft contents of his thorax on to the dirt.

Korolev processed the scene and finally absorbed the reality, he reached for his jacket on the back seat and the Tokarev T-33 semi-automatic pistol within. The sound of sword slicing through flesh, bone and sinew, punctuated by the gargled death throws of his troops hastened his reach. He grabbed the handgun from the waist pocket, and ignoring the wailing hysterical woman in the adjacent seat, he thumbed the mechanism to release the magazine. He quickly assessed the contents – a full sleeve of eight rounds. He pushed the clip home with his palm and flicked the selector to single shot mode, then methodically aimed his weapon.

A double tap to the chest flung a sabre-wielding tribesman into the tailgate of the truck. The Arab crumpled to the floor. Korolev worked his aim to the right, and finding another target, fired twice into the next man's torso with good effect. Another assailant materialised from the far side of the truck, with swirling black robes and a turban of the finest cloth. The man held a shamshir in each hand, scything his way through the rank and file. Korolev took aim and fired. Simultaneously, the ambidextrous warrior spun round a trooper. The bullets thudded home into the Soviet uniform. The Arab finished the job with a deep slash across the soldier's throat. Korolev snorted back rage and emptied the magazine in the direction of the attackers. The double-handed swordsman took a round in the shoulder, but adeptly slipped from sight under the truck.

Korolev discarded the empty magazine and dug frantically in his jacket for fresh ammunition. He bellowed at Emily as he did so, 'We are leaving! Climb into the back seat and pick up my leather satchel! When I have reloaded, we go out the driver's side of the car and take our chances on the cliff!'

He retrieved a full magazine from his crumpled jacket and pushed the rounds home, clicking one into the barrel. 'Now! We must move now!' He nodded in the direction of the rear seat.

Emily swallowed hysterics and finding a trace of reasoning, she struggled through the gap, banging her head on the crumpled ceiling. Silent tears smothered her face. She grabbed the briefcase, folding it against her chest with her left arm and leaving the other hand free to work the rear door. 'Got it!' she yelled.

Korolev needed no second invitation. He fired a couple of rounds over the bonnet and using the distraction to good effect, pushed open the driver's door. He braced himself against the doorsill and scanned the near vertical slope for any means of decent. He spied a fissure running diagonally across the rock face. It would give purchase enough for his feet and some meagre handholds.

Moments later the rear passenger door flung open. He shouted through the door, 'Emily, we go now. You first! Follow the crack in the rock to our right. We head down the slope for the river and the border! Understand?!'

Emily whined a reply, 'Alright, I am going, going now!' She discarded one of her leather sandals down the rock face, then the other. A second later she lowered herself feet first from the car and, sliding her belly off the rear seat, she dragged the case with her body from the vehicle. Her toes pushed into the substrate. She willed them to find a decent foothold and then shuffled sideways, lowering herself a few feet at a time while haphazardly grasping the satchel. As soon as her head had disappeared below the edge of the road, Korolev followed. He tucked his weapon into the back of his trousers and likewise slipped on to his belly and out of the car, then feet first on to the ledge.

He tentatively slithered a few feet down the slope and urged Emily on, 'I am right behind you. Move! Keep moving, don't wait for me!'

He watched as Emily responded with renewed urgency, with her skirt hitched above her knees and with the benefit of her long legs, she quickly established a rhythm and pulled away. Satisfied that she was making good progress, Korolev concentrated on shuffling his feet down the fissure and then moving his hands to find the next possible anchoring point. Suddenly, small pebbles and rivulets of sand trickled from above, coating his head and shoulders in a fine debris. Blinking dust from his eyes, he squinted upwards. A giant of a man climbed effortlessly towards him. Black robes billowed more dust into the breeze.

Korolev flicked his eyes down the cliff. Emily was making good her escape, even with the handicap of the briefcase. He weighed up his prospects. He lacked her agility, the Arab would soon catch up. There was nothing else for it – he reached for the TT-33 pistol in the back of his waistband. Grappling a sweaty, dust-caked palm around the stock, he eased the weapon from his belt, then dug his free hand into the crevice as best he could. He fired up the rock face into the sun. The bullet ricocheted harmlessly away. He leant backwards for a better view and fired again. The recoil of the weapon shuddered down his arm, twisting his back. He lost his footing and let the weapon clatter from his grasp as he scrambled desperately for a handhold – but it was too late.

'No!' He screamed with primeval terror as he fell into the void, tumbling past Emily, dislodging rock and scree as he did so and then cascading with the avalanche of rubble and sand into the valley below.

Mohammed Al-Ruzi stood over the precipice, wiping blood from his sword. He busied himself cleaning the last of the Russian filth from his weapon while his subordinate waited for orders. He sheathed his shamshir into its jewelled scabbard and then paused, 'Kill any that remain. Push the vehicles over the cliff.'

The minion bowed, 'It will be done,' and made to move off about his business.

Al-Ruzi suddenly raised his hand, 'Wait – bring the girl and the documents she carries.'

'Yes, my Shahzadeh. What of the other man?'

Al-Ruzi looked down at the figure of Colonel Korolev far below, then up at the buzzards riding the thermals. 'The desert will take him. Let the vultures feast on his flesh.'

The man gave a curt bow and turned to set about his task with brutal efficiency.

CHAPTER 20

Ravine

Nash dropped back the throttle on the stolen German motorcycle and allowed the machine to come to a slow stop on the side of the desert road. He stalled the engine on the BMW R75 and then stepped off the bike. He massaged his palms into the small of his back for a few seconds and then lifted the leather goggles on to his forehead, blinking. Dirt and compression scars marked the outline of the eye shields on his face. His make-shift headscarf fluttered in the heat, but remained in place thanks to a strip of parachute cord tied around his head. He rubbed the bristles on his chin and squinted up the valley into the sun.

The vista of rough gravel and sand, strewn with a plethora of small rocks, did nothing to raise his spirits. There was no sign of life, save for the dried out remains of the occasional gorse bush and the dirt track-come-road snaking into the distance. He raised a palm, shading his eyes and peered into the heat haze. The faint outline of rock formations shimmered on the horizon, or at least he thought they did.

He shook his vision clear and looked again. There was definitely something there – the beginnings of a mountain range or something else, perhaps an approaching dust storm. He clicked his jaw and exhaled, then walked around the front of the motorcycle and leant over into the sidecar, retrieving a map from the cargo net in the footwell. He spread the map out over the light-tan camouflaged paintwork and estimated his position.

They must have come this way – it was the only road going north east towards the Soviet Union. He quickly eliminated lesser routes on the chart. If this was the main drag, it was bad enough. The alternatives were nothing more than old goat paths – and they had left in vehicles. He dismissed the notion of managing a three ton truck across the rough terrain. It was this road or nothing, but where were they?

He checked his watch.

They'd had a head start, by some four hours or so. The bike had been very rough going so far, but not that much slower than a truck. He studied the map, running his finger along the weaving line that marked the desert road. It eventually came to steep contours, cutting into a ravine. He checked the scale bar, estimating the distance – some ten miles to the foothills which rose steeply thereafter into a range of mountains with long knife-edge ridges; the toughest of terrain with the road disappearing into the middle of it. He traced his finger over the map. The route twisted for miles along the valley, before emerging on to the plains below the Black Sea. A thin squiggle of blue marked the floor of the ravine – the River Aras. Nash followed the flow of the watercourse on the map. The slow trickle of water had carved a deep gorge over millions of years, the only crossing place was a bridge on the far side of the range.

He folded the chart, placing it back into the sidecar in exchange for a water bottle. He took a couple of slugs from the metal container and stoppered it, then mumbled to himself. 'Roasting hot, not much water and too many places to be ambushed. Thank fuck for German engineering.' He patted the barrel of Spandau heavy machine gun mounted on the sidecar. It would even the odds nicely when the time came.

Nash resigned himself to a few more hours on the road. He mounted the bike, kicking harshly at the starting lever. The

BMW roared into life. He gunned the throttle, listening to the throaty sound of the engine, then replaced his goggles.

He needed to catch up with Emily and Korolev's little convoy soon. He *had* heard the Major Weiner correctly. Something was arranged and from the tone of his voice it had sounded final. Money had also been mentioned – for hired help of the worst kind – local mercenaries. Still, it made no sense. Why risk poisoning the very trade deal the Nazis had themselves initiated? Or was that what they wanted British Intelligence to believe? Korolev had said it himself. New allegiances were forming between the Soviets and Germany. The Colonel was old school and a friend of the British. A political dinosaur; that made him expendable – and Emily too. Or maybe the Russian engineer had been dazzled by the offers of new technology from the Germans? It didn't matter who was pulling Korolev's strings, either way, Emily would be dead. The Germans, the Russians – no witnesses would be left – at least none that would be able to talk.

Nash thwacked the accelerator and spun the wheels back on to the road. He headed for the horizon with only a meagre four hours until nightfall.

Sergio Korolev felt the blistering on his cheeks, his eyelids were heavy, but registered fleeting glimpses of the world. Baking sun and then relative shadow, creatures squawking, tugging at his shirt collar, stabbing at his flesh. It wasn't troublesome. There was a pleasant numbness and no will or ability to move. He closed his eyes, appreciative of the darkness and thoughts of Mother Russia. How she had served him, he had served her. What was set and what might come to pass, a matter only for the living. It was cold, so very, very cold. As it had been all those years ago …

He sat in the rusting Nizhegorodski automobile with the engine running and cursing at the heater under his breath. He took a long drag on his Belomorkanal cigarette and choked out a cloud of smoke to add to the toxic atmosphere inside the vehicle. He rubbed the glass on the driver's window with his gloved-hand, scratching a fresh viewing hole in the iced up interior and peered through the frosting into the twilight. He mumbled to himself, cigarette still dangling from his lips. 'Only a lame dog would be out in this weather. Minus twenty-seven for fuck sake!' Despite his cursing, he realised the Politbureau hadn't yet managed to screw him up completely – for some reason there was still optimism. He scanned through the snow-covered pine trees on the edge of the road and looked for movement on the flat expanse of the lake. Snow flurries gusted back and forth, adding a soft top to the solid surface of the water body. He glanced sideways through the window, catching sight of a wild hare digging for roots in the tundra, then huffed. He'd been there for bloody hours.

At last, rounded headlights loomed in his rear view mirror, then stopped a few meters behind his car. Korolev sucked another lungful of tobacco smoke, then continued to bitch as he did up his sheepskin coat. 'They must think I am some kind of senile Bolshevik. Fucking NKVD have no manners these days.' He took off one glove and pulled the Beretta from his pocket, checking the magazine and then the safety. He shoved the foreign weapon back into his coat and then replaced his glove. He leant on the door of the Nizhegorodski. It creaked open under protest. An icy blast immediately found its way under the sheepskin.

Instinctively, Korolev pulled up his collar to meet the fur lining of his hat and thumped his hands together to get some circulation going. He dragged on the remains of the smoke still attached to his lips and eyed the new arrival. The driver, inappropriately suited for a day at the office, tiptoed around the front of the vehicle, holding the front of his suit together in a futile attempt to conserve warmth. He opened the rear passenger door of the Ford Sedan. A man wearing an expensive-looking woollen trench coat stepped from the car and donned his polished cap of the People's Commissariat for Internal Affairs. The NKVD trudged closer in the snow, pulling on his leather gloves as he did so. The insignia on his shoulders came into focus as he stopped a few feet from Korolev's position – a General no less.

The NKVD spoke in a clear but harsh tone. 'It is a cold night is it not?' He patted his gloves together then dropped his hands by his sides. The General stood firm and upright. 'I expect you are wondering why you are here? It is still, Major, isn't it? Yes of course, Major Korolev.'

Korolev dropped his cigarette into the snow and looked directly at his superior. 'Yes to both questions.'

The NKVD kept a blank expression. 'As you know, we like to keep matters of government and the Party in good order, and this requires the loyalty of all, especially the Red Army as your English friends like to call it.'

Korolev shrugged, 'I am just a soldier. I don't have any friends.' He paused and thought better of speaking further, 'Sir.'

The NKVD smiled, 'Your loyalty has been called into question, or so it seems.'

Korolev inched his left hand towards his coat pocket and the Berretta as he spoke. 'I have always been loyal. This you will know, as others do.'

The NKVD shrugged. 'Comrade Stalin is well … concerned that the process of command works efficiently and that certain officers have not been corrupted by their privileges, such as foreign travel.'

Korolev casually placed both hands in his coat pockets and began stamping his feet. 'Forgive me, General, but I have worked tirelessly for many years. It will only be a matter of time before our engineering projects bear fruit. We have some good progress on our rocket motors and other components.'

'Comrade Korolev, my point exactly. It seems we have less time than we thought.'

'Less time?'

'Our intelligence reports show, shall we say, interesting developments in Germany. And yet you waste your time on the British.'

Korolev worked his hand on to the stock of Beretta and wormed his gloved index finger cautiously under the trigger guard. 'The British?'

'Yes, Sinclair's woman. A married woman at that. Do you think that wise, Comrade?'

Korolev took a deep breath in through his nose, and gritting his teeth snorted several short lungfuls of cold air. He struggled to keep an even tone. 'She is a Russian, born of Moscow. A Soviet through and through.'

'Perhaps, but she did marry an Englishman – an intelligence officer – and one that is now very senior in his organisation. Don't you think that is strange?' The General paused, eyeing Korolev up and down. 'It is strange, is it not?'

The Major stood in silence and deliberately maintained a blank expression.

The NKVD formed a slow, contrived smirk and opened his palms at his side. 'I have no need to keep my hands in my pockets, Comrade ...' He slowly raised his hands to waist level, 'Neither do you. I simply make an observation.'

Korolev eased off the trigger and gingerly removed his hands from his sheepskin.

The General continued, 'That's better,' he arced his arm in a friendly gesture, 'Come – walk with me.' He turned towards the lake, not waiting to see if Korolev would follow.

Korolev sighed and trudged after the NKVD, placing his footsteps into the man's ahead to make the going easier. By the time he reached the lakeside the snow was knee deep. Korolev stopped next to the General, both men stared out into the wilderness. The General spoke first.

'Come, I have something to show you.' The NKVD strode off on to the frozen expanse of the lake.

Korolev followed. The windswept sheet crackled under his feet. He peered nervously at the route ahead, unable to discern the strength of the ice through the latest covering of snow. Regardless, he kept moving, alternating his sight between the frozen substrate and the back of the General's coat. He put his hand into his pocket, feeling the weight of the Berretta. If he was going to shoot the bastard, then now would be a good time.

The NKVD abruptly stopped and turned. He waved Korolev forwards.

Korolev let his hand slip from his coat pocket as he picked up the pace. He came to a halt facing the General, but glimpsed a raised, yet symmetrical patch of snow to the left. His mind raced. He forced outward calm and spoke in monotones. 'What is it that you would like to show me, sir?'

The General gave a sardonic smile and stepped over to the raised block in the ice, rubbing away the fresh snow from the surface of the knee-high structure.

Korolev followed the outline of the block – it was rectangular and clearly man made.

The NKVD stepped back, 'Take a look.'

Korolev hesitated.

The General growled, 'Take a look, Comrade Korolev.'

Korolev stepped tentatively towards the carved block of ice and leant over to examine the spot the NKVD had cleared. The cryogenic remains of a beautiful woman stared back, her eyes devoid of life and yet perfectly preserved; even the flesh had a pinky whiteness to it. Korolev stood upright, giving nothing away. 'Who is she?'

The General tilted his head. 'You don't know her?'

Korolev shook his head. 'No.'

'Look again, Comrade.'

Korolev peered at the body. Her features were very familiar, even frozen in the snow. 'I've never seen her before,' he lied.

'She was not a Bolshevik you understand. In fact, rather the opposite. One of the last surviving members of the Petrochov family, or so I am told.'

Korolev seethed inwardly, but pretended to frown and puzzle at the new information. 'Petrochov?'

The General stood in silence for a few seconds, then spoke. 'Come now. Do you want the Sinclair woman to follow her sibling?'

Korolev suddenly flushed, he stamped his foot in the snow, then slammed his first into his palm. He roared. 'Where is she?! Where is she?! What have you done to her?!'

The NKVD mused, 'She is well and in safe keeping – for now.'

The Major stepped forwards, craning his neck towards his superior, he menaced. 'You will not harm her.'

The NKVD chuckled and with lightning speed grabbed Korolev by the scruff, simultaneously apply an armlock. He slobbered in Korolev's ear through gritted teeth as he pushed him towards the icy coffin. 'Take a good look, Major. If you want to see the remaining Petrochov again, then you will do as I ask.'

Korolev tensed his muscles and heaved backwards, snorting rage as he did so, but the General anticipated his move and tightened the armlock. 'You have spirit, Major, but she has made her bed, a wife to the British Intelligence Service.'

Korolev spat, his face red. 'No! That is ancient history. She left him – you know this – she returned to Mother Russia. She is loyal. For the love of Lenin, she even left her own daughter behind!'

'How convenient,' the NKVD gave the trapped arm a wrench. Korolev screwed his face up against the pain. The

General continued, 'Your regard for this woman and her daughter vexes me. Why is it so?'

Korolev grimaced, then gave a forceful reply, despite the armlock. 'She may once have been a Petrochov. None of us can help what family we are born into. She *was* loyal to the Great Revolution, she *remains* loyal. I speak the truth and you know it.'

The General maintained his vice-like grip and hissed. 'You *will* do as the Party requires. Or shall we speak of a slow death in the Gulag for you and the Batyrka for her. You understand how they treat women in such places. Otherwise …'

Korolev hyperventilated frustration, wincing at the pain in his arm as the General tipped him forwards, dislodging his hat and planting the side of his face on to the ice. 'Argh!' Korolev screamed defiance as the searing cold burnt his face and ear.

Nash pulled up short of the next bend and slipped the clutch on the bike to idle the engine. He planted both boots on the gravel, but remained straddling the BMW. The last vestiges of orange sank behind the mountain, casting a shadow over the valley floor. The undeniable heat of the day still radiated from the mountainside, but even in the fading light it wasn't difficult to pick out the curls of dense smoke up ahead. He caught a whiff of the black vapour on the breeze – gasoline.

His mind conjured an image of death. Emily lay twisted and soiled amongst burning debris. He forced the thought aside and busied himself with a weapons check. Withdrawing his pistol, he disengaged the magazine on the Sauer 38, confirming the contents before ramming the casing back into the weapon. He flicked on the safety and shoved the handgun back into the waistband of his khaki trousers. He then re-tightened the lower strap on his leather knife pouch, taking comfort from the feel of the blades pressing against his thigh. He glanced at the Spandau, but dismissed the idea. There was no prospect of steering the bike and operating the heavy machine gun at the same time. Instead, he shoved a spare pistol mag into each of the breast pockets on his shirt: an addition to the rounds already bulging in the leg pouch of his khakis. He only hoped the local tribesmen hadn't up-graded from slings and stabbing weapons to firearms, all courtesy of the German Army. Judging from the smoke, they probably already had a few Mosin-Nagant rifles – and even in the hands of a beginner the Soviet-made gun would be accurate enough.

He twisted the throttle a couple of times to refresh the engine and slipped the bike into gear. He focussed on the plan, swallowing another image of Emily – this time lying with her throat slashed at the roadside. He trusted his instincts. Korolev was seasoned enough. They would be either both alive, or both dead. If it was to be the latter, the Russian would have given a good account of himself before the end. Nash eased the bike towards the next rise and the spirals of burning diesel only half a kilometre away.

His heart raced – she *had* to be alive. He worked the BMW amongst the potholes, finding the best line around the steep bend. He held back the urge to blast along at full speed and scanned the immediate surroundings for any sword-wielding Persians. Piles of scree and rocky depressions obscured numerous aspects of the roadside. Nash conjured another pleasantry – this time a real possibility – a single swordsman leaping from nowhere to cleave his head from his shoulders.

None came.

He finally stopped the vehicle on the last brow and took in the view of the dirt road stretching along the valley. The track was still rising, following the contour of the mountainside, but nonetheless snaking along with less twists and turns than before. He quickly fixed on a position some five hundred yards ahead. Bodies lay scattered across the route. His brain numbly registered the corpses of the Soviet troopers – at least a dozen or more. The occasional black-coated figure lay, unmoving amongst the Russian casualties. He reworked his eyes over the contingent, flicking from corpse to corpse. She wasn't there. Moreover, neither was Korolev's staff car. Perhaps they'd made good their escape?

Two, maybe three fires vented smoke across the scene, burning within a few yards of each other, but off the side of the road – and probably coming from the bottom of the ravine. He craned his neck. He couldn't tell. He cautiously roved an eye over the terrain again: no movement save the smoke, no ill-placed glints of steel or patches of undue darkness – nothing. If the enemy were present, they were well concealed.

He eased the bike into first, then second gear, and trundled towards to the remains of the battle. He stopped ten yards short of the first body, withdrawing the Sauer from his belt as he did so. He clicked off the safety. The engine hummed, keeping a steady idle. He arced the weapon back and forth across the road. No target appeared. He dismounted, leaving the BMW rattling gently. He moved tactically, working a double-handed grip on his pistol, snapping his weapon to his left, front and right; and then to the rear. He eased forwards, stopping at the first casualty, targeting each body in turn and seeking out aggressors. A sudden breeze swirled grit on to the bloodied uniforms. Silence had long since replaced the groans of the injured. No pleading eyes, no raised hands begging for medical attention – nothing – only solitude and the reek of excrement from the disembowelled.

Nash edged sideways towards the ravine, still half-marking targets amongst the dead. He stopped at the precipice and worked his weapon down the cliff face. A few bodies lay scattered below. One of the Russian trucks was upturned at the bottom of the gorge only yards from the river and with plumes of smoke rising from the remains of the cab. Another debris field was strewn down the cliff, culminating in an engine block and chunk of the chassis at the bottom of the ravine, marking the remains of the other lorry. A solitary tyre burned in the metallic ruins of the last vehicle, wafting a carbon smog over the wreckage. Nash extrapolated along the fragments of the convoy. Where was the staff car? He shifted his gaze up and down the river, and then over the battlefield.

No car, and no Emily – at least as far as he could see. He would have to check over the bodies on the road and those below. Any chance was worth exploring. He squinted forlornly down the cliff, searching for a feminine form. What had she been wearing? Skirt and sandals? He wasn't sure. He studied the rock face. It wasn't looking good. A narrow crumbling scar led at a steep angle, eventually reaching the bottom. He didn't fancy his chances, not in the dark; but he would be climbing down there all the same.

CHAPTER 21

Desert Camp

Emily Sinclair lolled about in the saddle, partly slumped forward, with her long hair matted over her face and her grey skirt almost up about her waist. Her head thumped with fatigue and the constant reminder of dehydration. Hooves clicked and scraped over the rocky ground. Her wrists rubbed raw against the rope binding her to the horn of the ornate leather saddle. The horse jarred. She vaguely registered the discomfort, moaning with her eyes closed and bare feet that lost purchase on the worn stirrups. There was only darkness, the smell of the animal and the fragrant odour of polished leather. Heavy eyelids beckoned the salvation of sleep, but only a comatose rendering was offered.

Her mount abruptly changed stride. The clack of hooves on rock was lost to the tumbling of loose stone as the beast slid downwards with the motion of the scree. The stallion whinnied, shaking its mane as it took to the descent amongst the boulders, only to land hard at the bottom. Emily crashed about in the saddle. Her chin thwacked into her chest as the horse leapt for a more secure footing on the flat ground ahead. The metallic taste of blood throbbed from her lower lip. The horse snorted as it trotted on to softer terrain. Emily willed herself upright and forced her eyes open to a squint. She moved her head slowly, barely observing the vista.

The surprising moonlight reflected an expanse of sand and shadows in the clear night air. Jackals, or perhaps some other demonic creature, gave a disturbed cackle in the distance. Her horse stopped of its own accord. Her eyes caught a small, but flickering orange glow on the horizon. A black stallion stopped adjacent to her mount, snorting protests against restraint. A flush of adrenalin washed through her body, bringing a degree of alertness. She looked across at the magnificent animal and worked her gaze up to its master. Mohammed Al-Ruzi sat authoritatively yet at ease in the saddle, pressing the soft leather of his handcrafted boots gently against the flank of the horse. He held the reins in one hand and pushed back his robes with the other, producing a jewelled dagger.

Emily flinched at the sight of the weapon, unable to conceal her torment. She watched helplessly as he seizing her bonds. She squealed as he adeptly flicked the razor-sharp blade over the rope. Strands of the bloodied hemp fell to the floor. The realisation of tentative freedom dawned, and with a look of subservience, she began to massage her wrists.

An elegant deep voice spoke to her for the first time. 'Please accept my apologies. It is not our way to treat women in such a manner, but it was necessary. You are weary, but we will soon be at my camp.'

Emily mumbled through parched lips. 'Water. You have water?'

The Persian leant into his saddle bag, producing a deer skin pouch. He pushed the full bladder in her direction. 'Drink a little to refresh your parched throat, but take only small sips. We have but a few miles to travel and then you may rest.'

Emily hesitated, despite a raging thirst.

He shook the skin gently, nudging the offering towards her. He spoke softly, 'Drink.'

The water sloshed enticingly within easy reach. She grabbed the vessel and fumbled the ivory stopper from the container, then tipped her head back, gulping several mouthfuls of the warm liquid.

Al-Ruzi guided the bottle from her lips with his free hand. 'Small amounts. Your body must become reacquainted.'

She panted gently, her palate still lusting for moisture. She pushed the tips of her fingers against her lips, dabbing the last drops of the precious liquid into her flesh, then looked at the Persian. His features remained hidden by shadow and the folds of his turban, but she assimilated an impression of the man. She spoke quietly as she handed back the water skin. 'Thank you.'

Al-Ruzi nodded, dropping the strap of the water bottle over the pommel of his saddle. He shifted his eyes into the night, avoiding the fleshy whiteness of her long legs.

'Where are you taking me?' she asked.

Al-Ruzi maintained a fixed gaze on the firelight in the distance. 'As I have said. We go to my camp and there you will rest.'

Emily suddenly found good voice, 'But where am I? Why me?'

The Persian turned sharply to face her, but retained his composure. 'You are in the desert. If you behave, you will remain free of your bonds. Please, no more questions.'

'Then I am your prisoner? Why? I have done nothing.'

Al-Ruzi took a breath, then replied. 'Know this – it is many miles to the nearest road. The searing heat of the desert plains are your prison. Escape will simply herald your demise. The vultures would pick at your flesh, devouring all. Not even your bleached bones would remain.'

Emily remained silent as the Persian stared down at her. He gave a gentle flick of his reins. The stallion obediently moved to a trot. She watched as the haunches of the beast disappeared into the darkness. Her mount instinctively followed. She remained slack in the saddle as her horse found its rhythm. The animal steadied to a plod. She focussed on staying upright, vertigo and the cotton wool-like feeling in her limbs put all thoughts of escape aside – at least for now.

Nash worked methodically down the rock face, taking care to place each foot securely before adjusting his grip. He stifled the urge to speed climb in the darkness and used the excuse of feeling out for the next hand and footholds to avoid thinking about Emily. He wedged his hand into the rock and formed his palm into a fist, finding enough purchase in a modest fissure to rest. He took a deep breath. Sweat dripped from his brow. The weight of the small canvas haversack seemed to prise his centre of gravity towards the abyss; but it was a necessary addition to carry water, some field dressings and spare ammunition. He peered down into the ravine. Only the occasional flicker of burning rubber penetrated the darkness. Smoke wafted ever stronger on the rising air. He estimated the distance – it couldn't be more than three hundred feet to the bottom – all the same, plenty high enough for a man to fall to his death. He exhaled and pinched a fresh hold in the slab of sandstone and stretched his foot towards the next anchoring point. He continued climbing down into the ravine.

The silhouette of jumbled rocks eventually came into view. He worked down a few more feet and then dropped on to the curved top of a large boulder. He laid himself against the smooth rock, extending his arms with palms flat and fingers stretched over the surface. He gingerly lowered himself, scraping his belly on the sandstone, searching for any kind of irregularity below to secure a toehold as he went. His feet suddenly lost purchase, and dangling in the void, gravity took control. He slithered down the boulder, hyperventilating through gritted teeth as he pressed his fingertips hard into the geology. Fresh blood welled up from under his nails, hard cuticle separated from the flesh.

He fell through the free air for a split second, then landed hard on his back. Winded, he writhed in silence and waited for the pain to subside, but thankful for the haversack braking his fall. He rolled over on to his belly, and then on to all fours, with sweat dripping from his brow, he shook his head clear and mumbled. 'Christ! That's right, break your bloody neck – you nugget.' He shuffled a few feet to the lip of the slab. Muscles contorted, rippling waves of discomfort tore down his spine as he moved. He cursed under his breath. 'Keep fucking going. It's only pain.' He dismissed the prospect of fractured vertebrae and peered below.

Vertical protrusions of splintered and jagged rocks marked the way ahead. He steeled himself and got to his feet, wincing. He tightening the straps on the haversack, then stepped forwards on to the first section of the laminated strata. It was now more of a scramble than a climbing descent. Emily flashed into his mind's eye. She smiled.

He paused, scanning the rock for a half-decent route. 'Bollocks to it.' Disregarding his injuries, he suddenly moved quickly from rock to rock, taking temporary handholds and arching his body like a chimpanzee over each sharp obstacle. Nash moved down the slope, abandoning any notion of a tactical advance – besides if the enemy were waiting, they would have heard him by now.

The striations in the geology gradually became less oblique with the descent. Ragged fingers of sandstone gave way to slabs of smoother rock. Nash warmed with the exercise, allowing his body heat to penetrate the knotted muscles in his torso. He jumped from slab to slab, keeping a firm grip on the shoulder straps of his rucksack. Smoke thickened as he made good his descent. He jumped from the last step in the rock, landing in a crouching position on the sand. He drew his weapon, surveying the debris in search of the enemy. He worked his pistol slowly over the field of view, forcing back the urge to rush. If she was here, dead or alive, he was determined to find her.

The first ellipse of the rising sun issued lasers of reddish yellow light over the landscape, giving a rosé complexion to the small sand dunes that formed incessantly on the windswept plain. Emily staggered a few feet ahead of her Arabian chaperone, rubbing exhaustion from her eyes as she followed the line of spent cast iron braziers leading towards a Bedouin-style tent. The flap of the tent suddenly opened. A wizened hand held back the canvas. She dipped cautiously under the awning, coming face-to-face with a man servant. She paused, taking in his dry scabs, halitosis and the hideous deformity that remained of his nose. The old man stared back from under pristine white robes that were at odds with his condition. One black sunken orb looked her up and down, the fleshly remains of the other eye socket attempted to follow suit.

She concealing her revulsion and stepped forwards into the surprising expanse of the tent. Cantilevered poles, carved with ancient hieroglyphs and polished to perfection, held the black canvas aloft in the rectangular atrium. The canvas sloped into the four corners to be met by the finest Persian carpets. Animal skins and silk cushions lay scattered about the floor. A raised platform made a seating area that arced along the length of the tent. A wicker sofa occupied centre stage, draped with blankets and a plethora of golden fabrics. An assortment of incense sticks added a sweet perfume to the air, mixing with the waxy odour of the candles. Two man-servants, dressed in plain white robes, busied themselves preparing refreshments at a small bronze table in the far corner of the room. A tall, athletic-looking sentry stood monolithic adjacent to the seating area, wearing polished boots and black robes. His turban partly obscured his features. The soldier kept his right hand firmly on the pommel of his shamshir.

Al-Ruzi wafted by, then stopped, placing one boot on the edge of the small step leading up to the platform. He turned, offering her an outstretched hand.

Emily remained stupefied.

He flicked his palm, gesturing her forwards. 'Come,' he ordered in a polite tone, 'Sit'.

She stumbled forwards over the rugs, bracing a hand against one of the tent poles as she did so. Her eyelids sat heavy as she willed some rational thought. She mumbled, 'Where am I? What do you intend to do with me?'

Al-Ruzi beckoned, ignoring the questions. 'Come, sit,' he repeated in a slightly more determined but nonetheless pleasant tone.

Emily moved sheepishly, taking Al-Ruzi's hand as her resolve crumbled in favour of the comfortable-looking furnishing. Her delicate fingers slid easily into the palm of his spade-like hand, and yet she detected no roughness, despite his very masculine nature. She followed his guide and fogged by exhaustion, dropped on to the sofa.

The Persian took position next to her, with his knees folded up and showing the leather of his boots against the rim of the low chair. His large frame nestled appropriately in the corner of the seating. Then, he leant back with one arm stretched over the head of the sofa. He brushed back the edge of his turban, partly revealing his face in the candlelight, and then spoke quietly with a respectful tone. 'There are refreshments. Will you take some water, or tea perhaps, and some dates?'

Emily nodded avoiding his gaze. She rasped a quiet reply. 'Yes please.'

Al-Ruzi clapped his hands. The servants moved briskly in his direction. One carried a brass tray containing tea glasses, a pot of steaming liquid, and a bowl of dates. The other, much shorter, stooped forwards with a ceramic jug and matching cup.

Animal instinct took over. Emily sensed the water, taking the cup eagerly from the servant's hand. She watched, mesmerised, as the clear liquid flowed from the earthenware jug, filling her cup to the brim. She gulped down the contents and without standing on ceremony, presented the cup again, glancing up at the servant as the cup was re-filling. She jolted stiff with a double-take of the man's face. Rotting remains stared back. Barely able to take a breath, she pierced a look at the Persian.

Al-Ruzi spoke in a matter-of-fact tone. 'We are but humble people. Every man finds his place, doing what he must.'

Emily remained sat forwards, frozen with her fingers around the cup. She gaped, but no words would come.

'Do not concern yourself.' Al-Ruzi maintained an impartial expression. 'It is dry leprosy. Drink from the cup.'

Emily perched, motionless.

Al-Ruzi spoke with a calm voice. 'Drink. Is it not your custom to accept hospitality?'

She forced a smile at the eroded servant and moved the cup gingerly to her lips, and despite her yearning for libation, she took only a hesitant sip.

'Do not be fearful, quench your thirst.'

Emily nodded gently and moved her lips to the cup. She swallowed a few mouthfuls.

'Drink your fill.' Al-Ruzi nudged the cup towards her mouth.

She gulping down the remainder and quickly thrust the empty cup towards the servant. Her face grizzled an involuntary contortion.

Al-Ruzi nodded appreciatively. 'You have spirit.' He gave a barely perceptible glance at the taller servant, carrying the bronze tray. 'Some sweet tea and a few dates will refresh your body further, then you will rest.'

Emily concentrated on the man's robes and then the tray. The dark steaming liquid emitted a strong, yet familiar odour as it filled the tea glass. She took the hot vessel by the rim and smiled politely as the man offered the bowl of dates. She took one of the fruits and bit into the flesh, allowing the sweet paste to melt on her tongue. Then washed it down with a sip of tea, almost scolding herself.

Al-Ruzi waved the servants aside. They departed silently, leaving the tray on a low wicker stall next to Emily.

She took another sip of her tea, and suddenly finding an appetite, devoured the date. She reached for another.

Al-Ruzi continued as she chewed on the fruit. 'Many of my men died to bring you here; and the documents you carried of course.'

Emily paused and took another date from the silver bowl. She stared at the tea tray, struggling to muster a reply. 'Why did you bring me here? I mean, why not just take the documents and leave me for dead with the others?'

Al-Ruzi leant across, invading her personal space as he plucked a fruit from the bowl. He popped the date in his mouth, chewing for a few seconds, before more or less swallowing it whole. He clasped his hands, absently rubbing his knuckles and then nodded slowly. 'Yes, you would like to know, but I have already told you that it is not our way to harm women. Simply be thankful for what God has provided.'

'What will you do with me? Keep me in the desert?'

'For now, you are my guest.'

Emily ruffled, despite her exhaustion. 'Prisoner – the word you are looking for is prisoner.'

He smiled and placed his hand on the white of her knee.

Emily stiffened.

He worked his palm gently up her thigh. 'Your delicate white flesh, so tender, so vulnerable. The sun would scorch it from your body in a single day.' He slowly removed his hand and flattened his palms together, as if in prayer. 'My servants

187

will bring you more suitable dress. You will be more comfortable.'

'Thank you, but I am still your prisoner, am I not?'

Al-Ruzi shrugged, 'I keep you safe from the desert, accept my hospitality.'

Emily reached for another date.

With lightning speed the Persian grabbed her wrist, easily achieving a vice-like hold. 'You are distraction enough for my men. Some have not seen their wives for many weeks. It would not be wise to test their patience.' He stared into her eyes.

He released his grip and then eased himself from the comfort of the chair. 'You will rest now. I will return at nightfall and we will speak again after I have studied the documents. Then, Nina Akimov, you can tell me who you *really* are and why you have chosen such Russian friends.' With that Al-Ruzi gave a curt nod, turned on his heels and marched briskly from the tent.

Nash eased forwards, keeping a double handhold on the Sauer 38. He peered into the twilight targeting the shadows and the thick eddies of smoke for signs of insidious movement. He stifled a cough as a fresh swirl of acrid fumes emitted from a burning lorry tyre up ahead, but edged towards the smog, catching ever-stronger whiffs of bubbling rubber laced with tar. He crouched a few feet from the choking soot, and keeping his weapon up, systematically scanned his arc of fire with the German pistol. He waited, jaw slightly open, listening. Sizzling rubber, the intermittent pop of resin bubbling from crusting axle grease, and the rasps of his own breathing filled his ears. He kept the weapon on target as his brain instinctively filtered the scene for the slightest background noise: the *click clack* of a rifle bolt, the slip of a boot on gravel, the tug of a grenade pin.

Nothing.

His palms sweated against the stock of the semi-automatic weapon. He curled his boots gently on to the sand, and maintaining utter silence, he risked a glance through the smouldering remains.

Still nothing.

He stepped forwards, standing slightly taller and weapon up. The unmistakeable odour of spilled diesel filled his nostrils. A symmetrical structure loomed from the darkness. Nash eyed the target, then moved his weapon sharply to the left, then to the right and also to the rear. He made his way across the sand, taking cover behind what seemed to be part of a flatbed truck. He caressed the edge of a running board, feeling the grain of the timber, confirming the solidity of the object. Definitely one of the trucks from the convoy. A muffled, barely audible sound emitted from the far side of the planking.

Nash tilted his head, listening – it was hard to tell, two, maybe three soldiers – or perhaps something else? Tensing his index finger under the trigger guard, he turned the corner of the wreckage and waved his weapon at target after target, all moving amongst the shards of planking and canvas. A muffled squawk and scratching emitted from under a torn section of the canopy. Nash threw back the covers, poking his weapon into the centre of a feathery mêlée.

Bollocks! *Fucking vultures*!

A flea-bitten bird flapped its wings momentarily and then tilted arse-upwards to resume its meal. A scrawny juvenile gobbled down a string of intestines, adding greedily to the slick of congealed blood that coated its face and neck.

Damn it to hell!

Nash kicked out, sending the birds scattering. He peered down at the corpse. Offal protruded from the rib cage, viscera draped from the remains of the body cavity – but the uniform was still recognisable – a Russian trooper. Nash exhaled a sigh of relief and raised his weapon, searching the twilight for casualties, while keeping a weather eye on the scavengers marking his perimeter.

He moved forwards, finding another body and then another. He edged along, following what seemed to be a debris field of young soldiers and fragmented woodwork. As soon as distance allowed, the vultures hastily closed in behind to resume their meal. Screeching and flapping issued from the rear as the creatures jockeyed for the best position and the tastiest entrails.

Nash cursed the scavengers and focussed on the end of the debris field – the cab of one of the lorries. He approached cautiously, despite the vultures having announced his arrival at the crash site. He made a circuit around the vehicle, moving the pistol ahead of his arc and up and down over the superstructure. Satisfied with the perimeter, he moved towards the cab.

He steeled himself as he shuffled the last few feet, his weapon up and trained on the crumpled door. He wrenched it open. The driver slumped out, bloodied and broken, dangling head first towards the sand. Nash jumped back, quickly waving the Sauer over the compartment. Finding no threat, he eased off the trigger and lowered his weapon.

He clicked the safety on his pistol, hissing between clenched teeth. 'Fuck it!' He slammed his left boot into the wheel arch, adding another dent. He huffed and turned away from the vehicle, marching towards the sound of water and the river. He stood on the bank collecting his thoughts. It was time to face facts – the enemy were long gone, leaving only the dead. There was no Emily and no Korolev.

'Come on, come on. Think!' He absently rubbed dirt from his forehead with his thumb and forefinger. He creased his brow and mumbled to himself. 'Don't be a nugget, what would the old bastard do? A substantial firefight, dead on both sides. The local tribesmen know the desert, so he wouldn't run for it on foot. No sign of his staff car. Bollocks!' He shook his head. Climbing down into the ravine in the pitched black had left him none the wiser. He looked up the cliff face towards the skyline, the first rays of morning light gave an orange fluorescence to the top of the escarpment. There wasn't much of a choice. He would have to continue searching the ravine in daylight and if the Arabs wanted his head – well, they'd have to come and get it.

CHAPTER 22

Weiner and Al-Ruzi

Major Weiner squinted against the glare and cursed as he crunched the gears of the *Kübelwagen*. Choking on his own dust, he tugged down the rim on his khaki cap in a futile attempt to keep the grit from his eyes and steered the jeep around the next hairpin bend in the dirt road. It was almost noon and there was a schedule to keep. He gunned the accelerator, forcing the light vehicle up the steep incline.

Bloody Arabs. The task had been straightforward enough. All the Arab had to do was recover the necessary documents and slaughter the Russian convoy – leaving evidence that would point towards local insurgents. With so many my tribes and religious factions in the area the Kremlin would give the appearance of retaliation by wiping out a few of the locals. After all, Iranian Azerbaijan was bandit country. The Soviets certainly wouldn't risk insulting the Führer by challenging the integrity of the German delegation. The Reich Chancellery would offer assistance at such a tragic hour – the Russians would politely refuse – and that would be that.

Weiner nursed the vehicle over a sizeable scour in the road. The meeting with Al-Ruzi had to be away from prying eyes – but this was ridiculous – a rendezvous in some godforsaken shithole, high on the Iranian plateau. The Arab had changed the plan, sending a messenger in his stead to Tabriz. Arrogant bastard.

Weiner thumbed the gear stick into second. The VW engine protested as the vehicle lurched forwards. He clenched his jaw, fuming. His memory banks suddenly conjured the feel of the Arab's blade against his throat. He mulled over their first meeting outside the mosque. Yes, he'd initially underestimated the Persian as some relic from another age; a mindless savage that would do his bidding for the price of a few second-hand rifles. On the contrary, Al-Ruzi was an intelligent and seasoned fighter, but did the Arab think him a fool? Come alone, meet in the middle of the damned desert. The Persian's usefulness was coming to an end. Weiner smiled at the thought, and glanced at the ruck sack on the passenger seat. The new-fangled Donarit type II high explosive would do the trick.

The *Kübelwagen* jostled on its soft suspension as the Major steered the vehicle around the last bend and on to a narrow, potholed strip that excused itself for a road. He took his boot off the accelerator and allowed the jeep to trundle to a halt. The engine idled in the heat. The route snaked along the natural contours of the cliff face. The dirt road seemed to get tighter, with barely enough width for a horse and cart, never mind a military vehicle. He leant over the driver's door, checking the clearance of the wheels from the precipice – a foot at best – then a sheer drop of some five hundred metres to the valley floor.

Fucking Arab.

He snorted back his contempt, and gingerly let out the clutch, focussing on keeping the wagon against the rock face. Bending the paintwork would be the least of his problems if the Donarit cooked in the sun for much longer.

Nash picked out the distinctive curvature of the radiator grill amongst the smoke. His stomach knotted as he paced towards it with the pistol in a double handhold and sweeping his arc

193

of fire for targets as he went. It had to be the Soviet staff car – it couldn't be anything else. His heart raced. He swallowed back adrenalin, struggling to stifle the desire to sprint to the wreckage. He edged closer. The vehicle was up turned and crumpled, as if screwed up and tossed aside by the Gods. His brain went into overdrive, estimating the survivable space inside the wreckage, while scanning the terrain for the enemy.

He reached the side of the GAZ M-1, and gradually worked around the vehicle with his weapon up.

No threat came.

He clicked the safety on the Sauer 38 and shoved it into his waistband, then moving like a demented ferret, he searched the bodywork for an opening. He settled on the rear panel, wrenching the metal just enough to create a space. He stuck his head through the gap.

Empty.

He slumped backwards into the dirt, holding his head in his hands, hyperventilating. He willed his breathing to steady, then chastised himself through gritted teeth. 'Bollocks! Assess, plan, act. Fucking bollocks!'

He stood abruptly and trudged towards the river, not bothering to draw the 38. He dropped on to one knee and cupping a handful of water, splashed the relatively cool liquid on to his face. He took in a slow, deep breath and exhaled, then stared into the river, mulling over the problem. He'd systematically searched the crash site, and despite the many bodies, none were Emily or Korolev. The sun was now up. He'd retraced his steps over the rougher parts of the ground, searching for possible hiding places, back tracked; but still no Korolev and no Emily.

He splashed another handful of water over his face and then took a drink. There were only a few remaining possibilities: they'd been captured, escaped into the desert on foot and were heading east towards the Soviet border, or they were holding up somewhere else in the ravine. He had to admit, in the absence of bodies, capture seemed the most likely scenario. Being on foot in the desert? Forget it. The Arabic horsemen would have cut them down in minutes. Nash racked his brains, 'Come on, Korolev … what would you have done?'

Nash looked up, staring across the river at the rock face on the other side of the ravine. He mumbled to himself. 'They're still in the ravine. The river. The Russian bastard's used the river!'

He stood, peering up the line of the river, checking both banks.

Nothing seemed out of place.

He turned, examining the river as it flowed downstream. That had to be it. The river was their only chance. He glanced over his shoulder towards the mangled compression that was the remains of the staff car. There weren't in the car and they weren't at the bottom of the ravine. Nash fixed on the improbability of escape, and pulling the Sauer from his waistband, he strode purposefully, southwards. If he stuck to the river, he would find them soon enough.

The jeep chugged along in first gear, slow and steady. The gritty substrate crunched under the stiff tyres. The occasional *clack clack* of stones told of the rock slab crumbling under the modest weight of the vehicle. Weiner turned the wheel carefully, easing the vehicle around the last narrow spit that cantilevered off the cliff face. He cursed the Persian for the hundredth time as he cleared the corner. The road opened out on to a rugged escarpment, dotted with ancient sandstone dwellings carved into the rock face. He trundled the car a few more metres to get a better view of the village, if you could call it that, and turned off the engine.

He sat motionless in the driver's seat, assimilating the terrain. The hot breeze whistled through the long-since derelict habitations. Buzzards nested here and there on the open window sills of the single storey cave-like homes. Guano and spent feathers caked the frontage of the stonework, and even at this distance the rank whiff of ammonia caught the back of his throat. A line of steps cut into the escarpment marked the main thoroughfare between the ruins. The upper tier seemed to have a few building that were in marginally better shape, with doors and shuttered windows; albeit with the wood bleached by the sun and worn smooth by decades of abrasion. Weiner opted for extra caution and sat observing and listening for a good minute.

Nothing.

He stepped from the Jeep, brushing a cloud of dust from his baggy khaki clothing and casually rolled up his shirt sleeves. He scanned the dwellings for signs of life as he did so.

Still nothing.

He snorted, wiping dust from his mouth and made a show of checking his sidearm. He re-holstered the pistol, leaving the leather flap open against his waistband, then leant into the vehicle, picking up a canvas haversack from the passenger seat. He shouldered the small, but heavy bag, and then grabbed the MP 40 sub-machine gun, instantaneously judging the weight of the weapon with its long clip. If they wanted to piss about, five hundred rounds per minute from the MP 40 would see off the best swordsman the Arab's world had to offer. He shoved two spare magazines into his leg pouch for good measure and cocked the weapon.

He bellowed, not bothering to conceal his malcontent. 'Al-Ruzi! Major Weiner, show yourself!'

His voice echoed about the escarpment. The buzzards squawked and flapped at the sudden disturbance, but otherwise remained unwilling to leave the relative shade of their nests. Weiner stepped forward, pushing up the brim on his cap. He trained the weapon on the building up ahead, his patience fading. 'Al-Ruzi! You called this fucking meeting place! Show yourself!'

Weiner stopped. He scanned the ruins for a response, movement, the slightest glimpse of cloth or shimmer of steel.

Nothing.

He moved forward a few more steps, keeping his weapon up.

Abruptly, Al-Ruzi stepped from the shadows, walking into full view on the flat roof of one of the dwellings in the middle of the village. His cloak flapped in the breeze. He stood majestic with his hand on the pommel of his shamshir and spoke in a loud, clear voice. 'Major Weiner, I am pleased that you have arrived. I trust your journey was difficult enough to dissuade others from following?'

Weiner growled a reply, 'I come alone. Enough of these games! Do you have the briefcase or not?'

Al-Ruzi folded his arms and laughed, almost politely. 'Major, I would not drag you to such a place without upholding our bargain. Yes, I have the case.'

Weiner pointed the MP 40 firmly in Al-Ruzi's direction. 'And the Russians?'

'Dead, all dead, exactly as we agreed.' Al-Ruzi moved athletically, descending across several rooftops and eventually landing on the stone steps leading to Weiner's position. The giant Arab strode down the stairs, paying no heed to the machine gun.

Weiner took aim. 'And, Colonel Korolev?'

Al-Ruzi smiled as he skipped down the last few steps on to the sand. 'He joined his comrades in the afterlife. None remained alive.'

'What about the girl?'

The Persian stopped a few metres from the German, keeping a firm grip on the pommel of his sword. 'Alive, for now.'

Weiner made a show of his weapon. '*Where* is she?'

'She is my guest.'

He fumed, barely concealing his rage. 'That was not the arrangement. You should have killed everyone, *including* the girl.'

'We do not murder unarmed women, Major Weiner. She has spirit: even for a Russian – or should I say an Englishwoman.'

Weiner grizzled, tensing on the MP 40. 'English? What is this? You don't know that.'

Al-Ruzi allowed a thin smile, 'I have not always been a savage, Major. I achieved an education overseas. Let's just say I know how an English lady would drink her tea. Think about it – the British wish to know of your meeting with the Soviets. A spy infiltrates the grounds at the Ambassador's residence – an English spy. Only a fool would not put an observer within.'

Weiner nonchalantly waved the machine gun, 'Alright, so the girl might know something of value.'

'The desert is her prison, she cannot escape.'

The Nazi snorted, 'I want the girl *and* the documents in exchange for German weaponry.'

Al-Ruzi maintained a polite exterior, 'Indulge me for a moment longer, Major Weiner. Let me demonstrate my part of our bargain.' The Persian slowly retrieved a scroll of paper from under his silk garment. 'Please, Major, take a look.' He waved the paper enticingly.

Weiner took a deep breath and exhaled, scanning the terrain briefly before deciding to lower his weapon. He hitched the MP 40 on his shoulder and walked firmly up to the Persian, snatching the document from his grasp.

Al-Ruzi stood motionless.

Weiner strolled a few yards away from the Persian to keep out of thrusting range of the shamshir. He opened the roll of paper, quickly appraising the contents. He turned to face the Persian. 'So, you have a technical drawing from the many pages of documentation in the briefcase. How do I know you have the rest?'

'The girl was captured with the briefcase in her possession. I expect she has knowledge of both the Soviet's and your affairs. Perhaps even communicated it with the British.'

'Alright, so you have the case.' Weiner hastily folded the paper, cramming it into his pocket. 'Where is the girl exactly? How do I know she is still alive?'

'Perhaps this will give you some reassurance.' Al-Ruzi pulled a photograph from under his cloak.

Weiner snatched the picture. He examined the black and white print, looking back and forth at the Persian has he did so. The image showed the woman sitting on a large wicker sofa surrounded by silks. Weiner furrowed his brow.

Al-Ruzi chuckled, 'What is it, Major? You do not expect a tribesman of these lands to own a camera? We do not shun the modern world entirely you know.'

'When this was taken? The woman could be rotting in the desert for all I know.'

'Observe,' Al-Ruzi slowly raised his left arm and then lowered it. Suddenly, a tribesman appeared from amongst the ruins.

Weiner instantly ditched the photograph and swung the MP 40 off his shoulder, securing a firm position. He menaced with the MP 40. 'What the fuck is this? We agreed: *come alone*.' He twitched the weapon back and forth between the choices of targets.

Al-Ruzi stood in silence, as his fellow tribesman approached.

Weiner tensed on the trigger of the MP 40. 'Explain, quickly if you value your life.'

Al-Ruzi remained calm. 'Please, I only wish to prove to you that the girl is alive.'

Weiner puzzled as the tribesman stepped on to the sand and took position next to his master. The man seemed to be carrying a camel hair blanket. The tribesman opened a fold on the blanket, revealing the contents.

Weiner stood firm, weapon at the ready. 'We agreed – *alone* – how many other men are you hiding in this pathetic hovel?' He took up the final strain on the trigger.

Al-Ruzi spoke in a matter-of-fact tone. 'We are both cautious are we not? I secrete but a handful of men in the mountainside. Of course, they prefer to carry their traditional Scythian Horse bow. You are not without military education, Major. Our bow proved its worth against the might of the English longbow in the Crusades. At this distance, bone and flesh are no obstacle to its path.'

'As is the Mauser rifle or my MP 40,' Weiner growled.

Al-Ruzi allowed a gentle smile. 'Come now, Major, your snipers have the stealth of juvenile goat herders. They have spent the night on the plateau for no purpose and yet they still live – only because I allowed it so.'

Weiner, flicked his eyes up at the ridge. Uncertain of calling the Persian's bluff.

'Please, Major, you see these garments.' He waved his arm towards the contents of the blanket. 'The grey skirt and other clothing – the same ones as in the photograph – and without appreciable blood stain. You know I speak the truth.' He paused, 'She is alive and well, resting much more comfortably in proper clothing for the desert.'

Weiner held on to the machine gun all the same. 'Alright, so the woman is alive. Our agreement is now to exchange the documents *plus the woman* for German weapons.'

Al-Ruzi snorted gently, 'Guns, money, nonsense. We do not seek the trinkets of The West, but something of far greater value.'

Weiner menaced, 'No more games, our arrangement was clear. Speak plainly, if you wish to see another sunrise.'

The Persian took a deep breath, puffing out his substantial chest and ignoring the jibe of his Nazi inferior. 'I seek to trade this so-called, Comrade Akimov, and the documents for one person – a woman who resides in Paris under the mighty heel of your Führer.'

Weiner frowned, his eyes flickered, revealing uncertainty. 'Woman? Paris? What woman?'

'The daughter of Ahmad Shah Qatar, heiress, and the rightful ruler of all of Persia.'

Weiner stood perplexed. 'Ruler of Persia? What the hell are you talking about?'

Al-Ruzi nodded respectfully. 'Our mighty Shah took refuge in France, while the English and Soviet dogs squabbled over the spoils of the Great War, dividing our lands amongst themselves. They stole our nation, soiled the pure flesh of our women, and starved our children. I will see that the word of God is followed and our lands restored.'

Weiner fired low, spraying bullets across the sand inches from Al-Ruzi. 'Enough!' He aimed the weapon at the Persian's gut and slipped off the rucksack; pulling out a solid block of explosives wrapped in brown wax paper and with a pencil-like detonator in place. He raised it in the air and called out in a loud, clear voice for all to hear. 'You mess with me, or interfere with my men – then everybody dies. Donarit Mark II! The very latest in German explosives! There is enough here to bring half the mountain down on our heads. *Everybody will die – everybody*, do you understand? Show yourselves!'

Al-Ruzi raised his arm slowly and waved his men from cover. Tribesmen dotted the ruins and the escarpment above. He spoke in a quiet voice. 'We do not fear death or seek your kind of vengeance.'

'Just bring me the woman and the documents. The oasis, ten kilometres due south of the escarpment. Be there at dawn, two days from now.'

Al-Ruzi folded his arms. 'And if I do not?'

'You hate the Russians and the British,' Weiner shuffled backwards, still holding the explosives. 'You don't have any friends left. If you want this French woman, you will do as I say.'

'Persian, not French. It is but chance that she resides in your occupied territories. Do not think yourselves better than the English or the Soviets. You are all cut from the same cloth it seems.'

Weiner backed up towards the car, sporting the massive lump of Donarit and the MP 40. 'Bring me the documents and the woman. Two days. Otherwise the Wehrmacht will show you the true meaning of deprivation – on this matter you have my word.'

Weiner carefully placed the explosive charge on the dash, and gently slid the rucksack on to the passenger seat, while keeping the machine gun trained on the Persian. He opened the driver's door and gingerly lowered himself into the car. He propped the weapon over the door jam, keeping his finger on the trigger and turned the ignition with his free hand. Miraculously, the VW started first time. He trundled the vehicle forward a few feet, turning the wheel in towards the settlement; and then crunched into reverse, backing up just enough to complete a full turn. He revved the engine and looked firmly at the Persian. He shouted, 'Two days, the woman and the documents – be there.'

With that Weiner sped off faster than he intended, risking the abyss and hoping to make the first corner before a storm of Scythian arrows could pierce his skull.

CHAPTER 23

Steinhoff and Weiner

Steinhoff paced back and forth across the hotel room, habitually pushing his glasses on to the bridge of his nose with his index finger. He stared at the floor as he assimilated the new information. 'So let me get this straight. We've signed the trade agreement, securing the special materials we need. These materials are secreted amongst a long list of natural resources needed for the war effort and Director Krauch has long since departed for Berlin, taking our copy of the agreement with him?' Steinhoff suddenly stopped and turned towards Major Weiner.

Weiner stood by the sofa, bristling. 'What do you expect? He is a senior official of the Reich Ministry. The trade agreement has been signed and Krauch is a busy man.' Weiner shrugged, 'Of course, unless you prefer to keep the Reich Ministry waiting?' The Major took a long drag on his smoke and exhaled contempt.

Steinhoff panted slowly, with perspiration dripping from his furrowed brow. 'No, but meanwhile everything is falling apart!' He flicked a dismissive hand in the air. 'Some religious fanatic of an Arab has copies of my work and now wants to make a new deal so that we can get back *our own papers*?! And *you* hired him! You're supposed to be in charge of security for the project! Why not just kill the bastard?!' The scientist resumed pacing back and forth, hunched over, fuming expletives to himself as he went.

'No, Doctor Steinhoff – he has what we *wanted the Russians to see* – a few technical drawings of part of your device – proof of a considerable leap forward in military technology.' Weiner snorted a quick breath and then took another drag on his cigarette, 'Besides, do you want your titanium and whatever else you need or not?'

Steinhoff paused at the drinks cabinet. Then, grabbing the nearest bottle of spirits, he unscrewed the cap. 'You know we cannot proceed to full-scale production without them. We *must have* the raw materials.' He poured a generous helping of vodka into a heavy crystal tumbler, then continued. 'With the materials we can mass produce – and if we mass produce, we win the war.' He took a gulp of the spirit then slammed the glass down, almost splashing the remaining contents over the rim. 'It's that bloody simple, Major! Or should my next technical report to the Führer indicate that I was over-ruled by a caveman and our most guarded secrets are now passed to the Russians?!'

Weiner ambled forwards, then slowly and deliberately picked up the scientist's glass of vodka, swallowing it in one gulp. He pantomimed refreshment as he placed the empty glass back on the tray. He gave Steinhoff a blank look and spoke in a low, steady tone. 'Russians that are now all dead. Perhaps you would like to join them? You have no concept of military tactics, *Doctor Steinhoff.*'

The scientist backed off mumbling, shaking his head. 'Well, no matter, the Arabs have my drawings. I must have them back.'

Weiner continued in a matter-of-fact tone, 'You will. The Plenipotentiary returns to Berlin in preparation for the Soviet's response to the Reich Chancellery. Naturally, assistance will be offered in hunting down the tribesmen who committed such a treacherous act, along with the suggestion that the Soviets extend their control from the north east into the region – to keep order, protecting everyone's interests, and so on.'

Steinhoff slumped into the sofa, suddenly drained. 'What am I supposed to do? I cannot progress. I cannot even think straight. The drawings are part of my most important work. I am lost with worry and we have spent so much money. It is illogical to give something so precious away.' He shook his head and stared despondently into nothingness.

Weiner gave a disgusted look. 'Like I said – you know nothing of military tactics. The Soviets will graciously decline our offer of assistance, but nonetheless take the opportunity to seize a new territory with the blessing of their closest ally. Thus, the Führer draws Stalin closer into the German-Soviet pact. The Russians occupy a worthless pile of rock and dust, saving us the trouble. Furthermore, any plans that the British may have had of extending from the south would also become instantly redundant. The Middle East will be divided between Germany and the Soviet Union, at least for now. You get your materials, the German war machine is fed with vital resources – everybody is happy.'

'I don't know, I still need to recover the drawing. You should have killed the stinking Arab while you had the chance.'

Weiner moved closer to the sofa and drew his *SS* dagger. He turned the blade over in his palm. 'Have you ever killed a man, Doctor Steinhoff? You know, got close up and personal?'

Steinhoff sank back into the cushions, raising his legs off the floor into a foetal-like position. He looked sheepish, 'Well, no, of course not. I am a civilian.'

Weiner paused, taking the opportunity to watch his charge squirm. 'No, I don't suppose you have, but you will have the chance soon enough.'

Steinhoff looked perplexed, 'I, I don't understand? What are you talking about?'

'We meet with the Arab tomorrow at a nice secluded oasis.'

'So, I will get my documents?'

Weiner towered over Steinhoff. 'That depends on *you*. What are *you* prepared to do? Kill or be killed for your cause?' Weiner lunged, stabbing the blade into the soft furnishing, an inch from Steinhoff's head.

The scientist yelped.

Weiner withdraw the dagger and return it to its scabbard. 'You don't have the stomach for it – I'd always thought so.'

Steinhoff reddened, but remained cowering in the corner of the sofa. 'You could have killed me!'

Weiner chortled, 'I should be so lucky. Perhaps if you can't kill a man, a woman might be more your size.'

Steinhoff gaped confusion.

'The Akimov woman – she's alive. We collect her from the Arab at the same time. Then you can ask her what she knows about your precious drawing, if you have the balls for it.' Weiner huffed contempt, 'But clearly, it seems that you don't.'

He marched for the door, not bothering to wait for a reply.

CHAPTER 24

River Bank

Nash glanced at his watch and then increased his pace, striding along the bank of the river with his thumbs wedged under the straps of his canvas haversack. He got a rhythm going, letting his body settle into an efficient yomp. His boots crunched into the damp gravel, leaving watery footprints that even a blind man could follow – but none of that mattered now – he had to find Emily and Korolev. He needed to cover more ground, and do it before the enemy reappeared.

He squinted against the morning sun, scanning the rocky landscape that made the ravine and stomped ahead. The prickly warmth on his forearms told of skin already starting to cook. He huffed, and without breaking his stride, rolled down his shirt sleeves and then adjusted his grubby shemagh to shade his cheekbones from the worst of sun. Not that it would do much good in the coming hours. The sides of the ravine were already reflecting heat, and with the sun creeping overhead, the length of the valley would be a blistering cauldron long before noon. 'Bloody desert, work with me for once.' He pressed on, subconsciously registering shapes, textures and hues for anything out of place.

He suddenly halted and pierced a look ahead. There was certainly something there, roughly a thousand yards out. He pressed the side of his palm against his forehead and forced his eyes wide open. He strained at the object; low and flattened, yet warped by the shimmering thermals. Definitely not a rock – and positioned at the edge of the water.

He broke into a run. The sand shifted under his feet, sapping momentum, but the object took form, transforming from shimmering obscurity to tangible reality – it was a body, definitely a body. He snorted resolve and pulled the Sauer 38 from his waist, clicking off the safety as he ran. A uniform with a tan shirt and red pips on the shoulder – a Russian officer – Korolev!

He dashed the last few yards, and slumping to his knees with Sauer 38 still in hand, he rolled the body over on to his lap. He stared down at the greyed features of Colonel Korolev, then bent over the old Soviet, pressing his ear towards the man's lips. He listened for any signs of breathing, searching the chest for movements. Nash furrowed his brow, concentrating.

Alive, but only just.

He roved an eye over his casualty: head wound, bleeding from the chest, rib bone protruding, numerous cut and scrapes, right ankle turned – most likely broken. Nash cursed his diagnosis and gently lowered the Russian's torso to the deck. Still on his knees, he shoved the Sauer in the front of his waistband and quickly pulled off the haversack, producing two field dressings. He ripped open the brown wax paper of the first dressing and curved the soft pad into a roughly doughnut ring shape and eased it gently around the protruding rib bone. He unwrapped the second dressing, and gently placed the pad over the first, then rolled the remains of the crepe bandage as best he could around the Russian's chest.

Korolev groaned.

Nash hurried, removing his shemagh and soaking the filthy garment with clean water from the canteen in his rucksack. He dabbed the make-shift cloth on the Russian's face and spoke softly. 'Colonel? It's Major Nash. Can you hear me?'

Nothing.

'Open your eyes.'

Still nothing.

Nash dabbed more water on to the Russian's brow. He shook the Soviet's shoulders gently. 'Colonel?'

The Russian gave a pathetic spasm, red, congealed spittle emerged at the corner of his mouth. His eyelids formed narrow slits. Nash shook him again.

'Colonel, it's Nash. Where's Emily? What happened to Emily?'

He groaned, moving his head slowly from side to side.

'Emily? Where is Emily Sinclair?' Nash repeated.

Korolev gasped a shallow breath, his eyes slowly opened. He rasped, 'Taken …'

'Taken? Taken where?' He roused the Colonel gently by the shoulders. '*Where* has she been taken?'

'Tribesmen … attacked convoy …' Korolev coughed, fresh blood oozed from his lips. 'Arabs have her …'

Nash sat up, and taking the canteen, dribbling more water on to Korolev's face. 'The convoy was attacked – you're certain it was tribesmen? How many?'

Korolev crackled a more audible reply, 'Arabic dress, swords.'

Nash swallowed back the lump in his throat. His voice wavered, 'They have her?'

'Yes,' Korolev hacked; blood and fragments of lung tissue issued from his lips.

Nash wiped the rag carefully around the Russian's mouth, 'Where did they take her? Which direction?'

'Into the desert.'

Nash reeled, but forced some composure. 'Direction – which way?'

Korolev shook his head.

Nash looked blankly into the river, then at the Soviet, 'Please, Colonel, think …'

Korolev winced, 'No time to defend … the briefcase.'

Nash took a sharp breath, 'They have the German documents? And Emily?'

Korolev dribbled more blood from his mouth and suddenly grabbed Nash by the shirt. Redness wicked from the field dressing. Korolev gritted his teeth, sweat soaked his matted hair. 'More, much more ...' He snorted blood, barely able to catch a breath into his remaining lung. 'Emily's mother ... in prison. You ... *must*, help her.'

Nash looked perplexed, 'What?'

'The Batryka. She's in the Batryka ... Get her out!' Korolev collapsed back into the sand, gasping like a fish out of water.

Nash lifted the Colonel into his lap, cradling the Soviet's chest wound with his free hand. Blood oozed through his fingers. '*The Baryka*? What does this have to do with Emily?' Nash suddenly shivered, despite the heat. He gripped the Soviet's torso. '*What have you done*? Tell me – *what have you done*?'

Korolev quietened, his voice barely audible against the trickle of the river water. 'Her mother ... aristocracy ... Petrochov.'

Nash puzzled, 'So? Emily? My mission?'

Korolev, rattled through gritted teeth. 'A test ... her mother ... not trusted.' He gave an ironic, painful chuckle, 'Ex-wife to an English spymaster.' Blood dripped from his mouth.

Nash adjusted his grip on Korolev's wound, blood pulsed between his fingers. He took the shemagh, and pushed the cloth deep into the injury.

The Colonel snarled pain.

Nash chased the train of thought, 'Something to do with Sinclair, with London?'

The Russian spat blood, 'No, *my test*. Pass, and the doors of the Batryka ... open. She ... would be freed.' He shook his head slowly.

'The Kremlin's using you? *For what*?'

210

Korolev grasped Nash by the shirt collar. 'You don't understand. *I loved her*. I still love her.'

'Tell me,' Nash glanced at the wound. 'While there's still time.'

Korolev rasped, 'My test was simple – to turn the daughter of my master's enemy: Emily.'

'You took advantage? Dropped Emily in it as Miss Nina Akimov – but you must have known – she would never work for the German-Soviet alliance.'

Korolev countered, blood now dripping from his nostrils. 'Thought I could save them both.' He began to sob, 'Start a new life together. I had to know, *had to know*.'

Nash furrowed his brow, 'Know? Know what?'

'*Emily is my daughter*.' Korolev slumped, blood gurgling in his gullet.

Nash kneeled, rooted to the spot, whispering to himself. '*What*? Emily, *your daughter*? A Russian?' The penny dropped, but it still didn't make any sense. Korolev gave a spasm, blood splattered from his oral cavity. He held on to Nash, gasping. 'Her mother rots in the Batryka. It was the only way to save her …'

Korolev began to fade.

Nash frantically shook the Russian. 'Save her from what?! From what?!'

Korolev smiled, and gave the quietest of whispers.

Nash leant his ear against Korolev's mouth.

'NKVD was right … They were never going to hand it over. Russia needs that propulsion system. Understand – *I needed it*! My pocket … in my pocket.'

Nash followed the Russian's eyes and pulled a small notebook from the Soviet's trouser pocket. Blood stained the worn leather cover. Nash opened the clasp of the tiny book to reveal thin pages with detailed notes and sketches. 'What's this?'

'D-Wing ... the most secret ... Soviet project.' He shuddered a breath, trailing a last whisper. '*Find Emily. Go to the Batryka. Save them both.*' Air rattled slowly from his torso, his body went limp. Colonel Sergio Korolev departed from this world.

CHAPTER 25

Oasis

The transmission whined as the Mercedes-Benz truck gathered momentum. The driver pushed firmly on the clutch, shifting the vehicle into top gear. His skinny frame of dark olive skin clung to the steering wheel. His head seemed to nod in a random fashion with every bump in the road, shaking the long black tassel of his fez. He gave Weiner a toothy white grin, apparently pleased with his progress.

The Major returned a blank stare for a few seconds and then shook his head. The Muslim Brotherhood – not one of the Führer's greatest decision – but needs must and they were short of men in Middle East. Still, the fez looked ridiculous. Its grey fabric did nothing to dignify the cap badge of the German eagle over skull and crossed bones of the Waffen-*SS*. Nonetheless, if the current escapade required sacrifice, it was better to lose a few peripherals rather than the true Aryan breeding of the *SS*. Weiner turned his gaze to the grit and dust on the windshield and the desert beyond, trying to ignore the discomfort of the poorly sprung bench seat.

He checked his watch, then looked down his nose at Steinhoff. The scientist sat in khaki shorts and a shirt, with one elbow on the open window of the passenger door as if going on Safari. He was studying a map, half-folded in his lap. The spectacled runt had tested his patience enough already. The little bastard had better tow the line today.

213

Weiner simmered, 'Where are we? We can't be more than a few miles out?'

Steinhoff pressed a digit on to the map. 'I think we're here, about three kilometres to go. We should see the oasis after the next long bend in the road.'

'About fucking time.' Weiner pulled his Luger from its leather holster and checked the magazine, then returned the weapon to its pouch. 'How's the other truck doing?'

Steinhoff stuck his head out of the window and looked back into the dust trail, adding another coat of sandstone grime to his face. 'Fifty metres behind us.'

'Good.' Weiner reached over his seat and thumped three times on the wooden slats at the rear of the cab with his fist. He bellowed, 'Make ready, five minutes!' He pivoted round to a more comfortable posture and mumbled to Steinhoff. 'Let's hope our little troop is up to the job. Remember, we take the girl and the documents. Our Muslim friends here,' Weiner jerked a thumb towards the driver, 'get to kill the rest.'

Steinhoff shrugged. 'What about the French woman? We come empty handed, except for a crate of guns and a letter pledging her release by the Reich Chancellery. What if your Persian swordsman wants his girlfriend back?'

'It doesn't matter. A letter is all he's getting – for now at least. Anyway, it's just a fucking headache. It's not as if we don't have enough to do in the occupied territories, without wasting my men trying to locate some upper class bitch that might, or might not be, residing somewhere in Paris. For all I fucking know, she's dead, or more likely shagging her way through half the bloody Panzer Division.'

The driver suddenly pointed towards the road ahead, jabbering in his native Egyptian tongue. He applied the brakes, slowing the vehicle to a stop.

Weiner sat forwards, peering through the windscreen, waiting for the dust to settle. The diesel engine hunted for air. The particulate haze drifted on the breeze, gradually revealing the terrain. There was a pocket of lush greenery about two kilometres up ahead. The oasis nestled at the base of a weathered sandstone escarpment. The rising thermals seemed to fracture the vertical crevices in the cliff face behind the oasis. Weiner reached for a pair of binoculars, cursing the Muslim prayer beads sitting on the dashboard. He pushed the binoculars against his eyeballs and focussed the lens.

The oasis consisted of a few white-washed buildings clustered around, presumably the watering hole. Low shrubs and scrub plants thrived on the perimeter of the settlement, punctuated by the occasional half-collapsed dwelling, long since taken over by livestock. A herd of goats occupied a corral, a few Khuzestani buffalo ambled amongst the dusty vegetation. A group of women worked on a parched excuse for a vegetable plot, but otherwise everything looked quiet – too damned quiet.

Weiner pulled the binoculars from his eyes and took in a long slow breath, then exhaled. 'Alright, no sign of Al-Ruzi, but we go in as planned. Remember – the girl and the documents – let me do the talking.' He gave a sharp nod to the driver. The skeletal Egyptian let out the clutch. The two-vehicle convoy moved along the narrow dirt road at a modest speed, but nonetheless sending a dust cloud into the atmosphere to announce their arrival.

Nash gently turned the throttle, and using his left leg, he fended off rocks as he coaxed the bike up the steep incline of the goat track. The sidecar jolted over small boulders, scraping the axle and causing the Spandau machine gun to rattle about in its mounting. Several ammunition belts for the heavy weapon and his haversack slid about in the footwell. Scree slid under the rear wheel with each twist of the throttle. Regardless, he edged the BMW forwards over the rough ground. There had been no time to gather proper intelligence.

He had to admit, he'd been relying on gut instinct and titbits of information gleaned from the locals.

The Arabs would have headed into the desert and most likely west or north west to keep clear of the Soviet occupied territory in Azerbaijan. This had to be connected to the Persian he'd encountered in Istanbul and then in Tabriz. The Germans were using the local tribesmen to do their dirty work; but at some point they'd have to meet up to hand over the goods – including Emily? He was banking on it. But it didn't make any sense. Why make a trade deal with the Soviets and then muddy the waters by having the Russian delegation murdered on their way home? Korolev had been pressurised by the NKVD, but had the old Soviet being working under direct orders from the Kremlin to steal technical documents from Director Krauch or Doctor Steinhoff? That would certainly be cause enough for retribution, but what about the Arabs? Either way the Persians were on the losing side, with the might of the Germany Army to the west and the Soviets to the east. Unless of course, they secured themselves a bargaining chip – the German documents to be sold to the highest bidder? If that was the case, Emily was an expendable trinket.

Nash flicked the accelerator. The BMW progressed along the goat path. The track turned left, following the contour of the hillside, eventually to reach an expanse of rocky debris that marked the rounded hilltop. He dropped the bike to a low gear and allowed it to trundle a few feet shy of the summit, then turned off the ignition. He dismounted, dropping his leather goggles on the handlebars and pulling the filthy shemagh up over the crusty blisters on his face. Then fishing around in the sidecar, he dug the binoculars from the top of his rucksack. He placed them over his head, being careful to tuck the lens into his shirt. He drew the Sauer 38 from his waistband. Then hunching over, he scrambled the last few yards to the summit. He dropped on to his belly in a suitable

216

shallow depression. Heat radiated from the substrate into his abdomen and thighs, adding to the discomfort already cooking his shoulders. He eased on to both elbows, and with the Sauer still in hand, took in the view of the desert below.

He froze to the spot.

Two trucks moved along the main highway that bisected the large expanse of desert, and creating a dust cloud as they went. Nash followed the line of sight of the small convoy. It seemed to be heading for a settlement at the base of the escarpment on the other side of the valley. Nash pushed the Sauer into the back of his trousers and lifted the binoculars to his eyes. He settled into the dirt as he positioned the eyepieces and then focussed the lens on the lead vehicle. The lorry came crisply into view. There was no mistaking the Mercedes-Benz flatbed truck – German – and definitely for military use.

He zoomed in on the driver's cab. Dust and reflected light obscured the details, but the driver wasn't alone, with at least one other person sitting up front. Nash scanned along the side of the vehicle, picking out the heavy canvas that covered the rear. He estimated the capacity – room for six or seven men on each side of the vehicle, so at least fifteen in each truck, possibly more. He lowered the binoculars and grimaced to himself, then resumed the surveillance; this time tackling the lorry at the rear. The canopy rattled with each rut in the road and the axle seemed to bounce a little more freely, perhaps the second vehicle was empty or simply carrying a light cargo? The dust obscured any proper view into the vehicle.

Nash snorted and shifted the binoculars towards the wadi at the base of the cliffs and quickly assimilated the village, if you could call it that; searching the white-washed dwelling for troops, swordsmen, anything out of place. A few old women stooped, labouring a vegetable crop from the arid soil. Goats milled about amongst the scrub and crumbling out-buildings. There was plenty of cover for hiding an Arabian militia amongst the ruins.

He shifted his gaze back to the convoy. The lead truck was already trundling off the main drag and making the last few hundred yards to the wadi. Nash decided to wait a few more minutes. If there was going to be a reception committee, at least he'd know how many he was up against – and more importantly, whether or not Emily was amongst them.

Weiner braced himself against the wooden dashboard as the truck swung in an arc and came to an abrupt stop. The creak of the tailgate and the thud of boots on timber heralded the *SS* troop of the Muslim Brotherhood decanting from the back of the vehicle. The men quickly took up defensive positions as the second lorry squealed to a halt. More fez-sporting Nazis piled out of the latter vehicle; Mauser rifles in hand, instantly fanning out around the convoy.

Weiner clicked the safety off his Luger and donned his canvas cap of the Waffen-*SS*. He waved his pistol towards Steinhoff, 'Let's get a move on. Remember, let me do the talking.'

Steinhoff slid off the seat on to the running board and stepped methodically from the edge of the cab. Weiner followed a fraction of a second later, jumping from the door sill and planting both boots on the sand at once. He strode forwards, brushing dust off his breeches as he did so. His leather knee-high boots crunched on the gravel. He aimed the pistol here and there into the dwellings as he went, allowing time for the last of his men to take up positions.

He halted, then shouted towards the main cluster of buildings. 'Al-Ruzi! Major Weiner, here we are again! Show yourself!'

He waited, eyeballing the terrain, feeling confident. His men knelt in silence, coiled, ready to defend their arc of fire. A sudden breeze rattled through some wooden shutters causing the hinges to creak. Weiner pivoted towards the noise, cocking his weapon as he did so – a small dust devil turned the corner of the nearest building and then dissipated. Weiner strained on the trigger mechanism. He bellowed again, 'Al-Ruzi, show yourself! No fucking games this time.'

A goat trundled into view, absently chewing on some parched scrub. Weiner pulled the trigger. The ruminant exploded crimson against a mud wall and collapsed. The shot echoed around the escarpment. He raised his pistol over head and fired twice more, 'Al-Ruzi!' He grimaced malcontent at the ruins.

The Persian suddenly stepped from the shadows. His black cloak hung neatly about his tall, solid frame, with his dark turban partially obscuring his face. His right hand rested on the pommel of his jewelled shamshir. He walked several paces into the open. Weiner sensed a new caution in the man's stride, then noting how the Arab stopped some five metres in front of the first truck and keeping a good few body lengths between himself and the German forces – not that it would make any difference.

Weiner stared at the Persian for a few seconds.

Al-Ruzi remained silent with his feet slightly apart and his hand resting on his sword.

Weiner sidled backwards a few steps, opting to maintain a respectful distance from the shamshir and then made another scan of the rooftops.

Nothing – not a single tribesman.

Weiner pointed the Luger squarely at the Arab. 'Call your men into the open.' He clicked back the firing hammer on the pistol. 'Do it now.'

Al-Ruzi stood motionless for several seconds, and then nodded appreciatively. 'The eye only sees what it wishes to find. A patient man can observe much, he only has to take the time to look.' The Persian lifted one hand into the air, keeping the other firmly on the shamshir. He flicked his wrist twice, making a sharp circular motion with his free hand – dozens of

Arabic swordsmen appeared around the perimeter; many on the open ground as if miraculously sprung from the very earth under their feet. They stood dressed in Egyptian cotton, apparition-like, dusty and perfectly camouflaged by their surroundings. All were armed with swords. Many carried rifles. The *SS* troopers held their positions. Some fidgeted, glancing incredulity at their comrades, while others responded by haplessly shuffling their rifle bolts before settling down. A few simply took a firm aim on the nearest target.

Al-Ruzi chuckled as he gave another flick of his wrist – bowmen appeared, occupying positions on the rooftops and high ground. He lowered his arm. 'Seek and ye shall find. Is that not what your Christian bible says? Mathew 7:7?'

Weiner kept the Luger's aim, levelling it towards the Persian's forehead. 'I am not one for philosophy. I prefer to let my pistol to do the talking – have you brought the Akimov woman and the documents?'

'I see you are direct as ever, Major Weiner. We are here to bargain. Do you have our supply of weapons?' He looked over the trucks. 'And where is the princess?'

Weiner spat sideways into the dirt. 'We have weapons as agreed. My friend here,' he jerked a thump over his shoulder towards Steinhoff, 'would like his diagrams back.'

Steinhoff moved sheepishly, stopping a foot or so from the Major, almost using his companion as cover.

Weiner gave Steinhoff an evil stare and then continued with the Persian. 'You're the mercenary, remember – we hired you to kill a few Russians in exchange for hardware, that's all.'

Al-Ruzi contrived a smile and shook his head slowly, he folded his arms as he did so. 'Life is never as one expects, especially in war – you should know that, Major.'

'That's all bullshit as far as the Wehrmacht is concerned. Your guns are in the back of the truck – just hand over the documents and the Soviet woman, then be on your way. Unless of course, you prefer to be on the receiving end of such superior German technology.'

The Persian remained unflustered. 'Come now, Major, we both know our arrangement was never about a few German rifles. You have what you wanted from the Russian delegation – all of whom are now dead.'

'That was the deal. So, now all you need to do is return our documents.'

Al-Ruzi reached under his cloak, producing a brown leather folder. 'These documents?'

Fuelled by the prospect, Steinhoff hastened forwards over the sand, coming to stop almost ahead of the Major.

Weiner offered a disapproving sideways glance, but kept his pistol aimed at the Persian.

Steinhoff mustered enough courage to speak. 'The documents. I must have them back, by order of the Reich Chancellery.' He held out a pathetic arm.

Al-Ruzi took a couple steps, patting the document wallet against his palm. 'Ah, you see, there is the dilemma. It's all a question of security. The Soviet delegation are dead and now my people await the wrath of the Soviet Union. It occurs to me to hand the documents *and the girl* over to the Russians. Appeasement for the sake of the innocent: the women and children in our villages, you understand.'

Steinhoff stood gaping.

Weiner cut in, 'That will not be necessary. I have already agreed to exchange weapons for the papers.' He lowered his pistol and turned about, yelling back to the nearest trooper. 'You! Take four men, bring the cases up front.' The Egyptian nodded a toothy smile from under his fez and scurried off, shouldering his rifle as he did so.

Weiner whispered to Steinhoff as he moved back to face the Persian. 'Herr Doctor, *I said* leave the talking to me, or are you trying to get up both killed?'

221

Steinhoff lowered his gaze.

Satisfied that his minion was at heel, Weiner took up the negotiations. 'These are not second-hand goods, but brand new weapons with a full compliment of ammunition and spare parts.'

Al-Ruzi shook his head and smiled, while placing the leather document wallet back under his cloak. 'I don't doubt that, Major, but *where* is the princess? The Akimov woman and the documents for the princess and some firearms was our new bargain, was it not?'

Weiner shrugged, 'We can at least trade on the weapons and documents today. Besides, why would I be interested in the Akimov woman? She is just a civil servant, aide de camp. Perhaps you should have killed her along with the others.'

'So be it.' Al-Ruzi raised a hand.

A swordsman stepped into view on the furthest rooftop. He held a young woman by the scruff of her brightly coloured silk vest. Even at this distance Weiner could tell from the whiteness of her face, and the flowing brown hair that had dishevelled from her matching scarf, that she was European. The swordsman held a long blade against her throat, stretching her body, with her feet almost dangled on tiptoes from the hem of her silk dress.

Al-Ruzi gestured towards Weiner, 'Major?'

Weiner stood in silence, slowly raising his pistol, targeting the giant Persian.

Al-Ruzi repeated, 'Major, should I kill the woman?'

Weiner pointed the Luger at Al-Ruzi's chest, then risked another glance at the woman – it was definitely her – the girl from the Soviet delegation. He waved his pistol at the Persian, 'I'll take the documents in exchange for the weapons.'

Al-Ruzi lifted his arm further, tempting. 'We both know she is not really a Russian. I wonder what secrets the late, Colonel Korolev, shared with her – and what superior German technology she now feeds to the British? Still, if you do not wish to know, I have but to command and her throat will be slit. What is your decision, Major?'

Steinhoff interrupted. 'No! Wait!' He gabbled a pleading look at Weiner, 'He's right. The girl may know something.'

Al-Ruzi kept his hand raised. 'Major, what is it to be?'

Weiner hesitated and then lowered his pistol. He stared at the scientist and then at the Arab. 'Alright, in addition to the weapons, the Akimov woman for the princess.'

Al-Ruzi flattened his palm in a firm gesture, then slowly lowered his arm. The distant swordsman removed his steel from Emily's throat, but tightened his grip on her arm. Emily yelped.

Weiner observed the woman for a moment, then turned to the Persian. 'Bring the girl down. I'd like a closer look, then we can discuss the princess.'

Al-Ruzi fixed a stare at the Major, 'I can assure you, she is unspoilt.' He turned momentarily, signalling stiffly with his arm. The swordsman released his grip, and gestured for Emily to move across the low roof to some decaying steps cut in the side of the dwelling. She walked unevenly, rubbing her arm. The hues of green, red and blue in her flowing skirt contrasting with the dull sandstone. The swordsman firmly ushered her descent.

Weiner broke in, 'So, the Akimov girl is alive and well. But there is a protocol to follow: Berlin you understand.'

Al-Ruzi frowned, 'Protocol? What protocol?'

Weiner shrugged, 'We have located Her Royal Highness,' he lied, pulling a folded sheet of paper from his the breast pocket of his shirt. He held out the paper. 'A letter from Berlin, pledging the return of your princess. Bureaucracy, everything takes time and then there is the matter of safe transportation of the princess to your homeland.'

Al-Ruzi spoke in a matter-of-fact tone. 'This is not a proper bargain. How do I know you will keep your word?'

Weiner waved the letter. 'You must understand, I am a middle ranking officer. I do not have the authority to move the princess at short notice, but my Führer does. This letter from the Reich Chancellery is the will of my commanders. Arrangements are being made for her release to you.' He held the letter out at arms length. 'It is proof that Germany has pledged her release and will make it so. Take it, as assurance.'

Al-Ruzi moved purposefully, retaining a handhold on his sword. He stopped in front of the Major, and tentatively took the letter and then retreated several metres. He stooped over the document with his back to the Germans and examined the contents, then turned towards Weiner, 'I should speak with your commander. It seems you lack the authority?'

Weiner shook his head. 'No, I am the senior officer in the field. No matter who they send, the decision is from Berlin. It has been made and we must wait a little longer for the princess to arrive.'

Al-Ruzi tucked the letter into his cloak. 'We are not able to complete the trade it seems, so I will keep this Akimov woman; but do not take too long, Major Weiner. There are others who would bid for her. I am sure the Soviets would like to know who she really is. A spy certainly – that would not please the Kremlin.' He increased his grip on the pommel of his sword.

The first crate appeared from around the side of the truck. Two skeletal-looking *SS* Muslims shuffled through the dirt, straining at the weight of the coffin-like container, while trying to keep their rifle straps on their shoulders. They dropped the crate to the deck and waited.

Weiner picked up the negotiations, sensing the opportunity slipping. 'Let's not be so hasty. I am sure the princess is important to you – as she is to me. As a gesture of good will, I offer these weapons in exchange for our documents – then we will meet again for the girl.'

A third soldier appeared with a crowbar. Weiner issued instructions under his breath, 'Open it, quickly now!' The soldiers went about their work as Weiner continued uncomfortably with the sales pitch. 'The weapons are first class, better than we issue to our own troops, and with a generous supply of ammunition.' The crack of splintering wood punctuated the monologue. Weiner waved his pistol loosely over the crate as he spoke. 'The technical notes are of no use to you. It makes perfect sense to trade now, take these weapons, the ammo, spare parts, the lot.'

The lid finally gave way. The two troopers slid the top off the case, letting it clatter to the sand. Weiner stepped forwards to show off the prize. He peered into the case. It was stuffed to the brim with rifles, light machine guns, grenades and ammunition. 'There you see, more than a match for the Soviets. Take the weapons, defend your homelands.' He lowered his pistol, forcing a blank expression as the Persian approached. Weiner encouraged, 'That's it take the weapons … then we bring you the princess.' The sudden cry of a female voice interrupted his soothing.

Emily stumbled down the last few steps on to the sand. A swordsman held the flat of his palm on her shoulder, guiding her towards Al-Ruzi and Weiner. Steinhoff hovered in anticipation. She shuffled forwards, pouting misery, glancing over her shoulder at her jailor. Weiner smiled and clicked his heels in mock salute. 'Fräulein Akimov, it seems you have got yourself into some difficulty.' He gave a rough smile, 'Of course, the good doctor and I are here to assist.' His faced flattened and his voice suddenly hardened, 'But only if you fucking behave yourself.'

Emily strained at the leash, giving Weiner a drop-dead look, but remained silent.

Al-Ruzi rubbed his chin, his dark eyes narrowing, 'Major, the letter offers some security, but perhaps this woman is not enough surety.' He nodded towards Emily, 'The daughter of Ahmad Shah Qatar is of great importance to our nation.'

Weiner maintained a calm exterior. He allowed his eyes to drift from Al-Ruzi to his own contingent of enlisted Waffen-*SS*, and then the swordsmen standing off but intent on closing his perimeter. A hot breeze swirled dust and grit over the gathering. The men stood in the baking sun, motionless, apart from their breathing. Weiner felt a hot flush of sweat trickle down his back as he contemplated the odds.

He *could* kill Al-Ruzi, grab the girl and the documents, and then pile into the truck. If it started first time – and it often didn't – they could make a turn and be heading out of the village before the sword-toting Arabs were upon them.

The tightening of catgut on leather and the eking of wood straining against the grain permeated his thinking. A dozen Scythian Horse bows held tension, pointing in his direction. He stammered, clearing his throat, then stood upright, taking a deep breath and with his chest out. 'Gold sovereigns – portable wealth is always of value in times of uncertainty – there's a war on and even you have to eat.' Weiner eased up his shirt with his free hand, pulling a canvas belt slowly from around his waist, still holding the Luger with the other hand. He held the belt dangling, then spoke clearly and loudly for all to hear. 'Coins – one belt of several at my disposal – in total worth some three thousand Reichsmarks.' He turned about, allowing the men to see the offering. He called to the swordsmen, 'Take this gold for insurance, feed your families, do the right thing! Prepare yourselves for the future, for you know what lies ahead: the Red Army will rip these lands apart, leaving none alive. We are your friends, *Germany* is your friend – take control of your future against the Russian hordes.'

The sound of an engine revving, deep and throaty, drifted into the corral. The BMW with its sidecar offered a single dust trail as the bike hunted for purchase on the dirt track into the wadi. All and sundry turned their attention towards the lone rider, his allegiance hidden behind a grime-laden shemagh and dusty fatigues.

Al-Ruzi lifted his palm urgently, 'Hold!' Bowmen obediently tracked the target. Not a single arrow was loosed.

Weiner squinted at the intrusion, registering a streak of familiarity with the German machine. His eyes widened at the sight of the Spandau machine gun resting across the driver's lap.

The motorcycle broke through into the relatively open space of the village and accelerated, the holed exhaust creating a din, the engine rumbling and assured. The driver swerved around the flatbed trucks, jolting the sidecar and plastering the assembly with gritty detritus. The brakes squealed, adding another shower of dust.

Men blinked dirt from their eyes as the *click clack* of the Spandau focussed their attention on the prospect of death.

CHAPTER 26

A Royal Allegiance

Nash pointed the heavy Spandau machine gun, hoping the elaborate coils of the bullet belt resting over his crotch wouldn't jam when he hit the trigger. He pushed the shemagh aside, uncovering his mouth and nose and spat into the dirt, then gained a measure of the hosting through his filthy googles, arching the heavy weapon towards the German officer and his companions. His heart leapt at the sight of her – breathing, alive, walking – tantalisingly close, almost tasting her perfume on the air. Adrenalin filtered through his flesh, drawing fatigue like sepsis from a wound, pushing all else aside. His mind slipped into total clarity, a crystallinity of thought that could only be found in battle.

He offering the barrel of the Spandau with the bike idling beneath his thighs. 'The girl, hand her over.' He edged the weapon over his targets seeking a response.

Emily winced, folding her shoulder as she squirmed under the firm grip of her Arabian captor.

Al-Ruzi replied, 'Englishman, we meet again. I trust your wound is healing?' He offered the thinnest of smiles.

Weiner stood perplexed, 'What the hell?'

Steinhoff slunk cowardly behind the Aryan bulk of his Major.

'I am just here for the girl – nothing else,' Nash said.

Al-Ruzi turned calmly towards her, then rounded slowly on Nash. 'You are English … *She* is English.' He tilted his head back and belly laughed with almost genuine mirth. 'I am afraid you are very gallant, but rather late.' He swept his arm towards Weiner, 'I am on the cusp of an agreement with the Major, here. So perhaps it is he you should barter with, but then I forget … Germany and England. You are sworn enemies, are you not?'

Nash shook his head, 'So, make a new bargain for the girl and I will let you live.'

Al-Ruzi mused, 'You'll have to do better than that, Englishman. If it is our destiny to die together this day – so be it.'

Nash continued, 'The German documents – they're details of a devastating new weapon – a weapon they would rather not see in the hands of the Soviets.'

'Or the British?' Al-Ruzi countered.

'Yes, or the British.' Nash agreed, 'But it is the Soviet's that threaten you the most. Your homes are too close to the Soviet Union for comfort. Make your peace with the Russians. I have something of value. A notebook belonging to Colonel Korolev. The Russians will want it back … I could give it to you in exchange for the girl.'

Weiner growled, 'He's a liar. Just kill the English pig, he's bluffing. There is nothing to offer.'

Nash snarled, 'Major Weiner, your predecessor, Commandant Kessler, didn't think so; and your Doctor Steinhoff … well, he's been on the receiving end of British Intelligence before. First at Peenemünde, then in the Carpathians. *I know* what the Russians want to do with your device.'

Steinhoff hissed from the seclusion of Weiner's shirt tails, 'He does know – he knows *everything* – let him take the girl for the Russian notebook. If what he says is true … well, we need to stay ahead!'

Weiner lashed out, instantly finding the bridge of Steinhoff's nose. The doctor crumpled to the earth with blood

229

gushing from his face. Weiner seethed hatred in Nash's direction. 'You might cut me down, but you will not leave here alive – on that you have my word.'

Al-Ruzi interrupted, 'Enough!' He turned slowly, focussing on the Spandau as he spoke, 'Englishman, your motive to rescue the girl is righteous – there is one so cherished that I also seek.' He paused, dark eyes fixed on Nash for several seconds, before returning to Weiner, 'Major, our bargain was for weapons in exchange for the lives of your so-called Russian friends. Yet, everyone is your enemy. Now, I see your true nature.' He pulled the letter from under his cloak. 'You have no intention of releasing our beloved Heiress.' He screwed up the paper, tossing it aside. He turned towards Nash. 'We will make our peace with the Russians using the secrets of your Colonel Korolev. Take the girl, go, and leave this place.'

'No!' Steinhoff reddened. Weiner pushed him back to the floor, and then menaced his Luger towards Nash and then the Arab. He bellowed, 'Al-Ruzi! What about our deal?!'

The Arab rounded on the Major, hissing, 'I will hold you to our original bargain – take the good doctor's notebook.' He offered a look of disgust towards Steinhoff who was still snivelling in the dirt adjacent to the packing crate and then fixed on Weiner. 'Leave the guns.' Al-Ruzi took a leather pouch from under his coat, 'Take your German documents,' and tossed it into the crate of weapons. 'Go back to Germany, Major, you outstay your welcome in our lands. I will seek a higher authority to negotiate for the release of the princess. I am sure the Iranian Ambassador would be interested in your treachery.'

'Nobody move!' A tense voice whined, all eyes turned to the blood stained features of Doctor Steinhoff. He knelt over the ammunition crate, holding a grenade between both hands, and with one digit wrapped around the firing pin. 'I am leaving with *my drawings* and the girl! Or we all die!' His hands shook with uncertainty, but remained hovering inches above the explosive contents of the ammunition crate.

Weiner held his pistol firmly, glancing back and forth between Steinhoff and the Arab. Perhaps Steinhoff really had it in him to pull the pin, but there was no point hanging around to find out. 'That's right, we're leaving and we'll take the girl to ensure our safe passage – we don't want anymore little accidents on the road.'

Al-Ruzi held the Major's gaze for a second, then turned towards Emily as she struggled a thin protest under the palm of her Arabian captor. 'Release the girl.' Al-Ruzi tightened his grip on his shamshir.

Emily moved sheepishly. Her eyes pleading to Nash and then with loathing towards the Germans.

Steinhoff stood up, holding out the grenade. He flicked his head to the rear, then spoke flatly at her. 'Get in the truck. Do it now.'

Emily dragged her feet, walking morosely. The ammunition crate blocked her path. She ambled around the obstruction, coming close to Weiner as she reluctantly headed for cab.

Al-Ruzi seized on the distraction, instantly turning about, and in one fluid movement locked the Major's pistol arm. He smashed the pommel of his sword into the German's neck. Al-Ruzi screamed, 'Allahu Akbar! Allahu Akbar! Allahu Akbar!' He flung the Major aside and instantly cleaved the head of an approaching *SS* trooper.

Steinhoff gaped like a cod-fish, first at the Major sprawled at his feet and then at the severed head. He watched morosely as Al-Ruzi cut down another German soldier. Blood sprayed on to his face. He flinched, losing his hold on the grenade. The hand-held explosive rattled harmlessly into the crate. Steinhoff dabbed his fingers in the fresh blood covering his cheeks and grasping the new reality. His gazed into the weapons crate. Opportunity dawned – he lunged for the

231

document wallet, grabbing it with both hands and then scuttled backwards away from the fighting, eventually crashing into the radiator grill of the lead truck. He held the documents tightly against his chest. A fez-wearing *SS* man appeared around the side of the truck, taking up a knee firing position at his side and then firing steady shots in quick succession. A second rifleman dropped into position to cover Steinhoff's other flank.

Steinhoff rallied, 'The girl! Get the girl into the truck.' The first man scooted off, then the second. The yelps and protests of a female voice told Steinhoff that the troopers were carrying out his orders. He looked over the mêlée. The giant Persian glided amongst the *SS* troops, scything flesh from bone. The *SS* rank and file of the Muslim Brotherhood pressed their advantage, but despite being outnumbered, the Persian held. Arabic swordsmen closed quickly from the perimeter. An arrow thudded through the gullet of one young Muslim *SS* trooper, then another shaft. Al-Ruzi sunk his blade through the chest of the nearest man.

Steinhoff didn't need to be a military strategist to see the tide was already turning. He roared in Weiner's direction, 'Major! Major, we need to leave! We need to leave *now*!'

Weiner shook his head, rubbing at the throbbing sensation in his neck, he forced himself to stand. Quelling a wave of nausea and with eyes watering, he stooped, picking up his Luger from the dirt. He grasped the weapon, working the mechanism frantically. The pistol jammed, scraping flesh from his knuckles. He tossed it aside and dived at the nearest MP 40 sub-machine gun in the weapons crate. He rammed home its long, thin magazine, fuming and pumping up adrenalin. 'Enough of these Arabs!' He roared, flicking off the safety and spraying a long volley, killing swordsmen and Muslim *SS* alike. Satisfied with the slaughter, he adjusted his aim finding the Persian in his sights. It was a pity, he almost admired the man's prowess with the blade, but the Iranian had

232

out-lived his usefulness. Weiner pulled the weapon into his shoulder and reached for the trigger.

Took-a-took-a, took, took-a-took-a, took, took-a-took-a, took!

The Spandau tore a path through the German line, cutting down half a dozen *SS* adjacent to the Persian and swathing around the ammunition crate. Bullets and splinters flew asunder. Heavy rounds tracked in Weiner's direction.

Weiner rocked at the pain as one of the bullets hit home, stumbling, and almost dropping the MP 40. He reached into his shoulder, feeling the deepness of the wound and withdrew a bloodied hand. Panting, he staggered towards Steinhoff and the relative sanctuary of the truck, with the MP 40 dangling from one wrist. He balled at the doctor, 'Start the engine! Fucking move!'

Steinhoff registered the instructions and dove head first into the cab, ignoring the *SS* trooper spatting with the women now detained in the middle of the passenger seat. He probed manically around the steering column and then the wooden dashboard, 'Keys!' He slammed about amongst prayer beads, maps and general detritus, 'Where are the keys?!'

The silvery items emerged from the rot. Rounds tick-tacked into the open driver's door. Steinhoff squatted low in the driver's seat and plunged the key into the ignition, then vigorously pumped the accelerator, cursing at the steering column. 'Come on! Come on! Come on!' The truck sprang to life. He revved the engine, belching soot from the rear, then pulled the driver's door shut and poked his head out of the window, roaring. 'Major! Now!'

Steinhoff crunched the gear stick into reverse, not bothering to wait. The passenger door swung open as he dropped the clutch.

Major Weiner tossed the skinny *SS* trooper out the door by the scruff, and piled in, sandwiching Emily in the middle of the cab. He pressed a palm over his wound, 'Drive! Go! Go now!'

Steinhoff swung the vehicle in a violent reverse arc. The flatbed rattled from side to side as the scientist dropped the clutch and sought first gear.

Emily screamed, writhing in the seat. Weiner smashed a backhander into her face and bellowed across at Steinhoff, 'Drive!'

Steinhoff hit the accelerator. The truck sped forwards, engine whining. He jolted it into second. The lorry gave another spurt, pushing past the combatants. He glanced across at Weiner. The Major sat grimacing, holding his wound and spitting blood. The vehicle suddenly broke through the fracas and on to the dirt track. Steinhoff dropped the clutch again, finding third, and then floored it – speeding as fast as possible away from the battle.

Nash stood tall, with his legs apart and keeping a firm grip on the heavy machine gun. The Spandau whined empty, still smoking, and then cackled slowly to a stop. He watched as the dust cloud swallowed the German truck and Emily along with it. The gamble hadn't paid off. He tossed the Spandau aside, and ripping off his googles, grabbed the Sauer 38 from his waistband, smoothly dropping to a knee firing position as he did so. He fired a double tap. An *SS* trooper dropped. He took aim, systematically killing another, then selected a fresh target. Before he had a chance to fire, multiple Scythian arrows pierced the man's chest and back. Nash paused, roving an eye over the remaining *SS* troop, then lowered his weapon. The *SS* soldiers bunched up. The Arabs closed in on their prey. Nash watched as Al-Ruzi sliced another jugular and respectively lowered the moribund trooper to the floor.

The Persian eased towards the encircled remnants of the Waffen-*SS* Muslim Brotherhood, spreading both his arms wide and still holding his shamshir. Persian longbows held the perimeter, strings taught, awaiting final orders. The Nazi troop jostled, some lowered their rifles as Al-Ruzi came to a stop. He rested his sword arm, speaking in an almost pleading tone. 'It is God's will that you few remain – you are outnumbered.' He shrugged, 'The battle is over. Your officers have left the field. Now put down your weapons or join your comrades in the afterlife.'

A few rifles clattered to the floor, hands went into the air.

Al-Ruzi offered encouragement, 'Surrender your weapons or die.'

The last few troopers tossed their weapons into the open ground. Then hesitating, they raised their hands in the air. Al-Ruzi nodded a silent command towards the nearest swordsman. Three Persians glided into the void, hoovering up the discarded weapons, before slipping to the rear. Al-Ruzi sheathed his sword and turned towards Nash.

Nash rose to meet him, keeping a grip on the Sauer at his side.

The Arab spoke calmly, 'Englishman, your careful aim …' He smiled, beckoning with his massive palms uppermost. 'Well, you have saved my life.'

Nash offered a thin smile, taking a measure of the Persian, 'No, I was trying to save the girl.'

Al-Ruzi shook his head, 'No matter, you have saved my life – for what purpose only Allah can reveal. Nonetheless, I am now indebted to you and I vow an oath of allegiance until such time as the debt is repaid.'

Nash nodded appreciably, he spoke quietly, 'Then help me find the girl – and find her before it's too late.'

CHAPTER 27

Airstrip

Emily Sinclair moaned. Consciousness beckoned. Her throat grated, parched and gritty, brain thumping dehydration from behind her eyeballs. She tried to lift her hand to the throbbing in her cheekbone, but couldn't. Her eyes blinked open, momentarily at first, then coming into focus. An oily rag bound her wrist to a solid surface. She turned her head slowly – both wrists. She tugged pathetically. The arms of the wooden chair creaked. She fought to raise her head, feeling pain in her back as she did so and squinted into the void. Spots of light registered and then something large. Sounds bounced, echoing like seashells in her ears. She took a shallow breath and tried to open the slits that were her eyes a little further. She fixed on the side of a flatbed truck – yes – a truck. She remembered now, there was a lorry. The desert road and … and Danny!

Her eyes flashed fully open.

Abruptly, she strained at her bonds, head back and crying with frustration. She slumped for a few seconds. Then summoning fresh concentration on her right arm and gritting her teeth, she tightened her muscles. Nothing – it wouldn't budge. She exhaled, almost exhausted, and looked about the place as she struggled to recover her breath.

The hanger took shape. A corrugated tunnel, the ceiling sparsely populated with utilitarian single hanging bulbs – the military kind with green metallic shades on a length of flex.

236

Two small windows to the right offered pockets of blinding whiteness, each casting a funnel of light on to the concrete floor. The Mercedes-Benz truck sat skewed at an angle some twenty feet away. At the far end of the space, a vertical crack of light revealed the hanger doors slightly ajar. Something crackled to her rear. She strained her neck, peering, catching a glimpse from the corner of her left eye – a work station – some sort of desk in the otherwise empty space. The crackle changed pitch. A sudden whine, then more crackling. There was no mistaking it – a radio.

Shadows moved from the right. Abruptly, the hair on her head was bunched up, and painfully so. A hand tugged at her scalp and pushed her head backwards. She stared at the corrugated ceiling and the single bulb immediately overhead, whimpering. The ill-defined visage of a stranger eclipsed in and out of the light. His voice spoke from above.

'Welcome back, Comrade Akimov, I am so glad you could join us.'

She tried to focus on the face. The voice, German, male, not familiar – but she'd heard it before. Where? London? The radio crackled. No, the desert, the wadi. She gasped a breath, adrenalin jolted her to awareness. Fresh beads of sweat secreted from her hairline – *Doctor Steinhoff*.

Her eyes took full focus on the German scientist. She gasped the warm, dry air of the hanger. Her neck bones crunched under the pressure of his grip. She strained in retaliation, searching left and right with her eyeballs – for salvation, release, anything.

His voice reverberated in her skull. 'Ah! Let me enlighten you – you're wondering where you are?'

She stiffened, breathing rapid shallow breaths. The features above began to move.

The voice continued, 'Yes, an old aircraft hanger in the middle of the desert. There's no escape – but then for you – there never was.' The voice paused, 'In a few hours I will be on a plane to Germany and you will be dead. That is – after you've told me everything I want to know.' The man's face disappeared, then eased back into view, but there was a difference, intangible at first, not exactly the same. He was carrying something? Slender, silver, sharp-looking. A knife – no, a scalpel.

'Argh! No!' Emily screamed at the prospect and writhed. The chair scuffed and jolted on the concrete. She twisted her wrists and ankles against her bonds to no avail and leaving friction burns from the ragged ties. She felt her vertebrae grind as Steinhoff applied pressure. Clumps of hair tore from her flesh. The visage of Doctor Steinhoff suddenly crisped even closer. The razor edge of the medical instrument hovered.

'Ah, Fräulein Akimov. It is so tiresome, don't you think?' He spoke nonchalantly, 'Let's start with a proper introduction. You know who I am, Doctor Steinhoff, so it would only be polite.' His voice suddenly menaced, he pressed the cold, flat edge of the scalpel against her skin, 'If you could tell me your *real name.*'

Emily snarled through gritted teeth, 'Just you wait, he'll rip your heart out,' she defied the abrupt agonising tug on her hair, '… then ram it down your Nazi throat – so go to hell!'

'Now there was I thinking you were a lady of some breeding. I was obviously wrong.' He nicked her bruised cheek with the scalpel.

She stifled a whimper, her back arched momentarily and then subsided.

'Tell me *your name.* Why are you working for the *Russians*?' Not waiting for a reply, Steinhoff, took another slither of skin.

'Argh!' She writhed and then slumped. 'Alright! British! I am British.'

He released his grip.

She shook herself free, feeling the warm sticky liquid trickle from her cheek and down the side of her neck. She stared daggers at the German.

Steinhoff paced slowly in front of the chair, waving the scalpel like a magician with a wand. 'Yes, I know – you're English. That makes you a spy and a soon-to-be-dead spy: so why don't you tell me about Colonel Korolev and the contents of his notebook.'

She hissed, straining forwards in the chair, her skin prickling. 'I don't know anything about a Russian notebook. I was there to record your meeting, then report back to London – so the RAF could bomb you to hell!'

Steinhoff looked to the heavens and took a long slow breath, 'You see, that's the problem – I am afraid you'll not be allowed to report back to London, but you do need to tell me about the Russian's notebook.' He suddenly changed pace, moving quickly to the chair, leaning in close. 'What was Korolev planning to do with my device?'

Emily faced down her enemy and spoke flatly. 'I don't know, and even if I did, I wouldn't tell you.'

Steinhoff lifted his brow, 'Oh, I wouldn't be so sure, but you *will* tell me your name, Miss?' He raised the scalpel to her face. '*You're name.*'

She spat defiance, 'Sinclair, Emily Sinclair … but I promise you this – you'll lose here, you'll lose the war – and when they find me, he'll cut your heart out.'

Steinhoff nodded, 'Yes, yes, I am sure he will.' He moved closer with the scalpel.

Emily screamed.

Nash shifted uncomfortably in his saddle, adjusting the reins, and holding his mottled grey and white steed on the summit of the dune. He pulled the grubby shemagh back from his face to get a better view of the terrain below. The modest dunes ebbed into the low scrub and stones that made the valley floor. The relatively flatter terrain below was some three kilometres wide, and hemmed in on the far side by a rocky escarpment. The airstrip was clear of large stones and gorse for most of its length, but the encroaching sand would soon return it to the wilderness. A single hanger occupied a space adjacent to the nearest end of the runway.

He lifted his binoculars and scanned the construction – corrugated metal sheeting, no air vents, no smoke trails, or other signs of habitation. A single scaffold pole protruding from the far side of the roof supported an aerial. He zoomed the lens along the run of the cable: intact, black flex, new looking – somebody had made some repairs. A radio. A rendezvous point. But had the Germans already left? He moved the binoculars over the utilitarian windows on the side of the building, only to scorch his retinas on the harsh reflection. He rubbed his eyeballs momentarily and then worked the lens over the front of the building; it was hard to tell from this oblique angle, but the large sliding doors seemed to be open a crack. Either the place was already abandoned with nothing of value inside, or somebody was home. His heart skipped a beat – tyre tracks in the dirt – the kind a flatbed truck would make.

He lowered the binoculars, blinking, and rubbed the stubble on his chin, wincing at the possible options. Dust billowing on the breeze. He turned in his saddle towards the Persian. 'No movement around the building, but they have a transmitter. A plane could be on its way, or has already left.'

Al-Ruzi sat upright on his black stallion, eyes fixed on the valley below. 'These Germans think they can hide themselves in the desert and then make their escape – they should think again – these are my lands. All is seen. All is heard. They leave a trail that even a clumsy child could follow.'

'What about a plane?'

240

Al-Ruzi shook his head, 'No, not yet, the buzzards are the only creatures to have circled the sky of late.'

Nash tilted his head and puzzled, 'You read the carrion feeders?'

Al-Ruzi chuckled, 'No, just the absence of markings on the runway.' His features tightened, he pointed a finger into the distance. 'And that black fleck on the horizon moving against the wind.'

Nash sharpened, and pressing the binoculars against his eyeballs, he quickly adjusted the focus. A small, twin propeller aircraft approached; its livery of grey scale camouflage pinpointed against the azure blue sky. He mumbled a commentary as he studies the aircraft. 'You're right, it's a transport – light aircraft, not a fighter. I don't recognise the make.' He shrugged as he lowered the binoculars, 'Not British or French,' then with more urgency, 'it has to be *them* – I need to get down there.'

Al-Ruzi nodded and pivoted in his saddle, waving an arm to the rear. Horsemen moved up the dune, urging their mounts against the undertow of the ever-shifting substrate. Some twenty riders gathered upon the sandy ridge, dressed for battle, sporting their Scythian Horse bows and curved shamshirs; some with Mauser rifles and their chests draped with ammunition belts. Robes billowing in the wind. Nash sat grimy, sweating, feeling the steel of the Sauer 38 in his waistband. He lifted the thin strap of an MP 40 over his head, laying the weapon comfortably in the small of his back. He glanced up at the plane, and then at the distance across the valley to the hanger. Even if he made it down the sand dune without losing his horse, there was some half a mile or more of open ground to cover – and even at a gallop – that would leave plenty of time for the Germans to pick them off.

Nash gripped the reins of his stallion as the Arabian troop took silently to the advance. He tipped his horse forwards on to the liquid flow of the sands, leaning back in the saddle as

241

the drone of the German Siebel Fh 104 aircraft reached his ears.

Weiner stood over the wireless set, keying the handheld microphone against the static. He spoke in an overly loud and clear voice, suppressing an overwhelming desire to smash the good doctor to a pulp. 'Yes, that's confirmed – two passengers,' he glanced at Steinhoff mincing next to the woman with his hands on his hips like some effeminate school boy-come-prefect. Emily sat slumped and bloodied in the chair, 'And one prisoner, a female.'

A voice crackled another question. Weiner barely got the gist as the airwaves bounced around the hanger. He squinted into the transmitter, 'What? Destination, you say? I'll tell you when we're airborne.'

Static phased in and out, broken words, the sound of the twin propellers turning.

'What?! Say again,' Weiner thumbed the button on the handset several times. 'Say again, Weiner, over.' He waited impatiently as the set whistled and waned a plethora of variable tones. 'This is, Major Weiner, are you receiving me? Over.'

More static.

He tossed the microphone on to the bench, 'Useless crap,' and exchanged it for the sub-machine gun resting against the table leg. He checked the magazine, slapping the mechanism about and then clicking on the safety. 'Our transport, we're leaving.' He nodded at the girl, while aiming the automatic weapon deliberately at the scientist. He spoke gruffly, 'Why not get rid of her? We're done here.'

Steinhoff pushed his glasses on to the bridge of his nose and whined a reply, 'She knows about Korolev's work. I need more time.'

Weiner spat, 'Alright – but she's your baggage – you carry her.' He paused with the machine gun, observing as Steinhoff stepped towards the girl and began fiddling with the oily rags binding her wrists to the chair. The screech of rubber pierced from a distance, then again. The throaty rhythm of the twin engines, powering up and down, got louder. Weiner shouldered his weapon and reached down, pulling out his boot knife. He marched briskly over to the chair and slid the blade under her bonds. With a quick sawing action, he severed one tie, then the others. He shouted as the sound of the German aircraft intruded from outside the hanger. 'Two minutes. We leave with or without her.'

Weiner moved off towards the hanger doors at a steady jog, catching site of the Siebel aircraft trundling past the windows, and taxiing into a turn. He'd just about had enough of this Iranian shithole. The dust and relentless heat, and the snivelling Steinhoff. The little worm had half the Reich Chancellery scurrying about, with minor diplomats filing paperwork, signing this or that transaction for goods and services. Then there were the logistics of moving materials from the Soviet border and halfway across Europe. It was a bloody nightmare, and the ungrateful swine could do nothing but moan about some bitch who might, or might not, know something about the Russians – if it was relevant at all. It was time to remind the snot of his responsibilities. The good doctor would be working until he dropped; and from the moment they arrived back at Wolfsberg. He would make sure of it.

Weiner pushed on the right-hand door, leaning his shoulder into the metalwork. The runners protested, scraping metal on metal as he forced them to slide open a few metres. He jogged back across the entrance to repeat the process with the remaining door. On taking up position, his eye caught movement in the desert. He flinched, then squinted into the heat shimmer. Lines thickened on his brow. Black figures,

243

some three hundred metres away, moving over the open ground at speed – and in this direction. Men? Yes, men on horseback. But from where?

The Persian.

Weiner hollered back into the hanger as he took the machine gun off his shoulder and clicked off the safety, 'We got trouble! Move it!' He squeezed off a redundant burst in the direction of the approaching cavalry as the bulk of Siebel Fh 104 aircraft trundled to rest, blocking his view. A violent shower of grit and debris swirled up from around the rotor blades, stinging his eyes. A small aluminium door, curved like the main superstructure of the aircraft, sprung open on the side of the cockpit. The pilot beckoned towards the over-wing entrance with a firm wave of his arm, still revving the engines. The aircraft hunted against the brakes. Weiner glanced into the hanger – Steinhoff moved at a modest pace, half-dragging the girl, with one of her arms pulled over his shoulder. Weiner cursed and dashed towards the aircraft bringing his weapon up as he did so – they needed more time. He threw himself into the dirt under the main fuselage, screwing his eyes up against the localised sandstorm and engine noise. He took aim with his MP 40. Arabian horses thundered through the scrub, the riders were low and expertly shielding themselves behind the thick necks of their steeds. The seismic gallop of hooves and engine noise vibrated into his chest. Closer now – one hundred and fifty metres. He glanced down at his leg pouch, regretting the limited supply of fresh magazines and then flashed a last look towards the hanger. Steinhoff was halfway to the airplane, hauling the half-spent woman along by her waist and arm. Was the bitch stalling or really out of it? Either way he needed to buy some time.

Weiner pulled one of the spare ammunition clips from his pocket and placed it carefully at his side. He pushed the sub-machine gun into his shoulder, and at sixty metres out, hit the trigger, offering steady bursts along the enemy line. Horses

244

tumbled, whining and kicking. Riders fell – some to their deaths under the massive bulk of their animals. Others, as if well trained gymnasts, somehow rolling and gliding to their feet, despite losing their mounts. His weapon clicked empty – forty metres – he deftly removed the spent cartridge and slammed home the fresh box, instantly spraying rounds.

The charge lost momentum, horses tangled, bloodied and lathering. Others wheeling in terror as the plane engines revved loudly almost deafening, billowing sand and grit. Mauser rifles fired. Arrows loosed, falling only inches short of their mark. Weiner took to a crouching position, edging backwards under the metallic belly of the aircraft, switching his last magazine as he did so. Rounds flick-flacked in the dirt, hastening his retreat. He gave one long burst, then ducked clear of the undercarriage to find Steinhoff bundling the woman on to the stubby wing of the aircraft. Weiner snarled, backing up and holding the sub-machine gun in one hand against his hip. He shoved the woman hard with the other. She tumbled on to the wing. The pilot reached out grabbing her by the scruff as Steinhoff quickly pressed from the rear. Weiner shifted attention back to his weapon. Backed up against the wing, he menaced rounds in short strategic bursts. He bellowed, 'Move it! Get a fucking move on!' Then gave another burst, rattling bullet casings on to the sand.

Steinhoff and the woman bundled through the door. The engines resonated a new urgent tone, the fuselage stiffened. Weiner felt the aircraft wing dig into his back. Needing no further invitation, he shuffled on to the wing and then coming to a stop sitting against the cockpit door, he offered bursts of the nine millimetre rounds to any who appeared. The plane lurched forwards as his last bullet was spent.

Nash jolted hard in the saddle as his horse missed a step and half-cantered over a fallen stallion. Rounds tore into flesh –

equine and human alike. Horses screeched primeval fear, some thrashing out with their front hooves and raising on to their hindquarters; others bolted forwards retaining their riders. He glanced at the German aircraft some thirty yards away. *Emily*! *No*! He couldn't allow it. If she was taken … it was unthinkable. He dug in his heels and urged his horse onwards, and gripping the reins in one hand, lifted the MP 40 across his chest. The weapon bounced and jarred, there was no useful aim.

The metallic drone of the engines thickened as he approached the fuselage. Sharp grittiness stung in the air. Light dazzled blinding from the cockpit glass and aluminium surround. The horse abruptly swerved, digging in its heels, and giving a shrill whine. Its hooves slid in the dirt, with its legs becoming tangled. The horse concertinaed into a twisting roll. Nash let go of the reins and rolled his arms up, barely protecting his head as he was thrown from the saddle. He hit the ground hard, smashing his shoulder into the compacted gravel on sandstone, ribs and jaw shaking. He remained in a tuck, spiralling several more yards before sprawling to a stop in the dirt. Gashed on both elbows, shemagh half choking his throat, and with skin grated bloody and raw on his right shoulder, Nash pulled himself to his feet; finding the MP 40 still dangling across his chest. He lifted the weapon and let rip a high volley, firing along the top of the aircraft towards the pilot, who seemed to be leaning out the far side of the craft. Rounds cracked the heavy glass of the cockpit. He caught a fleeting glimpse – hair – long brown hair, and grubby but definitely coloured clothing.

Emily!

The engines gave a renewed whirl to the rotors. The aircraft shuddered then began rolling faster. Nash shot at the cockpit. Then hesitating on the trigger mechanism, he arced his weapon right towards the fuel tanks: then thought better of it. Still holding his MP 40, he ran at a stoop, ducking under the belly of the aircraft. He doubled along underneath the plane, keeping pace with it, waving his weapon about and seeking the enemy. None came. Momentum picked up overhead. Sweat dripped from his brow, foreboding filled his heart. 'Think! Think! Damn it to hell!'

He ditched the MP 40 in favour of the precision of his Sauer 38. He checked the slide on the weapon and taking a deep breath, swung out to the far side of the fuselage, instantly bringing the pistol up in a double-handed grip. He instinctively half-jogged in a backwards motion, staying ahead of the wing, searching with the weapon and quickly finding the grizzled bulky frame of a German officer – *Major Weiner*.

Nash fired, hardly getting off a shot before the German's spent machine gun clattered into his face. Nash winced and checked his aim to stay clear of Emily in the small passenger compartment behind the cockpit. Shadow loomed. He pressed the trigger as the heavy weight of two sized-twelve German boots planted squarely into the middle of his chest crunching his sternum and forcing air from his lungs. He fell backwards into the dirt and almost simultaneously, an anvil punch collapsed the cartilage in his nose, spraying blood in all directions. A vice-like grip found the wrist of his pistol arm. He fired as his knuckles were pummelled again the hard earth, then fired again. The Sauer slipped from his grasp as an alternate massive blow smashed into his brow.

The aircraft wing rattled over their heads.

Abruptly the weight lifted from his chest and the grip on his arm released. He kicked out and rolled on to his knees, blinking blood and dust from his eyes and then groped in the dirt for his pistol – but not finding it.

The engines roared.

Nash looked up as the huge Major launched himself at the aircraft wing. The plane tilted momentarily with sudden extra load, but continued on its path. The German scrabbled belly first on to the wing and with one leg dragging in the dirt. The plane picked up speed.

'No! Emily!' Nash broke into a sprint, drawing a stiletto from the pouch in the small of his back. He pumped adrenalin, head down and charged towards the rear of the wing. The plane hunted briefly, then found more speed. The German struggled for purchase on the edge of the wing.

Nash lunged, burying his knife deep in the back of the Major's calf and twisting the blade for good measure. He grappled for a handhold on the Major's clothing with the other. The solid earth dragged at his ankles, stones cracked into his shins and the rough terrain threatened to rip them both from the aircraft.

Weiner rolled sideways.

Nash held on and pulled the knife free and plunged the blade again into the German's thigh. He yelled, '*Stop the plane*!' He stabbed again.

A heavy boot jarred into his jaw, then again. Flesh tore numbly on his ear. His neck crunched with each blow. Boot, blood and dust blurred his vision. He peered at the German figure. Words roared in his direction, punctuated by heavy duty footwear, '*Scheisse, Ficken Engländer*,'

Nash pulled the knife free, half-blinded, and rammed it home again as Weiner's boot found his jaw line: cracking teeth, tearing sinew. Nash shuddered an involuntary spasm as his neck snapped back against the humongous force and with his shoulder dislocating. His fingers released, no longer able to grip on the German's belt. He clawed at the German's leg as gravity and another generous helping of Nazi boot leather forced his from the plane.

248

CHAPTER 28

London

Danny Nash lay on his bunk, having not bothered to undress, dishevelled in crumpled combat trousers and a khaki woollen shirt. He stared at the ceiling, feeling vacant and bemused. Frustration simmered to a boil just below the surface. Perhaps he'd just been kidding himself. If he had the guts for it, he'd acknowledge the truth. Tell it like it really was. His mission had failed, *he had failed*. He couldn't beat this one out of his system – not this time. No amount of weapons drills, beastings at the gym, or hard runs could flush the failure away. It kept playing over and over in his head like a Pathé newsreel. The dumpy Siebel Fh 104 transport, moving down the airstrip. Its squat wings shuddering, wheels bouncing once, twice, three times over the rough ground. Then the shrill of the engine as the aircraft finally lifted off – taking with it Germany's most guarded secrets and maladjusted ambitions – but most of all, taking her. Taking Emily away to a place of certain torment and likely torture. To be discarded once all useful intelligence had been gleaned. Her voice still ringing in his mind's eye, pleading, calling his name, again and again. Then the prospect of her prison cell, dank and lonely. Brutish German soldiers ravaging her pale flesh, taking turns to intimately abuse the prisoner.

Nash bolted upright on the horsehair mattress, sweating and his heart pounding. He swung his feet onto the floor and pinched the bridge of his nose, then shaking his head clear. His mission had been to *watch her back*. Sinclair's words echoed in his skull. *Watch her back*. He should have tried harder, anticipated the enemy, and been more prepared. He laced up his boots and stretched to a standing position. Then limped across the empty billet, passing three other utilitarian metal cots devoid of bedding, and towards the workbench at the back of the room. He picked up his pistol, quickly dismantling it into its individual components. Then, dabbing a tiny drop of gun oil on to a rag, he began cleaning his weapon.

He'd find her, no matter the cost, no matter how long – or how many lives he'd have to take on the way. Remorse, guilt, vengeance, aggression, and then desolation: the cycle always had the same ending. Alive, but not living. A squat in Bermondsey, but no friends. Loneliness, with only memories of those already departed. A veneer of self-reliance that kept it all from crashing in. She could break the cycle. She *had* broken the cycle. He'd been a fool to not let her in, closer, to where it really mattered. To the place where he could be … well, just a man. Normal. Nash fumed as he reassembled the weapon. He worked fluidly: slotting the mechanism and slide into place, checking the spring, eyeing the clear barrel, slamming home a magazine, safety off, then cocking the weapon. He pressed the trigger.

Click!

Twelve seconds.

Was that it? Was that all there was? To drill, wage war and to die?

Perhaps not even that.

Steinhoff sat weasel-like in his brown laboratory coat. The grease marks on his sweaty face spoke of determined industry. The breast pocket of his overall stuffed full of

250

assorted screwdrivers, callipers, pencils and scraps of notepaper declared his status. He pushed his thick glasses back on to the bridge of his nose and stared at Emily Sinclair across his desk. She sat looking nervous on a utilitarian chair. The heavy clink of metal on metal, the movement of chains and the occasional burst of an industrial lathe, echoed into the small space from the shop floor.

'Fräulein, you should really consider your predicament. You are in an underground fortress and surrounded by guards.' He opened his hands and pouted, 'So, you see your friends will not be coming for you.' He paused eyeing her up and down, pleased with her figure in the short black skirt and white blouse. He'd selected the clothing himself. The bruising on her face was unfortunate, but par for the course, and the stitches on her cheek would leave a nice little scar. 'There is no escape so you may as well cooperate. If you do, you will be treated fairly – and if you do not.' He slowly clasped his hands together resting them under his chin. He offered a sickly smile and then reached into the pocket of his overalls, withdrawing a sharpened pencil. He toyed with it in his hand. 'You appreciate my position of course. I do need to understand what Korolev shared with you. It's a matter of policy for Berlin.' His voice suddenly hardened, 'But for me it's personal.' He stood up and walked slowly around the desk.

Emily sat stiffly with her knees together, back upright and hands clasped tightly to the edge of her seat. Her hair was tied back with what looked like a bootlace. Her voice was broken, dry, yet the tone offering a modicum of defiance. She gave a deathly look. 'To hell with Berlin and I've already sampled your notion of *being fair*.'

Steinhoff placated, smiling, choosing to mask his irritation. 'I am willing to overlook your little tantrum in Iran. If you tell me about Korolev's notebook, then there will be

251

hot food waiting for you in your cell, even some soap and warm water.'

She spat a reply, burying her fatigue, 'Damn you and your bloody Adolf.'

Steinhoff shook his head slowly, mocking. 'There you see. You make it difficult for us to get along.' He gripped the pencil in his right hand and leant over her, placing his free palm heavily on her shoulder. 'Why did Korolev want my device? What did he intend to do with it?'

Emily played deadpan, 'I don't know.'

'What did Korolev need, why was he really in Iran? *Why*?'

Emily flinched, but remained silent.

Steinhoff snarled, edging closer to her face with each question. '*What* did Korolev tell you? *What* was he working on? *What* was in his notebook?'

Emily grimaced, 'I'll keep my answers brief so that even a moron like you can understand.' She hissed, 'I don't know! I don't know! I don't bloody know!'

'You test me too much, Fräulein.' Steinhoff almost whined, 'Please give me a proper answer.'

'I already told you a thousand times. I don't know!'

'I will ask you again, what was Korolev planning? To use my device? In what way?'

'You're the engineer, you figure it out.'

Steinhoff twisted a wretched expression and then exploded, 'You will tell me – *Bitch*!' He plunged the pencil hard into the top of her knee cap, twisting it, splintering the wood and simultaneously applying pressure to her shoulder to hold her in the chair. Blood frothed from the wound. She snorted deep breaths, mouth closed tight and stifling the agony. Silent tears rolling down her face.

Steinhoff held over the pencil. His voice found a sudden calm. 'Let me guess. Korolev has made a Soviet rocket or supersonic aircraft. He needs my device to make it fly? Doesn't he?'

Emily flicked her eyes back and forth.

'I'll take that as a yes … The Russians want my device for a superior weapons system of their own. Fräulein, you could have saved yourself a lot of trouble. Tell me about this Russian technology. Korolev was ready with something, wasn't he?'

Emily sobbed in silence.

'It's something special, I can feel it … yes … Korolev is clever. What did he make – a supersonic aircraft, big and destructive?' He paused answering his own question, 'Yes, too big. He couldn't get it off the ground. Am I getting warmer, Fräulein?' He pulled the remains of the pencil from her knee.

Emily screamed, doubling over with the pain.

'How big is the Russian craft? Did Korolev mention its range? Its payload? What about his notebook? Sketches, drawings? What did you see?' He stood in front of the woman as she grovelled in the chair.

Her sudden movement barely had time to register.

Agony erupted in his groin, electrifying his spinal cord and stunning his brain. Steinhoff collapsed to the deck, gasping, 'You bitch!' He hunted for breath, 'You fucking bitch.' He squirmed on the floor with his hands over his genitals.

A figure briskly filled the doorway.

Steinhoff looked up amid flushes of pain. Major Weiner stood tall in a pristine new uniform, his biceps bulging in the jacket. He tossed a file on to the desk.

Weiner beamed a smile down at the scientist. 'I see you're getting to know your girlfriend.' He took pleasure in his minion's discomfort for a few more seconds, then glanced at the young woman. 'It seems she's useful after all.'

Steinhoff tried to focus through sharp pulsations, 'What are you talking about?'

Weiner scoffed, 'Take a look in the file. One Emily Sinclair. Mother, a Soviet citizen. Father, an Englishman – but no ordinary Englishman.'

Steinhoff puzzled, 'What?'

Weiner fixed Emily with a firm stare, 'A decorated naval officer and head of British Intelligence – Admiral Sinclair is it?'

Emily blanched.

Weiner nodded and spoke evenly, 'Yes, you've every right to show fear. If you think Doctor Steinhoff here is a nasty piece of work, you'll soon be begging to come back to him. It seems *SS* Division in Berlin is interested in meeting you. They're on their way now.' He knelt down next to her and continued in almost a whisper. 'Above my rank to interfere you understand. They're sending a real specialist – you'll experience the true meaning of suffering before they allow you to die … that's of course if they let you. They can keep a prisoner hanging to life by a thread for days, even weeks. Believe me, you'll be begging for death long before the end.'

Nash slunk up the stairs, two steps at a time. His boots clomped on the Paisley carpet. It was already late into the evening and preparations had taken most of the day. He cleared the top step and moved at a pace down the corridor, passing several office doors. The dark oak monoliths with their years of wood stain and old furniture polish felt dull and stuffy. Only the freshly polished brass of their door knobs, and the office nameplates, offered some cheer. Nash shook his head. The world was falling into utter chaos and yet someone, somewhere, still cared about the polishing. He rolled down the sleeves on his green army-issue pullover and adjusted the canvas waist belt around his middle as he approached the end of the hall. The door to the Soviet office was ajar. He cleared his throat, wrapped on the door twice and then entered. He shuffled a couple of feet and came to an uncertain stop as he looked across at Emily's desk. Sir Hugh Sinclair sat stretched out in her chair, with the collar of his silk shirt undone and his tie missing. His jacket draped over the radio on the desk. He held a crystal glass in one hand, gently swirling the amber contents. A bottle of single malt sat on the desk amongst a pile of large photographic prints. Nash decided not to comment, 'Sir, you wanted to see me?' He roved an eye over the thick volumes that lined the bookshelves and then the papers stacked in boxes about the room as he waited.

Sinclair waved him over, his voice a little subdued. 'Yes, come in, Danny, a scotch?' He poured another glass without waiting for a reply.

Nash stood at the end of the desk and accepted the glass. 'Thanks.' He took a sip, the smoky heat of the spirit burned his gullet. He waited a few seconds, before speaking. 'Sir, I have assembled the troop. They're good men, reliable, and very capable. We've been rehearsing manoeuvres all day: tactical assaults on heavily defended positions, close quarter battle, and fighting withdrawals. But it would help to firm up the plan. How we make entry into the target and the most vulnerable points to concentrate our assault.'

Sinclair took a swallow of his whisky, then winced, 'Vulnerable points? It's a stronghold. Mostly subterranean and heavily fortified – the enemy don't have any weak spots, except for one.'

Nash puzzled, 'Sir?'

'They have to breathe – and in an underground facility with that much traffic there will be ventilation shafts. That's your way in.'

'Sir, how do we know that's an option?'

'We have some intelligence from the RAF, thanks to a couple of free Polish airmen who were willing to take a big risk.' Sinclair sat forwards, placing his glass aside and moving the bottle of scotch. He pulled a large print from the array of photographs on the desk. 'The resolution is just about enough. See here,' He ran his finger over the aerial image. 'Patches where the trees have been felled. Cuboidal structures, clearly man-made and recent; not very big, likely a yard square.'

Nash perched on the edge of the desk, staring down at the grainy black and white for several seconds.

Sinclair spoke with an optimistic tone. 'What else could they be?'

Nash picked up the photograph, almost pressing his nose into the image as he squinted at the detail of the structure. 'I am not sure, sir. They could be air shafts, but then again, they might just be concrete blocks?'

Sinclair shook his head, 'No, not concrete – look at this.' He offered another picture, pointing to a large wall near the main entrance to the facility. 'The grain and hue is different. This is concrete.' He prodded the photograph, then looked at Nash. 'Those cubes are not, they're alloy or something similar, but not concrete.'

Nash considered the prospect of an air shaft with its vertical smooth surfaces, no grip and utter confinement: a single casualty could block any advance, or indeed escape. It was a rat trap. He kept the thought to himself. 'Alright, sir. Let's suppose these are ventilation shafts of some kind – we still don't know what's on the other side of the grill. We could be hundreds of feet off the cavern floor, follow a shaft into a locked store room, or worse – land in the officer's mess.'

Sinclair nodded slowly, 'Yes, I am afraid so. You'll just have to take pot luck. There aren't any other choices.'

Nash took another sip of scotch and shook his head slowly, exhaling, 'I just wish we had a bit more intelligence. Our only advantage is the element of surprise, getting in and out quickly will define the outcome. We don't even know if she's there …' Nash suddenly felt helpless, filled with remorse.

Sinclair dropped the photographs on the desk and rubbed his eyes, exhausted. 'Where else would they take her? They've gone to the trouble of bundling her into a plane to Germany. They think she knows about Korolev's work. It makes sense to go where the construction is. It is secure, she's potentially a high value prisoner, and any information gleaned can be put to use immediately. *She has to be there*.'

Nash wanted to explain. Say how he felt about Emily, about Sinclair – the closest thing he'd ever had to a father figure – about regrets, not telling Emily that he loved her and not having the guts to ask for her hand in marriage. She was the best thing to ever happen, and he knew it. 'Sir, I … I wish … I mean … I.'

Sinclair cut him off with a wave of his palm. His voice had a broken edge, his bloodshot eyes almost pleading. 'She is there. Your task is to get in and bring Emily out.'

Nash studied Sinclair's face and then spoke in almost a whisper, holding back tears 'Sir, I … I will find her. Not matter what happens, I will find her.' He repeated.

Sinclair nodded appreciatively, 'Danny, I know, if anyone can …' He suddenly took a deep breath and became more businesslike. 'Well, we should keep a clear head and focus on the mission parameters.'

Nash shook himself from the doldrums. 'Yes, yes, of course, sir.'

Sinclair continued, 'But that's not all. The operation has been sanctioned on one condition – we maximise disruption of their factory and incapacitate as many of their engineers as possible.'

Nash forced a modicum of composure. 'Sir, this is a rescue mission – if I stop to fight, I'll lose the element of surprise.'

'That's why I am coming with you.'

Nash did a double take, 'Sir? You're what? I don't understand.'

257

'I know it's a little irregular, but I will be leading the second team. You'll have thirty minutes to infiltrate the enemy and make your escape. After that …' Sinclair opened his palms and gave a wry look.

Nash furrowed his brow, 'You're going to level the place? But there'll be no time to set proper demolition charges, not without more men.'

'You're right and the underground complex is likely too large to cover in the time available – that's why our strategy will be area denial.'

'Area denial? I don't follow you, sir.'

'The intelligence from you're little trip to I. G. Farben ruffled a few feathers in the Cabinet Office. The Germans have their *Zyklon B*, which our boffins say is designed for chemical warfare. We'll be giving the Nazis a taste of their own medicine – area denial – we're going to make the place so badly contaminated as to render it unusable for decades.'

Nash stiffened, a grim expression fixed. 'Sir, there must be some other way? You've acquired their *Zyklon B*? Gas is indiscriminate, my men, *Emily*?'

Sinclair shook his head, 'I know … I know. If there was any other path, I would take it – but there isn't.' He paused and stared hard at Nash, then swallowed. 'We use mustard gas, and Lewisite from the Americans. We parachute in under the cover of darkness. Travel light, move fast.'

Nash blanched, 'Sir, Emily will be in danger. Besides, any use of such chemicals will infuriate the Russians and give the German High Command the opportunity to strengthen their pact with the Soviets – we will never win this war if that happens. The Red Army could march west into Eastern Europe with the blessing of that madman, Hitler.'

Sinclair gulped back the remains of his scotch, then hardened, 'Thirty minutes, Major Nash, after that we poison the place – and as for the Russians – I am sure they'd like to know about the chemical agents their so-called German allies have been making in secret. No, the Soviets will turn a blind eye as long as they get Korolev's notebook back. Even if I have to take it to Moscow myself.'

CHAPTER 29

Wolfsberg

Nash felt the freshness of the light wind as he descended and a little ungainly with the weight of his rucksack dangling between his legs. The harness tugged at his shoulders with each twist and turn of the parachute. He pulled gently on the control cords and looked up into the silk canopy, cursing its crystalline reflection in the moonlight. He coaxed the parachute across the breeze, desperately trying to correlate the map he'd memorised of the terrain with the blackness below. The landing site had to be there. They'd come in from the east, using the mountainside for cover. With any luck their arrival would go unnoticed. He glanced to his right, barely able to pick out the next man descending through the drop zone. A silent commando of the finest men, but they needed the element of surprise. Everything depended on it.

His feet suddenly brushed light and airy over a treetop. Branches rustled. A stand of silver birch, then a clearing. He raised his knees, pulling harder on the control cords, stalling the chute. The canopy billowed momentarily then swung like a pendulum. Nash twisted the control ropes and plummeted the last fifty feet as he committed to the landing. He hit the ground and sunk into the boggy meadow, then flounced over the soft terrain, being dragged by his harness for several yards before coming to rest. Wet moss and grass instantly soaked his combat fatigues. He rolled on to his knees and quickly gathered in the canopy, then unclipping his rucksack and the harness. He bundled the parachute tight, placing it under his left knee, then efficiently donned his backpack and positioned the British-made Sten sub-machine gun across his lap. He checked the long thin magazine, replacing it in the side of the automatic weapon and clicking off the safety. Then remained hunched, at the ready, waiting, as gentle thuds in the cool night told of more commandos arriving in the drop zone.

Shadowy figures moved in the darkness, working methodically. A layer of ground mist seemed to dampen down the sounds of their arrival. Nash whispered harshly, 'On me, Nash, Major Nash!'

Men gravitated towards his position. Faces and hands were blacked up with camouflage cream. Scarf commando caps covering their heads. Some carried climbing ropes, others rucksacks – all heavily armed with Sten guns, grenades, pistols and stabbing weapons. Nash checked the luminous dial of his *Kreigsmarine* watch: two a.m. Three and half hours before sun up. They'd need to be in, out, and well on their way to the rendezvous point close to the Ukranian border by then. Korolev's notebook was some insurance policy – and a bad idea. He only hoped Sinclair's little conversations with Moscow had filtered down to the Red Army in the sticks.

A bulky apparition approached. Nash tensed on the Sten gun and then relaxed – Al-Ruzi. The Persian squatted at his side, dressed in tightly wound jet black silks. Slits in the garment revealed only the cold eyes of the assassin. He carried a climbing rope across his chest. Nash noticed the handle of a short sword poking from a fold in his clothes, and wondered how many other razor sharp instruments of death the Persian carried. He whispered to the Arab, 'You made it down alright?'

Al-Ruzi nodded, only the whites of his eyes moved, he spoke softly. 'Indeed, I look forward to reacquainting myself with the Major Weiner.'

261

An agile streak moved into the huddle. Nash looked across at the new arrival. 'Sir?'

Sinclair stared back. 'Everyone down safely?'

Nash replied in a whisper, 'Yes, sir. I think so.'

Sinclair checked the mechanism on his machine gun, then scanned up the slope of the small mountain. 'We'd better get going, we need to be on station in no more than one hour. We move in our teams as planned.'

Nash rasped a reply, and got to his feet, holding the machine gun low across his chest. He moved off across the clearing and into the tree line. Men followed at three yard intervals; disciplined, fit and ready for war.

Emily Sinclair panted gently, controlling her breathing as she rolled up the sleeves on her over-sized boiler suit. The black garment clung in folds to the moisture on her back and chest. The insoles of her threadbare plimsolls, presumably taken from one of the slave labourers, stuck to her bare feet. She adjusted her grip on the metal tube that once served as a table leg and look about the cell. A single bulb provided a dull glow, extenuating the unevenness of the chiselled rock. The single mattress on the floor offered no utility or means of escape. The now broken, small alloy table listed against the wall.

She stared determination at the steel door and jammed the table leg into the narrow gap between the locking mechanism and the solid frame and worked the alloy pole against the curved edge of the retaining bolt, scraping metal on metal. The bolt jostled in the mechanism, but otherwise remained fast. She withdrew the table leg and flattened the alloy into a better wedge shape, then tried it again, squinted at the lock and feeling for the slightest give. She dragged metallic scratches over the bolt and eased it back a fraction of an inch, before it snapped back into place.

Damn it!

She withdrew her make-shift jemmy and repositioning the instrument, then applied pressure at a slightly different angle. The latch bolt moved on its spring, but only fractionally. She walked the pipe another couple of millimetres, keeping up the pressure. The bolt moved back a little more – then sprang closed. The metallic sound echoed around the cell.

Bloody hell! Damned it to bloody hell!

A voice suddenly drifted from outside, getting louder, but not urgent. Boots shuffled against stone.

Emily froze with table leg in hand, panting, and with her heart in her mouth.

The voice complained, mumbling German and then the sound of keys rattling into the lock. The mechanism turned.

She lifted the table leg over her head, grasping it with both hands and pumping up the adrenalin, then stabbed out with all her strength as the door opened.

The guard gasped silent surprise, dropping the keys and groping for the jagged alloy protruding between his collar bone and jugular. Blood thickened from the wound, soaking his shirt as he sunk to his knees, gaping.

Her mind raced. Her stomach churned. Frantic, she pressed all her weight on to the make-shift weapon forcing it further into the man's chest.

He stiffened, gurgling more fluid and then collapsed forwards.

She felt sick and horrified. The plan had evolved as far as getting the door open and killing the guard wasn't part of it. She swallowed back the bile filling her gullet and willing herself forwards, she grabbed the moribund soldier by the shirt collar; hauling the flaccid body into the cell and smearing a red congealed stickiness across the sandstone. She stepped over the warm corpse, closing the door ajar, then stared at nothing for several seconds, hyperventilating.

Think! Think!

She grabbed the bunch of keys from the floor and bundled them into her pocket. Then, all fingers and thumbs, she scrabbled about the German's waistline; finding a canvas pouch. She hastily withdrew the soldier's sidearm from its holster and then remembering her training she clicked back the slide, chambering a round and then put the safety on. She rested the weapon in her lap as she searched the poor soldier's pockets, gathering a spare 7.65 mm pistol mag, a pocket knife and a metal whistle. She shoved the items in her overalls, then picked up the handgun. The German FN Herstal felt light enough and the slim pistol grip seemed to fit neatly into her palm. She checked the safety again, this time leaving it off. Satisfied, she eased to her feet and feeling regret for the expired guard, headed for the door.

She pushed it open and moved cautiously from the cell. The gangway was just about wide enough for two people. Naked bulbs were screwed into a cable at random intervals in the low arched ceiling. The air smelt of damp and earth. She craned her neck to the left, then to the right. The undulations of the hand-chiselled passage limited her vision to some twenty yards in either direction. She gulped back fear and pulled the door quietly to a close. Then, with her weapon up, she moved strategically down the corridor – exactly as Danny had taught her.

Nash stared down the square shaft. A cube of brightness marked the bottom of the construction some fifty feet below. The walls looked neatly excavated in the rock, and thankfully, only the upper reaches were lined smooth with alloy sheeting. He stood upright and then turning his back to the shaft, tugged on the half inch thick climbing rope; hoping the anchoring point on the adjacent tree stump would hold. Then, pulling the green commando scarf cap tightly on to his head, he slid the Sten gun under his arm and against his neat rucksack. He instinctively ran a palm over the small of his back, checking his pouch of stiletto throwing knives, then examined his waist belt to ensure the pistol was properly holstered. Grenades and spare magazines bulged in his thigh pouches. He took up the slack on the rope and stepped over the metal rim, pressing his toes into the metalwork and leaning backwards. The rope creaked under the strain.

He glanced at the Persian wondering if they would make it – he didn't doubt the man's ability with a sword, but this was going to be a different fight. The Arab had made a blood oath. Nash somehow felt comfortable with the change of allegiance: any battle-hardened soldier could understood a debt of honour and his gut told him it was genuine. Sinclair had even recognised the cultural significance of the Iranian's pledge. The Arab also had a vested interest in seeing the Russians placated with the return of Korolev's notebook. Still, it looked as if the Persian had his own method of commando-style warfare. 'You sure you want to bring that thing with you?' Nash nodded towards the Scythian Horse bow and quiver of arrows on the Persian's back.

Al-Ruzi chuckled, 'Indeed, range, silence and accuracy for when we need it, Major Nash.'

Sinclair interrupted, stepping up to the rim of the ventilation shaft, sweat and camouflage cream steaked across his face. He prodded a staccato-like finger at his wristwatch, hissing at Nash, 'On my mark!' He counted down.

Nash checked the luminescent dial on his *Kreigsmarine*.

'Mark!' Sinclair growled. 'Thirty minutes, Major. After that, this shaft will be a poisonous fume.'

Nash nodded a silent reply and turned Al-Ruzi, 'I'll see you at the bottom of the shaft – wait until I am clear of the rope.' He slipped the stop knot and disappeared into the void.

Nash pressed the edges of his boots into rock and ducked down between his own legs, gripping the wire grill with both hands. The weight in his rucksack pressed down on his neck and threated his balance. He pushed gently at the grating, getting a measure of it, and then jolted his left arm forwards, forcing the grill open. The metal grid dangled on flimsy hinges. He adjusted his footing, and taking a handhold on the rope still dangling in the shaft, he peered below.

The factory floor came into view, with the noise of industrial lathes, drills and machinery abruptly filling his ears. Men in brown overalls, others in white laboratory coats, were dotted about the place. He scanned the scene moving his eyes methodically from left to right. A large expanse of rock had been excavated to make the cavern. He estimated the dimensions – some seventy yards long and around sixty feet wide – about the size of four tennis courts, only this wasn't Wimbledon. The space was divided into open plan concrete bays that ran the length of the large tunnel. The place looked busy. Each bay contained tools and materials, some with gas bottles and welding equipment, others with machinery for cutting metal sheeting. His eyes fell on the central section of the factory floor and froze.

The German device.

Only bigger than the one he'd seen at Peenemünde. Three of the bays each hosted tubular missile-like structures. Cables ran from the sides of two of the devices, like technological placentas giving life to the monstrous creations. One of the beasts was awake – a red plasma glowed hot in the centre of the furthest device. A man stood next to it, making notes on a clipboard. The man wore glasses, dark hair and the way he moved seemed familiar.

Was it *Steinhoff?* Perhaps. Suddenly, the hollow metallic sound of heavy boots clunking on steel penetrated his thoughts. They were close and rhythmic, at least one pair of boots. The vibrations got louder and with metal squeaking with the footfalls. Nash darted his head back into the void and eased the grill almost shut.

Bloody fool!

He'd nearly missed it – a steel gantry running behind him, only a few feet from the ventilation shaft. Nash watched through the grating as a German trooper walked past, rifle slung on his shoulder, but keeping a steady pace and glancing periodically down at the factory floor; going through the motions but nonetheless alert. Nash waited as the footfalls faded into the distance and then glanced up the shaft to Al-Ruzi. The Arab stood braced against the shaft, holding the rope firmly. Nash whispered, 'It looks like we're in business. There's a steel gantry just behind us – cover me.' Without waiting for a reply, Nash eased the grill open and risked a peek in both directions along the aerial walkway. The section seemed clear, although twenty yards to his right, the structure turned in front of a small office space, blocking the view. Stairs ran down from the office to the factory floor.

Nash tested the metal rim of the ventilation shaft. Fine grains of rock crumbled from the edges. It would have to do. He repositioned his Sten gun under his arm. Then pulling the straps tight on his rucksack and gripping the metal rim with both hands, he dropped through the hole and flung himself at the gangway.

He landed hard and catching his rucksack on the railings. The gantry shuddered. He flattened his stomach and chest against the open mesh flooring and remained motionless, waiting for the vibrations and sound to dissipate. He looked through the floor grid, cold sweat dripping from his brow. Two engineers continued their work below, seemingly oblivious to his arrival.

He slowly retrieved his Sten gun and shifted gingerly to the rear wall of the gantry, pressing himself against the damp rock. The place was enormous. How was he supposed to find her amongst all this? Clicking the safety off his machine gun,

267

he nodded up towards the shaft. Al-Ruzi appeared, and in one fluid ghostly movement, swung on to the walkway barely making a sound. The Persian crouched at his side, bow in hand, gently resting an arrow on the string with his forefingers.

Nash grizzled, 'We move. Down the gangway, check the offices first. If no luck, there must be some kind of holding area, cells or storerooms.'

Al-Ruzi nodded towards the shop floor, 'Are those the deathly new weapons you speak of? They seem almost ready.'

'Yes, the bastards have a production line. We'll do what we can – but the girl first. Understand?'

'Down!' Abruptly Al-Ruzi pushed Nash to the floor, adeptly loosing an arrow from a kneeling position.

The shaft thudded home into the gullet of a trooper. The man dropped dead on to the gantry, his rifle clattering on the mezzanine.

Nash stiffened, then nodding a quick thanks, before moving off in half-crouching monkey run and holding his Sten gun in both hands. Al-Ruzi followed, placing another arrow on his bow. They made the distance quickly. Nash pulled up adjacent to the window frame of the first shed-come-office space. He glanced inside.

Empty.

He ducked low, stopping at the door of the next room. He pushed it open and stomped in, showing the Sten gun about the place.

Nothing.

He shuffled backwards out of the door and on to the decking and then turned, aiming his weapon down the stairs. He tensed on the trigger, heart pounding, with rapid shallow breaths, his eyes flicking up and down the factory floor, then back to the stairs.

Where is she?!

He descended the flight of steps at speed, keeping the machine gun at the ready and then dropped to one knee at the bottom, holding the ground and allowing Al-Ruzi to glide past. The Persian took up position next to a lathe, offering the tautness of his bow to their perimeter. Suddenly, a middle-aged man in overalls turned the corner. He looked up from his clipboard, pencil slipping from his grasp as he registered the giant Persian.

Nash crouched, coiled, finger on the trigger. Al-Ruzi held the technician in his aim, but didn't take the shot. Instantly, Nash leapt from the sidelines, crossing the Persian's arc of fire. Then forcing a hand over the technician's mouth, he wrestled the man to the ground and simultaneously drew a blade from his knife pouch. Nash twisted the weapon home, shredding kidney and severing abdominal arteries. He held on as the engineer thrashed and finally expiring. Then he whipped the blade from the corpse, giving the Persian a questioning look. Nash hissed as he stowed his knife, 'Where were you?!'

Al-Ruzi closed, targeting the bow across the concrete bay as he did so. He spoke without looking down, 'Doctor Steinhoff, I caught a glimpse. I am sure it was him.'

Nash hunted an eye amongst the machinery and concrete divides. 'Where!?'He took up his Sten gun.

Al-Ruzi gestured with his bow, 'Two bays along on the left, maybe three.'

Nash scrambled to his feet and scurrying to the edge of the adjacent concrete plinth, glanced into the next bay. On the far side, two engineers in brown overalls worked at a bench, their backs keeping them oblivious to the threat. A single trooper stood a few feet away with his rifle at ease on his shoulder and looking disinterested in his surroundings.

Nash pointed at the soldier, 'I'll move on three, then you take him down.'

Al-Ruzi flashed a silent reply and took aim.

Nash counted in his head, showing fingers at his side. *One ... two ... three.*

An almost silent whoosh of air passed his ear as he broke from cover. The arrow struck, burying into the soldier's chest, then another. The trooper toppled backwards. Nash sprinted for the bench, drawing a stiletto. One of the engineers turned towards the sudden commotion, his brow furrowing. Nash swiped the blade across his gullet, severing windpipe and major blood vessels, and then moving in a fluid arc grabbed the remaining scientist by the throat. He pushed the engineer backwards over the bench, forcing the man off balance and plunging the throwing knife into his heart – but too late.

'Argh! Argh!'

A scream issued, gurgling at first, but then roaring, primeval and echoing around the cavern.

CHAPTER 30

Last Man Standing

S hots rang out, singularly at first, then more. A rapid burst came from the gantry overhead. Al-Ruzi turned, loosing arrows in quick succession – two troopers fell to their deaths. Nash let rip, spraying the metal decking with rounds from his Sten gun, then bellowed towards the Persian, 'We get Steinhoff! He'll take us to her!' He rattled the magazine empty, then dropped to one knee, flipping out the spent cartridge and slamming home another. He offered another burst to their rear.

Soldiers filed on to the gantry at the far end of the cavern. Shots echoed from multiple positions across the factory floor.

Nash fired controlled bursts, 'We move!'

He turned the corner, sprinting into the next bay and letting the Sten gun do the talking. The massive alloy tube of the Nazi superweapon loomed centre stage. Rounds flick-flacked off machinery. Engineers scattered in all directions, discarding their tools and swerving to avoid automatic fire. Nash slid to a halt against the massive timbers cradling the device and found cover. Resting his machine gun against the woodwork, he tore off his rucksack and fished inside. The device *was* bigger than the prototype he'd seem at Peenemünde, and complete. Could it travel further? Target London? Certainly. Perhaps even New York. And with a heavier payload, what new level of destruction could the weapon bring? He flashed a glimpse at the power cables running from the ignition plate in the side of the weapon and found what he was looking for as Al-Ruzi rolled to his side, firing arrows in quick succession.

Nash held the beehive mine in his hand and then stood up, ramming the three metal prongs on the base of the conical explosive charge into the side of titanium alloy skin of the Nazi device. The shaped charge would do the trick. Working quickly, he took a copper timing pencil from his rucksack and forced it into the top of the charge.

Al-Ruzi towered at his side, still firing. 'Major Nash! We cannot stay here! What about the woman?'

Nash shouted still concentrating as he found the pliers in his pack, 'Almost done!' Then pressing gently, he partly crushed the copper tube of the timing pencil and the glass vial of acid within. The corrosive liquid would soon eat through the thin wire holding back the firing pin, blowing everything to smithereens. Nash shouldered his rucksack and grabbed his weapon, 'Let's go!' He didn't wait for the Persian to reply.

Scooting low and using the device for concealment, Nash rounded the end of the timber cradle, then ducked back almost immediately. Automatic fire splintered wood into his cheekbone and deafened his ears. Numbness took the side of his face. He shook his senses clear. The large open tube of the device pulsated. The structure seemed to beckon. Its gleaming titanium alloy exterior contrasting with the black carbon-coating within. The lumen of the creation sapping energy, offering utter darkness, all consuming – the secret of its monumental power. He changed out his magazine and flicked back the slide on his weapon and glanced at his watch.

Seventeen minutes – then Sinclair would turn the place into a toxic wasteland.

Where the hell was the Persian?

He leaned out from cover, firing a burst from the Sten gun. Rounds flashed back, tearing up the timbers in reply. Nash squatted, almost under the cradle and keeping a firm grip on his weapon. He peeked up at the gantry – troops, twenty yards, approaching fast. The enemy were closing in on all sides.

Bollocks!

Digging into his thigh pocket, fuming, he produced two grenades. He pulled the pin on the first charge with his teeth and tossed the grenade across the bay. Then he lobbed the second. He hollered, tucking up, 'Al-Ruzi! Cover!'

The shock wave cleared a path. Nash leapt to his feet and sprinted for the next bay, firing his weapon as he rounded the concrete partition. Figures in brown overalls moved haphazardly around machinery and another massive device resting on its cradle. The external alloy of the second machine sat pitted with fragments of shrapnel and decorated with occasional debris, but was otherwise intact. Nash rattled off a long burst arcing across the bay, seeing off the last of the technicians. He ran towards the huge weapon, with rounds suddenly snapping at his heels.

Nash zigzagged, roaring, adrenalin rushing, accelerating. Bullets tore a line through the concrete as he dove behind the cradle of the second device. Chunks of wood splintered from the bench. He kept his head down as heavy machine gun fire came to his position. Rolling along the floor and coming up against a thick timber, Nash snorted for breath, changing out his magazine. Then leaping to his feet, he fired the full compliment in a steady stream at the gantry.

'Argh! Argh!' The Sten rattled hot and smoking, his chest vibrating. It clicked empty. Nash dropped behind the bench. Only three magazines left – he'd have to make them count. Slapping home a fresh box of ammo into the weapon and rolling left, he came to his feet, pressing the trigger. Bullets spewed into the gantry: raking down the German advance, pounding flesh, fragmenting bone. Bodies fell at the front of the line, bunching up the troop. He keep firing, emptying his weapon, and with the barrel scorching ducked back into

273

cover. More troops appeared on the gantry. They held the high ground. He couldn't last – the rat trap had been well and truly sprung.

He switching over magazines, rolled to his feet and hit the trigger on the run.

'Argh! Argh! Argh!' He emptied his magazine at the gantry and made ten yards. The heat of the barrel burned his palms. The German MP 40s replied with a torrent of bullets. Grimacing, he flung himself on the floor behind the end of the device, and changed out his last magazine. There were no options left.

Fuck it!

He found three grenades remaining in his thigh pocket and leant over the end of the bench and tossed two grenades, firing pins still secured, into the device. The grenades rattled inside the giant tube. Then, gritting his teeth, snorting defiance, he stood up, blasting the Sten gun for all his worth. Rounds poured at the approaching troopers for the several long of seconds before it was empty. Then, discarding the spent machine gun, and then pulling the pin on his last grenade. He bowled it into the belly of the second device; then instantly backed up, simultaneously pulling his pistol from its holster. In a double-handed grip, he fired well-aimed double taps at the enemy as he retreated to the rear.

Suddenly the huge Persian appeared, moving towards Nash's position, firing from his bow; once, twice, three times, then moving and firing again. Nash renewed his efforts, offering covering fire to the Iranian.

The grenades exploded. A dull thud, as if immersed in a barrel of water. The device jolted on its mounting brackets, a pulse of static electricity prickled the air.

Al-Ruzi loosed the last of his arrows towards the gantry as he levelled with Nash, then tossing the bow aside and withdrew his Webley revolver. He worked methodically, taking single shots to the chest of the closest targets. 'Major?!'

Nash was fresh out of choices.

Abruptly, a shaft of red plasma pierced bright and steady from the end of the machine. The superheated lance sliced through German torsos, cauterizing flesh and severing limbs.

Nash hollered, 'That way!' He gestured towards the third bay. 'We find a small tunnel, where their numbers will count for less!' Nash moved sideways, taking advantage of the scorching plasma. Barely making five yards, a streak of grey caught his peripheral vision. He reacted instantly, dropping a shot behind the Persian. A German trooper clattered to the floor at their feet. Nash swivelled, firing again, taking another at almost point blank range; then sprinted clear, still firing.

His pistol suddenly clicked. 'I am out!' He crouched in the open. 'Changing pistol mag!'

Al-Ruzi stepped up, his heavy relic of a pistol showing its worth at close quarters. Single 0.45 calibre rounds tore into flesh, bone and sinew; the momentum of the shots throwing each victim backwards in disarray.

Nash leapt to his feet, simultaneously taking aim, and with a double tap from his pistol finding the chest of a closing trooper. Nash roared, 'Come on!' He backed up, conserving ammunition, discharging at the most efficient targets.

Al-Ruzi fired a last round and deftly tossed the revolver into the approaching mêlée. He followed after Nash, drawing a curved short sword from under his cloak, then another. The jewelled weapons glinted, razor sharp. He retreated several yards, then turned smoothly on to the German advance, parring aside the barrel of Mauser rifle and slicing a throat. Using the spent trooper as a human shield, he thrust his sword into an adjacent chest, then cleaved a random pistol arm at the wrist; before unzipping the guts of another on to the floor. He pushed the injured back across his path, before pivoting on the balls of his feet and running after Nash.

They turned the corner together and suddenly scuttled to a stop.

The Persian hesitated in a defensive stance, blades dripping with blood.

Nash turned sideways on to the new threat, legs apart, probing with his pistol at four or five targets. His aim came to rest on a tall, muscular blond figure.

Major Weiner.

The sound of multiple weapons cocking issued from the gantry overhead. Troops closed the circle from behind. The large tubular structure of the third device hummed in the middle of the bay: the titanium alloy gleaming, a red plasma hovering in the void of the device. An eerie static filled the air. Voltage spilled snake-like bolts of red from the ends of the device; its deadly tendrils seeking a route to earth.

Nash stood panting, face gritted and bloodied, sweat congealed on camouflage cream. A metallic sulphur tasted on his palate. He clicked the hammer back on his pistol, keeping the Nazi squarely in his sights.

Weiner took a cautious step, with the MP 40 machine gun resting in his hand. 'Put down your weapons.'

Nash held his aim, growling. 'I'll drop you.'

Weiner shrugged, 'Perhaps, and then you will both die.'

Nash menaced with his pistol, 'Where's the girl?'

Al-Ruzi jutted back and forth. German troopers respected the reach of his sword arm.

Nash repeated, 'I want the girl. Where is she?'

The sound of a single pair of hands, clapping slowly, echoed about the cavern. All eyes turned towards the noise. Doctor Steinhoff strolled into the proceedings, coming to a stop at the edge of the circle, a few feet away from Weiner and his captives. He placed his hands deep into his lab coat pockets and nodded with satisfaction. 'Well, well, well. This is a rather unexpected reunion.' He gave a sickly smile. 'You're along way from home, Al-Ruzi. Shouldn't you be desiccating somewhere in that godforsaken desert of yours?' He turned a thin look towards Nash. 'And your friend, not so lucky without his motorcycle and Spandau machine gun. Persistent, I'll give you that. You should both be dead – but don't worry,' He shook his head slowly, still smiling. 'That's something we will soon remedy.'

Nash held his aim, ignoring the jibes of the scientist. 'Major, *where is she?*'

Emily Sinclair grasped the FN pistol in both hands and moved along the narrow passage, keeping her back to the wall and scanning for targets. Sweat dripped from her brow, her mouth parched and stomach churning. Her pulse abruptly raced.

There it was again!

The sound of gunfire, echoing, then dissipating into the rock. The prospect of escape urged her advance, but self-discipline and some weapons training checked her step. Words repeated in her mind, Danny's words.

Safety off, chamber a round, tension on the trigger, weapon and eyes as one: search, clear, move.

He'd made her remember it.

Working methodically down the dimly lit passage, the echoes of gunfire becoming more frequent and louder. Automatic weapons mixed with single shots as metallic smoke insidiously tainted her nostrils. Repeating the drill, shifting her aim robotically, she covered the ground. The passage took another undulating curve, then streaks of brightness broke the shadows on the rock walls. The arch of the roof broadened out.

A pulsating boom suddenly shifted the stale air.

Emily flinched.

There were flashes of red. The hairs on her arms stood up, but not with fear, it was something else. She puzzled. Static took her clothing. She moved steadily towards the light with

277

its new intermittent crimson, her footsteps punctuated by ever-louder bursts of machine gun fire and then pistol shots. She increased her pace as the passage expanded into the cavern beyond.

Crouching at the entrance of the large cavern with her FN Herstal in one hand, she quickly assimilated the scene. Single rounds of gunfire thundered about the excavation, with bursts of automatic weapons becoming less frequent. Machinery partially blocked the view across the factory floor. A scattering of soldiers seemed to be moving towards one of the central bays. A haze of cordite-laden white smoke hung over the place and slithered along the curved ceiling towards air vents. Soldiers lined a high gantry on the far side of the factory, with their weapons pointing downwards. Bodies lay draped into the void at their feet. Others were strewn bloodied and motionless on the stairs. The smell of burnt flesh mixed with that of spent gunpowder.

The shooting stopped.

Emily eased forwards, walking tactically in a double-handed grip. She worked the weapon over the immediate perimeter: taking in lathes, wooden shelving stacked with curved alloy sheets, coils of copper wire heaped on the floor, welding equipment, and boxes of supplies dotted about the place. She used the advantage of the cover, eventually emerging between a bank of industrial lathes, and took up position behind a greasy oil drum, training her pistol on the back of the gathering. Soldiers formed a loose semi-circle facing into the bay. Shades of red illuminated the concrete, demonising the troopers on the walkway overhead. She paused, listening and watching. There was an exchange of voices. Whatever was happening seemed to be reaching a conclusion. If she was going to make her escape, now would be a good time.

She shifted her attention to the rest of the cavern. Another reasonably large tunnel exited from the corner of the space,

278

some thirty yards away. A narrow gauge railway track was embedded in the floor – that had to be it. *The way out.* She pushed herself to her feet, then gasped, dropping back into cover.

Doctor Steinhoff!

Recovering some composure, heart still racing and suddenly smouldering with hatred, her eyes followed the scientist on his route between the machinery. The bogus intellectual walked with his hands deep in the pockets of his white laboratory coat and was heading towards the central bay. She aim the FN Herstal at his upper body. The weapon dallied in her hands, drifting on and off the target. She screwed up her face, fuming.

She'd have to get closer to be sure of killing him – or she could just leave while there was still a chance. The place was a treasure trove of intelligence, and intelligence the war effort badly needed. She conceded, escape and getting back to London with the layout of the place was the right course. It was just a matter of getting through an exit tunnel likely full of armed guards. She scanned the cavern for alternative prospects. Her brow suddenly furrowed. Had she imagined it? She squinted through the white fog at the ceiling – the nearest ventilation grill swung silently on its hinges. Someone was there? She glanced across at the next ventilation shaft. A shadow moved in the space, the grill was missing. There *was* someone there.

Then she heard it. Just a snatch of vocabulary – but it was enough – *Danny!*

All thoughts of escape blotted into the recesses of her brain. Her mind wrenched towards the improbable, the impossible: Danny Nash was here? The voice repeated amongst the gathering. This time she heard it clearly – it *was* Danny – *Danny Nash!*

Gritting her teeth, she stood upright holding the pistol in a firm double-handed grip. She snarled silently as the back of

Steinhoff's laboratory coat came into focus. She stepped forwards, keeping her weapon on target. It would be good to kill the bastard after all.

CHAPTER 31

Commandos

Emily Sinclair moved at speed, closing the distance and utterly fixed on the white laboratory coat amongst the line of army uniforms. The doctor's shoulders moved. He seemed to be speaking, but she'd didn't hear the words. Only the barrel of the Herstal mattered as she weaved around obstacles scattered on the concrete floor.

Twenty feet.

She tensed on the trigger taking up the second pressure.

Ten feet.

A flash of grey registered from her left eye: a soldier turning, shouting, pushing others aside. His rifle barrel cumbersome, slow to rise in the confinement.

A surge of adrenalin palpitated her ventricles, she lengthened her stride and pulled the trigger on the move. The recoil of the pistol tugged her senses to a sharp relief. Sounds flooded in, her eyes reporting in real time, her mind crisper. The loudness of the pistol reverberated in her ears. The spent round clanked hot over her knuckles and cordite stung her nostrils.

The shoulder of Doctor Steinhoff turned inwards, spinning him around. His face contorting and his thick spectacles falling to the floor. His arm reaching across to the dark crimson wicking into the white fabric of his laboratory coat.

She pressed the hot metal of the Herstal against his forehead and cocked the hammer with her thumb. She allowed her momentum to push Steinhoff backwards. She followed through, breaking into the circle of men.

She screamed in fluent German, 'Nobody move! Otherwise Steinhoff gets it!' She glanced around at the assembly, ramming the weapon into his skull. 'I'll blow his brains out! I swear!'

The guards on the shop floor held their rifles, looking uncertain. The nearest *SS* troopers on the gantry retrained their MP 40s.

Emily twisted the nose of the Herstal into Steinhoff's forehead, and shouted into the crowd. 'Think about it! Where would your nasty little project be with the brains of the operation spread up the walls?!'

She flashed a brief look at Danny. He stood covered in grime, bloodied and sweaty – but very much alive. She buried the urge to run to him and forced an icy composure, then menaced a harsh whisper at Steinhoff. 'Gone on, dare me. You know I'll do it.'

Steinhoff blinked, his eyes roving, unable to find focus. He panted slowly, barely managing the pain in his shoulder. Blood seeped through his fingers. He pressed his palm more firmly over his wound. 'You shot me?' His brow lifted, he muttered. 'I am shot … I am actually shot.' He swallowed, his breath short, face pleading. 'Alright, alright, just hold on, wait.' He stood more upright, with the gun still pressed on to the middle of his forehead, and spoke in a broken but loud voice over the crowd. 'Do what she says … by order of the Reich Chancellery, do what she says!' He gasped another breath, leaning into his wound, almost exhausted.

Emily felt the adrenalin soaking away from her muscles. She pressed the gun hard into the scientist's skin all the same. Now what? The Major Weiner couldn't be trusted. The moment she released her aim, his men would attack. And the Persian – what the hell was the Arab doing here?

She forced bravado and spoke in a clear German voice, 'I am walking out of here and this sack of shit is coming with me!' She reverted to English, commanding less harshly. 'Danny, let's go.'

Nash shook his head and maintained his aim on Weiner, 'Major, what time is it?'

Weiner hesitated, frowning. 'Time? What? The time?'

Nash waved his pistol. 'Yes, the time. The time now, Major Weiner.'

Weiner lifted his wrist, still holding his MP 40. He looked at Emily and then at Nash. He spoke in a measured tone as he inched his fingers towards the trigger of his automatic weapon, 'Why do you need to know the time, Englishman?'

Nash stood in silence.

Emily gave a quizzical look.

Suddenly a canister dropped from the ceiling. It bounced one, twice, then rolled across the floor. A hissing sound emitted, then a rush of thick red smoke, then another canister and another. Canisters fell from multiple air vents as commandos roped in, firing their Sten guns from their hips.

Steinhoff felt the pressure of the pistol lessen on his forehead and decided to take the chance; swiping out in desperation with his good arm, he dislodged the barrel from his face. The handgun discharged. The deafening pressure wave ruptured his eardrum. Flecks of powder scorched his neck and earlobe. 'Argh! Argh!' He lashed out at the blurred image of Emily Sinclair, sweeping his arm back and forth. Agony erupted on the bridge of his nose as the rugged handle of the Herstal connected, crunching cartilage. Steinhoff staggered backwards, catching his heel on something soft, tumbling, landing hard on his backside and then scuttling to the rear; but miraculously placing a hand on a familiar object. Still shuffling, he grabbed at his spectacles and hastily organised them on to his face as the next blow landed.

His jaw slapped sideways with the metallic thump from the body of the pistol. A not unpleasant feminine scent mixed with the throbbing of his cheekbone. He stared up at his assailant, getting just enough focus on the dark of her overalls to register the sound of the hammer clicking back on her weapon.

He gazed at the cocked pistol, then snarled, snatching at the weapon with his good hand. His fingers found the barrel. He twisted with all his strength, 'Argh! Argh!' And kicked at her soft ankles. The pistol scattered to the floor. He punched out, finding only air. Abruptly, a knee smashed hard into his face almost lifting his buttocks off the deck. Sliding backwards, he landed concussed and deranged under the cradle of the working device.

The hum of the molten plasma was somehow calming, offering resolute defiance. The crimson hue radiated a warmth intended only for its master. His creation, holding court against the insignificance of percussion weapons. Why did these cretins think they could win? It was preposterous: like pitting Neanderthals with sticks and stones against the technological might of the Roman legions. There could be only one outcome. Steinhoff reached into his pocket, producing a small vial of the finest black powder. He removed the stopper and held the tube in his lap, panting, laughing at the irony of it all. Blood and snot dribbled from his nostrils. The bullet wound in his shoulder now seemed irrelevant. He stared at the Englishwoman as she closed in, studying her movement and timing as she stooped low with her fists bunched. He darted an arm out, grabbing her by the throat and closing his fingers hard around her windpipe. He snivelled victory at her pretty little face. 'You see. No matter how many times I explained it, you simply don't understand do you?' He stared deep into her blue-green eyes. 'The Gods quiver at the power I wield.' He tightened his grasp, hissing. 'Herald the bringer of death. Your world … is no more.' He tossed the tube of carbon sixty into the device.

The plasma expanded, roaring, suddenly filling the full width of the massive tube. The searing hot gases changed hue from red to a brilliant yellow – boiling, churning about itself like the surface of the sun. He held Emily tightly, snorting, then cackling as he pushed her towards the superheated torrent of laser light and flame. Impotent fists pounded at his ribs.

He increased his pincer-like grip about her throat, and shoving her hard towards the blinding hot light, he sneered victory. 'Feel the beginning of creation, bitch!' He thrust her towards the plasma.

Suddenly, pain erupted in his shoulder wound. 'Argh! Argh!' He half-rotated his torso, catching a good look at the penknife as she twisted it into his flesh. His balance shifted, he tilted sideways.

Emily shouted venom-like into his ear. 'You first, shithead!' She kicked out, dislodging his arm and pitching him off centre towards the flames.

The primeval liquid flashed tendrils of scorching heat, a malevolent force reaching out for its master. Steinhoff resisted, swallowing pain with defiance. The sound of hair crackling and the smell of singed flesh filtered into his senses. He snarled, 'You cannot win! You know that!' His skin burned, he hissed. 'We will *always* be superior to *you*.' He felt himself tilt towards the heat, 'No! No!' He slipped a bloodied palm to the floor, seeking purchase. He stared at the plasma and its superheated hues of yellow and orange, then growled defiance at the girl.

'Kill me and another will take my place. You have already lost. You don't have it in you, do you?' He gazed at her features as she contorted with anger, or perhaps it was disgust? Her hair silhouetted against the glow, like a visitation

from the Gods. His body tilted. 'No! Wait! There's more …
so much more.'

Emily snorted, 'No, not for you there isn't.'

The side of his face boiled as she pushed him into the
volcanic plasma.

Nash reacted with cat-like reflexes, bolting from the deadly
engagement and towards Emily's position. Rounds from
Weiner's MP 40 scored a fragmented line across the rock,
snapping at his heels. Nash piled forwards, taking in multiple
threats and firing single shots on the run. His rounds found
their targets. Two soldiers crumpled on either side of her. He
covered the distance in seconds and bundled expertly into the
fray, locking a German arm over his shoulder before firing a
single shot under the man's chin. He felled a second trooper
with a head butt, before discharging his weapon in quick
succession into two more German chests. He fired his last
round at point blank range, exploding the skull of an *SS*
trooper. Then deftly removing the slide on his pistol, he
planted the jagged metal into the eyeball of another, ripping
the soldier's machine gun from his grasp. Cocking the
German weapon, Nash ploughed a furrow through the Nazi
infantryman firing until it was empty, then discarded it. He
turned towards Emily, grabbing her by the wrist. 'Come on!
Let's go!' He glanced down at the scorched features of Doctor
Steinhoff, then at her. 'Are you hurt?'

She shook her head.

Nash dipped to the floor, probing the waist belt of a spent
soldier and producing a pistol. He flicked off the safety,
chambering a round and then handed it grip first to Emily. He
collected a Mauser rifle from an adjacent corpse and hurriedly
checked the magazine. Nash assessed the battlefield as he
pressed the rifle butt into his shoulder. Al-Ruzi appeared at
his side, chest heaving, sword bloodied anew.

Red smoke whirled intermittently across the cavern. A handful of commandos had hemmed in the enemy with the brutal efficiency. The heavy exchange of Sten guns against MP 40s had taken a toll on the *SS* troopers holding the gantry. Bodies piled up, blocking several sections of the walkway. Several injured *SS* men remained at their posts. Ropes dangled from the ventilations shafts. The concrete bay lay strewn with the dead and wounded. The roaring drone of the Nazi device pained his ears. He searched the field for the Major Weiner – no luck.

Nash half-shielded Emily and shouted at the Persian, 'We go out the way we came in!' Then nodding towards the ventilation shaft some thirty yards away. 'We head for the stairs!'

Nash edged forwards, discharging careful rounds from the Mauser, then moving a few more yards and firing again.

Emily shuffled at his side, conserving rounds, offering single shots from their flank.

Al-Ruzi shielded Emily's rear with nothing but his flesh, dispatching any who came within reach of his blades. Two commandos fired their Sten guns from a high vantage, hanging on their abseiling ropes dangling from separate ventilation shafts as they strafed the enemy below. The desperate party snaked into the second bay, working around the corpses and debris as a squad of infantrymen suddenly blocked their escape.

Nash dashed forwards, heart in his mouth, closing the distance and firing the Mauser rifle in quick succession. His first round hit on target: tearing flesh and then protruding bone from the man's chest. The second shot drifted, catching a second German in the guts. Nash fired again, then his weapon clicked empty.

He snarled, throwing the spent rifle at the nearest troop and putting his head down for the charge. 'Argh!'

He rammed into the cluster, pushing two troopers to the floor and tumbling to the ground with them. He smashed a fist into the nearest face, sending the man's head back, then chopped a blow across his gullet. The soldier choked, grasping his windpipe in retreat. Whipping a blade from his pouch, Nash planted a stiletto into the chest of the next man, then stabbed with the weapon again, desperate to make the kill. Two grey figures loomed at the edge of his vision. Half lying on the floor, Nash flung his knife in a backhand motion. The blade sailed through the air, glancing harmlessly off the nearest man's tunic. The two soldiers turned their rifles. Nash scurried to his knees, seeking another blade – but he knew he couldn't make it.

The sound of systematic pistol shots deafened his ears.

Abruptly, the nearest soldier stiffened, with incredulity passing across his face as redness seeped from his tunic. His weapon clattered to the floor. He toppled.

Nash squatted, momentarily perplexed. He flicked an eye towards his benefactor. Emily stood firm, her pistol smoking.

The second trooper turned, discharging his weapon in her direction.

Nash hollered, reaching for a knife, 'No!'

Emily doubled over.

Ratta-tat tat, ratta-tat tat!

Nash tucked up against the sudden deafening roar, spent shells bouncing hot off his shoulders. 'Emily! Emily!'

The remaining German flew sideways in a hailstorm of bullets.

Nash looked up. A bear-like commando filled his vision.

'You alright, sir?' Nash's Number One stood square, gritty determination showing from under his camouflage cream. The barrel of his Sten gun glowing hot. His canvas webbing crammed with grenades and other goodies. He quickly offered Nash a sidearm.

Nash took the weapon with a silent nod and instinctively made the weapon ready as he jogged to Emily's side. She leant stiffly on one leg, pressing her palms on to the other thigh. Blood oozed between her fingers as she sobbed back pain. Al-Ruzi had already sheathed his swords and took up her pistol, protecting their rear.

Number One covered their position from the front, and hosed down the bay with his almost full magazine for good measure.

Nash yelled over the din as he took Emily on to his shoulder, placing one arm around her waist. 'Can you walk? We have to move!'

She nodded sharply, and gasping a breath, forced herself more upright.

'Good, that's good!' Nash tightened his grip.

Number One leant in with a shout as he changed out his magazine. 'Ready?!'

Nash raised his pistol, firing a double tap overhead. A trooper fell against the gantry. Nash nodded to his Number One. 'Your orders were to wait, not attack.'

The sergeant cocked his weapon. 'Beggin' your pardon, sir, but bollocks to that.' He fired a burst at their perimeter, clearing the way ahead. 'Shall we?'

They hurried across to the concrete recess that marked the next bay. Nash bunched close behind his sergeant, almost tasting the man's cheap aftershave mixed with sweat and the aroma of gun oil. Nash pulled Emily close, firing rounds to cover their flank, then up on to the gantry, adding the last of the stragglers to the pile of bodies on the aerial walkway.

Number One halted at the perimeter of the bay and pressed against the concrete wall. He kept his weapon up, assessing the way ahead. The coast seemed relatively clear. 'We move on three! One … two … three!' He stepped out into the final bay, spraying rounds from his Sten gun and carving a route to the stairs alongside the massive device. His weapon littered a few more corpses against the sides of the huge wooden cradle. Satisfied, the sergeant moved off.

Nash followed, offering his pistol up on to the gantry and eyeing for a path up the stairs amongst the bodies. He half-jogged, dragging Emily along, ignoring her yelps of pain and frustration. Al-Ruzi pressed at his back.

They halted at the base of the stairs. Nash took a defensive stance, panting, holding Emily off her bad leg. The sergeant rattled his Sten gun up the stairs, then flew up the mezzanine steps two at a time. Nash waited, glancing upwards, as Number One installed himself at the top of the stairs with a fresh magazine loaded into the Sten gun. A commando offered a rope from the ventilation shaft only a few yards along the aerial walkway. Nash took to the steps, pulling her with him and almost tasting the prospect of freedom.

'Ow! Ow!' She cried, flushing with pain as her leg dragged on the steps.

Nash grimaced, then suddenly stopped. 'Stay with me! Take the pain! Use it! We keep going!'

He hauled her up a few more steps.

Emily collapsed, panting heavily, skin pale and clammy. 'No. No, I can't. Need to rest … Just a few seconds.' Her eyes squeezed shut, deep furrows carved her brow.

Nash held on to her, barely four feet from the top. He glanced across at Number One steadfastly holding the high ground and then down at Al-Ruzi who stood firing single shots from the German handgun. The Persian covered the length of missile-like Nazi device with his pistol, blocking any easy route to the stairs. Nash returned his attention to his casualty. 'Emily! We have to move! Come on!' He shoved his gun into his waistband and hauled her to her feet, placing one hand about her waist and the other on the scaffold handrail. Then inched up the steps.

A shout went up from below. Nash paused on the penultimate tread, seeing the Major Weiner round the corner with several men. Nash call down to Al-Ruzi, beckoning retreat. 'Come on!'

The Persian offered a gentle smile, 'Go! Goodbye, Major Nash,' then turned towards the enemy, tossing the pistol aside and unsheathing both of his swords.

CHAPTER 32

Debt of Honour

Mohammed Al-Ruzi allowed his hanker to rise, pulsing steady and wanton through his veins, his muscles taut from the long discipline of war. His flesh, blood and sinew made ready to honour the occasion. He muttered a fitting prayer for the souls of his enemy, '*La hawla wala quwata illa billah.*' There is no transition or strength, except through God. He increased his pace, moving lightly on his feet, giving a shrill cry '*Allahu Akbar*! *Allahu Akbar*!' God is great!

He charged at the enemy, keeping Major Weiner centre stage and suddenly hurling his left-hand sword at the nearest trooper. The jewelled blade spiralled through the air. A flashing blur. Then thudded home. The soldier collapsed to his knees, wailing, clutching at the massive steel protruding from his chest. Almost simultaneously Al-Ruzi produced an ivory dagger from under his cloak. The curved stiletto of the *Pesh-kabz* knife was light, familiar and perfectly balanced. He let the weapon fly.

A soldier choked as the blade buried in his gullet.

Al-Ruzi rushed forwards, closing the gap and retrieving his knife, leaving the trooper gushing and collapsing to the floor. Then in one fluid movement, raising his sword and swivelling on the balls of his feet, he hacked clean through the barrel of the Mauser rifle belonging to an adjacent trooper, before shoving the pommel into his opponent's face. The soldier staggered to the rear, with nasal cartilage smashed and bloodied. Another instantly took his place. Al-Ruzi adeptly shuffled his weight and position, cleaving his sword through the guard's helmet. He flexed the blade free as if splitting coconuts.

A voice bellowed close to his head. 'Enough!' A muscular pistol arm came up. 'Time to die, fucking Arab!'

Shots rang out.

Al-Ruzi felt the pressure wave flatten his ear drum. Charred flecks of silk singed from the tight bindings of his ebony headgear. He swirled about, sticking his knife through tendons and finding the bone of Weiner's forearm. With his ear ringing, he brought his shamshir sharply to rest over Weiner's right shoulder, pressing the razor edge of the sword against exposed flesh. He panted with exertion, sweat soaked the cloth covering his brow. His dark eyes stared through slits in his black silks.

'I vowed that you would one day feel my blade, Major Weiner. That day is upon us.'

The beehive exploded.

Weiner crashed into the wall and then fell hard to the floor. Winded and dazed he lay sprawled on his belly, gritty cement fragments stuck to his face. Pain flashed from his left thigh. The smell of scorched clothing mixed with gunpowder. He smarted at the knife wound in his arm and rolling on to his back, looked upon the *Pesh-kabz* still protruding from his flesh. He tightened his jaw, then stiffening his whole body, he pulled the knife free.

'Argh!' He hunted for air, holding the soiled blade in his hand and grimacing. He sat up and registering the shredded and smouldering remnants of his uniform. Multiple incisions scratched sharp discomfort down his left side. He reached out for one of the larger twists of shrapnel buried in his leg. He gave it a tug, 'Argh! Fuck!' Agony pulsed from the injury as the metal stuck fast. Accepting his wounds, he swallowed smoke and dusty air, willing his senses to the fore. He reached for his pistol holster.

Empty.

He glanced about his position, then began hauling himself across the floor towards the remains of the large wooden cradle and Steinhoff's device. The tube of the massive weapon sat skewed with its long wooden cradle partly destroyed, scorched by the blast. Small flames licked at the timbers. Debris lay everywhere. A concave hole in the side of the device marked the point of the explosion. The skin of the weapon was breached, but not destroyed. High voltage arced violent sparks from the impact zone. The plasma was a raging torrent; shuddering abrupt colours, flashing red, green, brilliant white and then orange.

Weiner dragged himself against one of the better timbers and rested his back on the wood; at last able to draw some kind of breath, despite his lungs being raw and smarting against the cordite-ridden air. He ducked involuntarily as the breach in the device spewed a random protest of sparks and mercuric baubles of red hot plasma on to the floor. He coughed, spitting blood and then pulled himself to his feet, keeping a firm grip on the *Pesh-kabz*. Leaning on the woodwork, he quickly scanned the scene.

'Al-Ruzi!' Weiner stared across at the Persian. The Arab stooped in the open on the far side of the device, clothing torn, sword held limply at his side.

Weiner snarled, throwing the knife.

Al-Ruzi laboured a response with his sword, deflecting the knife and sending it scattering into a pile of detritus.

Weiner rounded the end of the bench, dragging his bad leg as he went and then suddenly stopped short. A gleaming and bloodied shamshir lay at his feet. He picked up the sword, feeling the weight of the weapon, slashing it a couple of times

294

across the air. He snarled an ugly look at the Persian. 'You had to ruin the deal. You could have had it sweet.' Weiner hobbled with increasing speed towards the Persian, growling contempt. 'A stock pile of German weapons to rule your own little slice of desert; but instead you try and fuck me over.' Weiner raised his sword, 'So, now you fucking pay for it!' He lunged at the Persian, swinging the sword with surprising accuracy and power, using the advantage of his muscular shoulders.

Blades crashed heavily, sharp edges scraping and sliding. Weiner pulled in close against the Arab, menacing, pressing harder as the Arabian swordsman equalled his hold. Weiner hissed shaking his head. 'You're done, Al-Ruzi. Your princess: dead.' He gritted his teeth, grinding blades with the Persian. 'Your people – we'll wipe them out – gone!' Weiner shoved with all his strength. And making a space, he swiped heavily for the Persian's middle.

The blade found nothing but air as the Arab stepped clear. Weiner growled at the slits in Al-Ruzi's turban. 'Die like a man. Show your face for once.'

Al-Ruzi pulled a couple of wraps from the garment and tossed it aside, then brandishing his sword towards the German. 'I fear for your destiny, Major Weiner. Allah has you on a different path.'

'Argh!' Weiner rushed forwards, whirling the blade, demented.

Al-Ruzi absorbed the attack with rapid parries, stepping backwards with each blow.

Weiner broke off, both men stood panting.

Al-Ruzi lifted the tip of his sword a few more inches. 'We will not meet again in the afterlife.' He steadied his breathing. 'Goodbye, Major Weiner.'

Al-Ruzi attacked.

Weiner snarled, meeting the assault, moving with desperate agility. Blades clashed in quick succession. Weiner held on, despite the knife wound in his arm.

Abruptly, the Persian changed tack, offering an upper cut and alternate rhythm with his blade.

'Argh!' Weiner retreated a few steps as the tip of the blade sliced across his chest, cutting neatly through his tunic. The wound opened instantly, seeping a steady flow of crimson. Weiner looked down at his wound, enraged. 'Bastard!' He swung his sword over his head in a double-handed grip, powering hard for the Persian's skull. 'Argh! Fucking hell!' Weiner rained down multiple blows, berserk.

The Persian held his breath, moving his feet, reposing, allowing his opponent the torrent of abuse, then sensing the lull after the storm, stepped sideways drawing his sword across Weiner's back.

'Ooaah!' Weiner staggered away from the Persian's blade, taking a long arc to recover his position. He turned, stooping, bleeding and panting heavily. He waited, recovering his breath. The Persian seemed to keep a respectful distance, or perhaps the Arab was also showing signs of fatigue?

Suddenly, a foreign voice shouted from one of the ventilation ducts overhead. Weiner glanced upwards. The English girl bundled into the shaft. His ears caught the clank of a canister dropping from above, then another. Adrenalin pushed the pain aside, his eyes sharped as one of the canisters rolled into view at the edge of the bay. An acrid yellow mist issued forth, and even at this distance, his flesh tingled with chemical irritation. He urgently shifted his attention to the Persian, searching for a weaker flank, anything.

Weiner charged, bringing his blade down from above and then with manic powerful swipes from the side to side. Pressing close, he dragged his blade violently across the Arab's bicep. 'Yes!' He pulled the edge of his sword through his opponents wound with satisfaction and rounded to make ready for his next attack.

He stared at the Arab. The Persian stood half-sprung, blood glazing the torn silk of his sword arm. Yellow mist curled in the air a few feet from their position. Weiner shifted sideways to avoid the deadly cocktail, his opponent followed. Weiner rasped, placing a free palm over his mouth, his eyes watering.

Al-Ruzi tugged a wrap of silk up over his nose before silently gesturing the Major forwards with a flick of his palm.

Weiner eyed his opponent as another canister rolled across the floor. Thoughts of self preservation intervened. He could make a run for it and let the Arab choke to death. After all, others parts of the complex would be in lockdown. Safe areas, well-contained and with the prospect of medical attention. He considered his wounds. He could make it to the safe area – or he *could* do the right thing.

Weiner held his breath, and curling his lip into a snarl, he flew at the Persian; pressing hard with his weapon, slicing and hammering for the slightest gap in the Arab's defences. The Persian dropped back close to the device. Weiner sensed the upper hand, roaring, 'Argh!' He chopped down with his sword, again and again, taking the foreground and forcing his enemy into reverse. Weiner hacked, making contact with the alloy skin of the device, sending sparks asunder and cleaving chunks from the timbers where the Persian had stood but a shadow, milliseconds before. 'Argh! Argh! Argh!' Weiner frenzied, uncontrollable, lifting his blade high in the air and scything it down.

The Persian dodged and parried.

'Argh! Fucking Arab! Argh!' Weiner savaged, fast, repeated blows, increasing the tempo as the Persian sidled in retreat along the device.

At last Weiner loomed over his target, certain of his aim. 'Time to die!' He delivered a massive double-handed blow.

Al-Ruzi ducked under the blade and thrust his swords upwards.

Weiner stiffened, dropping his sword and staggering backwards; coughing blood from his lips. The Persian's shamshir protruded from his chest. He watched confused as the Arab approached. Al-Ruzi looked odd, with almost a kindness about his face. Weiner shuddered as the Persian pulled the blade free. Foamy liquid gurgled a protest for his throat. He felt light-headed, cold and with his legs suddenly weak. He dribbled blood and roved an eye over his rendered chest, and then looked up vacantly at the Persian, whispering. 'I almost had you … almost.' The Arab stood with both blades in hand. There was a swish of steel, a flash of light, then vertigo. Pin points of light turned to darkness.

Weiner's head separated from his body.

Mohammed Al-Ruzi stood over the headless corpse as the poisonous fume of Lewisite and mustard gas snaked inches away. He sheathed his swords and lifted several layers of silk over his mouth as first contact with the toxin blistered the severed head. He mumbled at the remains of his opponent, 'Allah will judge you now, if you are worthy.'

With that, the Persian turned on his heels and headed for the stairs.

CHAPTER 33

Home

Danny Nash turned the corner and stopped, then glanced up at the street sign that had been painted out on the dull brick of the nearest terrace. It seemed about right. *Parklands Road*. He swallowed back his apprehension and stared down the street. This was it – real life. Terraced houses lined both sides of the road, each with their own postage stamp-sized bit of front garden. Some with flowers in bloom. Despite the war, the pavements were fairly neat and mostly unbroken. The occasional hawthorn tree added a splash of extra greenery outside a few of the homes. He tugged the string of his canvas duffel bag on to his right shoulder and then counterbalanced his small cardboard box of possessions under the left arm of his grey coat.

Moving house.

All done in one go. Everything he owned, easily carried on the bus, and walked the last few hundred yards of the journey. He shook his head and grimaced, then smiled. He mumbled to himself, 'What the hell are you doing, Nash?' He huffed and continued his personalised rant, 'Getting a life – stupid. Remember, a fresh start. Or do you want to screw that up as well?'

He smirked and looked down at the regulation boots that were partly hidden by his brown corduroy trousers. The transformation to civilian clothing was never going to be quite complete, but at least he was trying. He'd even swapped his rough khaki shirt for a cotton one: red and black with a lumberjack-style pattern.

He took a deep breath and strode down the road. His boots clipped rhythmically on the pavement. The sun warmed the last of the morning chill from his face. House sparrows darted busily between fence posts and tiny hedges, some nibbling on stale bread crumbs. Empty milk bottles sat on a few doorsteps.

People actually live here, with neighbours.

Nash counted up the house numbers in his head.

Ten ... twelve ... fourteen ... sixteen ... eighteen.

Maybe living wouldn't be so bad after all. But the concept of other people? Having neighbours for Christ's sake! What would he say? How would he even begin?

Hello, my names Danny Nash. I kill people for a living on behalf of His Majesty's Government, and then some.

Forget it.

He stopped outside number twenty-eight. The garden gate and picket fence was made of roughly cut timbers; functional, but nonetheless pleasant. The front garden was three yards square, with a few plants growing in the border along the fence, and a patch of grass. A front door in need of a lick of paint and a tiled step marked the entrance. Nash propped the cardboard box on the gatepost and fished in his trouser pocket for the keys. He produced a loop of string containing two keys; one for the front entrance and a solid-looking key for a deadlock, likely the back door.

He picked up the box and opened the gate, then walked up to the porch. He dropped his things on the doorstep and put the key in the door, then turned the handle and allowed the door to swing ajar. This was it. Civilisation; albeit rented, but that didn't matter. It was still a house of his own. A back door, stairs, and more than one room. A place to sleep that was separate from where the food was prepared. Even his own toilet in the backyard.

He wondered if he really needed the extra space, and decided that he didn't, but he'd go along with it anyway. It was all part of his plan; well, Emily's plan. To be something other than Major Danny Nash. Being plain old, Mister Nash, when he wasn't at work.

He muttered to himself as he stepped over the threshold and dropped his coat on the peg in the hall.

'*Mister Nash*'.

It didn't sound right.

He clunked along the wooden floor. His boots echoed about the empty house. He stopped at the base of the stairs, which marked the intersection of the ground floor rooms. A small living area was on the left and a kitchen to the rear. Nash took in the smell of stale air and walked into the living room. The place was a decent space without any furniture in it. He glanced down at the worn, but clean carpet, and then remembered his boots. That would have to be a new habit – boots off in the hall.

Bloody hell – even slippers!

Nope, he'd draw the line at slippers. The new Danny Nash wouldn't stretch that far.

Suddenly the clip clop of hooves and the rattling of a cart roused Nash from his thoughts. He about turned, and headed out the front, pausing dumfounded at the gate. A Shire horse stood chewing on its brace. Dull reins led back to a flatbed wooden cart. A scruffy and wrinkled old man sat holding the leather strops. A cloth cap covered his balding head. Nash ran a weary eye over the delivery. The wagon was loaded with a few bits of furniture: a table, at least four chairs, a chest of drawers and something else under a canvas – large – probably a wardrobe.

He leant on the gate, furrowing his brow suspiciously. He hadn't ordered anything.

He rolled his eyes heavenwards as Emily appeared from the far side of the horse and then widened to his best grin. 'What's all this?'

Emily stood in slacks and a woollen herringbone jumper, then smirking as she patted the horse gently on its nose. She gave sly look, smiling. 'A few basic essentials.'

Nash raised an eyebrow, 'Essentials … really?'

She tittered as she sauntered towards the garden gate, 'Yes, really, and what would be more civilised than being able to sit down at a table to eat a meal with friends?'

'I don't have any friends,' he smirked.

'That's because you don't have a table from which to show your hospitality.'

'Oh, hospitality now is it? Blimey! One thing at a time.'

She eased up to him over the gate. 'You can't eat out of mess tins all your life, Danny Nash.'

He smiled, 'No, I suppose not …'

She smiled back.

He swallowed, glancing at the second-hand furniture, then at her, but said nothing.

Emily ignored his uncertainty and tilted her head with a coy look. 'Well, Mister Nash, are you going to let me in?'

Danny lifted the latch on the gate, and then sheepishly moved back, swinging the gate open. He looked her in the eye. 'It's a lot of furniture. I mean, well, it's a big house and it'll be just me most of the time.'

She moved closer, pulling herself into his chest and almost whispering, 'Then perhaps I can stay over now and then …'

He looked down at her beautiful face and took in the smell of her perfume, 'That would be alright by me.' He kissed her gently on the lips.

The *having a life* idea suddenly seemed less scary. Besides, he was in too far now. So why not give it a shot?

Emily thrashed sporadically in the twilight world of slumber. Her clammy limbs tangled in the bed sheets. Her unconsciousness screwed her face up and clenched her fists into the mattress. She felt an unpleasant heat, burning, radiating from within her chest and suffocating. She fought for air, struggling against the engulfing darkness. Then nothing. Only a cold dampness and the gritty loam of the underworld stuck to her skin. Her voice echoed in the void. Then there was the water; the constant dripping of water and utterly maddening.

Drip, drip … drip. Drip, drip … drip. Drip, drip … drip.

Then the demons would come.

Drip, drip … drip. Drip, drip … drip. Drip, drip … drip.

A malevolent creature boomed from the abyss. 'You wanted something – *didn't you?*'

Drip, drip … drip. Drip, drip … drip.

It whined, sneering, as it clambered over the rocky threshold, '*Something more …*' The creature laughed a deep satisfying belly laugh and then jabbed a skeletal finger in her direction. 'Something more!' Its tone changed to a sudden poisonous vitriol. 'And you go it! More than you can imagine. *Didn't you?*! But what will you do with it now, *Miss Sinclair?*'

Emily squirmed.

'*Murderer!*'

The creature revealed itself in the gloom. The visage of Doctor Steinhoff, twisted and burnt. It chortled, 'No? Perhaps you prefer another?' The creature's face transformed, showing all those that had been. Cold and grey. The bloodied corpses of German troopers: one, then another, and another.

Emily curled into a foetal position, naked and alone, feeling the chill of the cavern. The beast towered over her.

'These men had wives, *children*. What does that make *you?*' The apparition mocked, 'Murderer! Murderer! *Murderer!*'

Drip, drip … drip. Drip, drip … drip. Drip, drip … drip.
'Murderer!'
Drip, drip … drip.
It spoke more quietly as it turned away, 'Murderer!'
Drip, drip … drip.
Then fading into the distance, it hissed, 'Murderer!'
Drip, drip … drip.
Then just a whisper, 'Murderer …'
Drip, drip … drip.
Only the cold, the sharp gravel-like earth and the constant moisture remained.
Drip, drip … drip. Drip, drip … drip. Drip, drip … drip.
Her leg throbbed, dull and steady at first.
Drip, drip … drip.
Then painfully.
Drip, drip … drip.
Agonising pain. She curled up, squirming her white flesh against the volcanic soil. Her hands clasped over her thigh. Pain, only pain now. She stretched the injured limb, massaging it, but no respite would come.

She removed her hands from the wound. Blood dipped down her fingers into her open palms. Thick, congealed and like molasses, the crimson liquid stained her skin; then flowing over her wrists and soaking her arms.

The souls of the dead chanted, '*Something more … something more … something more. Murderer!*'

Emily screamed and a sat bolt upright in the bed. She felt her hair matted against her face, almost obstructing her breathing. Her cheeks blushed with the conjured fever of nightmares. She blinked her eyes open. Then parting her tangled locks, she examined her fingers, turning her palms over and over.

She sat hyperventilating and uncertain.

Then looked up.

The room came into focus, slowly at first.

A bed. She was in a bed. White sheets and a thick blanket. A bedside table. A lamp.

She clicked the light on.

Flowery wallpaper stared back. Curtains hung closed over the upstairs window.

Her voice crackled, a parched whisper, 'Danny?'

There was no reply.

She pushed her fringe back, then gulping down a few lungfuls of air and huffed. Her shoulders sagged, but she was grateful for the reality of wakefulness. She looked about the bed.

Yes, Danny's place. Safe.

She let the thought sink in, relieved.

Suddenly, Nash appeared around the doorway. He stood dressed in a green pullover and his only pair of corduroy trousers, and carrying a steaming brew in his right hand. He stepped towards the bed with a worried look on his face, 'I left you sleeping. Are you alright?'

Emily tentatively smiled.

Nash saw through the façade. 'Cup of tea?'

Emily nodded, groggily.

He sat on the edge of the bed, then handed her the cup. 'You're still having nightmares? The same one?'

She took the cup and swallowed a hot sip of the refreshing liquid and then nodded. 'Yes, the same one.' She took another sip, 'When will it stop?'

Nash allowed his face to mellow. 'I don't know. In time, perhaps it will fade.'

Emily shook her head slowly, 'The bruises, scrapes and cuts are gone. Even my leg has more or less healed within a month. But this goes on?'

'Don't beat yourself up. Give it more time. It's early days yet,' Nash smiled.

'But, Danny, I haven't slept properly for weeks, not since we got back. I don't know … I just don't know. How can I

305

function with no sleep?' She bowed her head, staring into her tea.

Nash squeezed her forearm gently, 'You need more time, that's all.'

She looked up, suddenly fixing a harsh glare. 'How do you deal with your demons, Danny? How do you make them go away?'

Nash swallowed, then shrugged, 'I don't do anything in particular. I just leave it. When I need to sleep, I sleep.'

She grimaced, 'You're not a good liar, Danny. I've seen your notion of sleep, remember. Tell me … will the terrors always be with me, as they are with you?'

Nash took a deep breath. 'Yes and no. It depends. For me, I recognise them for what they are – just dreams, bad dreams. I don't try to think about it. I put them aside. If you try to analyse things, you'll drive yourself to madness. Forget dreams. I just rationalise the insanity with reality: I am sent to do a job and I do it. Orders are orders.'

'But you still have nightmares and you have killed so many. Danny,' silent tear formed in her eyes, 'does it get worse with each life you take?'

Nash glazed over. 'So, you *really* want to know? How I deal with it.'

'Yes.'

He held his breath for several seconds, then exhaled. 'Alright. The truth is, I'll always remember the first one, and sometimes the last. The rest is a blur. My dreams serve only to twist the memories in my head until they become nonsensical, an unreality. Sometimes I can't remember if I killed a man, or if I dreamed it. The who, what, when and why for, become irrelevant because I can't tell reality from the nonsense inside my skull. I am screwed up. SIS has screwed me up.' He shrugged, 'But what can I do? I just accept it. The army has made me who I am. So I embrace what I have become – and use it to do good.'

306

She whispered, her voice broken. 'You kill more of the bad men, just to make your demons go away?'

'Yes, but not just my demons,' his voice dropped a barely audible whisper, 'nor to set right what has been made wrong. Perhaps I fight so that others don't have to.' He paused pinching the bridge of his nose and then looked directly at her. 'In the end, I ... I don't know anything else. I am just a soldier.'

'If I work in the field for SIS, will my nightmares recede?'

Nash shrugged, 'Perhaps – but only if you have someone or something to save.'

Emily nodded slowly and took a sip of her tea, 'Yes, I do. There is always something or someone worth saving. Isn't there, Danny?'

CHAPTER 34

Epilogue

Emily Sinclair sat in the rusting Nizhegorodski and pulled her thick woollen overcoat more tightly across her chest. Only the fur of her Soviet hat offered insulation against the bitter northerly winds. Ice frosted the windscreen. Her cheekbones were raw and chapped from several days of the freezing cold. She stared at the notebook on the dashboard and then shoved a bulky finger under the wrist of her leather glove.

Six a.m.

She took a deep breath and exhaled foggy moisture, then picked up the notebook. She tapped the small leather bound volume in her gloved palm for a few seconds, inhaled another deep breath, and then buried the book in her pocket. She shoved the door of the   Nizhegorodski open. An arctic blast instantly penetrated her coat.

A solitary man stood on the pavement across the empty street, with his portly middle-aged frame wrapped in his Soviet Army winter coat. The red hammer and sickle of his Ushanka hat was the only colour in the drabness of the morning. The Soviet moved off. Shuddering, she crossed the road, crunching through the ice encrusted snow, following at a discrete distance.

A flurry of fresh snow swirled amongst the dilapidated buildings. The few shops were either not open yet, or boarded up and long since gone out of business. The Russian skulked, head down into the wind, keeping a steady pace. Emily balled her gloved hands, then flexed her fingers, but no circulation would come. Her wrist bones ached with the cold. She glanced apprehensively about the street. There was no threat, only isolation. She returned her focus to the pavement. Barely keeping her footing, she tracked after the old Soviet.

After some two hundred yards, the buildings began to thin, giving way to high walls topped with ancient rolls of barbed wire. The Batyrka prison loomed, grubby and oppressive. The Soviet kept walking, eventually coming to stop some twenty yards from a pair of huge iron gates. The industrial iron railings bristled with sharp welds and assorted metal spikes. The gates seemed to mark the end of the street as well as the entrance to the prison. More barbed wire filled the inside of its perimeter. Two soldiers slinked back and forth across the front of the gates in a well-trodden depression of compacted snow.

The Soviet leaned against the wall, sheltering a match from the wind and lighting up a cigarette. Emily caught a whiff of the rough tobacco as she approached. She slowed, hesitating to a stop a few feet from his position and placed her hands in her pockets. She grasped the notebook between her thump and forefinger, comforted by its presence. A bargaining chip of sorts. The Sauer pistol weighed down her other palm.

She forced a short smile and nodded towards the old technocrat. She spoke calmly in fluent Russian, her breath visible in the cold. 'I am Sinclair.'

The Soviet grunted, 'Of course you are.' He took a slow drag on his cigarette. 'Do you have it?'

Emily fixed a blank expression, 'Yes.'

The Russian put out a palm, 'Good.'

'No, first I want your word.'

The Soviet grimaced, 'There's a war on. I don't have time for this.'

Emily remained firm, '*Your word.*'

The Soviet shuffled his feet and took another puff of his smoke, 'Alright, damn it.' He turned towards the gate and raised an arm, then pushed the cigarette between his lips and put his hands in his pockets, stamping his feet. 'We wait a little while. You will see.' He suddenly smirked. 'You like our Russian weather, no?'

Emily remained silent, peering through the brisk flurries of snow and towards the prison gates. The sound of keys clanked. There was movement in the courtyard and a lamp shining. She craned her neck. The guards were moving off their beat, turning towards the activity within. She waited, her heart pounding.

The Russian spoke, 'Show me the notebook.'

She retrieved it from her pocket, holding it out for the old dog to see, then pressed it tightly to her chest. 'Do as we arranged and the book is yours.'

The gates of the Batryka creaked open, just enough. A lone figure in ragged clothes, half-draped in a rough blanket, stepped through the gate. The lamplight glowed orange against the turquoise ice and snow. The figure crumped a few feet away from the threshold, then stood sheepish in the snow. The gates gave a loud metallic groan and then clanked shut. Keys hurriedly secured the padlock. The jailor scurried off back towards the bowels of the prison. The two sentries remained behind the gate, with their rifles slung on their shoulders.

The lone figure looked back and forth across the gates and then walked a few steps further away, then faster, hastily moving from view into an alley and away from the prison.

The Russian grumbled, 'There, it is done. Now the notebook.'

Emily countered, 'How do I know it is her?'

The Russian took another suck on his cigarette and stubbed it under his foot into the snow. 'We are not animals you know.

Now the book, otherwise she goes back inside – forever. No release. Would you like that, English?'

Emily stepped forwards, handing over the book.

The Russian flicked through the first few pages, grunting to himself, then looked up. 'Good, very good. Colonel Korolev's work is returned to where it belongs. You have made a service to the Kremlin, Miss Sinclair.'

Emily shrugged, 'What happens now?'

The Soviet placed the notebook deep inside his breast pocket and then took out another cigarette, he cupped his hands around it as he struck a match and worked up a glowing ember. He flicked the match in the snow and spat a fleck of tobacco from his lips. He nodded appreciatively, 'What happens now?' He hissed, 'War, Miss Sinclair, *total war*!'

Nash held in the shadows, pulling up the collar of his grey coat against the drizzle, and breathing steadily. The smell of coal dust, diesel oil and the heavy vapour of industrial chemicals teased his nostrils. Rain glistened on the cobbles under the solitary street light. A half-track armoured vehicle rumbled past, its canopy bristling with soldiers and a Spandau heavy machine gun out front. The tracks squeaked and clattered along the road. He peered after the heavy truck as the roar of its engine dissipated into the night, then checked the road for stragglers.

Nothing.

He waited, allowing his hearing to readjust in the night: the low hum of machinery, the venting of pipework, the rattle of chains and the occasional sound of metal chinking against metal issued from the factory. He took in the brick wall that made the perimeter of the chemical works. It was some ten feet high. He tightened the straps on his small haversack full of explosives. He'd have to take a run at it.

The factory roof outlined for some distance behind the wall. White acrid clouds billowed from smoke stacks dotted amongst the pipework. The intelligence from the files in Frankfurt had made things clear. There was definitely unfinished business with one Director Krauch of the I. G. Farben Corporation. Nash recalled the blistered flesh, weeping boils and festering airways at Wolfsberg. He pushed aside his revulsion. All from half a dozen cans of Lewisite left over from the Great War, mixed with a little mustard gas. It had put a stop to production of the device at Wolfsberg, at least for a while. Sinclair would have to wrestle with his conscience on that one. But this place? What the Nazis were doing here was on an entirely different scale. An abomination.

He took out the Sauer 38, screwing on the custom-made silencer and returning the weapon to his coat pocket. He ran his fingers over the pouch of throwing knives resting in the small of his back, then paused before sticking his head out. The road seemed quiet. No vehicles, no patrols. He took several deep breaths, pumping up the adrenalin, then ran hell for leather, throwing himself up the wall, scraping his boots on the concrete and digging his fingers into the top of the brickwork. Finding purchase, he scrabbled over the top and dropped down the other side, landing hard on to a concrete standing. He tucked low, catching his breath, mouth open, listening.

Nothing.

He pulled the Sauer from his pocket and flipping off the safety, took in the scene. A narrow service lane curved into the twilight between the main building and the piles of coal, crushed limestone, and other raw materials heaped against the perimeter wall. The side of the long building supported a myriad of pipe work and gantries leading into what looked like a mezzanine level or perhaps a second floor. Clusters of storage tanks nestled against the factory wall. The nearest vessel gleamed with condensation, its shining aluminium skin

312

just as new as the pipework forcing a path through the red brick. Steam abruptly vented from a stack on the adjacent façade. The smell of rotten eggs mixed with the aromatic odour of benzene. Nash checked to his left, following the line of the nearest pipework and found what he was looking for.

He dipped from cover, crossing the raised camber of the cobbled access road, then took shelter under a gantry. He worked the Sauer methodically over the metalwork, then satisfied, moved off cautiously towards a large cylindrical tank.

After some ten yards he sidled to a stop, pressing his shoulder against the curvature of the storage vessel. The metal surface emitted the steady vibration of industry and the occasional glug of vitriolic liquid from within. He slipped off his pack, retrieving an explosive charge. Then, keeping the Sauer close to hand on a smaller girder, he wedged the new plastic explosive into the metal frame of the tank and pushed in a time pencil. He fished into his map pocket for a pair of pliers and carefully crimped the copper tubing. He picked up his pistol, and re-shouldering his pack, he checked his watch.

Twenty minutes.

He edged around the tank, finding a small flight of concrete steps leading up to a doorway. A subdued yellowy glow issued from its surround. He aimed the Sauer in a double-handed grip and placed a boot on the first step. Sweat trickled down his back as the general hum of the factory encroached.

Light suddenly spilled from the doorway. Nash fired.

Plimf! Plimf!

A German officer toppled, headfirst, down the steps and coming to rest at his feet. Another single shot into the soldier's forehead secured the outcome. Nash flicked his weapon back over the entrance. A man paused on the threshold, laboratory coat showing in the light and clipboard in hand. Nash squeezed the trigger as he closed the distance, trampling over the body of the dead officer and taking the steps two at a time.

Plimf! Plimf!

The scientist sprawled against the doorframe, then slumped, devoid of life. Nash waved the Sauer through the open door, feeling exposed as he kicked the body clear of the woodwork and into the drizzling rain. He stepped through the door, instantly taking in a powerful chemical odour, and shifting quickly into cover behind some machinery. He shortened his breathing, listening and watching, showing the Sauer about the place. A handful of scientists busied themselves, some wearing protective clothing around large vats in the middle of the factory floor. Liquids simmered in two of the industrial cauldrons. Banks of gas cylinders lined the far wall. Pipework ran overhead, with vertical drops bolted against the near wall; some labelled with large arrows, clearly marking the direction of flow for the toxic brew. Skull and crossed bones stated the obvious on the side of the nearest vat.

He quickly changed out his magazine and taking shallow, economical breaths, set off. Sidling low between the machinery and working his away across the perimeter to the far wall, he ducked into the lee of some gas cylinders. Sweating, eyes smarting, he slipped a block of plastic explosive from his rucksack and wedged the malleable green substance between two of bottles of industrial methane. He pushed a time pencil into the middle of the charge, the almond-like essence of the high explosive greasing his fingers as he did so. He wiped a hand on his thigh and then crimped the copper tube with his pliers.

He peered inside his rucksack.

Three more charges, ten more minutes.

If he worked quickly, he might just make it.

The tailor fussed, brushing down the lapels and smoothing the shoulders of the jacket, then ran a keen eye over the fall of the exquisite fabric. The golden buttons on the tunic were not too overstated. It had been the right choice and would go well with the medal – the most prestigious of honours. Order of the German Cross, no less. He glanced towards the recipient across the dressing room. The man stood facing the deeply polished oak panelling, with the crisply ironed pleats showing on the back of his shirt. The man struggled to fold down his starched collar over the silk tie. The tailor concealed his revulsion, and with bile churning his stomach, forced an adequate smile as he lifted the jacket from the clothes stand. He moved across the room with an accustomed dignity, and held the garment open. He mustered faltering encouragement, 'Sir, your jacket. All ready and fully adjusted to meet your ... specifications. If you please, sir.' He shook the clothing gently, poised like an effeminate matador. An appendage, heavy and crusted, moved awkwardly into the sleeve of the jacket. The tailor shifted sideways, guiding the pristine garment into place and offering the other sleeve to the gentleman's good arm, then adjusted the shoulders to make the best of the man's alien posture.

The grizzled creature turned. Greasy wisps of dark hair protruded from the relatively human patches that remained of his festering scalp. The scar tissue lay thick and mottled on his left side, partly obscuring his face. A mound of historically liquefied flesh was all that remained of his earlobe. A new leather eye patch covered the most offending orb. The man dribbled slightly as awkward tones issued from his deformed palate. 'I said, no mirrors!' He tossed a small hand-held glass across the room, then slobbering on to his good side and calming slightly. 'Am I ready?'

The tailor stepped back, rubbing his chin thoughtfully. 'Yes, sir, I believe you are.' He offered a respectful bow, only just holding on to his stomach contents, then forced a polite smile. 'The Führer awaits your company on this most historic occasion … Professor Steinhoff.'

Printed in Great Britain
by Amazon